He heard half of what she'd said as he watched the liquid slide down her throat, the way it moved under her soft skin as she tipped her head back, spilling a thick wash of brunette hair over her shoulders. Her jacket was on the chair. The low, bluish lights in the room from the monitors practically made her sheer blouse see-through…the lace beneath it caught his attention and sent his line of vision over her breasts. He had to close his eyes as his gaze slid over her tight nipples. Good Lord, he remembered her in his arms…every agonizing moment.

She glimpsed at him from the corner of her eye and nearly choked on her pop when his eyelids became heavy and he slightly turned his head away. This calm, discreet man was not the Barron Maverick she knew. Suddenly, she felt too exposed without her jacket on. Just knowing that he'd been looking at her that way made her nipples sting. Lord, she remembered those fevered nights with Barron … under the moon and stars, his deep, baritone growls sending chills down her spine…the way he made love; hot, intense, and impassioned until there was nothing left to do but sob from pleasure.

Vegas Bites:
A Werewolf Romance Anthology

L. A. Banks,

J. M. Jeffries,

Seressia Glass,

Natalie Dunbar

Parker Publishing, LLC
www.parker-publishing.com

Noire Allure is an imprint of Parker Publishing, LLC.

Vegas Bites: A Werewolf Romance Anthology
"Heat" copyright © 2006 by Leslie Esdaile-Banks
"The Hunger Within" copyright © 2006 by Jackie Hamilton and Miriam Pace
"Double Down" copyright © 2006 by Seressia Glass
"Out of the Dark" copyright © 2006 by Natalie Dunbar

Published by Parker Publishing, LLC
12523 Limonite Avenue, Suite #440-245
Mira Loma, California 91752
www.parker-publishing.com

ISBN 10:   1-60043-001-5
ISBN 13   978-1-60043-001-5

First Edition

Manufactured in the United States of America

Heat

by

L. A. Banks

Acknowledgements

This wild and crazy story is dedicated to Jackie and Miriam, two wonderful sister-authors who coaxed "the animal" sensibilities out of me (LOL), and to my agent, Manie Barron, who told me to "Let the Dawgs out!" I'd also like to thank my family, especially my daughter, who accommodated this project during the Holidays— when I'd promised, *no mas, por favor*. Thank you, Parker team, as well, for the hard work in pulling this all together under fun auspices! As they say, it's ALL good.

Chapter One

Las Vegas, Nevada… French Quarter Hotel and Casino

Butch Maverick sat in the central bar ignoring the poker and tournament tables, staring down into his glass of Dewar's. He hated coming to Vegas. The incessant ring of the slot machines gave him a headache. It was hot as hell and dry as a bone… a hundred and three degrees in the shade. Even under the air conditioners, he was still sweating. He hated being boxed in, having to stay indoors during the day just to catch the frigid AC temps. At least it was cool at night in the desert, where he could run wild and free.

But what was with the air conditioners in the casino? It seemed like Malcolm had them on full blast, but he was still burning up. Vegas was not him at all. The vibe, the climate, and everything else simply went against his basic nature. Worse, there was always some bull when he had to bounty hunt here. He could already smell Laurel's sweet scent, and he'd just walked in the damned door.

He took another sip of the dark liquor and winced, determined to stay focused on his mission: find out who'd been wreaking werewolf-style havoc throughout the Midwest.

His brother in Philly had given him the tip, cop courtesy by way of blood. The job was out of his brother's jurisdiction and crossed state lines in a way that an East Coast detective would be hard-pressed to explain, if he started hardcore investigating. That's where he came in. Freelance hunters had no boundaries.

They both knew the deal. The casino owners were about to retire, and the last thing Mom and Pop Temple needed was a hostile pack takeover of an establishment they'd held onto since the fifties.

Yeah… this was potentially a family matter. Preternatural Po-Po didn't need to get involved. Internal affairs of the pack were just that, private, and no human cop interventions ought to be in the mix.

But with a rogue gang doing home invasions, robbing banks, savaging civilians, and basically running amok, it wouldn't be long before humans would take matters into their own hands. Then it would be an all-out wolf hunt. The fuckin' vampires would love it. This had to be solved like the past three attempts to take the casino had been. Mobsters quietly disappeared into the dark of night, never to be seen again. So had another foolish pack that had tried the French Quarter, and a shady international businessman was only a withered carcass when they found his stupid ass.

The cash trail led here, where new shipments of methamphetamine were coming in strong through Cutter, Fang, and Mad Dawg. Everybody knew they ran the drug thing in Vegas, but you couldn't smoke a man for his black market operations—as long as they kept that bullshit on their side of town. Problem was, he wasn't sure they had, which meant he'd have to look up an old friend with the loveliest set of fangs that could make a man shiver from across the room. Like her working name, Ecstasy Jones was all that—practically a drug herself. Correction, she was definitely that, but nowhere near a controlled substance. Girlfriend was ecstasy personified, out of control, and could make a man jones for months after getting with her.

Butch knocked back the rest of his drink and stood, his gaze roving the slot machine rows before slowly scanning the poker area. This was exactly why he hated coming to Vegas. If he looked up Ecstasy, the high-roller vamps that were her primary clientele would be hissing and spitting like bitches. If he followed his first impulse and went to see fine-ass Laurel, he might have to rip Guy's face off, and then tangle with his boyz Troy and Oliver. That's the last thing the family needed right now, a split in pack ranks. Any sign of weakness or dissention in the family was a bad thing, especially when there was a potential coup in the wind. Damn, it was hot! His shirt was sticking to his skin.

A woman as fine as Laurel had a way of making even the most reasonable man act stupid, especially near a full moon when she was going into heat. Laurel didn't need to be running security; shit, *she* needed security.

That dumb bastard, Guy, was always snarling about marketing the casino better to humans to boost revenues and complaining about keeping any supernatural incidents on the DL... sheeit. He was about to have a serious public relations problem up in the joint if his Gaming Manager and Pit Boss Manager got in his face today with Laurel's thick scent opening his nose. That bull between him and Guy shoulda been squashed about a hundred years ago, anyway. It wasn't his fault that the woman wouldn't mate him on the regular. Laurel didn't do any guys that worked for the family. Period.

Butch let out a heavy exhale of frustration and glanced around. Why did these elimination jobs always have to come his way near a full moon? Fate had a serious sense of twisted humor. He had to find Marcus, his homeboy that ran Public Relations. Had to get the low down on the underground buzz on the situation while he was still lucid. Good thing there was one brother in the clan that still considered him family.

Malcolm was also cool. Had to be, to keep the hotel biz running smooth. At least those brothers always had his back, and Laurel didn't mess up their cool. Mated males could hang, it was just the solo brothers that got messed up by her—but he wasn't gonna let her mess with his mind today. When the moon came up, he'd figure out a way to cope. For now, he had business to attend to.

Sliding a twenty across the bar, he decided against another drink and began walking. One drink was cool; a second one would relax him too much. The Dewar's had definitely been a necessary distraction to get his head right before going up to the offices, though... where Laurel's scent would get even thicker. Where she'd play with his mind; would probably try to signify on his occasional rendezvous with a female vamp hooker. Ecstasy was good people...all pro. Not a hooker, a prostitute, and yeah, there was a difference.

Laurel needed to get off it—he'd left the inner pack with good cause, and she didn't need to still be salty about it after all these years. It was either that or kill a clan brother for her. Besides, if she wasn't giving up tail, then hey. What was a man supposed to do?

Butch kept walking with purpose, winding his way past the French Quarter Restaurant, zigzagging in a lope through the roulette and Black Jack tables toward the elevators. Scents from the restaurant made his stomach rumble. The sizzling cuisine in there, as well as those wafting toward him from the Voodoo Café and Big Easy Cajun joint, almost made him stop. But he pressed on. The day of a full moon was always a bitch.

· Forget the elevator to the second floor. He needed to walk off the wood just thinking about Laurel had given him. The stairs could work.

He flashed the security guard a family badge, opened the door, and bound up the steps in two strong lunges. Oh, yeah, this was not a good sign. It wasn't even four o'clock in the afternoon, and a shape-shift was trying to come through against his will.

Butch exited the stairwell and set his jaw hard, his eyes hunting the Administrative Office door. He tilted his head and allowed the scents behind it to flow over his palate. Secretary... cool... Marcus was in. No competitor and no Laurel, for the moment. Cool. No drama.

"Yo," he said with a slow smile as he entered the office.

Janet glanced up at him with a big grin. "Stranger..." she murmured, and then looked him up and down. "Long time, Butch."

"Hey, what can I say, baby. Been on the road." He passed her desk, issuing her a sly wink, and told himself to keep moving. Foxy thang had a buttermilk biscuit booty that would stop traffic and make a man wanna sop up his own drool like it was gravy. That was the last thing he needed with Laurel already on a mission. "My boy Marcus in?" He knew the answer, but just asked as a courtesy.

"Yeah…" Janet said, still looking him over while chewing on the end of her pen. "I'll buzz him for you, hon."

"Appreciate it." He stopped short of Marcus' office. It was a territorial respect thing, but he definitely wasn't trying to stand too close to Janet.

Before Janet's call connected, Marcus flung the door open and laughed. "Aw, man! Who let the dogs out? Thought I picked up your tracks—whassup!"

Marcus grabbed Butch into a familial hug, then they broke from each other's hold, play boxing for a moment.

"You doing all right?" Marcus stood taller, trying to compensate for the one-inch height differential between them.

"I'm good, can't complain," Butch said with a broad grin, squaring his shoulders, and reinforcing his six-foot five advantage over Marcus' six-four frame. "You got a minute?"

"For you, brother, yeah. Step into my yard."

Marcus gave Butch a sidelong glance, and Butch just chuckled. Now that the minor pissing contest was over, maybe they could get down to business.

"Been hearing things," Butch said once he'd closed the door to Marcus' office behind them.

"I know. We all have." Marcus rounded his massive walnut desk to flop down into the large leather chair behind it. "But I thought maybe you'd just picked up on Laurel's trail and were finally gonna—"

"Don't start." Butch held up both hands in front of his chest with a wide grin. "Not today."

"You mean not tonight, man," Marcus said, ribbing him.

"I came here strictly on business."

Marcus sighed and motioned for Butch to sit down. "You really should be talking to the head of Security Operations if you think there's a serious threat to the casino. I'm just your dawg in public relations."

"I was gonna go to Malcolm instead."

Butch watched Marcus make a tent with his fingers in front of his mouth and waited as he took his time to respond. They both understood how Laurel would take either of them sidestepping her authority.

"You really don't wanna have that conversation with her, do you?"

"Not if I don't have to." Butch looked out the window at the late afternoon sun.

"Laurel and I are cool... like brother and sister, and—"

"I'm not trying to put you in a position, man."

Marcus leaned forward. "Then before you go bloodhound on her turf and piss her off by giving her boss a heads-up before her, you might wanna have that conversation." He sat back and put his hands up in front of his chest. "Just an opinion."

"Shit." Butch stood and went to the window, rolling his shoulders to try to work the tension out of his neck. Instinctively, he knew Marcus was right—Laurel would bear canines if he didn't show her the respect of rank. But he damned sure didn't need the complication. "It was just a hunch, anyway," he hedged.

"Be real, man. If it was a weak hunch, you wouldn't even be in Vegas, right?"

Butch refused to answer the legitimate charge and kept his line of vision on the horizon.

"You know how she reacted the last time you rolled through here and got in contact with that vamp pro for a source without running the sting through her office," Marcus pressed on.

"I was solving a crime, man," Butch growled. "The vampires had a smooth identity theft ring going, blamed it on the ghosts— succubae, incubi, clientele the vamps love... so, I had to get on the inside with a sister that services the vamp high-rollers. You know that. And we got the rat bastards too, the ones claiming they had old world money so they didn't need to do petty crimes for a few million."

"I'm not arguing, man," Marcus replied calmly. "But it almost started the old civil wars again between us and the vampire nations—it went down very politically incorrect, feel me?"

"That's why I wanna talk to Malcolm before I bring this to his door." Butch glanced over his shoulder at Marcus, holding him with a glare. "As next in line and the man running the entire hotel operation, he needs a heads-up."

"True, but how would that look if he knows, and his Director of Public Relations has a prepared, canned speech for the Preternatural Authorities, and his head of Security Operations doesn't know jack about it?" Marcus let out a hard breath. "They're gonna have to have inscrutable evidence of who's behind the crimes before you smoke anybody on our premises this time, Butch—because nobody wants to be involved in potentially kicking off a supernatural war between vamps and were-clans that could spill over into the civilian human population. That's bad for business, and if human communities get nervous, they'll start the old wolf hunts again. All of which means, you're gonna have to go in deep, do your homework with an evidence trail that's airtight… which means you're gonna have to talk to the best tracker-hunter we've got in the family—Laurel."

Butch briefly closed his eyes and ran his palm over his close-cropped beard. He could already feel it had grown a quarter inch just being in the office boxed in by Laurel's scent, and the normally precise cut of it was getting ragged around the edges. He clasped both hands behind his back and willed himself not to pace.

"It's real bad this time, isn't it?" Marcus said with a half-smile, standing to go pour them both a drink.

"I just think it's strangely coincidental that at the same time major were-style robberies have gone down in the Midwest, meth labs out here are cooking and moving product like never before. My gut tells me they've got a new cash infusion way too close to our family borders here. They're building ranks and strength in numbers. Bad sign."

"I'm not talking about the coincidences of the crime," Marcus said, bringing Butch a Dewar's neat. "I'm talking about her affect on you. Look at your hands. You've practically got the shakes, brother. Damn. Play your cards right and you might get lucky tonight."

"I'm cool," Butch said, growing irritable. He accepted the drink and knocked back a healthy swig of it—hard. Wincing, he set the glass down on Marcus' desk. "I'm not even going there."

"Then lemme call her in, so she knows you aren't peeing on her tree behind her back. I'll fill Malcolm in, and I'm sure he'll support you and give you the nod to hunt on the property."

Butch paced away from Marcus. "Whatever." He didn't need this complication. When Marcus depressed the intercom buzzer, Butch battled for composure and had to turn to look out the window again when Laurel's melodic voice filled the speakerphone. Just hearing the way she said hello, all deep and husky, made his stomach clench. If she walked in the door trailing heat, she'd definitely give him the shakes.

"We got a situation, Laurel," Marcus said in a too-cheerful tone that grated him.

"I'll be right there," she said, her tone low and filled with authority.

He could do this. Butch set his jaw hard. It had been a while since he'd seen her, but wouldn't let it show. He had a nice cash bounty coming his way if he solved this case that the Feds didn't wanna touch and local Preter Po-Pop didn't want in their files. All he had to do was chill and do his job, then be out.

The moment he heard Laurel's soft footfalls loping past Janet's desk, he knew the second drink had been a mistake. Yeah, it had been, and he was sure of it when she opened the door to Marcus' office. Oh, shit… she looked better than he'd remembered.

Five-feet, eleven inches worth of drop-dead fine almost made him tilt his head as their gazes locked. She straightened and hesitated by the door. He watched her nostrils subtly flare, scenting him as she released a low, practically inaudible growl deep within her voluptuous chest.

The timbre of the sound made him stop breathing for a second. He kept his line of vision on her gorgeous, gray-eyed glare, but somehow it slipped and trailed down the bridge of her nose to her full, lush mouth and temporarily landed on her shoulders to study the gleam of sunlight that put red and gold highlights in her profusion of thick, brunette hair. His mind was jacked on the spot.

"You didn't tell me *he* was here," she snapped, cutting Marcus a hard look.

Marcus just smiled as she slammed the door shut behind her.

"Good to see you again, too, Laurel," Butch said coolly, really needing that second drink now, versus earlier.

Swiping his used glass off the edge of the desk, he opted for a third one to put more distance between them. He headed for Marcus's bar. No matter what, he wasn't going to allow her to see the effect she had on him. It was over. Her toffee-hued skin had always been his strange addiction, just like her long, shapely legs.

A moment of clarity was in order. He couldn't look at her again yet. Even covered up in black linen pants, they served to-die-for proportions… and no suit jacket and plain white silk blouse could hide the package underneath the loosely constructed linen fabric. Just a whisper of her lace bra peeked over the low-cut shell and had caught his eye just as he'd turned to fix another drink; the same way his nose had caught her intoxicating heat-scent mixed up with whatever incredible perfume she wore.

"So, you're sniffing around my damned yard again?" she said after a tense pause, walking deeper into the office to challenge him.

"The potential situation required it," he said without turning to address her. That wasn't possible now.

Thoroughly offended that he was giving her his back to consider, she slowly folded her arms and stared at him. She had to pull it together. What the hell was he thinking, coming to Vegas in leather? Why today, of all days, would he bring his fine ass into her casino wearing animal skin!

Laurel counted to ten, half to stem the rage; half to be sure her voice wouldn't hitch when she spoke. *Good God,* the man was an awesome specimen. Animal magnetism literally leaked out of his pores in his sweat. Shoulders built like canyon boulders… pure rock posing as sinew across each blade, just like the concrete blocks in his abdomen… chiseled back and that fantastic, tight ass of his that tapered into granite thighs beneath butter-soft black leather.

She turned and walked away, sending her scowl toward Marcus, who, by rights, should have warned her first. The fact that Marcus only smiled an apology irked her to no end.

No, she wouldn't even think about the way Butch's spine dipped into a deep valley before it gave rise to haunches that could just make a woman stupid. Uh uh. Not today. Screw him. That arrogant tail-chasing, disrespectful, double-dealing SOB was not gonna make her drown in those liquid brown eyes or touch that smooth, ebony skin he got from his African American-Choctaw blend. Nope. She wasn't ever again in life running her fingers over his thick, velvety, onyx waves that became long and magnificent curls under a full moon… like she would forget all the shit he did. Butch Maverick could drop that heavy, masculine pheromone scent and baritone voice on another sister that was trying to hear it—she wasn't the one.

"So what's the situation?" she finally asked Marcus once she'd recovered, her tone curt.

"Butch has a theory," Marcus said with a lopsided grin. "This is his hunch, so I'll let him tell you the dealio." Marcus rounded her and headed for the door. "I'll fill Malcolm in while, uh, Butch runs it down. You two play nice—no biting."

Both Laurel and Butch stared behind him for a moment, incredulous.

"Punk," she snarled under her breath as the door closed.

Butch took a sip of his drink. "You wanna sit down and talk or—"

"Just say what you gotta say," she snapped, too furious and too turned on to move toward a chair.

"I got a tip from my brother in Philly, and I've been tracking a series of hard core Midwest robberies that've left bodies. There's an eerie coincidence in the increased production of meth by a strong clan that's always had their eyes on this hotel gem. Thought I'd check it out to be sure there's no link that could cause the family long-term problems."

She casually leaned against Marcus's desk to appear nonchalant and unimpressed, but partly to keep her balance. She was done, or was it undone? There was no argument that the man could track his fine ass off. Had a mind like a steel trap. Problem was, right now she felt like she was in its teeth. It was the way he was looking at her over the rim of his glass as he slowly sipped his drink, like he wanted to eat her for dinner.

"All right," she said, conceding only enough to be civil, and knowing Malcolm would demand that. "We heard some rumors, too. We'll keep an eye out for any suspicious activity that comes our way. Thanks for letting us know you got a tip all the way down here in advance, *this time*."

He didn't immediately respond but just looked at her with a sexy half-smile. The dig had been her way of verbally backing him up, sending him the message not to even try her, and very necessary to keep her distance and to help her focus. She just wished he'd say something or argue with her to staunch the burn, but he just scoured her body with a spine-melting gaze.

Butch's burnt-gold collarless shirt was clinging to him like a second skin beneath his jacket, thoroughly defining his cinderblock chest. Its hue was a phenomenal contrast to his dark complexion and his eyes in the late afternoon sun... damn, the man didn't look a day over thirty-five. And he was definitely packing more than just a Glock nine in his shoulder holster. However, just because she was going into heat did not mean she was insane.

"Don't mention it," he finally said in a low rumble, his eyes never leaving hers, and then he took a deep swig from the glass and winced, flashing a hint of upper and lower canines that had begun to extend. "You look good, Laurel. Been a long time."

Just seeing that slight transformation made her stop breathing for a moment. Damn... the man had made her wet her thong, and the moon hadn't even crested yet.

"Then I'm sure you know our policy," she said between her teeth, refusing to address the compliment that released butterflies in her belly. "No bullshit on the premises that could spook humans. No wildass firefights, bar room brawls, or anything that could upset our hotel guests and alert civilian authorities. Vampires as hostages or entities to lean on for information are out of the question. There's already bad blood between the fila from the last incident—and since you didn't have full evidence, or a *credible* witness you were willing to disclose, tensions are still high with that group."

She pushed away from the desk and stood before him with her arms folded, resolute. "We can't have that this time, even if you suspect a competing were-clan. I want this done clean, without a raggedy aftermath."

He smiled. God, she was gorgeous.

"I'm serious, Barron Maverick." Her hands went to her hips.

He almost dropped his glass. Nobody called him by his formal name, but her. To everyone else he was just Butch. And the way she said it... the tone ran all through him.

"I want to know your *every* move," she said, pointing her graceful finger at him.

He stared at her hand and tilted his head. "My *every* move?" He'd meant the question to come out more like a challenge growl, versus the baby-come-here-and-I'll-show-you direction it took... but damn, she was blowing his mind. He remembered those nights with her like they were yesterday.

"Yes. I'm serious," she said, her pristine enamel extending in her mouth a fraction as she argued. "I'm not cleaning up after you again. The human authorities were crawling all over this casino for months after you left the last time."

"My bad," he murmured, unable to keep desire out of his voice. "Won't happen again."

"Not on my watch. It had better not... or I'll personally kick your huge ass myself."

An alpha challenge from an alpha female... he was in love.

"Baby, I—"

"What?" She cocked her head to the side and got up in his face.

"I meant Laurel," he said, breathing her in. "The history gets a little confusing this close to sunset."

She narrowed her gaze on him. "I'm not playing with you. Whatever's going on in the streets, handle it and clean it up, but keep it in the streets. That's your jurisdiction. But once it crosses my threshold here, it's mine. We clear?"

"Laurel, back up from me a little bit," he said quietly. "You smell *incredible*."

She turned abruptly and walked away to stand by the huge windows and hugged herself. "Don't start that shit on my job."

His gaze raked her from head to toe and settled on her firm, round ass. "I'm not trying to start nothing." He stalked over to the bar and set his glass down hard. He had to get the shape of her behind out of his line of vision. It was making his balls ache. "I'm just being real."

"Good," she said with a slight shudder to her breath.

"It always was, though, wasn't it?" He had to ask. She was making him crazy.

"It'll be dark soon, the vamp hookers will be out—you have options. Go roll one of them while you're on the hunt, and keep it in the streets and not my hotel-casino."

"So it's back to that, huh?" Now he was pissed.

"It never left *that*," she said, her tone lethal as she spun on him, her eyes beginning to flicker gold in the center. "Just like I never left you, but you can't say the same—can you?"

Why did she have to go there with change-fire in her eyes? Shit. He was dangerously on the edge of a full shape-shift to mate her hard if she didn't stop messing with his mind. After seeing her pretty irises burn with canines lowering and the spike of challenge in the air, her scent tearing him up, working his sinuses into putty for her, it was impossible to get the image of her on all-fours out of his brain… under the moon with her head thrown back, spine dipped, sweat running… Lawd. He wanted to howl.

"I'll keep you informed." He almost wiped his brow but still had some pride.

"Good. You do *that*." She lifted her chin, thrust her shoulders back and strode to the door, leaving her fantastic scent trail in her wake.

Rendered momentarily speechless, he just gripped the edge of the bar and shuddered as she slammed the door behind her. It was way too hot in the room. He felt like he was suffocating. Butch closed his eyes and breathed her in deeply through his nose, but refused to pant. *Man*, this was gonna be a long night.

Chapter Two

L aurel walked away from Marcus's office, fanning her face and gulping air. She couldn't respond to Janet's wide smile.

"*Girl...*" Janet said in a conspiratorial tone. "I hear you. If it was me, I'd be calling down the moon early."

Laurel kept walking; she had to. She couldn't even answer the comment and was thankful that Janet hadn't shouted the ribald remark like she normally would have.

There was only one way to get Barron Maverick gone—get the potential problem investigated with the quickness, the threat addressed quickly, and then she'd send his big, burly, incorrigible ass packing. That was all to it.

Damn, she needed some water.

He had to go eat. Period. He was hungry as a mofo. Laurel was filleting his mind and his judgment.

Butch left the office not worried about letting Marcus know his whereabouts. He'd get up with him later. Cajun steak, bloody to the bone, was calling his name. He bound down the fire exit stairwell and quickly crossed the gaming floor.

When he practically skidded to a stop in front of the "Please Wait To Be Seated" sign, the restaurant hostess issued him a welcoming smile that had an invitation embedded in it. He had to shake off the temptation. Too young. Summer college help and human. Uh uh. Too close to Laurel. Human on a full moon eve was a tragedy waiting to happen. Laurel. Too much drama. His brain was slow cooking in his skull.

"Can I get you anything to start?" she asked in a suggestive tone, seating him at a far table in the back.

Butch rubbed his palms down his face and let out his breath hard. "Just a steak, bloody—with everything you got on the side."

She sidled up closer to him, leaned down to show off a magnificent man-made cleavage, and flipped her long blonde hair over her shoulder. "Everything, sir?"

"Potatoes, uh, peppers and onions, whatever."

"Oh," she said, looking extremely disappointed and briefly bit her glossy, pink bottom lip. "Anything to drink, then?"

Butch closed his eyes and nodded. "Iced tea. Non-alcoholic—with a *lotta* ice and some space." He looked at her and pulled his cell phone off his hip.

She placed his menu down on the table hard. "In case you want anything else," she said in a crisp tone.

He hadn't meant to hurt her feelings, but was so jacked up he couldn't address it. Rather than watch her walk away, he hit Malcolm's number and waited. As soon as the call connected, he didn't bother with formalities.

"Did Marcus talk to you?"

"Yes," Malcolm said calmly. "And hello to you, too, man."

"Yeah, hey. We cool? I can do my hunt?"

"You can do your hunt, but the question is, are you cool?"

"Yeah, yeah, I'm good."

"You sound out of breath. Where are you?"

"Eating dinner." Butch held the phone away from his mouth for a moment and took in two, long inhales and let them out slowly.

"Little early, isn't it?"

Malcolm's tone held a level of mirth that grated him. He could hear Marcus laughing out loud in the background. He'd kick his ass later.

"I was hungry," Butch said flatly. "I'm downstairs."

"Whew… okay," Malcolm said, sounding cheery. "Might try to bring that down again tonight when the moon is out and it's better to hunt. Can't rush it."

"Talk to you later, man." Butch hung up and flipped his phone shut. Everybody was a comedian.

Food. Then to the Black Jack and poker tables to watch the floors for who might come through flashing a wad of cash. Then he'd go to work when it got dark.

The moment the sun set, he got up from the card table and began walking to the lobby entrance. He'd put in a cell voicemail message to Ecstasy, but didn't need to compromise her customer relations by having her seen on his arm. Some things just weren't done.

The vamp high-rollers didn't like sloppy seconds, which is how they thought of hooking up with a female vamp after she'd been with a Were for the night—elitist bastards. But they thought nothing of passing her around in ridiculous, multi-partnered orgies all night, as long as it was all vamps. Sick. Wolves didn't play that shit. Males squared off, battled for dominance, and then may the best man tag it. The poontang was his and his alone for the night. To his mind, that was the way nature had planned it.

Butch shook his head as he stepped out into the parking lot and stared up at the moon. The cool night air felt good against his face. Male vampires were some *foul* entities with sordid behaviors he could never consider. They'd do anything with an orifice. Same deal with those nasty-ass serpent demons.

Anacondas would do twelve males to a female all at the same time in a mating ball. Twisted, literally. Exactly why he didn't deal with succubae, they'd do anything in any shape, too… just like those damned transvestite incubi would. He shivered. Another good reason not to mess with that species. With the phantoms you didn't know what you were getting, male or female, and as an alpha male wolf, aw hell to the no. If he woke up and it was male, he'd have to kill it.

"Hey, lover," a seductive voice said in an airy voice behind him.

He turned quickly with a start. As fine as Ecstasy was, he could never get used to the materializing from mist thing that she did. He liked concrete sensory cues—like sound and hearing; something rolling up on him that had a definitive scent. But, she was still fine.

"Hey, baby. Called you."

"Uh, huh," she murmured, showing fang. "You're awful jumpy tonight." She glanced up at the moon with a knowing smile, then tapped her cell phone and shook her head. "You have my private telepathy down pat. All you had to do was howl it in your mind, and I would have picked it up as a stat call… 9-1-1 emergency, baby," she said on a breathy whisper, moving closer as she stared at his jugular. "Why—"

"I just called about business."

"Isn't it always?" She arched an eyebrow with a seductive smile. "Even while in-lair during the day, I could've sent you a little some-thin' somethin' had I known you were in such a state."

"I'm cool. I just wanna ask you a few questions."

He backed up, assessing her deep cleavage and the way her pretty brown skin had a bluish tint under the moon. Her taut brown nipples were showing through the black lace panel down the front of her outfit, and it made him absently lick his lips. The black dress was to die for, and the platinum thing she'd done with her short spiked hair was sexily bizarre. She was a petite package of curves that was worth considering, given the way Laurel was acting, but he had things to do.

"Want me to siphon it out of your mind?" Her eyes went to half-mast, glowing slightly red as her lids lowered.

"No," he murmured, not sure that no meant no. His gaze was trapped by the little gold ball tongue piercing. Uh uh. A telepathic connection with her was too hot, same reason he'd called by conventional technology. Ecstasy could send images into his head that made good phone sex seem as exciting as doing laundry.

She came closer, trailed her hand down his chest, lightly raking it with her nails until her palm landed on his groin. "How long have you been carrying *that* loaded gun?"

He chuckled and briefly shut his eyes. "All damned day." He swallowed thickly as she gently massaged his erection, making it throb harder. "But, listen... uh... I really need to talk to you."

"Okay," she whispered in his ear, her chilly skin brushing against his neck as her cheek grazed it. She kept her hand working between their bodies as her tongue flicked his earlobe. "So talk to me, lover."

He grabbed her wrist and stopped her hand, tilting his head from the delirium she was producing. "I can't talk, let alone think, while you're doing that under a full moon."

"All right," she said, nipping his neck, pouting. "But if you wanna take a quick desert run on all fours... I might not even charge you." She kissed the underside of his chin. "Think about it. It's been a long time, but my shape-shifts aren't that rusty. The last time was incredible."

"No lie," he said with an appreciative shudder. "But..." He glanced up at the moon, and then back toward the hotel.

"But, *she'll* have a problem with it." Ecstasy sighed, pulled her hand away, and studied her French manicure. "So, talk."

"Girl, don't be like that."

"How am I being, Butch?" She looked at him hard. "You saving yourself for her tonight—did she say she was gonna break down and hook a brother up?"

"That's not what I came here to talk about." He began to pace. "You know you make me crazy. But, there's this thing going down."

"And you want me to do what about it?" She folded her arms over her double-D cup chest. "Maverick, you do know that the French Quarter is hosting the Twenty Million Dollar Texas Hold 'em Poker Tournament?" She sucked her teeth. "Do you know *how many* Master vampire high-rollers will be coming to town for this? Can you say *billionaires*? So tell me why I'm standing out here arguing with your stubborn, Lupine ass about giving you some head or doing a shape-shift in the parking lot, when I could be taking telepathy transmissions for orgies all week?" She began to dissolve, serving him mist.

"Hold up, hold up, baby," he said, his voice low and firm. "They won't be here till near midnight, and it's early by their standards."

Her form became more solid, but she still kept her chin lifted, offended.

"And, uh, I know I haven't been through Vegas for a while, but there's something going down that could be dangerous to the fam." He touched her cheek, and then caressed it once he was sure she wouldn't bite his hand. "Why don't you go into my mind and pull it, to save time?"

She glanced up at him, and a slow smile crept across her crimson lips.

"Go easy on a brother. I'm wearing leather and gotta work all night."

She laughed. "If I go in, you'll howl... you sure you want me to pull up before you—"

"Please don't embarrass a brother out in the parking lot, and have me have to walk through a lit casino floor after busting a nut in my leather."

She brushed his mouth with a kiss. "I wouldn't do that, boo."

"Yes you would—for spite," he said, laughing. "You are *treacherous*, girl."

"I am, but, some things are just tacky. Besides, the other girls would say it was a sloppy job, might pick up my signature in it, and then they'd really talk about me... claiming that I, Ecstasy Jones, couldn't finesse a Lup. Would ruin business. So, you're safe... but will be horny as hell when I'm done."

"Gee thanks," he said, slightly salty about the dig regarding his wolf heritage.

"Aw… I was just messing with you. A lot of the others would cross over to get with you, darlin'. You know that. Those bitches would hiss about me because they'd be so jealous."

"Ecstasy, why are you always giving me the blues?"

She hugged him and found his jugular. "Because you're a natural, sexy, warm-blooded pain in my ass."

Her love bite broke his skin and went in so smooth that his knees buckled. The woman hadn't lied; his scrotum contracted to the pulse of her suckles against his neck and she pulled information out of his mind like a pro.

Tears were in his eyes he needed to cum so badly, but he let her quickly siphon the information she needed to get on the case. He'd spotted a few strange Weres in the casino at the poker and Black Jack tables flashing big cash wads and pulling C-notes off the knots to tip waitresses way too much. Letting Ecstasy take his throat was a necessary compromise, a barter that only vampires understood. Blood. A transaction as old as life itself. Yeah… it wasn't done between the species, and she'd have to gargle like hell so a snob vamp client wouldn't be offended, but he needed what only she could do.

He tried to focus on that while he held her delicate shoulders, and she writhed against him making him begin to pant.

"Oh, shit, girl, c'mon and finish up." He dropped his sweat-damp forehead to her shoulder. "You are dangerously close to breaking your word." A hard shudder passed through him as she pulled away from his throat and licked her lips breathing hard.

"Damn…" she whispered. "Nothing but pure testosterone and adrenaline running through you tonight, lover. You sure you don't wanna take a run in the canyons?"

Unable to answer her for a moment, he held the side of his neck and began to walk in a tight circle.

"It's been a long time since you've had a female," she said in a calm, smug tone, allowing the illusion of a thick, silvery mane to take over her hair as her ears laid back against her skull.

Gulping air, he held up a hand. "Don't. Aw'ight. I gotta work." He shuddered hard, shook off the sensation that was carving at his groin, then threw his head back and howled till he could hear it echo back to him. "Shit!"

Several return howls made him look into the darkness beyond the casino lights with longing. His attention fractured as he closed his eyes for a second, tilted his head and inhaled sharply, picking up females everywhere.

"I didn't mean to mess you up that bad," she said, covering her mouth and laughing.

Not amused in the least, he jerked his attention toward her.

"Damn, your eyes are glowing gold and shit, and you'd better pull it together before you go back inside. Canines in full effect. Humans can't deal with it, even though they know we're around."

"I told you, in and out!" he shouted, rubbing his jaw and pacing.

"Okay, so I lingered, 'cause I missed you."

He couldn't catch his breath as he balled his hands into fists and tried to summon calm, locking his jaw and willing the canines back with his eyes shut tightly.

"Count backward from a hundred," she said, floating around him. "Works for the male vamps. A client told me."

He snatched her and kissed her hard. "Shut up, Ecstasy." He let her go and walked away a few paces. "You gonna help me?"

"How much?"

He drew in a hard breath. "Twenty-five large."

"Oh, you have *got* to be kidding." She walked past him, bumping his body as she sauntered toward the casino entrance.

"Okay, okay—you say a number, then we'll discuss it."

She put her hands on her shapely hips and gaped at him with disbelief. "There is *nothing* to discuss. My prices are firm. Harder than your dick, in fact."

"That's a lotta money for—"

"Kiss my ass, Butch Maverick—not even for you!"

Ecstasy threw her hands up and paced toward him, pointing at him as she pecked her neck in a defiant rage. "You want me to shape-shift into a hot she-wolf, blow the minds of those animals in there flashing cash, siphon their minds to see if they're connected to some coup bullshit, then come back to you. Did I get it all?"

"Yeah, so what's the problem?" Indignant, he folded his arms over his chest. She might have made him hornier, but he still knew how to count money.

"On a primo vamp night... where I could be drinking a fine blood merlot, in a penthouse lair, with I don't how many illusion-casters that will do me in silk sheets and rose petals at a very fine price, and deliver a bite that will make me see stars?"

She walked away from him shaking her head, and then spun on him. "But instead, I'm supposed to be in a filthy canyon, outdoors, on my knees because you Lups like to get your run on before you get your swerve on, and I could get my entire throat ripped out if the guy isn't suave—which under full moon conditions, he won't be... and under a full moon, the son of a bitch, and I do put emphasis on the word *bitch*, will probably cum in three good thrusts—unlike a vampire—who has perfected seduction to the fine art it is... oh, yes, but a Lup will want it doggie style all night, over, and over, and over until the sun comes up, holding my ass hostage where I could possibly torch at dawn and—"

"All right, stop talking trash about my people, sis!" He walked deeper into the parking lot. The way she'd put it, by comparison seemed so crass. "We ain't all like that, and the part about three good thrusts is bullshit."

"Am I lying about the canyons, though?" Her hands had again found her hips and her mouth twisted in a smiling scowl.

Heat

"We like the outdoors; fresh air, okay? It's not silk and rose petals, but—"

"Seventy-five for the three of 'em or I don't work."

"What!" Incredulous, he glowered at her and raked his fingers through his hair. It was growing by the second through his fingers, and he yanked his hand away from his skull. "You wouldn't have to do more than the alpha, any ole way. The betas will back off or get beat down. So, what are you—"

"The alpha is the one I have to wear out first, to get him out of the way," she said coolly. "Chances that I'll get near his throat are slim. Think about it. The only reason I got to yours is because we're cool." She sighed and studied her French manicure again. "The alpha will shift, chase me, pin me down hard, mount me, and he'll be in the throat dominant position behind me. True?"

"True," he muttered. Her logic and his erection were wearing him out.

"And when he's done, he'll get up, nip me goodbye on my ass, and lope off to find another female for later after he eats if I'm not still available."

Her logic had trapped him and pinned him to a parked car. He simply leaned against it and released a weary breath.

"The betas will be in the nearby distance, too punked to actually challenge him for me, but walking in circles with their dicks hard and whimpering for whatever the alpha discards—which will be a non-permanent mate female; me. The moment he dismounts to go eat, they'll come sniffing in, heads lowered, and very, very hopeful... but since he'd marked me first, they'll be nervous, looking around to see if the big male was coming back and if I'll allow them to mount me after him." She calmly strolled closer to Butch. "You know how this works, baby."

She sighed. "One will stand watch to look out for the boss, the weaker one of the betas. The other one will nuzzle me, test for acceptance, and I'll nuzzle him back to let him know, yeah, I'm game." She leaned in closely and murmured her statement. "He'll already be so keyed up he'll almost bust a nut as I turn around for him. The other one on lookout might not even make it to the mount. He'll try to nuzzle my neck while jerking off after watching for a few seconds to hurry the other male along, while that male snaps and barks at him to back off, but not about to stop pumping."

"I get the picture," Butch said, looking away from her too disgusted. What she said was true; beta males had no self-respect.

"You've never been a beta, so you don't know how alluring an alpha's picked female is. Stupid betas could just pay another working girl and have their own female for the night... but, noooo. They gotta have the alpha's pick, if possible. It's the conquest of a lifetime."

She threw her head back and laughed low, deep, and richly when he didn't answer. "Oh, shit, you Lups are crazy. I'll siphon them during every aggressive, frantic nuzzle, and my bites will turn them on so badly the process will be a very quick information exchange... and then, I'll lift my head, look over my shoulder and seem panicked, like the big guy is coming back, and they'll scram. Survival of the fittest."

She was giving him a headache, but it was the truth, even though he didn't want to hear it in such graphic detail.

"Butch, baby, no self-respecting alpha pick would be caught dead with a beta male humping her after an alpha was done—*that's* a real slap in the face to a dominant male, enough to make a girl road kill. The betas won't know that I've been discarded, and even if I have, anyone in the big male's pack that dared to come behind him on a full moon night, would get his throat ripped out just on general principle. It would be a territorial issue and an authority challenge that he wouldn't tolerate. My *goodness*, you all get so primal during this phase of the moon! Vampires are much smoother about the whole issue of sexual territory—to them its sport to see who the most seductive male is... and if he can pull the bait with linguistic dexterity, then, whatever."

She batted her eyes and traced a finger down the side of his throat. "Theater darling... you came to the best; a mistress of illusion and seduction, which is all in a night's work. Female Lups don't have the telepathy and would get caught up in the moon thing, anyway. Phantoms can't be trusted, they work all sides of the house and would give up the ghost," she said, giggling. "I'm your only ace up the sleeve for this job. Or I could go do the vamps, and with them I'd multi-orgasm for the money, too. So—"

"Seventy-five," he muttered, pushing away from the parked car and stalking toward the casino. He needed space. He needed more cash, too, which meant going to Malcolm—which now meant he had a partner and wouldn't be a freelancer, the only way he liked to work... And since the cash would come out of Malcolm's security budget, Laurel would be alerted and start some bullshit he could *not* handle tonight.

"Glad we came to terms," Ecstasy said in a giggling echo and blew a kiss behind him. "I'll have word for you tomorrow night... and anything else you want. Toodle-loo."

Chapter Three

Laurel closed her eyes. She'd heard Barron's signature howl through the plate-glass windows of her office, and had to hold onto the arms of her chair not to answer it. The response call was bubbling up in her esophagus, but she'd managed to choke it down with extreme effort. No matter what, she was staying in her office tonight. Going down on the casino floor in this condition was too volatile. The huge tournament didn't need the disruption of a bar fight caused by a heat-scent, spiking clan-foreign alpha males into mortal combat.

Watching the rows of monitors from her safe position was best. She could send her staff out on the floor, stay in contact with them by two-way, and keep a sweeping gaze on any suspicious activity from where she sat—alone.

It always pissed her off to no end that Malcolm would make snide comments about her staying home for a few nights each time she went into phase. *Pompous jerk.* So what she loved him as family? That didn't matter, the sexist statement always led to a test of wills.

Anyway, what was different about her so-called "condition" than any male's? They acted like complete idiots when the moon waxed full, but nobody sent the entire retinue of male staff home then. So why in the hell did she have to go home just because she was feeling a little rammy during a heat? No. She was their full equal, and defied any male, alpha or otherwise, to challenge her authority.

Besides, it wasn't a real issue until that pain in the ass, Barron Maverick, had darkened the hotel's doorstep again. Before that, she'd gotten through every phase as cool as a cucumber. Well… almost. Still, none of the Lups she'd seen had impressed her. *Whatever.* She refused to howl at the moon from a mere Maverick sighting. *Not.*

Heat

Laurel focused her attention on the cameras, but then caught Butch's image loping toward the poker and tournament tables. He moved in long, fluid, graceful strides, and she had to remember to breathe in through her nose, and then let the air out of her lungs through her mouth. For a moment, her eyes abandoned the screens containing images from the second floor's pool, arcade, and banquet rooms. The shops, day spa, and amphitheater somehow slid away from her mind, along with the parking lot. It was impossible to hold her focus on the meeting rooms and nearly empty halls on the second and third floors, or any of the restaurants and bars.

Hundreds of people milled about, but for a very fleeting moment, there was only one guest in the entire complex... Barron Maverick. One set of wide shoulders and square-jawed profile that she could mentally process. One handsome face. One set of large, rough hands that picked up a fan of cards and coolly slid chips across the green felt, sending chills down her spine.

"All clear on one," a staffer said through the two-way, jolting her back to reality. "How's it look from your side?"

Panic made her quickly scan the first floor monitors. "Good. Good." She swallowed hard.

"You hungry?"

"Yeah, a burger, rare, would be most excellent right now," she said quietly, her gaze going back to the one monitor it shouldn't have.

"I'll bring it right up," her employee said in a hopeful voice.

Laurel groaned inwardly. All she needed was a very hopeful beta male in her face, right now. A sweet as he was, never. "No, that's okay, Stew. I can hold off for a little while." She kept her response polite...appreciative, but firm.

"It's really no problem, Laurel... anything you want, okay?"

Jesus, give me a break. "Thanks, Stew, but I'm all right." She dropped her voice an octave to squash the attempt.

Trying to wrestle her brain back to her job, she immediately called the rest of the security personnel on two-way and checked in with them, hoping the other monitoring stations that were secretly tucked in offices had been on-point during her brief lapse. This had to stop. Sleeping on the job was dangerous for guests and the entire operation, especially with high-rollers coming in near midnight for the tournament. What Butch had told her had already been a source of worry before he got there. Rogue bandits couldn't be tolerated. The casino was gonna be loaded with wealthy clients that could be easy marks under a full moon. The establishment needed that like a silver bullet in the head.

Laurel rubbed her palms slowly down her face, glad that all the security news, so far, had been benign. The negative roll calls from the beefed-up staff made her feel slightly better, but didn't relax her in the least. It also didn't help that she was so hungry right now that she was ready to gnaw on the side of her desk.

She sat forward, leaning on her elbows and made a tent with her fingers before her mouth, carefully watching the gaming floor. *What the hell are Cutter, Fang, and Mad Dawg doing here flashing large wads of cash in the Black Jack area?* They usually kept to the casinos in the brothels on the other side of town. Earlier, only a few new high-roller Lups she didn't know had been there, but where were they now? She leaned in closer. *Where is Maverick?*

Frantic, she began pressing buttons on the monitors trying to locate him. If he started some action in her shop tonight without telling her, it would be *on*, buddy! But she suddenly relaxed when she saw him leaving the Voodoo Café with the small restaurant's signature food parcel. Rolling her shoulders, she smoothed the baby-fine hair that was standing up on the nape of her neck.

"Better not," she muttered, and went back to intently watching the three guests that concerned her.

A knock at the door almost made her jump out of her skin. She stood, for a second not sure why, until she smelled him… along with a burger.

"Yeah, what do you want?" she called out in a surly tone, cocked her head, and closed her eyes, letting out an impatient breath when he didn't answer.

"Maverick, whatduya want?"

"I was hungry, ordered a burger before I sat down at the tables, and figured you might want one, too. I just picked it up—you want it now, or ya wanna wait till it gets cold?"

She strode across the room, unlocked the door and flung it open. "I'm working."

"I know, but are you hungry?"

Exasperated, she moved to let him in and slammed the door shut behind him. The smell of the food, along with the tantalizing smell of him, only stoked her ire. She locked the door.

Ignoring her outburst, he loped over to her desk and pulled a Styrofoam box out of the bag, set it down slowly and backed away. "Bloody, cheese, no onions, hot sauce, and fries on the side." He looked at her, and then extracted two root beers from the bag and held out one for her. "Something to wash it down."

Her stomach did flip-flops as she stalked over to him, snatched a pop bottle, and muttered, "Thanks."

It took everything within her to move around him and go to her desk, but she refused to immediately tear into the box of grub. No. She focused her gaze on a monitor while the delicious scent of near raw, flame-seared beef wafted up her nose. Her hands were practically shaking as she angrily twisted off the pop cap, threw her head back, and guzzled half the bottle.

He had to sit before he fell down. Rather than look like a complete idiot, he grabbed a nearby chair, turned it around backwards, and sat with a thud. It was either scarf down the burger or make a lunge for her. Opting for the sane choice, he set his root beer on an adjacent desk as calmly as possible and ripped open the bag to get his container of food. The huge burger was gone in three wolfing bites; albeit, he was slightly humiliated that he was practically slobbering on himself in front of her, but kept his expression nonchalant as he licked away the remnants of ketchup from his mouth... it would have been so nice if she had done that.

"You're not gonna eat?"

"In a bit," she said with attitude, not looking at him.

"Hey, if you don't want it..."

She looked at him and opened the box lid, irises holding a slightly glowing dare.

"My bad," he said, chuckling and began scoffing down his fries. "All a brother was trying to say was... if you weren't hungry don't let good grub go to waste."

"Thank you," she said after a moment, and finally picked up the burger, sniffed it, then bit into it hard.

The look on her face made him stop chewing. Her eyes had crossed beneath her lids, and the soft moan she released almost made him stand. But he had to be cool. Had to tell her that Malcolm was gonna sock her budget hard for a little undercover work that had to be done the way it had to be done. The call went down without resistance while he was ordering the burger. Once he'd explained Ecstasy's plan, all Malcolm had said was, "Damn... do it."

But he wanted that news to come from him, not Malcolm, and knew Laurel would shift and go for his throat when she heard it... no love-play in the lunge at all. The burger had been a peace offering, although he'd have brought her a dripping steak, if she'd let him.

"See those three guys at poker two," Butch said, trying hard to keep his focus as he watched Laurel eat. "Earlier, three weak alphas were sitting where they are now."

"I know," she mumbled through a bite. "Where are they? That's what I wanna know."

There was no good way to answer her legitimate question. "Cutter, Fang, and Mad Dawg usually don't show themselves around here," he said, choosing his words with care. "Don't you think it's mighty coincidental that they're here now... during a big tournament that starts tonight and about to run all week?"

"Yeah," she said, polishing off the burger, and washing down the last swallow with her pop. "But there's a lot of new faces here just for the tourney. That could be a sign, but might not be. But we do need to watch them."

He'd heard half of what she said as he watched the liquid slide down her throat, the way it moved under her soft skin as she tipped her head back, spilling a thick wash of brunette hair over her shoulders. Her jacket was on the chair, the low bluish lights in the room from the monitors practically made her sheer blouse see-through... the lace beneath it caught his attention and sent his line of vision over her breasts. He had to close his eyes as his gaze slid over her tight nipples. *Good Lord*, he remembered her in his arms, every agonizing moment.

She glimpsed him from the corner of her eye and nearly choked on her pop when his eyelids became heavy, and he slightly turned his head away. This calm, discreet man was *not* the Barron Maverick she knew. Suddenly, she felt too exposed without her jacket on. Just knowing that he'd been looking at her that way made her nipples sting. Lord, she remembered those fevered nights with Barron... under the moon and stars, his deep, baritone growls sending chills down her spine... the way he made love; hot, intense, and impassioned until there was nothing left to do but sob from pleasure.

"What do you make of it?" she said, quickly bringing her mind out of self-hypnosis, and beginning to munch on her fries without tasting them. She had to do something with her hands.

"I think the weak alphas came in and cased the joint, flashing money to make it look like they already came loaded," he said in a gravelly tone with his head hung back and eyes closed while inhaling and exhaling very slowly. "Then Cutter and his posse came in as a follow up recognizance to be sure, using the same pattern."

She couldn't speak as she watched Butch labor to breathe. Slowly and very methodically, she abandoned her fries and the pop on the edge of her desk. It was the sexiest, most primal thing she'd seen Barron do. The man was simply breathing, on focus with his words, but a repressed shift was clearly kicking his ass. He was making her remember too much tonight, and she was less than stable. Plus, he was right. What was happening on the floor smelled suspicious.

"You think they'll make a move tonight?" she murmured, and then watched his breath hitch from the sound of her voice.

"I hope not," he said, lifting his head slowly to stare at her. "I'm being real."

She squeezed her knees together under her desk to stave off the want that was burning between her thighs. "I have to watch the floors and be sure they don't try something stupid."

"I know; me too," he said in a low rumble, and then slowly cased the room, his gaze stopping on the technology and finally settling on the lock on the door.

"Oh… no, Maverick, don't even think it," she said chuckling softly, unable to force indignation into her tone.

"We can still watch the monitors. The door will be locked." His unblinking gaze and the serious tone of his voice held her for ransom. "I missed you. The moon is out, and I can't fake it. I can't forget. Being around you messes me up bad, Laurel."

"I missed you, too—but this is my gig, Mav… come on. Gimme a break."

"Then, when do you go on break?" he asked, slowly standing.

"I don't. Not with a potential threat in the casino," she murmured and stood.

They both stared at each other for a moment.

"You're standing way too close," she said quietly, her eyes searching his.

"I know," he murmured. "But I can't back up."

She swallowed hard. "Neither can I."

"You gonna call Malcolm… or your men on the floor… so somebody else can watch those guys for a few?"

"In a little while," she said slowly, as his hot palm cupped her cheek and seared it.

Heat

He shuddered when she turned her mouth against it and kissed the center of it as her eyes closed. "You wanna watch the monitors together?"

She nodded and placed her hand in the center of his stone-cut chest. "We can't shift in here, though—you know that."

He only nodded and stepped in closer to her. Initially it was impossible to speak as the words he was about to say got lodged in his chest under her warm hand. "You're burning up."

She closed her eyes. "So are you."

He allowed his trembling hands to fall to her shoulders. Heat fever was making her blouse stick to her body. He breathed her in, pressing his nose to her hair as she fit against him with a whimper that released a deep, guttural groan from within him. The moment her hands slid up his back, he sought her mouth hard, and could feel his vertebra beginning to separate for a massive wolf transformation. She pulled out of the kiss, gasping.

"You're shifting and—"

"I know, I know, I'm sorry," he whispered urgently, cradling her face and raining hot kisses against it. "It's just been so long without you, baby." His voice was bottoming out, becoming unintelligible. She felt so good; his body couldn't stop moving against hers as she gathered his leather lapels into her fists. He still had a gun on him, and couldn't even think about wasting time removing it. His hands were preoccupied in her velvety hair, then caressing her arms, her supple spine, and sliding over hips he'd missed until they covered the firm lobes of her ass. "Oh, God Laurel, get somebody in here to cover for you for an hour."

"I can't leave my post," she breathed out, her hands sliding up his chest and over his nipples, making him insane as she nipped his Adam's apple.

"The door is locked," he gasped on a ragged murmur.

"We have to watch the monitors. If you shift, I won't be able to."

He crushed her mouth again, nodding, wishing he could just drop to all fours, but knew she was right. If he went there, it would

be all night, no human reasoning capacity within him. She was sho'.
nuff about to make him go straight wolf.

She yanked away from him, spun around giving him her back,
and flattened both her palms on the desk. He lost it as her backside
slid against his groin. All he could do was blanket her with a groan,
cup her breasts, and slowly run his hands the length of her abdomen
to find her pants fastenings. It took everything in him not to shred the
fabric, but as she began to pant and grind pleasure into his groin with
her haunches, the consequences of doing that became a very distant
concern. Her head dropped back and the howl she held in made his
hands clumsy. His mind had one goal: get her pants down.

Agony produced sweat that ran in rivulets down his temples. Her
blouse was already drenched from her perspiration and suffering.
She helped him get her fastenings undone, and yanked down her
zipper; he quickly pushed her linen pants over the swell of her hips
and bit her shoulder as his palms drank in her warm, damp flesh. He
had no patience for the thong; it was gone with a sudden rip. His
fingers caressed her belly, and then slid between her thighs to sink
into her wet valley. It had been so long, the sensation made him
need to look at a monitor to keep the inner wolf at bay.

But it was the sound of her fractured voice that did it, along with
her frenzied attempts to get his belt unbuckled, and then work on his
pants hardware. He silently cursed himself for the complexity of
clothes as she struggled, and he tried to assist, but was unable to stop
touching that hot, wet, slippery place that smelled so good between
her thighs. Years away from her were making him foolish, but right
now he didn't care.

The moment she freed him, he knew they were both in trouble.
The burn of her skin as he pressed against her softness was so exquisite, tears blurred his vision. He could feel her howl working its way
up her abdomen as he gently extracted his hand from between her
legs, briefly held her hips positioning for sudden entry, and then sank
against her in a deep thrust. It was so damned good he yelped.

"*Barron*, it feels so good!"

Heat

The way she'd said his name blanked out all reason. The tight, slick sheath of her body was pure destruction to a man's will. He grabbed her around the waist hard with one arm, bracing on the desk with his free hand, as he nipped her ear and kept thrusting.

"Go 'head… shift for me, baby," he murmured between hot bursts of breath. "I'm right there with you."

But fragile clarity came to his mind as he threw his head back and glimpsed a monitor. Cutter and his crew were on the move. Damn it!

"I'm shifting," she wailed. "I can't help it."

"No! If you go, I'm gone," he said between his teeth, trying to hold it at bay. "I won't be able to shift back. If somebody knocks on the door, won't matter."

It was as plain as he could make it in short, choppy sentences laced with heavy breaths. If Malcolm barged in or there was a floor emergency, there'd be no way to preserve her dignity, shift back, and be cool. Not now. He knew she'd never forgive him if he took her there. And yet, at the moment there was only right now, sending spasms of acute pleasure through his rod, crossing his eyes, splattering her back with droplets of his sweat, a repressed howl at the moon bubbling within him. *Damn…* he was losing control.

She nodded quickly as though reading his mind and dropped to her elbows beneath him, reaching backward to stroke his hip, her fevered mouth pressing a kiss against his bulging bicep. If she hadn't read his mind, then she'd definitely read his body. When her spine plummeted and she suddenly lifted her backside hard to meet him, he bit his lip not to holler. She hollered for him. That set off a chain reaction of call and response that neither of them could fight. Her name was bouncing off the walls between each breath; her nails were pulling up desk walnut; he'd almost knocked himself out, his forehead colliding with a monitor while trying to drag her up onto the desk.

Heaven help any fool that knocked on the door. The hair on his knuckles was starting to grow, and he could feel it getting longer from his scalp, thick ringlets brushing his ears as he furiously rocked against her. The transformation was trying to come as hard and fast as he was. Her voice was changing, getting deeper with every moan, and then she shuddered so hard when she climaxed that his lower canines split his lip.

The seizure that shot through him was blinding; the howl was ridiculous. But there was no way to stop it. The mournful wail blended in with hers and left them both limp and winded on the desk with their eyes closed.

It took him a moment to peel himself up from her spine enough to gather his wits. She was sprawled out beneath him, the desk veneer ruined.

Laurel slowly lifted herself up from the desk, leaving a damp outline on it from where her body had been. He kissed the nape of her neck, allowing his hands to revel her breasts while nuzzling her now very long hair.

"That was fantastic," he murmured against her shoulder, still inside her, and feeling her body contract around him. This gorgeous woman in his arms was the only one that had made him feel this way; this complete. He couldn't stop kissing her.

She leaned against him with a sigh and reached backward to touch his face. "That was *crazy*-fantastic, Barron… You're the only one that makes me get insane like this." She released another satisfied moan and turned enough to kiss his shoulder. "Your hair and beard grew while we were at it."

He chuckled low in his throat. "Among other things. You have that effect on me."

"The fries and pop fell," she said with a slight laugh that made her canal tense, dredging whatever remained in his sack.

He shivered with a smile. "I'll buy you some more for the late-night munchies." Thoroughly content, he murmured the promise against her neck. "Then we can go till the moon fades. Remember that time… midnight till after dawn, and we were still out there going strong?"

They both tensed and he slowly withdrew. Oh... boy... *midnight*. The tournament. The rival clan. She didn't even have to say it. This had been nuts. Completely insane.

"I know," he whispered, now trying to help her pull up her pants.

She didn't turn around, but quickly zipped them up. He followed suit, but had difficulty. He was still too hard.

"We didn't watch the monitors," she said in an unnaturally calm tone, but still didn't turn around.

"Yeah, uh, I know." He let his breath out hard and stroked her hair, knowing she was freaked out beyond imagination. "But at least I kept my word. I didn't shift... not all the way."

He watched her hug herself and lean her head back. "Oh, my God... I didn't make you put on a condom, either."

He froze. "Ooops," he said slowly, and then let out a very quiet sigh. "Uh..."

She held up her hand. "My bad," she whispered.

He kissed her hand and turned her around. "It'll be cool," he said, forcing alpha bravado into his voice. He tried to lean down to kiss her, but her eyes held such quiet hysteria he hesitated.

She just looked up at him. "I'm *in heat*."

He closed his eyes and kissed her forehead. What could he say? He'd definitely dropped a full payload. They were both still breathing hard from it. He just hoped she was still on the pill, back then she was. Maybe they'd dodged another silver bullet? But something crazy was going on in his head—a part of him wouldn't mind if tonight made things more permanent.

"I need to clean up in here and..." her words trailed off as she glanced at her partially destroyed desk while trying to smooth her clothes. "*Oh, shit...*"

"Baby, don't panic. We'll get cleaned up; I'll fix the desk somehow while you go to your suite and take a quick shower. Then, uh, what I can do see, is uh, watch the monitors for you, and uhmmm. Oh shit. Uh, then when you come back down, all I gotta do is hit the men's room for a minute—then we can go talk to Malcolm, and—"

"Talk to Malcolm about what?" Her gaze was open; trusting, but becoming more furtive the longer it took him to respond. "I mean, we saw those guys casing, we *think*. But we weren't really watching long enough to know for sure. Right now, I don't wanna alert Malcolm unnecessarily until we see them doing something that offers ironclad proof they're up to no good." She ran her fingers through her hair. "God, the last thing I want is for Malcolm to come down here, see this very obvious mess, then start asking a whole buncha questions that we can't answer and get him all riled up for a speculative reason. This was really outta line."

The words *oh shit* imploded in triplicate within his brain. Now that the big head was doing all the thinking again, he knew clearly that this could not end well. He'd done everything in reverse, being so jacked up. He'd struck a deal with Ecstasy before consulting Malcolm; he'd called Malcolm first, before consulting Laurel; he'd made love to Laurel before asking her about birth control necessities; had entered her before putting on a condom, if one was required; had loved her hard before telling her about the seventy-five grand sting. Butch just closed his eyes.

"Baby, listen… uh, Malcolm needed more—"

Static on the two-way stopped his words. An efficient female voice he didn't recognize broke through the receiver and made him put rational distance between him and Laurel.

"Yo, Laurel. Heads-up. Malcolm is on his way about the request for more sting dollars. He's getting off the elevators now."

Butch couldn't even look at her now.

Chapter Four

Malcolm was at the door before Butch could barely get his shirt tucked in good. Laurel's eyes were so wide he thought the woman would pass out. She straightened her suit, raked her fingers through her tussled hair, snatched up the fallen fries and spilled pop bottle, and hurriedly slung it all into the trash as she dashed across the floor like something was chasing her.

Laurel yanked the door open so hard that it slammed against the wall. Butch hung back and leaned against the destroyed desk, trying to casually body shield it from Malcolm's notice.

The boss walked in, glanced around, and then brushed invisible lint off his navy-blue designer suit lapels as though needing somewhere discreet to send his line of vision for a moment. A wry smile tugged at Malcolm's mouth as he entered the room and calmly shut the door behind him, tilting his head.

Butch watched Laurel watching Malcolm as his nostrils flared just a tad, and he straightened to look at Butch. Two alpha males of approximately the same height and build, one a bit older, stared at each other, exchanging a silent understanding. There had been no territorial breach, per se, but Laurel was like Malcolm's baby sister. If a heat mating had gone down under Malcolm's roof, then it had better be a permanent one, unless Laurel wanted it otherwise. It was all in the eyes, a non-verbal warning etched in the cool glare Malcolm assessed Butch with. The silent statement was easy to read: *Don't play with my sister's heart or I'll butcher you, Maverick.*

"Then I guess you already told her," Malcolm finally said, swallowing his smile, "and I take it everything is cool with the arrangement?"

Butch cringed as Laurel looked from Malcolm to him. Oh… shit… this would end very badly indeed.

"Tell me what, Barron?" Laurel's voice was tight, her eyes losing the trust in them. Suspicion slowly replaced it.

"Uh, baby—Laurel, what had happened was—"

"You didn't tell her?" Malcolm looked at Butch hard, then glanced around the disheveled office, and shook his head. "Maybe I need to come back in another hour. I'll be sure to bring a body bag for your carcass." He narrowed his gaze on Butch. "Lay a canine on her while she kicks your ass and you know our friendship will be severely strained, right?"

Laurel folded her arms over her chest and stared at Butch without blinking. "Tell me something very quickly and very rational, Barron Maverick," she said in a warning tone. "So help me."

For a moment, all he could do was stare at her. A rosy tinge of embarrassment stained her cheeks. Her flushed face shamed him for putting her in this predicament. In all honesty, he'd only meant to come up to her office to make peace, but wound up making love. Now the boss was in the bull, and he knew she'd flip.

"I needed to get some deep, undercover information." Butch pushed off the desk and began to pace while talking with his hands. He had to ignore the way Malcolm's gaze slid over the desk and his eyebrow arched. This was raggedy; yeah, he knew it, but the circumstantial evidence had him framed. "So I asked a contact to siphon some information outta those first three Weres—"

"Stop," Laurel said, coming closer to him while holding up her hand. "You began a sting, in my yard, without telling me?"

"Well, uh, sorta—but, the deal is this—"

"It's seventy-five Gs, Laurel," Malcolm said flatly. "The source is reliable, we need to work with her, and only a female vamp can get that sort of 4-1-1 out of beta males that fast."

"You didn't…" Her hands went to her sides, and then slowly became fists.

"Laurel, uhmmm... what had happened was—in the parking lot, she explained—"

"In *the parking lot?*" Laurel whispered through her teeth.

Malcolm headed for the door.

"That was your howl out there, because of *that?*"

"I'll have accounting draft Ecstasy Jones a cashier's check, or does she want cash, man?" Malcolm said evenly.

"Cash," Butch said, looking out of the window.

The punch connected with his jaw so hard and so fast that it caught him off guard, knocking blood and spit from his mouth. Laurel was up on a desk, eyes glowing.

"I'll get it from the vault," Malcolm said coolly, opening the door. "Large bills or small?"

Butch dodged the lunge and leapt over a row of monitors and desks. "Don't leave me in here with her, man! Laurel, calm down. I can explain."

Two monitors crashed into the far wall as Malcolm gently pulled the door closed behind him. A desk overturned, and three chairs became rubble as they splinted from the impact of being hurled against the wall. He ducked behind the desk for a second, and then peeked out. The most magnificent creature, the only one in the world for him, was slowly advancing on him, her silver-black coat glistening, canine teeth fully extended into a beautiful snarl, eyes glowing gold inside her gray irises.

Just seeing Laurel that way did something very insane to his mind. He shifted instantly, transforming to his real self to stand four-feet at the shoulders in a thick, jet-black coat. Laurel lunged, got his arm, severely lacerating it, but he loved every minute of it as he finally flipped her to pin her down, his huge jaws poised over her throat.

When she stopped struggling, he cautiously pulled his jaws away, careful not to cut her with a canine. "I didn't do her in the lot," he rumbled, panting more from her being beneath him than the fight.

Laurel snarled and normalized into a naked woman under him, tears in her eyes. "This is just like before," she said, looking away, her hand absently stroking his coat.

"No it's not," he said quietly, dropping down to lay on her naked in his human male form.

She put her hand between their mouths when he leaned in to kiss her. "How much are you getting off this bounty hunt?"

He sighed. Money was the last thing on his mind, but he knew he had to oblige her. He owed her that. "A little over a quarter mil," he said, hoping she'd lower her hand.

"From where?" she asked in a brittle tone, grabbing a fistful of his hair to pull his head back to stop another attempted kiss.

Her body was burning up under his, setting his on fire. Seeing her shift had torched his libido. The moon was still out. An adrenaline rush was thudding in his groin. She was still so wet and he was oh so close to being inside her. Why did they have to fight now? "Baby—"

"Where?"

"Every municipality that got robbed had a bounty," he rushed out. "The Preternatural Authorities."

"Then you pay your own freight or I want a third of the bounty to reimburse my budget that you spent without my authorization. In fact, I want it paid back, regardless. We clear?"

"Yeah. No problem," he said, his hands in her hair. "Just…"

"Don't even think about it," she said, dropping her tight hold on his curls and shoving him off her. "You must be crazy!"

It was a valid assumption. A very true one, as he watched her saunter over to her pile of clothes and begin to tug them on. The plea that he was sure had to be in his eyes entered his voice. "You sure you don't wanna… I mean, it's… Malcolm didn't have a problem… and—"

"Put your clothes on."

She didn't even turn around. That was the worst part of it. Just watching her lovely ass move as she dressed. Begrudgingly, he got up and found his pants to yank them on. But the sound of male foot-steps made him snarl. The scent that came with it made him find his gun. Not tonight.

She turned as the door opened, hurriedly tucking her blouse in her pants, and froze.

Guy was standing in the opened doorway with a room service tray and a plate under an aluminum cover. "I bought you a steak because the fellas said you had to work graveyard shift tonight," he said, snarling at Butch as he slowly cast the tray on the only desk standing in the room. "But I see you already ate." He glimpsed around the room and stared at the barrel of the gun.

Laurel closed her eyes and hugged herself. "Guy, listen… it's not what you think."

Butch slowly set the gun down on a freestanding chair. "You wanna do this in the parking lot like old times?"

"Why not?" Guy growled. "Seems like everybody's tripping down memory lane tonight."

"Hold it," Laurel said, stepping between them. "If either of you do that, I swear, I'll tear both your throats out. Like I need this shit with everything that's about to go on in this hotel!"

Butch backed up. Guy's gaze raked his naked chest and then Laurel, but he finally backed up, retracting his canines.

"Thank you," she said, glancing at both of them, disgusted. "And thank you for the steak."

"Don't mention it," Guy muttered, then turned and strode away.

She gave Butch a hard look. "I'm going to take a five minute shower. When I come back, your ass better be down on the casino floor working to protect my seventy-five grand investment."

What could he say? Laurel had a right to be pissed. The casino was loaded, and the rival clan was definitely up to no good. An insane part of him still wanted Guy and his pit bosses to bring the noise. He needed to get that out of his system once and for all. The sex scent on him was already drawing beta females near, and, unfortunately, a few alpha females, too… which only made the males he passed glower with a curled lip.

His battered jaw looked like he'd been in a fight over a female and lost, or maybe punked down off his mount—since Laurel's scent lingered. That only made the nearby betas aggressive enough to openly challenge an alpha male that had been rank-stripped. The other alphas were serving him grisly expressions to further display their dominant rank over his, as though thoroughly disgusted that a male his size could've been so humiliated and still had the nerve to come out in public. Fuck 'em all, it wasn't their business.

But going up to his hotel room to take a shower had been out of the question. If Laurel came down first and didn't see him, then it would get real crazy.

His jaw hurt, and his lip was busted from his own canines and Laurel's blow. His arm hurt like hell. Her canine gash was still tender and probably would take twenty-four hours to heal. The Mardi Gras Bar opposite the entrance seemed like a good place for a man to go to lick his wounds. He could see the action from afar, have a drink, and try to chill.

"Didn't take half as long as I thought," a cool female voice said in his ear. "They must have been really messed up by the scent in the casino."

"Merlot?" Butch asked without looking at Ecstasy as she slid onto a barstool next to him.

"Darlin' that's only for show—you know I drink private label."

Butch nodded and hailed a bartender, but a hostess brought a drink over to Ecstasy before Butch could discreetly put in her order for blood-mixed private label.

"What's this?" she said, holding the glass with two fingers and looking into it with an arched eyebrow.

The hostess shrugged. "The gentleman over there sent you some Hypnotic."

She walked away, and Ecstasy sent her line of vision across the room. Butch bristled. True, Ecstasy wasn't his woman, but some things were protocol. He glanced where Ecstasy's gaze lingered.

"A new vamp high-roller wonders if I'm under a hypnotic spell, trying to pick up a thug werewolf. Creative expression. I like him. May have to do him later." Ecstasy set down her glass with precision and blew the challenging male a kiss over her shoulder.

Butch growled.

"Well, you do look like a thug, Maverick. What the hell happened to your lip?"

"Long story," he muttered, rolling his glass between his palms.

"I can kiss it and make it better," she said, chuckling.

"Gimme a break." He took a sip of Dewar's and flinched from the sting of alcohol in his mouth.

"I really can kiss it and make it better, you know," she said, accepting the drink the bartender wasn't sure why he'd made for her, but did. "Come here. We regenerate from nicks and scrapes... and fangs all the time. I already have your blood in my system, so a quick kiss will fix the lip and bruised jaw."

She slid a cool, graceful palm under his chin and turned his cheek so he faced her. "Ouch. The bruise that came with it was nasty, too. Did she do that?"

"No," he muttered, to embarrassed to go into detail.

Ecstasy leaned forward and tenderly brushed his mouth. "Liar."

When she pulled away, she ran the pad of her thumb over his mouth. "She benefited from all my prep work to get you turned on. I *so* envy her."

"Why, you wanna bust me in my mouth, too?"

She smiled. "Yeah, something like that."

He let out a heavy breath. "So, tell me, what's going on?" He needed to switch subjects. Feeling down in the dumps, a drink in front of him, the moon still up, and a gorgeous babe understanding it all beside him was a recipe for disaster.

"The betas were interesting," she said, twirling her wine glass and taking a slow sip. "Fast, but interesting."

"I don't need the gory details, just the facts."

She sighed and chuckled. "The increased meth production is for the vamps coming in."

Now she had his attention. Butch frowned and gave her a side-long glance. "I don't follow."

"You did *secure* my money, right?"

He took a sip from his glass and set it down hard. "Yeah, did I ever."

She sidled up closer to him and spoke in a private tone. "The high-roller vamps coming in tonight are billionaires. Therefore, their parties are lavish beyond your wildest dreams. The penthouses will be rocking until dawn, but before that, they all have to go to the special basement suites without windows."

"So, far, I'm not getting new information," he said evenly, glancing at her, and then going back to his drink.

"Those old boys are so decadent that they'll take anything to keep the party going past dawn in the special basement suites. Normally, you know we practically pass out at sunrise, correct?"

He looked at her from a sidelong glance. "Yeah."

She leaned in closer. "The batch is tainted with blessed sodium... like holy water and Red Sea salt, et cetera." She trailed her finger down his thigh. "Old Masters won't dabble in a drug that could reduce their performance while under the power of darkness... they own the night. But they'll take a hit of anything that can make them stay up past dawn."

"Whoa," Butch said slowly, not even feeling her lazy trail up and down his leg. "But those guys got a nose, they'd smell—"

"Uh, uh, ahhh…" she said, wagging her finger. "Seems the rival clan has been robbing banks and whatever to build up an arsenal and to pay a few witches off to create an aphrodisiac in earlier batches." She sat back with a triumphant smile when Butch's jaw went slack. "Very shrewd."

Butch leaned closer to her, glancing around, raising nearby hackles from fellow patrons. "This isn't normal were-clan style. They had to have a backer. Vamps normally won't trust anything coming from us—not anything to ingest."

"Correct," she murmured, sipping her Merlot-blood mix slowly. "The witches are expensive, and the initial batches had to be couriered over to a vampire the old boys trusted… and it had to be tested. Perhaps family from one of the guys you dusted that had been involved in the identity theft ring, hmmm? Anyway, word got around that the werewolves who were enemies with your clan had something that worked—and wanted to make peace to let the vampire nations know they weren't in the earlier incident. They had to make a credible separation."

"All right, so there's new get-high out there, but the vamps can create crazy drugs on their own. Why would they need the were-clan?"

"It's all packaging and witchcraft, lover. Yes, they can make their own drugs, but somebody got the chemistry just right."

"What does it do?" He had to keep his voice low and glanced around without moving his head.

"Think of it like daylight Viagra. Now, it's a hot commodity, but the old boys are always wary… will only take it directly from the manufacturers—never the underling dealers. Hence why Cutter, Fang, and Mad Dawg are here tonight, not to distribute, but to be present as a manufacturer's oath of approval… showing themselves as unafraid to be seen silently backing up their product warranty. Under normal conditions, if you screw a big buyer, you're dead. So, most reasonable manufacturers send a middleman. Their presence sends a message that they stand behind their product. The betas will hand it off during the tournament to the buyers' middlemen, and so forth. Then it gets couriered up to the penthouses while the old boys work the tables with their games."

"And after they do the drop off, they sit back and wait, then bum rush the lairs, right?" Tension was winding down Butch's spine as he practically held his breath for Ecstasy's confirmation.

"Oh… no…" she said, finishing her wine. "They wait for the bodies to be found tomorrow night. There will be an all-out assault on the hotel from the vampire nations, if a large number of their VIPs, again, came to an unhealthy ending in this establishment. And of course, since the bodies won't be robbed, and the rival clan will be there to backup the vamps with heavy artillery to minimize any vampire casualties… it will look like your family did it. You guys did something shady in the hand off, or the switch when it got up to the penthouses—that the hotel management has access to with keys."

"This set up is so freakin' foul…"

"Yes, Butch. It is. Very vampire-like. That's why I'm sure they received assistance from the identity theft ring of new money holders. Old world vampires wouldn't engross themselves in such machinations for a little hotel, but newly made, greedy bastards would. The old boys play for shares of *countries*, not a Vegas strip hotel." She shook her head. "This is small time, relatively speaking—even though I'm sure it means a lot to you."

Butch looked at her hard, not angry, just trying to wrap his mind around the scale of old money vampire life as he spoke. "If the Preternatural Authorities got wind of this, it would all come out in court, though," he said, taking a deep swallow from his drink. "You're right, though. This is big time for us. We can't have the family reputation screwed like that."

"If it went to a lawsuit, the vampires would *own* this jewel. But we know it won't come to a thrilling legal conclusion—these guys are old world and serve justice in a very medieval fashion. Feudal, perhaps, but effective. And they'll break off a share to those who supported them. The establishment will be co-owned by them and a clan that can produce a product that will draw dignitaries from even the international set. You follow now?" Ecstasy kissed his cheek. "You've been played."

She sighed as she stood, openly shaking her head for theater so that anyone looking would think she'd declined to service him. "Actually, your old bounty is what gave them the idea. The vamps had a grudge, and we *never* forget a wrong. Centuries can go by, and it's like it happened yesterday. The rival clan saw an opportunity to exploit the code of vengeance we hold so dear... and voilà." She kissed him again quickly. "I have to go, sweetie. Deliver my money tonight; large bills will be fine. You know the lair. I'll be working the hotel, but you be careful."

"Thanks, baby," he murmured and clasped her hand to hold her for a moment. It wasn't for theater. "You be careful, too, and get off the premises before morning."

She just smiled and sauntered away. Butch looked around at the victorious expressions of the leering male vampires and flashed them a snarl.

He had to call Malcolm from a very private place. This was urgent.

Okay, two could play this game. Laurel stepped out of her room wearing a strapless black dress with her weapon firmly affixed to her thigh. If Butch Maverick wanted undercover, then she'd show the man how it was done. A female werewolf trailing heat-scent on a casino floor was a pure force of nature.

Chapter Five

Malcolm wasn't in his office—damn! He'd wanted to tell the boss face-to-face. It was a full moon and Marcus' cellular was going straight to voicemail. Laurel wasn't in her suite and wouldn't pick up her cell.

Butch strode through the hallway on a mission and headed for the stairs. He needed to get to his room to place several red alert calls where there'd be no eavesdroppers. Couldn't do it anywhere on the floor where it might look like he'd left an informant and went right for the phone. Ecstasy would be at risk, and she'd never be missed until the next night. Her lair seal couldn't be opened during the day; the light would fry her if she was there, and destroy her body as evidence of foul play.

As he took to the stairs, he heard a door open on the floor above him and one below him. He rolled his shoulders, preparing for a fight, sensing one coming by instinct. Guy strolled down the steps. Troy and Oliver boxed him in.

"Not now, man," Butch snarled. "There's some serious shit going on with the family."

"You bet there is, motherfucker," Guy snarled and spat. "You come back here after being gone for almost five years and tag my lady right in the hotel where we both work?"

Butch just stared at him for a moment. The important message he was carrying battled with the direct alpha challenge. "Your ass is delusional. Had she been yours, nothing woulda went down… and after five years, you cocky son of a bitch, trust me, you oughta hang your dawg head if I could walk back in here like that and pull her during a heat."

Heat

Ball game. The gauntlet had been thrown down. Shapes shifted in a whir. Clothes dropped to the floor. Two huge combatants were in the air. Canines ripped at limbs. Cement walls crumbled in huge chunks as massive wolf bodies slammed against them and came away in a tangle of fur. Barks echoed in the stairwell from the beta referees urging the mortal combat forward.

Tumbling down three stairwell flights with jaws locked together, claws slashed at barrel chests, then the stalemate broke so that male wolves could circle, pant, and lunge again. The steel banister gave way to a two-story drop. Both combatants reared on their hindquarters. Butch threw a punch that blew Guy through the door and onto the casino floor.

Moon madness had Butch in its grip. He was up on a roulette table, jaws dripping blood and saliva. Guests screamed and rushed about, but to his battle-focused mind, they sounded like tiny, annoying birds scattering, so far away. He had another male Lupine in his sight, and they both turned at the same time to see Laurel's horrified expression. Her scent was in the air as the three alpha males that were competing for her attention stood, dropped human form and lunged.

It was on. Every male for himself, but the grudge match was really between Butch and Guy. Security tried to surround them, but couldn't get a shot off without injuring the wrong inner clan wolf. Tables crashed into splinters, dealers dove for cover, and vampires took spectator positions on the ceiling, enjoying the testosterone display.

Slot machines slammed into walls, spilling thousands of non-silver slugs. Phantoms squealed with delight. Beta males barked in agitated circles, while females eagerly awaited the victors, getting turned on by the blood lust as huge bodies tore at battle-thickened coats, trying to take a throat.

When Butch saw Guy go down under three foreign clan attackers with a yelp, something fragile snapped within him. That was still family—beef between brothers; outsiders were dog meat.

He leapt onto the first attacker's back, caught a wrist as it rose to claw out Guy's eye, and yanked the arm out of the socket. From the corner of his peripheral vision, he saw Laurel drop her dress and shift to jump into the fray.

She'd pinned an alpha and came away with a rib bone, but he'd punched her in the face and sent her sprawling. That was it. The offender's esophagus came away from his throat as Butch's jaws took it out from the Adam's apple. When he spun on the third attacker, Guy was able to scramble away.

The two hunting male wolves circled each other slowly. Laurel got back up and circled from behind, snarling, helping to box in Butch's prey. A pump shotgun blast made all wolf forms freeze.

"Not in my establishment!" Malcolm bellowed, casting off the silver slug-filled gun to an underling and shifting into a huge, gray wolf with glowing eyes.

The outnumbered wolf lowered his head.

"That's my sister!" Malcolm growled, "And my brother-in-law." He looked at Laurel and then at Butch two seconds before he lunged, flipped the attacker, and came away with entrails, snapping.

Butch slowly stood, and shifted back. Laurel did as well and came back to her luscious human form, holding her face. Malcolm rolled his shoulder, straightened, and spit out bits of intestines. Slowly, everyone who'd lost it shifted and stood calmly naked. One-by-one, hands came together in a steady, methodical applause.

"Damn straight," Malcolm said, leaning his head back and howling, "Family first!"

Rounds of howls sent shivers down Lupine spines as vampires and assorted entities passed curious glances.

"This is why we generally do not frequent these types of establishments," one very aristocratic vampire said, smoothing his ruffled shirt and extending his elbow to his wife. "It's not done quite this way where we're from. I'm afraid we'll have to withdraw from the tournament."

Heat

Butch watched the early arrival vampires slowly withdraw in a huff, taking their human helper population with them, as well as several galled phantoms. *Whatever.* His gaze slowly tracked Laurel as she calmly dressed, as did every other male wolf on the casino floor. It was definitely worth it.

Memory slowly came back about how it all got started as he glanced at Guy and couldn't help himself. The growl came out of nowhere, from some deep chamber in his chest. The crowd tensed again with nervous anticipation.

"She's mine. Period!" Butch said, pointing at Guy. "We can finish it to the death in the parking lot!"

Laurel tiled her head. "Have you lost your mind, Barron Maverick?"

Guy growled and began to circle him to shift again.

"Completely," Butch shouted, ready to go back to wolf on a dime. "I am very crazy right now, Laurel. You'd better tell your boy just how insane I can be!"

"Stand down," Malcolm snarled at Guy. "The man saved your life, and this time, I won't get in it if you challenge him for her—but will if anybody else tries to break the two combatants up." He snatched his suit pants from the floor and yanked them on. "If I don't break it up like I did when you were kids, and your betas don't assist, tonight I think you'll get your ass kicked—but do as you like, brother. The choice to die in a mate contest battle is always yours."

Guy hocked, spit and stepped back, sufficiently cowed.

"I thought so, bitch," Butch muttered, snarling at Guy and ignoring the appreciative glances of the females he passed. He didn't know where his clothes were. All he was sure of was that he needed space and distance before he killed somebody.

Butch stopped walking, passed Laurel with a slight shudder, and looked at Malcolm. "We need to talk, ASAP. Bring Laurel."

Malcolm nodded. "Meet me in my office." He looked around at the destroyed casino floor. "Clean this up," he said to his employees. "For those guests who are staying, the tournament will obviously have to be postponed. Rooms, drinks, and dinners on the house for this evening to anyone who wishes to stay. Vouchers to reimburse those leaving for tonight can be picked up at the Concierge's desk. Our apologies from the management." With that, Malcolm zipped up his pants and followed Butch and Laurel toward the stairs.

⚜

"What!" Malcolm yelled, pounding his fist on the desk and splintering the wood. "In my hotel?"

"Yeah… that's what she told me, boss." Butch walked in an agitated circle.

"Then why didn't we out them right on the floor in front of the vamps?" Laurel folded her arms, believing his story, but still battle-hyped.

"Because with the obvious dissention in our ranks, and without solid proof without outing my source—which could put her life in jeopardy with her own kind forever," Butch said, staring at Laurel hard, "and with an unknown factor of armed mercenaries from a foreign clan, if I just stood up on a table and blurted it out, shocking Malcolm, it would seem like I was the one who had fore-knowledge and was trying to take over this clan."

Butch looked at Malcolm with respect. "They would think that the brawl that began in the stairwell and spilled out into the gaming floor was from internal affairs of our clan going through a power struggle about whether or not to poison the vamps."

"Correct," Malcolm said between his teeth. "An attempt to poison them would be viewed no differently than an actual, successful group assassination. They would have begun the war right then and there with witnesses and under justified circumstances—and as Butch said; the traitors would have rushed in to back them up when we weren't expecting an attack like that."

"The vamps deal in absolutes, like we do," Butch said, spiting out blood and testing a loose canine between his fingers. "Any display of wavering loyalty is like a slap in the face to them."

"So what do we do?" Laurel's eyes sought Butch's, and oddly not Malcolm's.

Not wanting to overstep his bounds, Butch glanced at Malcolm.

"We call a family meeting tonight—a brief one." Malcolm let out a weary breath. "We make sure we have enough reinforcements of artillery, should there be an attempted attack. But we're gonna need a sample of this mystery meth—and catch the Lupine who's passing it. Meanwhile, I need to also let the VIP vampires quietly know not to touch any controlled substance given to them anywhere, because there's a bad batch floating around… this has to be done in a way that allows them to save face."

Butch nodded. "Yeah. Let them be a part of the sting so they know we're interested in the truth, and only that. But it has to come from Malcolm, or it'll look like a power fracture."

"Then, let's do this," Laurel said calmly, heading for the door. "You're gonna have to hang me out as bait for the remaining betas in Cutter's clan. You know the deal—the strongest one just stepped up after all three of the leaders went down. Every male out there is trembling from the post-battle adrenaline. It's a full moon. He saw me shift. He saw me fight. He saw me naked. I'm in heat. And due to the brawl, he hasn't been laid yet—probably never by an alpha female."

Malcolm and Butch just stared after her as she slipped out the door and closed it softly behind her.

"You okay, man?" Malcolm asked in a low, concerned tone.

Butch shook his head no, staring at the door. "You heard the woman… It's a full moon. I saw her shift. I saw her fight. I saw her naked. She's in heat… and due to the brawl…"

Malcolm simply nodded and landed a hand on Butch's shoulder. "Let's get the meeting done fast. After this shit, I need to go find my mate, too."

Butch could barely concentrate on what was being said, beyond the strength of their forces—everything else he'd already heard. The huge bruise on Laurel's face was the thing that stole his attention. He so badly wanted to get up and help her nurse it with ice, but that would diminish her worth as a alpha warrior in front of the pack, and he'd never do that to her.

But if Guy didn't stop cutting his eyes at him with Troy and Oliver, the bull would bubble over again and the family meeting would be disrupted. The family couldn't afford that again. Everyone had to be on focus, had to have their ears keened and their eyes opened. Malcolm was right. Distractions could no longer be tolerated. Easier said than done.

"So, until the main gaming floor is pulled back together, we'll use the convention center space on the second floor for tournament tables as well as Black Jack and poker tables. We can set up temporary bars in there to replace the central bar that got trashed. On the third floor," Marcus said, "in the meeting rooms, we can salvage whatever undamaged slot machines we have, save one for another bar, and also add a bar to the pool area. Essentially, the first floor— other than the restaurants that somehow made it, will be closed for renovations until further notice. The PR media spin will be that we're expanding for guest improvements. End of story."

Malcolm nodded, appearing satisfied. He then glanced at Laurel. "You ready to go in?"

She nodded. "Piece of cake."

Butch clenched his fists but kept his mouth shut. Not ever being a beta male, he had no real frame of reference for what happened in intimate encounters until Ecstasy told him. But now the thought of Laurel playing with a beta male disgusted him to no end.

Malcolm saw the slight bristle. "You're her main backup," he said to Butch as calmly as he could. "They heard you claim her, and when she's ready to come out of there, you know what to do."

Butch nodded, but the glare Guy shot his way put him on his feet. He pointed at Guy across the room, canines lowering and a dangerous shift eminent. "I thought we got this shit clear down-stairs!"

Eleven family members eased back, waiting for Guy's response. When Guy looked away, shoulders relaxed.

"Okay, then. Everybody knows what to do." Malcolm set a calming gaze on Butch and let out a weary breath. "Save it for the sting, man. Save it for the sting."

Butch walked beside Laurel, and then suddenly slung his arm over her shoulder in a possessive hold.

"I don't like it," he said.

"Neither do I, but I have to do it."

He stopped walking as they neared the elevators, and he gently touched her chin, turning her face to study her cheek. "You should put some ice on that."

"It'll heal by tomorrow," she said quietly, covering his large hand. She brushed his mouth with a kiss. "You were awesome."

He tilted his head and let his fingers tangle in her hair. "But you were magnificent," he murmured. "I've never seen you really fight since we were kids… and then it was just family scraps—not a death struggle."

She smiled and looked away shyly. "Sorry I savaged your arm."

"I deserved it," he said quietly, forgetting to depress the elevator button.

"No you didn't. You hadn't lied to me… and the info Ecstasy got for you was worth every penny."

"I didn't do her in the lot, Laurel. That I swear to you."

"I know… I was going from old memory, because the old Barron would have."

He laughed quietly. "Yeah. Sad but true. The old Barron would have."

"The howl ran all through me… I was just upset because I thought it was for me."

He pulled her into an embrace. "Oh, it was; trust me. It was."

She gave him a disbelieving smile. "I'm not angry, I was just…."

"It was for you," he repeated softly, leaning in to lick her earlobe. "When you waltzed into Marcus' office… damn… I was messed up. Before I even saw you, your scent had me walking in circles. Then you came through the door—this angry, ravishing, snarling beauty, and I couldn't breathe." He found a place on her neck and paid it gentle attention, loving how she melted to fit against him. "Then you got in my face and challenged me, and then stormed out. I thought I'd lose my mind… was half about to drop to all fours and chase you, girl."

She laughed quietly and ran her hands up his back. "I needed you to do that. I came out of that office panting."

"For real?' he said, beginning to nuzzle the side of her face that hadn't been injured. "You felt like that earlier today?"

"Uh huh," she whispered, nodding and holding him tighter. "I was soooo wet that I had to get out of there."

He shuddered. "Oh… shit…."

"Yeah," she said, nipping his ear and sending a raspy whisper into it. "I had to sit on my hands and force myself to stay in my office." Her head was beginning to lean back as her eyes slid shut. "And when you howled, Barron… it plunged into me like a knife. Then the hunger came."

"Really," he said, starting to pant. "I was so messed up that I practically agreed to any terms Ecstasy offered. I just wanted to get back inside, tell Malcolm, so there'd be no trouble, and then bound up the stairs to feed you. That's why I couldn't even stand out there and argue with her and haggle about money. I wasn't trying to undermine your authority. The moon was full; your scent was all over the casino... I had to get to you. Next thing I knew, I was telling the truth to the moon."

"For real?" She pulled back and looked at him, her eyes glistening with desire. "You couldn't even haggle terms with her because of that?"

He nodded and swallowed. She watched his Adam's apple bob in his throat.

"The whole way up to your office I was saying a prayer... please let her be in there alone. Please don't let some other male be in her face that she wants in her face. Please let her like this cheeseburger. My heart was slamming inside my chest like I was a kid in high school."

She kissed him slowly and smiled, dropping her voice to a low, husky tone. "For real?"

"Then you were there," he said, his voice becoming gravelly. "Alone. Hungry. Sniffing me for a lie. Hunting me with your eyes when I came in. Listening for unspoken words between sentences. My eyes were trying to tell you all the things my mouth couldn't say 'cause I was too choked up... how much I missed you, how I was a fool to ever leave you... how if you gave me one more chance to fix what I broke, I'd never break it again. Then I heard the lock click and almost shifted on you right then... oh, shit... you have no idea how close I was."

He hugged her tightly, more tightly than maybe he should have, if he was going to hand her off to another male. But it was reflex. She felt so right fitting there, and he needed to get it all out and said in case anything went wrong.

"I'm not gonna lie, in that moment that you locked the door, I forgot about the money. I started hunting you."

She gasped, and he felt it in his groin.

"You hunted me?" she whispered quickly, her breaths now shallow.

"Hell yeah…" he said just above a growl. "I wanted you bad. I scanned the room for an exit—there was none. The wolf mind took over. Mate her, and mate her hard. Period. There was no battling with the animal. It had won all but my outer skin, at that point."

He felt her tremble and it made him seek her hair with his nose. He pulled in a deep inhale and let it out through his mouth in a hot wash. "I began to figure out how to box you in a corner, trying to figure out which one, which surface, how to position you so you'd most enjoy it… 'Cause, see, the moon was coming through the window. I have excellent memory. My nose got it all, and you were in heat, burning me up just like you're doing now. Then you just turned around for me and dipped into the mount position, and my mind snapped. Next thing I know, we were half-naked, half-shifted, half-crazy, and howling. I wasn't trying to disrespect you or play you cheap, Laurel. It was be with you or stop breathing."

"I need another shower just from talking to you in the hall," she said on a strangled breath.

"Why'd you tell me that?" he said, aggressively taking her mouth, then backed off a bit, remembering her injured jaw. "I'm sorry… but…."

"Yeah, I know." She ran her hand down his chest and pressed it against his hard abdomen. "I wanted you to hunt me… chase me… make me dash through the desert under the silver moon. I wanted to turn into silver-black blurs of motion, running so fast and so free that I became the wind… with you on my heels in that fantastic, jet black coat—midnight itself."

"Oh, girl, stop…." He closed his eyes, unable to stare into her deep, luminous gray eyes that flickered animal wolf fire beneath them.

"I have a very good memory, too… because it all came back in that office." She clutched his back as her mouth neared his, and she licked his face. "Wolfen… Lupine lover… named Barron for the noble human rule… named Butch by the clan for the alpha male that you are… and claimed by *me*. Since you left, there's been no one in the pack worthy enough to follow you to mount me… and you have *no idea* what that's been like starving for you to come back—*that's* why I had an attitude," she said deeply in a low, feminine growl.

"Oh… baby… I'm no more good now." He couldn't breathe, couldn't release her, and could barely stand on two legs, needing to go to four to keep his balance.

"The ketchup on your face… and the hamburger blood was mine to wash away, Barron… I'm in full heat right now… just after midnight, and I can feel it making me very insane."

He stood there panting hard, then licked her face and nuzzled her injured jaw. "I'll eat again soon so you can do it. Anything you want; any place, any time, oh shit, anywhere, just tell me and I'll drag it still kicking over the threshold—will kill it in front of you, if you wanna see it die."

"Yeah.…"

"Baby… say it again like that with the growl in it."

"Barron…" she murmured, growling his name. "You don't know how much I wanted to find a private little place in the crags, high up to put us closer to the night disc in the sky, and throw my head back for you and feel your breaths in my ear… the weight of you against my back so divine that I howled till I cried and cried till I howled, until my shape-shift wouldn't even hold and I just broke down and became woman in your arms."

"Oh, shit, Laurel… I ain't letting you go down there for some beta male to even try to—"

"Shush," she said, stopping his words and pending kiss with the pad of her finger. "Hold that memory and extract me from that room well."

"No question." He looked at her hard. "Laurel, I'll be coming through that door on a take-no-prisoners rampage."

"Good," she said sweetly. "Kill them all. They came against our clan." She closed her eyes and allowed her head to drop back. "*Then hunt me*—after you're nice and bloody."

Her spine hit the elevator doors. He could feel her slapping at the wall to find the button. If the contraption had opened, they would have both fallen in and hit the floor. Malcolm's calm lope down the corridor wasn't even enough to break the kiss. He needed to mount Laurel so badly that his entire body was trembling.

"Man… you're gonna have to let her go in order for this to work," Malcolm said calmly, depressing the elevator button for them. "You two can either stay in the hall making out like kids, torturing yourselves, or do the job, and then head for the hills."

Butch tore himself away from Laurel's mouth, and she came out of the kiss with a gasp. He looked up at Malcolm with a pained expression and slowly unwrapped his arms from around her waist.

"Yeah, okay… I was just saying goodbye." Butch winced as he pulled away.

Laurel dabbed her mouth with the back of her wrist. "I was going downstairs in a minute."

The elevator doors opened and Butch held onto the wall beside them, swallowing down a forlorn howl as they closed her away.

"She's beautiful, Malcolm."

"I take it that we won't have any witnesses after this is finished?" Malcolm said in an even tone with a smile.

Butch just shook his head, staring at the shut elevator doors. "I don't think so, man. I really don't."

Malcolm nodded and began to lope away. "Okay. Cool. I'm not in a very tolerant frame of mind myself tonight."

Chapter Six

It wasn't hard to track a foreign clan member on the premises, especially having tangled with his alpha brethren in a brawl. Even human common sense said the new leader would be in one of three places; the remaining bars, the restaurants, or in a room getting it on, if not the hills. She just hoped it wasn't the hills.

But a promotion was a promotion and a conquest was a conquest—even if by default. Since her clan appeared to only be focused on the foolish combatants that entered a domestic dispute, it wouldn't give the rival clan reason to believe they'd each be hunted down for spite. Especially not when free food, liquor, and accommodations had been publicly delivered by a clan leader as a peace offering.

Laurel's mind assessed the potential threats as she rode the elevator. It was imperative to remain focused, something very hard to do after being in Barron's arms. Nonetheless, she had to wrest back her strategy and keep the details sharp in her head like razor canines.

No, the rival clan wouldn't be in the clubs partying; that would seem like a slap in the face to the pack members who'd died—but eating and drinking in a jovial wake was acceptable. Outright retaliation from them for the deaths of their two big alphas, and the severe maiming of a third who lost his arm, would be seen as low. After all, they were the ones who'd lost their cool and allowed their libidos to make them jump into a family dispute between pack brothers over an inner clan female.

If there was no alpha contender from her clan staking a claim, then, by rights, the alphas from their clan could have duked it out between themselves to win her. But to cross clan lines and go alpha-to-alpha over a rival clan's woman was severely out of order. Wolves had a different philosophical bent than vampires.

Laurel stepped out of the elevator and kept walking across the battered first floor of the casino, headed for the bar. Drink, eat, and be merry—that was a werewolf male's style. They'd go to the bar to raise a respectful toast to the dead after loading the bodies in a truck. Then they'd head straight for a restaurant to eat well, both in memoriam to the fallen and in tribute to the next leader. Then they'd be off to be merry with whichever female was down. The beta females would be fawning, and tonight the conqueror might take more than one. But if the alpha females were present and willing, which they'd have to be to keep the clan going, then he'd have to pick one—and that's who she'd have to brawl with first to get the new leader alone. Laurel sighed hard.

Why couldn't things just be cool, she wondered? Tonight of all nights, the last thing she felt like was a bitch fight. But so be it.

She surveyed the remaining, undamaged bar on the first floor. Just as suspected, food had been ordered and the drinking was going non-stop. They'd blended things together, obviously ravenous after watching the brawl, and had clearly decided to pass on the idea of moving the party to a restaurant. The little fracas that trashed the first floor would no doubt improve business in the long run—the Weres loved to see a good beat down, and the more blood and bodies involved, the better. This had been like WWF with no refs, no rules, and no pulled punches.

Heads turned as Laurel walked into the bar, and she spotted the newly installed alpha sitting in a booth with two beta females under each arm. The rival clan of Weres had a biker theme going, nothing but black leather, steel-studded collars, tattoos, and spikes, with hard attitudes to match. It was a far cry from her more corporate clan that preferred the laid-back approach. Okaaay... so negotiating by talking one's way out of anything would be impossible. Sophistication was not in the rival clan's grasp.

Heat

Laurel's eyes cased the perimeter and stopped. Loud music was making her temples throb. Bass lines were rattling her skeleton. The head alpha female was in the house. Not good that she was built like an ox. Cutter's wife was no joke. All the while the family meeting was going on, she'd been too caught up in her own heat to thoroughly work the logic from the female side of things. Major oversight. The moon was kicking her butt royally.

She kept walking, and made sure her movements through the crowd were fluid and non-threatening. It was important to appear nonchalant, as though she was just going to get a drink... possibly, for her man, nothing more. As long as she didn't make a false move, they wouldn't. But their distrustful, angry eyes were on her.

The facts were simple: her family males couldn't jump into a brawl between one of their females and those of a rival clan without that being considered a serious breech of conduct. It would start an outright war. Going after a rival clan's female in combat mode, when a female from their family crossed the line first, to go after the rival clan's alpha male? Hell no. The rival clan's females would be within their rights to attack the poaching female, en masse, which was why that generally never happened.

Tension keened Laurel's senses. In all the discussion, she hadn't factored in the huge alpha female on the rival clan's side that could possibly mop her ass up and down the bar. Plus, by all indicators, the sister had a squad that was not above jumping in it. Laurel's mind raced. Who did she have in her clan that was female?

Most other threats to the casino had been male inspired, and she had plenty of male security staff and family to deal with that—but this was an unusual situation. Probably why it had been overlooked as a hurdle. Everyone was battle amped, hyped up, thinking through testosterone and moonlight, and focused on how to handle what they'd believed to be the primary threat to the family and her safety: Dominant males. They forgot all about the basics—pissed off females with an axe to grind. Grudge match personified.

Okay, that left her with few options. Simone Temple, Malcolm's sister, who ran the club entertainment, was too classy to get down in a bar brawl. Simone had a Lena Horn vibration and hadn't shifted into a she-wolf to do battle for years. Scratch that option. Octavia, Oliver's twin sister who ran mall store operations, wouldn't help. No doubt, she was still salty about her choice of Butch over Oliver's alpha friend, Guy. Plus, Octavia had always been sweet on Butch.

Laurel tried not to sigh as she neared the bar rail. Claire might be with it, but she ran the food and beverages, and was busily re-establishing new watering holes up on the second and third floors with Marcus. After a big fight, liquor was serious revenue that couldn't be ignored.

That only left Iva in accounting, who was no doubt tallying losses and feverishly trying to be sure the cashier's booths and vaults, as well as the trashed slot machine revenues, were safely stashed. With all the chips, coins, and cash that went flying, and patrons who were complaining about interrupted bets, Iva probably had a line of snarling guests outside her office to contend with. The final alternative was Solange, the elder Temple's personal assistant. However, even as beautiful and awesome as Solange was, if she wasn't strong enough to be taken as a mate by Julius and Esther Temple's son, Malcolm, then it was very doubtful she'd fare well in a bar fight, either.

Laurel released a quiet sigh. No wonder she'd been made head of security. Tonight the responsibility weighed heavily on her shoulders as she kept her gaze roving and ordered a drink, keeping Cutter's wife in her peripheral vision. But the sister was cool, sipped her drink slowly and evenly, not even snarling yet. *Good.*

Part of Laurel wanted to offer her condolences for losing the big guy she'd come there with. Then another variable entered her peripheral vision. Oh, yeah, there had been three alpha males, and their pack was strong with three alpha females. Now there was a *big* problem, but too late to call any outer circle female family for backup. Not to mention, calling weaker, beta females in as backup would put those females in severe risk of being killed or badly maimed.

She assessed the new alpha male leader from a sidelong glance. Weak jaw structure, short canines—therefore short dick. Oh, yeah… these rival clan females were *not* gonna be happy with the new top dog, and he definitely wasn't gonna be able to control them for long. Laurel glimpsed him again. Almond complexion, pocked, with freckles. Small, nervous, hazel eyes, short reddish-brown afro, slightly thinning on the top. *Hmmm*… Judging by his height sitting down, he appeared to be about six-feet even. Damn even *she* could take him.

Laurel glimpsed his old beta girlfriends tearfully saying goodbye as he looked up and spotted her. The hunt was on.

She took her time leaning in to reach for her Dewar's on the rocks at the bar, making sure he saw her real good from behind, but kept her vision roving on the now alert alpha females sitting at the far end.

This wasn't the place to order a girlie drink—nothing blended, nothing foamy, and definitely nothing with a cherry on top. She'd be safe if the new male leader approached her and sniffed her, and she soon left. That would be his first right of refusal, and he'd bark down any females from his own clan that snarled—after all, it gave him bragging rights to have sniffed another rival male's territory.

Her mind was on fire as she brought the Dewar's to her lips and took a slow sip. Even though he might come sniffing, the weak rival alpha might not want to start a war by having the foreign female go home ragged from a bitch tussle. It would bring a foreign male back to him to get in his face about not being able to control the females in his pack, which this male couldn't, and the challenge for dominance would be on—ending in a severe male beat down, possibly even a pack takeover that they couldn't afford. So, no, the new alpha wouldn't allow his babes to just outright jump her, there had to be cause, given she knew instinctively that he'd pee his own leg if Butch lunged at him. That bought her time. That also made the new male take his time to get up and approach her. The man was obviously weighing the odds himself.

Laurel glanced at who would be coming for her. One was a burly chic, about five-foot-eight, two hundred pounds. Cutter's wife. Thick all the way around, and it didn't seem to be fat. She glanced at Laurel, and Laurel averted her eyes quickly, and then suddenly realized the potential hazard of the brief but profound submissive act. *Damn.* It was reflex. A pair of dark female eyes in a dark face set hard now hunted her, backing her off. The competing female flipped a set of long micro braids over her shoulders with a silent snarl. *Oh… shit.*

But Laurel held her ground and coolly sipped her drink. Another alpha female now gritting on her was a very athletic looking, mega-tanned blonde with spiked hair, serving biker gear to death. Her arms were longer than Laurel's, which meant she had by reach what the other one had by weight. That could've been Fang or Mad Dawg's woman, she wasn't sure. Mad Dawg had lost an arm; Fang had lost his life. Either way, whoever this broad belonged to was pissed off. Suddenly, the little black dress and sexy spike heels to attract the alpha male seemed foolish. She should've put on some combat gear.

The third female problem was about her height, but built like a brick house—all curves. Laurel focused on her moody dark eyes as they followed her. The challenger had cut her hair short and dyed it Goth black. Even though her face was pretty, and didn't have a keloid scar over her brow like Cutter's wife had, there was a definitely hardness to her cinnamon-hued skin that told of many street fights. It was in her eyes.

Okay, only the heavyset chic, Cutter's wife, had any tresses to grab if it got down to it before an all out shift, and her own head was vulnerable with her shoulder-length hair. Another problem.

Laurel sniffed the air discreetly. Other males were starting to position with interest, since the new alpha had seemingly passed on her. But none of the other females in the joint were in heat. One advantage. *Okay, work with what you've got.*

She glanced over her shoulder at the new alpha and risked giving him a suggestive pout, and then turned back to her drink. The action could be read in two ways; either, come here I want you or who you looking at asshole. She hoped the rival females read it as the later and would hold the line waiting to see what he'd do.

Circumstances would leave him curious, though, if he had any balls. She knew she'd been gone long enough from the casino floor and still smelled enough like Butch to make it seem like he'd had her, then had gone out to drag in grub. Her presence in the bar unescorted on a full moon during a heat could be construed as her misbehaving, looking for options after getting quickly and unsatisfactorily laid, and thus hunting the bars for some additional action while her big male was off providing. Tantalizing as a concept to a new power drunk male. The bourbon didn't help him, either. By the same token, the Dewar's and her state of missing Butch so badly wasn't helping her logic; it was making her bold; rashly so.

A beta male stepped to her, just slightly taller than she was, and leaned in near her at the bar. She looked him up and down with disdain and backed up, partly to hold out for the one she wanted to attract, partly because he was offensive to her, and partly because it would start an attack rush from the alpha females in his clan.

"Can I buy you another one?" he asked, trying to drop his voice to an octave he didn't own.

"I don't think so," she said evenly, looking at his slim, wiry build and unkempt cornrows that were fuzzy in the part.

"Why not, sweetness?"

She just stared at him for a moment. The list of reasons of why not was way too long to delineate and recite while sitting on a barstool. First of all, if she was gonna go with his weak ass, she liked her men well-barbered, and if he was gonna rock cornrows, at least let the rows be precise, greased to gleaming clean at the scalp. The thin, ragged goatee he had made her want to slap him for even coming over to her. How about a full beard, grown by pure testosterone, and cut down low to an eighth of an inch over a strong, square jaw with a straight-edge razor so sharp that it put tears in a woman's eyes? This brother had no pride. The biceps were lame, the chest pathetic, no six-pack in the abs, skinny legs, which meant no power thrusts, and no ass in his baggy jeans—couldn't jump. Then had the nerve to have such short canines that he'd put a platinum and diamond grille in his mouth! *Oh, no he is not in my face with a bling grille!* He didn't even smell good.

"Get outta my face," she finally said as she rolled her eyes at him and turned back to study her drink.

He tilted his head and scowled at her. "A brother can't buy you a drink? Whassup with that?"

Hard gazes were on her; the tension was so thick in the bar that side conversations had ceased. Only the loud music was creating sound. Someone in the back discreetly turned it down, most likely to be sure they didn't miss a thing.

"I got a man," she muttered and finished her Dewar's, knocking it back, and then set her glass down on the bar hard.

The loud statement was designed to send the rival females a message that she wasn't poaching, but to stoke the alpha male she wanted to a challenge. He took the bait. The new alpha stood up as the beta who'd tried her mumbled bitch under his breath, and stalked away. She let it ride. Under different circumstances she would have ripped his little diamond earring out of his ear. Tonight, there wasn't time for teaching a beta a miscellaneous lesson on things one should never say to a lady.

She could feel the presence of the new male looming behind her, but kept her eyes on the bartender, who'd hesitated refreshing her drink. The bartender's eyes went first to her, and then to a point just behind her, seeming to be waiting on who would order.

"My apologies for my posse's rude display," a rough, mid-range voice said from behind her. "May I buy you a drink to make up for it—peace?"

"Yeah, thanks," Laurel said without turning.

A barstool opened next to her as several males moved to allow their new leader maneuvering room. Laurel glanced at the now snarling alpha females, and noticed that the new alpha did, too. He shot them a glance that wasn't as firm as it should have been, she also noted. They didn't stop curling their lips, but had muffled the sound. This brother was in way over his head. Their pack had to know it. But she was cool.

"I'm Havoc," he said as the bartender set Laurel's drink before her. He glanced up, ordered himself a Wild Turkey, and then leaned in with a chipped tooth smile. "Didn't expect to see you down here tonight."

"Yeah, well, I got bored," she said in an icy tone that held a hint of mystery. "Sorry about what happened to your posse."

"It was fucked up," he said with a slight smile, reaching up to accept his drink without taking his eyes off her. "But... hey... shit happens. And looking at you, I understand how that did."

She let out a hard breath and ruffled her hair off her neck, now giving him direct eye contact for the first time since he'd sat beside her. "Dumb bastards are still up there fighting. The moon is out, I'm in heat, and they'll both be too ripped up to... hey, forget it. Thanks for the drink." She picked up her Dewar's and allowed him to take her statement as a subtle offer to rectify her problem, and clinked her glass against his.

He swallowed hard and leaned in closer. "A gorgeous woman like you shouldn't have to deal with bullshit like that, feel me? Why don't you just get away from it all?"

She gave him a half smile. "Wish I could... but, uh, that might cause problems. I just came down here to put some distance between me and the madness, get a drink, and try to figure out how to get through another lonely night... alone... you feel *me*?"

"There's no problem if you wanna hang out with us, sis," he said, his eyes seeking. He took a quick sip of his drink to wet his throat. "You eat yet?"

"Yeah, but I'm *starved*," she said, holding his gaze and allowing her eyes to rake him slowly.

"Bartender!" he shouted, "Order the lady another Dewar's and some ribs, stat." Havoc looked her over with a hot gaze. "Or you want a steak?"

Several loud snarls ricocheted through the bar. Laurel raised an eyebrow and downed her drink to prepare for the one that was quickly coming.

"I don't think they'd appreciate me hanging out long enough to wolf down a steak with you, baby. As it is, the vibe I'm getting is making me uncomfortable. I'll just accept the drink and be on my way. Maybe take it up to my room." She began to push away from the bar.

"Hold up, Ma," he murmured, touching her arm gently, and then allowing his fingers to trail up and down it. "There's no static." He turned on his barstool. "Is there?" he added through his teeth, looking at the three females that slowly stood. But his attention fractured before he'd laid down the law. "Damn, your skin is soft."

His clammy touch had put gooseflesh on her arms, but not for the reason he probably assumed. The guy was giving her the creeps. Laurel submitted to letting him touch her hair, but kept the females in her peripheral vision.

"Feels like velvet," Havoc said quietly. "I can see why they were doing mortal combat over you, baby." He inhaled sharply. "You just went into phase today, didn't you?"

She shuddered at the statement. It was true. The first eve was always the worst, but the shudder had been brought on by thinking of Butch. "Yeah."

"So, like, uh, when the ribs come... you eat, chill, and then, you know, maybe we can go somewhere and talk—get to know each other a little. You can tell me what's been going on in your life."

Laurel sighed. This brother had *no* original rap. "Okay, if everybody's gonna be cool."

"They will be," he assured her, leaning in to smell her again.

"The hell they will," a deep female voice said from across the bar.

"Fuckin' A-right," another growled.

"You must be out your damned mind," another muttered, followed by the distinctive sound of a female sucking her teeth.

Laurel shrugged and looked at Havoc and sighed. "Like I said, I think I'll just leave and take my drink to my room. It's getting thick in here. I'd better go. Thanks for the offer, maybe another time." She held his gaze for a moment with longing, and then slid off the barstool, leaving him with an erection.

He was off his stool and out of the daze in seconds, canines extended. Laurel hesitated as he whirled on the three females that had challenged his booty-call.

"I told you bitches to chill, didn't I?" he shouted.

Laurel almost laughed as they looked at him like he was insane, cocked their heads to the side, and hands went on hips.

"Say what?" Cutter's wife snarled, her eyes narrowing. "I know you did *not* go there." Her head bobbed with each word. "My husband is dead, I get your ass as a weak replacement, and you said whaaaa to me? After he's gone because of her in the first place!"

"For her?" The blonde spat on the floor, her eyes holding both fury and disbelief. "You will get your punk male ass beat down up in this bar so bad, 'cause if Fang was alive, trust me, you'd get nowhere near *real* alpha female tail—don't front."

"Mad Dawg might only have one arm, motherfucker, but still got more balls than you, and a longer dick too," the Goth female said, pounding fists with her girls. "I'd take his one-armed mount over your weak ass any moon. Call me out my name again, punk, and that's your throat."

It was interesting, really, as she watched it go down. The bar cleared, Havoc was left standing in the middle of the floor. Horniness had made him forget his reality. Males who had begrudgingly accepted his promotion smiled and gave way to see how he'd handle himself. The man was trapped between a rock and a hard place. A strong female alpha from a rival clan in heat was behind him with her man out on the hunt and liable to come back to take grave exception to what was going down; three very pissed off alpha females from his own clan ready to go for his throat were before him. Butch wouldn't have even been able to deal with this. Laurel laughed.

"Whatchu laughing at, bitch!" Cutter's wife shouted.

It was now or never. Laurel shifted, bound over Havoc's head, and alighted on the bar, bearing fangs. Being in heat had its aggression advantages, too. She was nuts. Moon off da chain. Any female with sense knew it. They might beat her by numbers, but they'd feel it in the morning if they lived.

Taken slightly by surprise that she'd been so bold to go for it without thinking, the three challengers backed up, and then shifted, holding their ground.

Laurel snarled, advancing slowly with her head down, her voice a resonant alto. "Bitch... was I talking to you?"

Cutter's wife was on the bar now at the far end, and had to make a lunge to keep her pride. The males in the room was slobbering on themselves and beginning to pace. Laurels' eyes narrowed, but Cutter's woman had no idea how much pent up aggression were in her.

Laurel left the bar before Cutter's wife could blink. She was on her and had body slammed her to the bar, slashing her face, but leapt back before one of the rival female's huge claws could rake her. Two more females went airborne, but Havoc, in distress that his in-heat female might be harmed, shifted and got into the fray, drawing them to attack him.

"Oh, shit, that was a punk move, man!" someone called out.

"Let the females go at it, and may the best one win!" another voice shouted over the din.

Havoc was caught in-between two females who were savaging him. Laurel had the big one down on the floor, pinned down, and had ripped off her ear. Tables and chairs crashed as thick bodies lunged, came down hard, and battled on the floor. A hard elbow caught Laurel in the stomach, knocked the wind out of her, and she was on her back, underbelly showing. Cutter's wife pivoted and came for her, but Laurel dug her claws in her chest and hit her pelvis with both feet, flinging her body up and over the bar to crash into shelves filled with bottles.

Shards of glass and liquor exploded everywhere. The big female was down, out cold, and missing an ear. Laurel jumped up and leapt onto a section of the bar above where Havoc was trapped. Barking loudly, she got the two females' attention.

"Back off!" Laurel shouted, and then lunged in to assist Havoc, taking the blonde wolf down in a hard roll. She stopped struggling as Laurel's jaws clamped over her exposed throat. Breathing hard, Laurel waited for the submissive, let-me-live whimper.

"Don't kill her, sis," a male shouted from behind. "You staked your claim, now let her up."

Trembling with battle rage, Laurel slowly removed her poised canines and leapt back. The female who was circling Havoc backed up, panting, and then shifted. She stood there naked and furious, but had to let it go. Havoc was stronger than her, and had a strong foreign female working with him. The blonde shifted to send the message that she too would yield. Laurel stalked back and forth on the bar, glancing between them and the unconscious she-wolf behind the bar.

"It's cool," Havoc assured her as he shifted back from the reddish brown and cream-hued, slim wolf he'd been into human male form. His lip was busted, his nose broken, and his chest was severely gashed, but he'd live.

Uncertain and too unstable now with a hunt pulsing through her, Laurel eyed him, still peering over the edge of the bar, and then at the crowd.

"C'mon, beauty," Havoc crooned, breathing hard. "It's okay."

"Damn… you see her?" a beta said with appreciation, pounding fists in the crowd.

"Man, I can't believe that's *you*," one of the others said, shaking his head. "You gonna tag that?"

Laurel snarled at the inference, but remembered the mission. She didn't want to shift back and stand before them naked, however, going to the next phase required it. The big brown female on the floor behind the bar stirred, Laurel lowered her head and growled low in her throat. The males on the periphery had begun to pant. Havoc was so turned on that he approached her haunches and attempted to stroke her while in human male form. She whirled on him, snapped, bearing canines, saliva dripping, which only made him whimper with need and walk in an agitated circle.

"Baby, shift back so we can get outta here," he whispered.

Cutter's wife got up slowly, her coat littered with glass and bleeding. Then she shifted into a human, breathing hard on her hands and knees. She looked up at Laurel with hatred in her eyes. "Later."

Laurel nodded, leapt down from the bar to circle Havoc's legs, brushing against them, and then nuzzled his hard groin. She glimpsed up, and he just nodded and closed his eyes. She shifted back, and a guy who'd been standing on the sidelines tossed her dress.

"Thanks," she said, catching it with one hand.

"Damn, baby, they make any more like you in your clan?" the guy who'd tossed her the dress said with a leering smile as she pulled it on.

"No," she said flatly, thoroughly disgusted. "Why you think they tore up the casino like they did?"

"True dat!" a peanut gallery observer hollered as Fang and Mad Dawg's women went to help Cutter's wife. "Make a man ready to bum rush your clan, if they did."

"Would you get me outta here?" Laurel said, looking at Havoc, who'd been too spellbound to even put on his pants.

"Sure, baby," he said, now moving with conviction, yanking his pants on in a one-legged hop. "Where you wanna go?"

Heat

"Your room. Now. Order room service. My man is out in the canyons. Can't risk it, but gotta get somewhere soon."

Chapter Seven

She didn't have to say it twice. Havoc practically dragged her to the elevators, and then walked in an agitated circle because one wasn't coming fast enough.

"We could take the stairs, you know." she said coolly, studying her nails and cleaning fur and flesh out from beneath them as she waited for the elevator.

"Yeah, but, your other man could be in there with his boyz," Havoc said like the punk he was. "I can smell 'em in there from before. That's where the fight broke out, right?"

"True," she said with a weary sigh. Then she had an idea. "You got anything for the head in your room?"

"Sure, sis. Weed, coke, E, dust, whatever. You know that's our trade."

She looked out the window. "I like things fast… you know what I mean?"

He nodded and hustled her onto the elevator, depressed his floor button, and then crushed her against the wall, grinding on her thigh. "Speed, you want some meth?"

"That could work."

"Damn, I can't believe you fought for me like that," he said, his hot bourbon breath coating her neck.

He leaned in to kiss her, but she turned her head. "Your lip is split, and one of your dead alphas hit me in my face. It still hurts." That was the truth, but not the reason she'd turned away.

"It's cool, it's all good," he said, running his hands up and down her sides. "My nose is broke and my lip is split anyway, like you said. Once you turn around, none of that will matter, though."

"Glad you understand it wasn't personal."

Laurel fought not to bite him in his nose and rip it off his face. She smiled as pleasantly as possible. He hadn't even mentioned the fact that she took a roundhouse in the jaw by a strong male. *Pussy.*

"Naw, baby, I knew that after I saw how you was down for whatever."

He shuddered against her, beginning to dry-hump her leg. *Betas.* Laurel sighed. The elevator stopped.

"Do me a favor and don't cum on my dress. My man will take serious exception, and won't understand."

"Cool, cool, my bad," Havoc said, backing off her to allow her to exit the elevator.

He ran ahead of her, fumbled with his wallet, got out the card key, and opened the door. She couldn't believe that he was practically puppy dancing, moving from foot-to-foot as she leisurely strolled down the hall and slipped into his room. Beyond disgusted, she willed herself not to flinch when he had grabbed her arm, spun her around fast, and pinned her to the door. He'd yanked her so hard that he'd knocked the wind out of her.

She looked up at the sprinkler system, trying to ignore the fact that he was now furiously dry-humping her ass. "Uh, the meth you were gonna tighten a sister up with?"

"In a minute," he said, trying to get to his zipper.

"Oh, so it's like that, huh? I put my life at risk, fight for your ass, go up against three hard alpha females, and I gotta wait till you cum before I can even get a damned meal or a little somethin' somethin' for my head—mind you, I'ma probably get my ass kicked when I get home for sneaking out."

"Oh, c'mon, baby, you know it's not like that. I—"

"See, I shoulda known...."

He backed up, and then finally rolled off her to thud against the wall with a groan. "Naw. I got it in the room."

"You ain't never been with an alpha female have you?"

He looked at her, straightened, and squared his shoulders. "Whatchu talkin' about? I been with plenty."

"Yeah, okay. That's why you can't be cool enough to go get me what I asked you for, first."

He glared at her and walked over to the closet, slung the door open, and squatted down to put the code in the room safe. "That ain't it," he argued, grabbing out several handfuls of plastic bags, brandishing them for her to inspect. "It's only on account of the fact that you're in heat… and we was fighting together and shit… and, damn, baby, whatchu want? I got a store right here."

Laurel smiled as his voice cracked. Part of her felt bad that it was gonna go down like it was, but hey. She came over to him as he stood panting and looked at the bags.

"What's the one with the purple tint running through it? That looks freaky."

"No, no, you don't want that," he said quickly, separating the bag out from the others and tossing it back into the opened safe. "That'll mess up your head, and the last thing I want tonight is for your head to be that messed up."

Laurel put her hands on her hips. It had to be what she was looking for. "Oh, okay, so you save the good shit for the VIP's, right? I ain't a VIP? Fuck you. Go find a beta female or jerk off, but—"

"No, no, no, you don't understand," he said, body-blocking her as she headed for the door. "It's no good. Shitty batch."

"Yeah, right," she muttered, trying to step around him. "Word in the hallways was that you guys had a special sex-blend for the male vamp high-rollers coming through. All the females in every species are talking about it in the ladies rooms. That's why I was fighting to get with you tonight… figured if you had a little aphrodisiac to blow my mind, along with your fine ass, damn… I'd be done. Would probably start howling before you put it in, if I let you. But since you're not sharing, I'm leaving. Boop—I'm gone."

"No, baby—don't bounce yet! Uh, listen, it ain't like you think, for real."

"Then how is it, Havoc? Talk to me real clear, so I understand." She looked at him hard and folded her arms over her chest as his eyes slid shut in agony. Conflict was eating him alive, she could feel it, so she pressed on with her bogus story. "You saw my man. Does he look like the kind of brother that would tolerate some shit like this? But if I came home good and high, and still tripping enough to make him forget why he was mad… you know, you know. I could live and maybe come see you again on the regular. Sneak tip. That is, if I was so inclined and had a reason. You haven't given me a good enough reason to piss Butch off yet and let you mount me."

Havoc opened his eyes and traced Laurel's cheek with trembling fingers. "Baby, I want you so much right now, I'm stupid. I'ma tell you something that's gotta stay on the down low, between me and you, all right? Let me explain before you just sashay your fine ass outta here. Baby, trust me, you could have anything I had in here, if it wouldn't make you sick. Can you do that for me? Just listen to a brother's plea?"

Laurel lowered her eyes and slowly unfolded her arms. "As long as you're not trying to play me… all right. Why can't I have any of your best stuff?"

"Because it's *poison*." He said quietly, now tracing her collarbone and staring at her breasts.

"Oh, man," she scoffed. "I can't believe you're one of those tired-ass dealers with a conscience—the whole 'I'll deal to the fools on the street, but don't want my lady to taste my product,' kinda rhetoric."

"No, that ain't it," he said, touching the V in her neck with the pad of his thumb, but not yet bold enough to just body-snatch her to him. "I mean its *real* poison. Will kill you in the morning, especially if you're a vamp. It's cut with a nasty mix in it."

"Then why'd you made some bullshit like that?" she said, beginning to pet his chest. Havoc leaned against the wall as her fingertips glided over his nipples. "Seems like a waste of good drugs."

"It's for the vamps," he said on a thick swallow, unable to keep his eyes open as her hand slid down his torso, then slowly stroked his belly. "Damn, girl, you're hot."

"Who cares about the vamps? Snob bastards. Why poison 'em, when you can probably rob their lairs blind in the daylight?"

"You'd be down for something like that in your clan's hotel?" he murmured in a heavy, impassioned growl.

She fought not to cringe and dropped her hand to his crotch. "Do I seem like a sister who's down for whatever?" The statement was non-committal, but at this point, he wasn't splitting hairs about semantics.

He nodded and began breathing through his mouth as her hand slid across his hard length. "Damn, baby, take it out."

"Oh, so now you can't hear me, huh?" She released a forced chuckle.

"I can't really concentrate right now."

She squeezed him, producing a moan. "I said, why are you wasting good drugs on the vamps instead of making the good shit for Were clans? I just wanna be sure you're not holding back on me, trying to mess with my mind."

He pulled her to him hard and found her neck, but had to come in easy or risk hurting his broken nose. "Although you've messed my head up, I can't hold back from you. There's something big about to go down. You want in on our side... wanna come with me and be my woman?"

"You serious, you'd try to break me out of here?" Laurel let out a hard breath; no way was she telling him she'd go against her clan or be his woman. But she could ask questions and get direct answers at this point. "How would you do that?" .

"It got a little delayed, due to the fight in the casino, but by tomorrow night, wheels will be in motion. That next morning, the bullshit will hit the fan. By that following evening, this joint will be under new management." He pulled back and looked at her hard. "So, lemme ask you again. You wanna be my woman?"

Laurel smiled as an elder, aristocrat vampire materialized behind Havoc in the bathroom. It was very cool how the European brother did it—no reflection, no peripheral vision cue. Smooth, wearing a tux, too... battle bulked with about seven inches of fangs in his mouth, eyes gleaming red fury while four more thick-bodied male vampires materialized behind him looking like bouncers. Their silent stealth was awesome, and she had to give the species their due. She finally nodded, but the nod was for the vampires. Her clan couldn't be seen as culpable to a werewolf setup.

As coolly as possibly, she led Havoc by the hand to position him in front of the opened bathroom door.

"All right, I hear you," she finally said.

Havoc let out his breath hard. "Good, then where were we, pretty lady?"

A chain flipped over Havoc's head so fast and caught his windpipe that he hadn't seen it coming. Laurel screamed for dramatic effect, which brought Butch and Marcus barreling through the door. Havoc released a strangled wolf cry that his clan heard. Vampires stormed the room from every direction as Butch pushed Laurel behind him, again, just for drama. This had to go down right. Malcolm and his clan's security forces were in the room with half of the rival clan within moments. VIP vamps brought human helpers brandishing silver-shell-loaded pump-shotguns and Uzis. It was a standoff.

"What's going on in my hotel, Sir Helmsley? Why do you have a were-clan guest in a threatening position? I demand an explanation!" Malcolm shot his gaze around snarling were-clans and hissing vampires, playing the sting ruse to the bone.

"I have him on treason," Sir Helmsley said coolly, tightening the chain against Havoc's throat as he futilely struggled. He looked down at his captive and snarled. "Shift, and I will snap your neck before fur forms, trust me. I have dealt with this before, as old as I am."

Helmsley waited until Havoc ceased growling and turning, relaxed the chain just enough so Havoc could breathe, then related everything he'd heard Havoc tell Laurel.

For effect, Butch squared off on Laurel. "Is that true, he said that to you?" Witnesses were an important part of vigilante justice, if one wanted to stem a war.

Laurel nodded, making her eyes tear. "I just asked him about the get-high."

"Then what were you doing here! You could've had him bring it to you in the bar." Butch looked at her and kept his expression hard, walking closer to her in a threatening way that only Were males would take as realistic.

All eyes were on Laurel as she cringed and took a submissive position, lowering her head. "They tried to jump me in the bar," she wailed, going girlie-girl on Butch for effect. She pointed at Havoc's clan. "Ask 'em, their three big alpha females jumped me while I was all alone, that's why I came up here with him. Shit, Butch, I was in heat, they were acting funny, and tonight, I needed something for my head!"

She waited for Butch to scan Havoc's clan, and as eyes slid away from his, the Temple clan growled. Good. The story was plausible and told in a way that would save Butch face, just in case rumors cropped up, and those always did.

"You tried to jump our female for no reason, when she was making a buy?" Marcus snarled, gaining nods from the other males in his clan, then scanned theirs. "That shit was low."

"Oughta kick your ass on general principle," Guy growled, but stepped back into the pack as Butch glared at him.

"I wanted to get high, that's all," Laurel said, sounding forlorn. "He asked me to be his woman, but I never committed to all of that—and *no*, I didn't give him any tail."

Butch glanced at Helmsley. Everyone on the were-clan inside knew it was important to preserve the alpha male's dignity by having the story corroborated by an uninvolved third party, if original power lines were to be maintained. An invisible vampire with an inscrutable reputation was just such an entity. All eyes went to Helmsley. This part was important to have as word on the street, in case any of the rival clan's members escaped or were allowed to live.

"The lady speaks the truth," the older vampire said calmly, dropping his hold on Havoc to smooth his tuxedo lapels and distinguished brunette hair, paying special attention to the neat silver-gray at his temples. "But he did try to seduce her." Helmsley smiled, clearly knowing that was reason enough for a death sentence served by Butch.

Havoc backed up deeper into the room, holding up his hands in front of him. "Yo, man, I didn't know that it was like that between you and her, and uh, see, what had happened was—that vamp bastard lied on me, man! For real!"

Butch walked forward slowly, stalking Havoc, glimpsing Havoc's clan's stricken expressions as he passed them. Their leader had been punked down, and their game was busted by some old-world vamps that now had a grudge. He snarled at Havoc, then suddenly rushed him and punched him in the face, sprawling him on the floor. Malcolm jumped between Butch and the limp body on the carpet.

"Okay, okay, Butch. Stand down. Your lady held the line and was obviously just up here for a little recreational—even though I don't permit it among my clan." He glanced at Laurel. "Your reprimand comes later, Laurel, and depending on my mood in the morning, I might let this slide given your condition… and may elect to chalk it up to your seeing all these brawls tonight. But we have a more serious issue."

Malcolm went to the safe and looked at the bags of dope on the floor, then focused on Havoc's clan. "First of all, nobody from my clan gave your clan permission to distribute illegal substances on our premises."

Malcolm's clan snarled and vampires slowly nodded their heads, red eyes glowing.

"Second of all, to poison VIP guests for no reason is a major felony. Attempted murder is a death sentence," Malcolm growled.

Havoc's clan began to back up, but they were boxed in on both sides of the hall—vampires had come in through the windows and walked through the walls on one end, Malcolm's clan was on the other end by the elevators.

"It wasn't us," Cutter's wife argued, holding the bloodied place were her ear used to be. "We got set up by the vampires."

Hisses greeted her statement as vampires and their human helpers leered.

"It's true!" Fang's wife shouted. "Jacques, Claude, family of all those guys from the identity theft ring were in on it—their families wanted to avenge their deaths. They said the old world dudes didn't protect them like they should have, and the Temple clan dusted them, so... They asked us to make the product, but what they did with it was their business!"

"You can't blame the manufacturers," Mad Dawg's wife yelled. "This is a war between the vampires, we ain't in it. We just supplied the weapons."

Malcolm glanced around. "That's up to Helmsley."

The old world vampire nodded and brushed invisible lint off his pristine white collar.

"All I know is," Malcolm said evenly, "I want your asses off my casino property forever. That is permanent banishment for even bringing this shit to my door. Me and Sir Helmsley go way back... we have respect for each other's way of doing business. Since you brought it here, but no damage happened, all I'll do is put you out." He looked at Sir Helmsley and both entities shared a knowing smile. "However, how he deems to handle it after that is his business. The Temple clan washes their hands of it and of you."

"You can't turn us over to vampires!" Cutter's wife shrieked, her nervous gaze ricocheting around the other standing were-clan members.

"In my world, which is very medieval, we have ways of making the night feel eternal... and we *will* get to the bottom of the extent of your involvement," Sir Helmsley smiled a slow, sinister grin. "Let us hope that you were only suppliers and not directly bearers of arms against us. For you know how we vampires think of treason... once a grudge has been lodged, it is *forever* written in blood. Ask Machiavelli."

"Oh, shit!" Fang's wife screamed and covered her head.

Instantly, black vampire transport clouds thundered down the hall in angry tornados with a screeching fury of red-eyed warrior bats in them. Rival clan members tried to shift into werewolves and break through doors, and those that panicked were summarily shot. Hundreds of vampire guards grappled with werewolves in the tornadoes that immediately swept the entire rival clan away. Sir Helmsley calmly adjusted his sleeves and stared at his manicure until the dust settled.

"Malcolm, let me buy you a drink," Sir Helmsley said. "This could have been very unfortunate and extremely embarrassing to the coalitions with our nations. You take Rémy neat, correct?"

Malcolm smiled. "Private label, in my office?"

"Done," Sir Helmsley crooned. "And I have dispatched a retinue of scythe bearers to hunt down those crass, new money vampires that would treacherously aid a plot like this. Hoodlums." He glanced at Havoc, and then his henchmen. "Make him disappear—permanently. A man should never attempt to put his hands on another man's woman, unless he's prepared to suffer the consequences—and do see that he suffers... all night." Helmsley smiled a sinister smile at Butch, then at Malcolm. "Thank you, gentlemen, for giving us the bodies and the warning. Since fair exchange is no robbery, how about if I repair your first floor and other losses?"

"Most appreciated," Malcolm said.

Butch nodded. "Y'all are deep."

"To be sure." Helmsley bowed, and then snapped his fingers hard.

The room transformed, all evidence of drugs, broken door hinges, spent rounds, and splintered wood was gone. The hallway and guest doors that had been battered in were repaired. Laurel could only imagine that the first floor had righted itself, too.

Helmsley smiled at her seductively. "Yes, milady. It has." He gave her an appreciative glance and chuckled softly as he briefly looked down at Havoc. "I do understand that poor bastard's dilemma, however." He sighed and winked at Laurel, letting her know that some things he would never share.

Laurel gave the debonair old vampire a subtle thank you nod and stepped back as Butch slid his hand into hers. Some things Butch didn't need to know, like the part about her stroking Havoc's crotch. But it was a sting, nonetheless. Marcus and the rest of the family gave her and Butch a look, while four huge vampires lifted Havoc and blew through the wall in a black energy tornado. The wall reconstructed immediately after they were gone.

Sir Helmsley straightened his spine and adjusted his diamond cuff links. "Riff raff and ruffians," he stated evenly.

"Can't have it on my premises," Malcolm said, entering the hall with Helmsley.

The entire Temple clan gathered around in the hall with them and stared behind the old leaders: one from one species, one from another, as they coolly strode toward the elevators side-by-side.

Butch turned to Laurel as Marcus gave him a wink. The family began to disperse in a slow file headed for the nearest restaurant or bar.

"You coming with us to eat?" Marcus called out, making the family hesitate.

"No, we'll catch up with you later," Laurel said quietly, staring up at Butch.

Everybody smiled and headed for the elevators.

"You know you weren't by yourself in that bar," Butch murmured as soon as the hall cleared. He touched her cheek. "The vamp squad said they wouldn't get in it unless you were cornered."

She smiled and pushed him away. "Didn't trust me? I should belt you for that."

He followed her toward the stairwell. "I trusted you, didn't trust them. Didn't want you to get jumped... be outnumbered... get your gorgeous face slashed by some brute sister... you know?"

She opened the stairwell door. "I had it covered."

"So did I," he said, glimpsing her backside.

She laughed. "I suppose you had the vamps shooting your head images of everything I was up to while in that bar?"

He let the exit close behind them and grabbed her arm, then pulled her to him slowly. "Yeah... you were phenomenal. But I got real worried when they lost the transmission when you came up to the room."

"I was all right," she murmured, kissing the underside of his chin.

"This sting wouldn't have gone down smooth without you," he said quietly, stroking her hair. "The set up was *lovely*... and you kept a war from going down. The teamwork was off da hook, Laurel." He took her mouth carefully, still aware of her bruised cheek.

She sent a soft moan into his mouth as their tongues dueled. Just to hear him give her credit and acknowledge her importance in the operation blew her away. She knew for a strong alpha male like Barron to do that took a lot, and she mentally played with the concept as his tongue played on her palate. Just knowing he'd be gone again very soon made her savor his mouth, imprinting the taste of it into her mind. His scent was already branded there.

He pulled out of her kiss and sought her hair to nuzzle as his hands caressed her back. "But the way you shifted and fought, girl... the transmission was so hot I was ready to blow everything and rush the bar."

She couldn't even answer him, could only find his mouth again, but this time more aggressively. Oddly, her jaw didn't hurt. Two A.M., the moon was still full; she was hours into a hard heat, and everything dropped down on her like a ton of bricks. She had multiple male battles and one of her own. Pack approval, Malcolm's smile that she did good. A war averted. Bad guys served justice. Her family was safe. Five… long… torturous years without mating. *Without him.* Butch's baritone making her wanna yelp. Seeing him shift into the gorgeous animal he was… the hot private confession by the elevators. His hands spreading a post-midnight burn across her back and ass… his hard body pressed against hers, making her writhe. Laurel threw her head back and howled.

Five years, was he out of his mind? Her howl tore one from his throat and crested his canines. He couldn't get her dress off fast enough and didn't care who might see. Five years because he wanted freedom—freedom from what? He could get used to Vegas and bounty hunt from here. Damn, there was so much he'd wanted to tell her while her butter-soft skin was stuck against his human form. He had to get it out before he went straight wolf and chased her into the desert. It came out as a panted stutter, but it was the pure truth. It wasn't delirium talking; he'd known it for a long time.

"Ain't been nobody like you, Laurel. Yours is the only heat I want. Marry me."

That's all he got out before she shifted, and he dropped to all fours, then bolted after her.

The Hunger Within

by

J.M. Jeffries

Acknowledgements

To Leslie: for your terrific sense of humor and willingness to jump on the carousal lending your support to this endeavor. This book would have been nothing without you.

To Seressia: for having so much faith and for being a true friend. Friends rule forever!!

To Natalie: for your commitment and willingness to take a chance.

To Angelique: This would never have been accomplished without you. You are more than the best, you are truly wonderful.

To Genice: She ready!!! Thanks for the snazzy cover and for being the voice of reason in the middle of the desert.

To Deatri: You go, girl, you're the best. Don't ever stop being you. You're level-headedness means so very much.

To Sidney: Thank you from the bottom of our heart for your eagle eye.

To Mary and Margaret: You are truly the best.

To Pam: We would never have gotten so far without your critical thinking and intuitive questions.

To Sherrie: Your support means so much. You keep us moving forward.

To Dianne: Quick Books is no longer a mystery. Well, mostly not a mystery.

To all the Wild Women Writers: Don't go away, we still need you. You're the best.

To Manie Barron: You're priceless.

From Jackie: Mom, thanks for being there and reminding me of what's important in life..

From Miriam:To my husband and children, thank you for allowing me to pursue more than my dreams. I dedicate my future to you.

—Miriam Pace and Jacqueline Hamilton writing as J.M. Jeffries

Chapter One

Solange Warwick paced back and forth across Esther Temple's opulent office as she tried to think of a way to tell her boss about her decision. She paused at the bank of windows overlooking the casino. A pall of uneasiness hung over the floor. Vamps, Weres and humans were not always a good combination, but the draw of twenty million dollars for the winner of the Texas Hold 'em tournament was enough to force a truce. Though the damage from the fight between the Temple clan and a rival werewolf gang had been repaired, the memory lingered. Marcus had pulled out all the stops on a publicity campaign to calm the public's fears and had finally enticed them back to the casino. Laurel's highly visible security teams on the floor were keeping the peace, but the humans were still skittish. Who knew when an all out war might erupt again?

She started pacing again. Solange had been Esther and her husband, Julius's personal assistant for more years than she cared to remember, and her decision to leave the pack had cost her a lot of sleep, a bucketful of tears and a bigger dilemma than she had ever thought possible. She glanced at Esther who was bent over her desk running a French-manicured fingernail down a row of figures.

Solange let out a pent up breath. "I've decided, not to go with you and Julius to Alaska." Her decision had resulted in untold hours of regret and worry Esther would never understand.

Esther raised her head, the silky black curls swayed around an ageless face the color of fine Baltic amber. She pulled on the sleeve of her blue Gucci suit. A sure sign she was displeased. "From talking about crawfish and jambalaya to leaving the pack is quite a leap in subject."

The Hunger Within

Solange put her hands behind her back so Esther wouldn't see them shaking. "I've been thinking how to tell you this for days now."

Esther leaned back in her black leather desk chair. "My, dear, Julius and I haven't even decided yet if we're going to Alaska. He's mulling something over in his mind and won't confide in me just yet. Though I'll admit it's intriguing to have all those open spaces to run in." The casino had been her life, and the desire to move on to something else had been difficult, but Esther knew she and Julius had to move on, and leave the casino in their son's more than capable hands if the pack was to survive. The time had come for Malcolm to prove himself. "I'm sure Malcolm will be delighted you're staying in Las Vegas."

Now came the really hard part. She felt safe and secure here. More than safe—happy and satisfied. "I'm not staying in Las Vegas either." There, she'd announced her intentions to leave the pack, to strike off on her own and brave the world.

Esther's eyebrows rose. "Where do you intend to go?"

Solange knew from experience this was the calm before the storm, she forced herself to stop pacing and face the woman who had raised her from child to woman. Okay, she was intimidated. Who wouldn't be? Esther Temple was a force to be reckoned with. "I don't know. Maybe I'll travel." She hadn't been to Europe since 1938. "Maybe I'll go to Paris, or maybe Maine." *Or Venice.* She had loved Venice at the turn of the century before the war to end all wars had cast a shroud on everything. "I have plenty of money."

Esther rose from behind her desk and planted her hand flat on the blotter, her face suddenly fierce as though she could intimidate Solange. "Don't you have a better plan than just living in Maine or Paris?"

Maybe not she admitted to herself, but anything was better than staying here and facing her humiliation, especially now Malcolm had made his intentions known.

Esther rubbed her forehead. "You're leaving because of Malcolm, aren't you?"

"Partly." Solange tried not to wince at the memory of the pity in Malcolm's eyes. "Malcolm is a good man. Good enough to know we would never match." She darted a glance at Esther who had hoped for a marriage between her son and Solange. But Malcolm knew the pack needed a stronger alpha female than Solange could ever be. Deep down she understood the needs of the pack had to come first, no matter whose feelings got hurt.

Esther spread her hands. "But, this is your home. We're your family."

How to make Esther understand? "I know you and Julius love me as one of your own, but I've never been—" Solange searched for the best words, but as always they eluded her. "—sometimes the others look at me and see," she paused to gather her elusive thoughts, "my human father." —the man who had contributed his DNA, but had given her little else.

"No one blames you, Solange."

"Regardless." Solange tried not to wallow in self-pity for something that had happened before her birth. "My human father was responsible for a great many sins." And Solange knew those sins had descended to the child.

When Esther and Julius had escaped from the Three Moons Plantation just before the Civil War, they had brought all the children they could, including Solange. Fleeing just ahead of the dogs and slave catchers through alligator infested swamps, they'd been found by a mysterious Indian tribe whose members had been impressed with their courage and given them the gift of the wolf.

"Sometimes, I think you would have been smarter to leave me behind." Being the master's half-breed daughter had brought her a lot of grief. Sorrow she had tried to bury deep out of loyalty to Esther and Julius. But she never truly felt as though she belonged. She was a liability and knew it. Time to move on.

Esther smacked her hand on the desk. "Had the war not ended, do you know what your destiny would have been had we left you behind?"

Even though Solange had only been a child, her father had already decided her future. "My father would have sold me to the highest bidder at the quadroon balls." The balls had been romanticized, but Solange had known the truth of the tawdry sale of women to young planters' sons who took mistresses and had children with them.

A low growl escaped from Esther as she walked around her desk to stop in front of Solange. "You would have been the play toy of some rich, white planter."

Solange forced herself not to take a step back. When they were alone, Esther never insisted Solange give her the deference befitting her alpha status. "I know."

"I couldn't let that happen to you." Esther grabbed Solange's upper arms.

Her life on the plantation was so long in the past she barely remembered it. Solange had recreated herself into a modern woman and liked what she was. "Esther, I'm a hundred and fifty plus years old. I can go out on my own. I go to the grocery store by myself. I bought a car by myself. I even managed to attend college by myself."

A tear ran down Esther's cheek. "But you're one of my babies."

"I feel more like a burden." The truth had to be said. "I'm the weakest link in this pack." More than weak. She was protected and kept from so much. In their own way, the pack had kept her a child. "You never let me hunt on the full moon. You never let me…" her voice trailed away. She knew they loved her, but the past was always a guest who never seemed to leave.

"You're gentle," Esther said, "and generous and filled with compassion."

All those wonderful traits would have made her a good woman in the human world, but they were a liability in a wolf pack. "In our world those traits are considered weakness."

Esther shook her head. "Have any of the other children ever taken advantage of you?"

No matter who they were, Esther still considered her adopted children, her children, as natural born as her own. "No, but...sometimes they look at me and see the past. A wall has always stood between me and them." A wall that might not protect her once Julius and Esther left. She was a reminder of the bad times. No overt action would be taken, but Solange was afraid the others would eventually drive her away or kill her. Unlike the human world, wolves were brutal to those who didn't fit in.

"Babycakes." Esther drew Solange to her, cradling her. "I wanted so many things for you. For all my children. I wanted Malcolm to choose you as his mate."

Solange rested her head against Esther's shoulder, still feeling the stinging pain of Malcolm's rejection. "He needs someone stronger than me. With you gone, the next few years will see the pack in flux until he establishes himself as leader." He was already a solid, dependable leader, but needed to prove himself worthy of the pack's loyalty. "I don't blame him for wanting someone else." The words stung and tears threatened to spill. "If I were in his shoes, I wouldn't pick me either. I thought because Malcolm was born after we escaped, I wouldn't have baggage with him, but I do, and nothing you say is going to change things."

"This is the first time you've ever defied me. You're growing up."

Solange laughed shakily, grateful Esther understood. "It's about time." Though she had a sense of direction, a sense of moving forward, she would miss the pack and the safety it gave her, but she needed freedom

Esther patted Solange's cheek. "You will always have a special place in my heart."

Solange kissed Esther and they broke apart. "I know, but I really do think you need 2500 crawfish. Julius likes his etouffee and will park himself by the buffet table and not share with anybody."

"Thank God we're werewolves, or he would weight 750 pounds."

"You would love every inch of him."

Esther's dark eyes sparkled. "Darling, I have."

Solange blushed. At least someone had a love life. Hers was pretty sterile at the moment.

Esther paged through her address book. "Would you like me to call Dan Castle in Toronto? His pack is small, but strong, and there are several unattached males."

"I don't need you to match-make for me." She wasn't doing a great job for herself, but some unwritten law stated she had to marry a wolf, and none of the males she knew suited her. She'd heard about a were-alligator running amok in a lake in California. Maybe she should contact him to see if he needed a mate, though she was more likely to end up as dinner.

"I can't help myself." Esther was the alpha female and tended to mother everyone. "It must be my age." She glanced at the mirror behind the bar as though searching for wrinkles.

Solange laughed. "You're only half way through your life."

Esther sighed. "I'm a middle-aged werewolf."

"Right. And by the way," Solange said with a half-smile, "Mr. Harry Belafonte himself called and told me he would love to sing with you at your party." In the early days when the casino was still getting off the ground, Esther had been the only lounge singer. With her sultry, Lena Horne voice, and her incredible good looks, she'd drawn an audience who remained faithful to this day. Though she occasionally still stopped by the Mardi Gras bar for a song, she didn't do it often enough for her legion of fans.

"Oh, be still my heart," Esther pressed her hands to her chest. "How did you do it?"

"I have my ways. Anything to make you happy." Of course Harry had wheedled a huge donation out of her for UNICEF.

Esther kissed her again. "You're my favorite."

Esther told everyone they were her favorite. She was the best manipulator. No one turned her down—ever—because they all wanted to make her happy. A tiny touch of guilt rose in Solange because she knew her leaving was not in Esther's plans. For the next hundred years, Esther would be sending subtle, underhanded gentle nagging to get Solange back into the fold. But Solange was going to be strong. She needed to make her own way in the world.

Jarred Maitland settled back in the old, over-stuffed chair and balanced a mug of coffee on his knee. He had a hole starting in the knee of his old jeans, and he smelled of stale casino smoke. He smothered a yawn. He'd intended to go back to his apartment after his shift, but Kenny Brooks had left him a message to come right over to his apartment. "What's the emergency?" The FBI didn't pay him enough to sip bad coffee. He was more in danger of dying from the coffee than from being undercover. He would have been in bed hours ago, except he'd decided to head to the office to file his reports and hadn't made it that far.

Kenny Brooks poured himself a cup of coffee. His lean six-foot frame barely fit into his rat hole of a kitchen. He walked out of the kitchen and sat on a green banged up sofa. Kenny smiled. His pale liquid silver eyes shone with something that made Jarred nervous.

Secrets—secrets Jarred didn't want to know. Kenny was a man who felt he should be the top dog in the food chain, and when the weres and vamps had come out of the closet, so to speak, he'd lost his status and couldn't seem to move beyond that.

As Kenny sat on the sofa, he pushed a wisp of blond hair back off his receding hairline. An old air conditioner wheezed in the window, but didn't seem to make much of a dent in the heat flooding in through the picture window opening over the dreary parking lot. Except for a large, elaborately embossed copper box sitting on one of the end tables, Kenny's apartment was as dull and dreary as the complex in which he lived.

Because of its elaborate scrolls and exquisite workmanship, the copper box stood out against the coarseness of the apartment. Jarred tried to focus on it, but his eyes kept sliding away to look everywhere else. The box left him uneasy, and he didn't know why.

Kenny was human with no ties to any of the preternatural societies, but he seemed to have uncanny abilities. The FBI knew he was responsible for the burglaries of a half dozen casinos in the last fifteen years, but had no proof. Which was the major reason Jarred had been given the assignment of infiltrating Kenny's gang. Las Vegas depended on its ability to create a playground, a fantasy, and Kenny had inserted a discordant note that left the city on edge.

"Greg was killed in a car accident last night," Kenny said without preamble, his voice flat and cold. "We don't have an inside man anymore, and we need those codes and blueprints of the sub-basements. More current than the ones Greg was able to get me."

Greg had been in security, and Jarred wondered if Kenny was lying. Had Greg really died in an accident, or had Kenny done something to erase him from the land of the living? On the surface, Kenny appeared like a regular guy, but deep down inside Brooks was just a touch on the freaky side. No one with an atom of sense would risk their life to rob a casino owned by a werewolf pack. At least not for twenty million dollars when they didn't need the money—like Kenny. So why take the risk? Jarred had come to the conclusion Kenny needed to be at the top of the food chain like he was before the world knew about vamps, werewolves, goblins and other ghoulies walked with the human race. "Are we walking away?"

"I'm not letting the robbery go."

Good, he's too much of an egomaniac to let it drop. Jarred wanted to burn Brooks so badly, he would commit the robbery himself and frame him. Too much hinged on Jarred completing this undercover assignment successfully. "What are you going to do?"

Kenny opened the manila folder on the coffee table and took out what looked like a photograph. "I have backup plans." He tossed a photo on the smudged coffee table. "What do you think?"

The photo was of Solange Warwick, personal assistant to Julius and Esther Temple, owners of The French Quarter casino. Anyone who spent any time around the casino knew exactly who the lithe, tawny-skinned beauty was. Kenny's candid photograph had caught her deep in conversation with Malcolm Temple. There was a touch of deference in her posture, every muscle knew this man was in charge…and something else. She was sad. Her shoulders hunched, her full mouth was turned down. *What a shame.* Beautiful women like her shouldn't be unhappy. A smart man would be spending all his time trying to keep a woman like her satisfied. So why was she sad?

Jarred glanced at Kenny. He assumed he'd gotten the job of snaring her because…well, women weren't Kenny's taste in play-mates. "Why Solange Warwick?" She was a werewolf; she could tear him apart with one hand tied behind her back.

"Seems like the beautiful Solange is in love with the owner's son and got kicked to the curb. Can't tell me a beautiful woman like her wouldn't like a taste of revenge."

"Trust me, if she was going after the owner's son, she isn't going to downgrade to a night club bouncer." *Or a human.*

Kenny smiled, giving Jarred an up and down appraisal. "You underestimate your charm with the women."

Which left Jarred feeling like he needed a shower. "Are you pimping me out?"

"For your share of twenty million dollars, hell yeah! I'm pimping you out." He pushed the photo of Solange across the table toward Jarred. "This is one beautiful woman. Frankly, if she did anything for me, I'd be on her myself, but I'd rather date you." He gave Jarred a flirtatious wink.

Jarred had gotten used to Kenny's flirtatious ways, but not even to bust this gang was he going to pitch for the home team. He picked up Solange's photo. She was a beautiful sister with high cheekbones, large chocolate eyes, buttery smooth skin and rusty black hair brushing the tops of her shoulders. He'd seen her around the casino enough times to know she was the type of woman he liked.

"You need to get to her fast," Kenny said.

"You really want me to seduce a werewolf?" He placed the coffee mug on the table and stood.

"She's still a woman."

"She could tear my head off."

Kenny shrugged. "She won't. So get to it. I need those codes."

"Why not you?" Even though Kenny went both ways, he had his own preferences.

Kenny glanced at the closed bedroom door. "Otherwise engaged," he said.

"Right." So Jarred would have to get in bed, figuratively speaking, with a werewolf, a woman who changed from human to animal and bayed at the moon. She was beautiful, and all he could hope for was not ending up dead.

With the Texas Hold 'em tournament having begun, the casino was stuffed to the gills with players—humans, vampire and weres, not always a good combination—legitimate guests and looky-loos dragging themselves in from the heat to watch the play for a few hours.

Though the traffic had been light because of a huge fight a couple days back, the hard-liners were still around. Which was why Kenny was interested in The French Quarter. The winner of the tournament was going to take home a sweet twenty million dollars, unless Kenny got his hands on it first. In fact, the owners had placed the twenty mil on display in a large glass case in the very center of the casino with four guards and a guard dog on duty. For sixteen hours a day the money was visible, along with the tournament trophy. The move had brought a lot of people through the doors.

Kenny stared hungrily at the closed bedroom door, licked his thin bottom lip. Jarred knew the time to leave, with his new instructions, had arrived.

He walked down the rickety steps to the parking lot, sidestepping a pothole and getting into his car. He started the motor and pulled out onto Tropicana. When he was a block away, he flipped open the glove compartment and pulled out his cell phone to call the office. Even though he was on loan from the L.A. office, he still had to check in with his new boss who just happened to be his old roommate from Quantico.

"Harrison Jones," Jarred's boss said on the second ring.

"Always the professional."

Harry laughed. "What's going on Maitland?"

"I just got handed a new assignment, romancing the Temple's personal assistant because Kenny's inside weasel, Greg, was killed last night in a car accident, or so Kenny is telling me."

"I'll check with Metro P.D. and see if I can find anything unusual. But I can't see Brooks jeopardizing his heist so close to the big day." The robbery had been scheduled for the second to the last day of the tournament, and Jarred was starting to get nervous. Everything about Kenny urged caution, and the longer Jarred was in his company, the more nervous he became.

"Brooks hides it well, but personally I think he has a loose screw rattling around in his head. Why would he leave a comfy life style in Philadelphia where his daddy owns half the city and take on a casino owned by weres who would eat him in a minute? He has five times the money in his trust fund than what he's stolen in the last fifteen years."

There were a few seconds of dead air from Harry's end. "That, my friend, is the difference between us. Why do I need this job when my daddy's a U.S. Senator? I could have ridden on his coat tails, taken a job on his staff and had a fine career in the political arena. But a political job would have been dull...deadly dull. But say whatever you will about Harrison Jones III, I'm not dull." Dull was definitely not a part of Harry's personality. He was Mr. Practical Joker. He was a good man, with a good personality and a good sense of fun, and Jarred was enjoying working with him. "Brooks may have all the money he needs, but we both know he's a sociopath and not too happy with his position in this new world order and social structure. And, inheriting money will never be as exciting as stealing it. Especially if he's taking from a were pack."

Jarred's traditional middle class upbringing said to work hard, and he'd get what he wanted. And what he wanted all his life was to be a G-man. Being with the FBI was the coolest job on the planet. Being undercover was more fun than he liked to admit. Every few months, he got to be somebody new, and always was the good guy wearing a white hat. And he'd need a white hat before this assignment was over, because he knew Solange Warwick was going to end up dead when Kenny was done with her. Kenny didn't leave loose ends.

Chapter Two

The employee cafeteria was crowded with the conflux of two shifts coming together. People moved along the buffet, pushing their trays. The French Quarter had always treated its employees well, and even though they worked for a werewolf pack, the humans had given their loyalty. Solange found an isolated corner table and watched as the night shift entered and the day shift got ready to head home.

Solange was surprised to see Laurel, head of security sitting around a table surrounded by her lieutenants. Since the big pack fight, her pack sister had been working non-stop keeping the peace, plus the fact her mate, Butch, had arrived in town. *How nice to see someone getting their happy ending.*

At another table, Malcolm and Guy finished their meal and stood up to leave. Guy tossed a flirtatious wink her way, but Solange knew it was more to irritate Malcolm than a come-on to her. Guy wouldn't gain any points by bedding her. Oh he'd have a good time, but that's all. Omegas were good for sex and errands in the werewolf world. At least no one treated her like dirt in this pack. No one wanted to answer to Julius or Esther.

Solange tried to ignore Malcolm, but she saw him scowl at Guy as if he cared. Then Malcolm turned to her, she couldn't read his expression, but she was sure it was pity. Solange's blood began to boil. How dare he humiliate her then feel sorry for her. Frankly all she wanted to do was walk over to him unsheathe her claws and slash them across his face. She could almost feel the blood dripping from her claws. Then she noticed all the weres stopped what they were doing and faced her. Oh God she must have sent out a very ugly scent to make the beasts stop eating. Not much got between weres and their food. Taking a deep breath she smiled as she tried to forget her utter humiliation. Malcolm gave her a brief nod as he passed, and she watched him head out the door. At least the pity was gone from his eyes. Score one for Solange. Although she knew it was a hollow victory, she let the pride wash over her if only for a few seconds. Fighting wasn't in her nature, she retreated.

More than anything else, what made her sad was the loss of Malcolm as a friend. No matter what he had to put the pack first, to keep the pack strong. In her heart she could accept his decision. If only her pride would let her, maybe she'd figure out a way she didn't have to leave.

She had to get away, to put the hurt behind her, to make a new life for herself. Though she was truthful enough to know she didn't love him in the way he needed to be loved, she did respect him and considered him a friend. The distance he'd put between them hurt.

The French Quarter's black Elvis impersonator entered the cafeteria. He wriggled his eyebrows at Solange and she found herself grinning back. She couldn't stay morose with Elvis around. Simone had hired him years ago. He'd not only been the first black Elvis in Las Vegas, but he also had the distinction of being the only black Elvis who was also a vampire.

A seductive musky smell tickled her nose taking her thoughts from Elvis. Solange inhaled deeply letting the captivating masculine smell wash over her senses. Her eyes widened when she realized a human male was behind the scent. Whoever the man was he smelled wonderful. Turning her chair she snuck a peek over her shoulder. A tall brother sauntered toward her. Solange felt her teeth sink into her bottom lip to stop the sigh wanting to escape. Normally a man carrying a pink lunch tray just looked plain ridiculous, but Mr. I'm-A-Stud just looked really hungry. Knowing he wasn't looking at her she let her gaze wander down his body. Long black braids hung over his muscular shoulders, which tapered down to lean hips and powerful thighs. God if he were a wolf, he'd be the baddest Alpha in the building. Still feeling safe staring, she trailed her gaze up until she stopped on the most beautiful full lips the gods ever made. The entire package of the man was wrapped in smooth almond colored skin.

And he was human. Shifting her gaze up she stared into deepest brown eyes she'd ever seen. But what startled her most were those magnetic eyes staring right at her.

Solange gulped finding herself unable to look away.

"May I join you?"

She gestured at the empty chair across from her, even as her head told her fraternizing with him was dangerous, but she just wanted to smell him some more.

He wore a black T-shirt with the Marti Gras logo on it and black pants identifying him as a bouncer at the nightclub "Thanks." He set his tray down and settled on the chair. "You're wearing a nice piece of amber."

She touched the heavy amber stone shaped like a pear hanging around her neck. "Thank you, it's my favorite. I collect amber."

He eyed the amber nestled between her breasts. "I've heard that anyone who touches amber, a piece of their soul is stolen."

Again, she was startled as she felt a tingle of awareness caress her spine. "You know the mystery of amber."

Lifting his eyes to her face he smiled. "My grandmother loved amber. She was a chorus girl with an all black revue that traveled around Europe in the late twenties and early thirties. She met this Communist guy who had a thing for her. He followed her all over Europe and showered her with amber. He even showed her the famed amber room at the Czar's summer palace at Tsarskoe Syolo."

His smile was friendly, but in his eyes she saw a hint of desire. Her stomach tightened. Solange started to tell him she'd seen the amber room, too, until she remembered she was a werewolf, and humans didn't like being reminded about the difference in their life spans. She, Esther, Simone and Julius had gone to Russia to negotiate a treaty with Russian wolves. They had stayed with the Czar and his wife. Her amber was probably older than this man's grandmother. "The amber room was beautiful." Which was as close as she could come to letting him know she'd seen it.

He lifted one eyebrow. After a moment, he gestured at the amber. "May I?"

She nodded her throat dry, and he reached across the table to caress the amber. His fingers were long and solid. His fingers lingered on the stone, and when he withdrew, there was a look on his face she couldn't interpret. For a split second she wondered what his fingers would feel like on her bare skin. An uncomfortable heat settled between her legs shocking her. Her nipples were peaked. Solange had the urge to get up and run away. No one human or were had sparked this kind of desire in her.

He smiled. "Now you have a piece of my soul forever."

She caressed the stone still warm from his touch and felt a blush steal up her cheeks. She felt were eyes on her. Oh my God, her hormones just exploded! Her eyes darted around the cafeteria. Black Elvis was smiling enjoying the show. Laurel's mouth was on the table including the two were males with her. Mike and Sam had their hackles up. "Ah yes." God she wanted to fan herself to cool herself down.

"By the way, my name is Jarred Maitland." He held out his hand, curling his fingers around hers.

Her immediate reaction was to pull her hand away, but she liked his touch. "I'm Solange." His strong hand sent heat up her arm. She hadn't dated a human male in a long time, and she'd forgotten how utterly captivating they could be. Dating were males was more primitive, more like a contest with each of them trying to figure out who would be the top wolf. Human men had the same competitive nature, but were more charming about it. She liked the human approach better. With human males she felt like a prize, with wolves she felt like a bone to be sparred over.

"I haven't seen you at the night club in awhile. Don't you feel like dancing?"

He'd noticed her? *What a surprise!* Normally she thought she just blended in next to her more flamboyant pack sisters. "With the tournament and Esther and Julius's farewell party, all I want to do at the end of the day is fall into bed. I don't have any excess energy to burn."

"I should be glad you don't come. The way you move just whips everyone into a frenzy and makes my job a lot harder."

"I'm sorry." She had no idea she had such an effect. She just liked to dance. The thought almost made her uncomfortable, but she did like the idea of him watching her. More than she should.

"Don't apologize. I like watching you."

This man was very appealing. He had a way of delivering a line that made her blush again. She sniffed delicately and could tell he was telling the truth. She could smell the hint of attraction on him. Her nose told her, he was interested in her, not what she was. Good, she hated human's who wanted to be were groupies.

"Don't be embarrassed," he continued. "Women usually dance for two reasons at a night club. Either they dance to impress, or they dance to entice."

Shocked, she needed to defend herself. "I go for different reasons."

He planted his elbow on the table and placed his chin on his fist. "Then why?"

"It's the only place I feel like I can let loose. I don't have to be me." A chance to leave her professional self at the door was priceless to her.

"I don't understand."

In for a penny…in for a pound. My God he was easy to talk to. He just had an aura that made a girl want to spill all of her secrets. This was not good. Or was it. "There are different Solanges. One Solange who has to be gracious, another has to be on top of everything and the third Solange has to keep the peace." She didn't always do a very good job. Uncertain how the last statement had slipped out, she snapped her mouth shut. She had always been the peacemaker in the pack and frequently grew tired of everyone's demands on her.

He dug into his food, and after a few seconds said, "I know how you feel. I have five sisters. Each one more beautiful than the next." He held up his hand. "I'm not bragging, but someone had to referee."

No wonder he knew how to talk to a woman. His sisters were probably gorgeous, because he was gorgeous. The tingle in her arms expanded up and down her spine. He was smooth and she liked his delivery. She couldn't remember being so attracted to a were male, much less a human male.

"I'm doing a short shift tonight," he said after he took a sip of his coffee. "I get off at ten. How about a late dinner so I can see you get a proper meal before you go off to bed after your energy sucking day."

For a second, Solange was too surprised to respond. Her heart started racing. Why would a sexy man like him want to be with her? She couldn't remember the last time she'd been propositioned so blatantly and so sweetly. Simone Temple entered the café and started toward her, the waves of anger bouncing off her.

"Yes," Solange said in a loud voice, "I'd love to have dinner with you." Maybe too loud.

Two beta males got up and stalked by them, their gazes flicking between her and Maitland challenge plainly written on their faces. Simone stopped, her mouth forming a surprised O, then she held up the thumbs up sign. Then she veered off and plopped down to speak with Laurel. Solange arranged her knife and fork, hoping to hide her nervousness. "Chef Marcel is making Beef Wellington tonight." She stopped; embarrassed, remembering he was a bouncer and probably couldn't afford a fine dining restaurant. "Never mind. We can go someplace else. You chose." She left the words, affordable, unsaid.

He leaned toward her. "Julius and Esther pay me a lot of money. I can afford Chef Marcel." He grinned at her and stood, his tray in hand. "Wear some amber tonight. It looks beautiful against your skin."

His words were said low and sexy. Their meaning undeniable. He was attracted to her. And she felt the niggling pulse of desire curling in her stomach. Heat raced through her. She nodded and grinned.

"Tonight." He walked away.

Simone slid into the spot vacated by Jarred. "My, my, my, big sister." The fact that Simone always called Solange big sister made her feel good. "He is one tasty man. I'm almost jealous."

"I'm allowed to have dates with regular guys?"

Simone chuckled. "When they look like him, yes. Look at that ass."

Solange twisted around to watch Jarred walk toward the exit. His rear end was two perfect moons moving in rhythm. She bit her bottom lip to stop the sigh. "It is a work of art."

"Not a bad piece to hang on any girl's wall," Simone said with a sigh.

Solange didn't want to talk about him with anyone. In a strange way she didn't understand, she wanted to keep him to herself. "Were you looking for me?"

"Yes, there's a problem."

She couldn't think of a moment when she didn't have a problem. "Don't let it be with the food."

Simone shook her head. "Nope."

"The entertainment?"

"Nope,"

"The tournament?"

Simone shook her head again. "Not the tournament. I need you to come play good cop. I'm the next big-thing, my shit-don't-stink, Danny Sawyer is here. Somehow, this little no-neck pipsqueak thinks he gets the Presidential Suite just because he decides to show up without a reservation, and insists we move Mr. Billionaire Vampire my-shit-don't-even-move-through-the-plumbing-into-the-basement. You need to go handle him, because mom and dad are going to eat him and his entire bimbo entourage. Then we'd all die from silicone poisoning."

Solange rubbed the side of her cheeks. She hated having to be Little Miss Suck-Up. "Tell the duffus we'll be happy to comp his room. He shows up unexpectedly because he knows he'll get free stuff."

"Can't we send him to the Luxor. I'll pay for the limo. In fact, I'll pay for everything."

Solange patted her hand. "You already know we don't do business that way. Why aren't you handling him?"

Simone pushed dark strands of hair out of her face. "Because last time I almost took a chunk of meat out of his thigh. It all started because I insulted his teeny, weeny pecker."

"How can you insult something that doesn't exist?"

Simone simply grinned. "I'll hurt him, and that won't look good as front page news on some tabloid."

Solange pushed herself to her feet. "Then I guess I'm on." She dumped her uneaten food into the trash, put the tray on top of the trash bin, and headed for the reception area, Danny Sawyer and his unpredictable temper.

Chef Marcel outdid himself. Jarred was a meat and potatoes kind of man, but the Beef Wellington was melt-in-his-mouth good. Solange enjoyed her food as well, though her beef was a lot bloodier than he liked. He wondered if it had been cooked at all. But then again, she was a werewolf, and she ate with relish. He discovered she was delightful company, even though she was the first werewolf he'd ever had a meal with. She was actually more human than he'd expected. Nor was he expecting how attracted he'd be to her. This was one of those times he hated his job. To get what he wanted, he had to use her. He hadn't felt this dirty in a long time.

"Why me?" Solange asked as the dinner plates were being removed. The waiter refilled her wine glass, and she took a sip.

For a second he didn't know how to answer her. Yes, she was a means to an end, but she was still a beautiful woman with a sad smile. And he wanted to make her happy, not just to get close to her. Everyone in the casino had told him she was kind, generous, and nurturing to all the casinos employees. Anyone who worked in the French Quarter knew, if you had a problem, Solange Warrick would make it better. What the fuck was Malcolm Temple's problem to not want a woman like her? "You're a beautiful woman. What man wouldn't want to spend time with you?"

She shook her head. "I think your motives go much deeper."

He leaned back in his high backed chair, studying her. This woman was not a pushover. She may have this delicate air about her, but she was sharp, and he would have to work really hard to get her where he needed her. Part of him also wanted her to like him. Maybe it was time for him to unleash Mr. Suave on her. Or at least let her take control. If he wanted to turn her then he needed to know her. "I didn't know I needed a reason other than the one that reminds me I'm a man and you're a woman."

She threw back her head and laughed. "I'm not your usual type of woman."

Okay the laugh shot him down a notch. "I don't know what you mean?"

"I get furry. You don't."

The wolf thing notwithstanding, she was every man's type of woman. She was the kind of woman you wanted to come home to. Make a life with. Damn, that scared the shit out of him. Thinking these kinds of thoughts got good agents in trouble. He knew he had to focus on the job, but all he wanted was to get up close and personal with her in a way not involving clothes. He was shocked at himself even more for wanting to bed a werewolf. "What type do you think I like?"

She studied him for several moments, her brown eyes seemed to be peering into is soul. "Fun-loving, no interest in commitment. I'm not saying you don't like substance, but I think you don't want anything too heavy."

Over the years, he'd concentrated totally on his career. He hadn't had time to set up housekeeping and start a family. Black men in the FBI still had a lot to prove, and working most of his assignments undercover didn't lead to commitment. Most women wouldn't tolerate a man who could be gone months at a time. "I've been busy."

A graceful batwing eyebrow rose and trained those soulful eyes on him. "Doing what?"

Okay lady break out the rubber hoses. Did she have any idea how hard it was to lie to her? Right now his attempt to lead her down the garden path was making him feel dirty like he was corrupting an angel. "Working." He knew the answer was vague, but he hoped it worked.

"You seem like an intelligent man, is a bouncer all you aspire to be."

He shrugged. "I like working at night."

"You didn't answer my question." She smiled, swirling her finger around her wine glass.

She made him want to come clean and tell her everything up to and including a desire for her so strong he'd risk his job. He couldn't tell his thoughts, but he still had to answer her question? He turned over several responses in his mind. "I don't dislike being a bouncer."

Her nose twitched. "You're lying."

Was she smelling him? Do lies stink? He was going to have to do some research on weres. He was so taken aback, he didn't have a response. "What would you like me to say?"

"Being a bouncer isn't all you're interested in."

The waiter brought Solange a slice of cheesecake; she flashed a mega watt grin at the man. She didn't order it.

"Thank you. Bill. You know what I like."

Must be a standing order with her. Jarred was going to slip the waiter an extra twenty just because he had good timing. Hopefully the act of eating the cheesecake would distract her from her inquisition.

"Well I'm waiting." She said then raised the fork to her mouth.

Sharpest tack in the drawer, his mother would say about her. His plan had failed, he thought. The sly smile on her full lips as she chewed told him she knew she'd outwitted him too. God, he liked this woman. "Okay, maybe I don't like being a bouncer, but it's gonna pay off." Okay, he'd just let something slip, and he saw her eyes go sharp and focused. "If something better came alone, I'd jump on it." Like a promotion back to the D.C. field office.

"You have an unusual way of phrasing it."

Okay, how did he salvage his slip? He smiled. "I got to meet you, didn't I?"

Again, she sniffed delicately, her nostrils flaring slightly. "You're good, but don't patronize me." She shook her fork at him. "I've been in the people business a long time and can smell a lie from across the casino. "

Okay, he thought. *How do I get out of this?* He leaned toward her. "Listen, we're having a good time here. The wine is good, the food is outstanding and the company is totally and captivatingly delicious. Let's not get into some of my emotional territory just now and ruin a good time. Let's keep this evening light and fun." He ended his speech, just keeping the pleading note out of his voice. "You have secrets and so do I."

"Fair enough. We'll keep things light. I can do light." She dug into her cheesecake again.

He found himself enjoying watching her eat. She didn't pick daintily at her food, but ate as though she hadn't eaten in two weeks.

Afterward, he took Solange for a walk down the strip. The French Quarter had originally been off by itself for many years, and the strip grown up to it. Instead of being a part of an almost slum, the casino was now in an area gradually up-scaling to better and grander things.

Solange swayed and bumped into him, sending his libido into overdrive. How could she be so beautiful, so sweet and delicate and be a werewolf. He didn't ask her. But he couldn't help a thrill of desire that swept through him at the danger she represented. He didn't feel physically threatened, but detected a more subtle emotional kind of risk he wanted to explore.

Despite the lateness, the strip was still alive with tourists heading toward wherever tourists went when they were being tourists. A kid in a black sweater and baggy pants gave Solange a blatant leer, and Jarred felt a spurt of anger. He wanted to slap the kid; instead, he held her hand possessively.

The kid smirked at Jarred and turned away, grabbing the hand of a girl and moving off.

The water show at the Bellagio started just as they approached. Solange leaned against the cement fence and cupped her face in her hands. Jarred couldn't take his eyes from her. She was so beautiful, so poised, and so friendly for being what she was. The were packs were known for their aggression, and here he was taking a midnight walk with one. Everything seemed so normal.

"It's a beautiful night," Solange said when the water show ended. "But it's time for me to be getting back."

Jarred didn't want the night to end. "It's a long walk back, how about a taxi ride?" he asked, though she didn't seem one bit winded.

"Works for me." A slight breeze fluffed her hair about her face, and she gave him a look that sent his libido into overdrive. The gentle scent of lavender invaded him. He used to think lavender was an old-fashioned scent old ladies used, but on her it smelled like desire. He wanted her. He didn't care she was a wolf. Right now, all he saw was a beautiful woman he needed to get into his bed no matter what the consequences.

"Then let's get back." He raised a hand and hailed a taxi. And, suddenly, he was more than anxious to see what developed next.

Solange couldn't believe she'd accepted an invitation to walk with this man. Was she crazy? She didn't need the complication. But she couldn't seem to keep her desire for him under control. What was it about him? They'd shared a meal and some witty conversation. She'd done exactly the same thing with plenty of men over the years. But she couldn't stop the feeling he wanted more. He seemed so intent on seducing her. For some strange reason, he knew all the right buttons to push. It made her feel so wanted.

The taxi deposited them at the front door of the casino. Jarred paid the driver, and the taxi roared off.

"Walk me inside." She couldn't believe she uttered the words. She was never so aggressive.

He slid warm fingers around her elbow and guided her into the casino.

Inside the tournament was still in full swing. This round wouldn't stop until it had narrowed the field a little bit more. Music blasted from the nightclub. Though the casino wasn't as crowded as it usually was, there was still a respectable crowd.

At the center of the casino, the glass case exhibiting the twenty million was empty. The money went off display at midnight and came back at six a.m. But the empty case still caused curiosity. A group of people clustered around the empty case, staring at it as they talked. Solange figured they were all dreaming about what they could do with so much money.

The tournament had been a logistics nightmare, but Solange had mastered it and pulled it together. She felt a sense of pride at all the work she'd done. Her job as the Temples' assistant was to get done what they wanted done. And with the popularity of Texas Hold 'em, they had gambled on filling the casino with not only players, but also guests. The hotel was filled to the brim, and for the first time an almost friendly cooperation between the vampires, the werewolves and assorted other creatures of the night had formed. With humans in the mix, the situation was more volatile, but nothing bad had happened, and Solange hoped nothing bad would happen.

At the bank of elevators leading to the family apartments, Solange turned to wish Jarred good night, but he forestalled her with a kiss. His lips on hers were warm and soft, and she swayed into him, her arms going around his neck. His breath fanned lightly across her cheek and he smelled of the night air and cinnamon. She thought about all the lonely nights she spent in her bed and knew she wanted him to go up with her.

The elevator doors opened, and he started to turn away. Solange grabbed his hand and pulled him in after her. They had the elevator to themselves. She found her eyes drawn to him. He looked at her as though she were the most precious thing in the world.

When her eyes came to rest on the hard ridge in his pants, sensual heat rose inside her, and her stomach somersaulted. God, she wanted him. She closed her eyes for a second, reliving the intense pleasure of his hands on her body, and his lips on hers. Jarred Maitland embodied every fantasy created in her love-starved imagination. She was crazy for going outside the boundaries of the pack, but realized she could not get away from him. She didn't want to escape. She couldn't wait for the elevator to open on her floor. When it finally did, she almost pulled him down the corridor to her apartment, opened the door with her keycard and pulled him inside.

When the door closed, Jarred braced his large hands on either side of her shoulders. Solange curled her hands into fists, forcing them to her side, not trusting herself to touch him. She inhaled the subtle, woodsy notes of his soap mixed with the heat of his body. She remembered the salty taste on his skin, the texture of his smooth flesh, and the hardness of his muscles. Shivering, she pressed harder against the door. "Tell me you want me."

Jarred took another step closer. He was only a half-inch away from her. "More than anything."

She tilted her head at him. "Have you ever been with a wolf?"

"I never wanted to be with one before." He pushed a strand of hair off her cheek, answering her with a silky smile. The tip of his finger left a trail of fire on her cheek.

Solange's knees buckled. She turned her head to avoid seeing the stark desire burning in his black eyes. A bit of common sense finally raised its ugly head. This could be dangerous. "We shouldn't be doing this," she murmured through a haze of desire. We don't know each other." Heat spiraled out of control from the core of her soul outward to each nerve in her body.

"You're not getting away from me now." He smiled. "I think we know each other just fine." He ran his finger along the ridge of her chin and down her throat.

Her body trembled, and the intensity of her emotions frightened her. "This might be a mistake."

"Maybe, but we'll never know until we do. I'm willing to find out." He kissed her neck, licked her.

Solange felt the tip of his hot tongue against her skin. She dug her nails into her palms to stop herself from reaching out, but she knew the battle had been lost a long time ago.

"The only mistake is not letting our attraction play itself out." He nibbled the spot where her shoulder connected with her neck.

A shuddering sound escaped her lips. Heat danced up her spine. She squeezed her eyes shut, wishing she could mark his seduction up to one of her flights of fantasy. But Jarred was flesh and blood real, not one of her nocturnal musings. He was so different from the males in her pack. He never looked at her with pity.

"Tell me you don't want me." He licked her lips, pressing hard against her.

"I don't think I can." Once started, she couldn't stop. Not now.

"This is how much I want you." Jarred guided her hand to the bulge in his pants, and then pressed her hand to his erection.

Jarred slid his hand over the exposed skin of her stomach. Her crop top and skirt gave him easy access to her body. His warm hand teased her flesh and eased upward beneath the crop top. Her belly quivered under his touch. Deep down inside, the beast growled and curled around, demanding to be released. A howl built in her throat, but she forced it back. She didn't want to scare him, to send him fleeing from her. She curled her hands in his hair.

Jarred held his breath waiting for Solange to push him away, to deny him, but the words never came. *This is insane*, he thought. He should take himself out of this place and run for all he was worth.

The velvet texture of her skin consumed him. He eased his fingers up her stomach, until the tip of his finger connected with the curve of her breast. He moved with deliberate slowness, enjoying the touch of her skin, the hardness of her nipples. Her head lolled back against the door, and her eyes closed. For a moment her face seemed to phase into something else, then returned to normal. He buried his face in her hair. She wasn't going to send him away. Her body was responding and eager to complete what they started. His whole body trembled from the sensual over-load.

She leaned toward him, and he fondled the sweet fullness of her breast. Her nipples beaded with anticipation.

Jarred drew in a harsh breath. Her lips had parted, revealing the tip of her pink tongue as she moistened her lips. He kissed her, drinking deep of the honeyed sweetness of her mouth. She responded in kind, her tongue touching his.

"Come on, Solange," he whispered hoarsely, "tell me you want me as much as I want you."

She fit her body closer to him, molding to him. "I didn't run, did I?"

"No, you didn't." He laughed and slipped his hands around her waist. He raised her shirt over her head, tossing it aside to gaze in wonder at her breasts. They were lush and beautiful. High, firm, and round, they were his ideas of perfection. He stroked her rosy nipples with the pads of his thumbs.

How had such a fiery, seductive woman managed to make a place in his life so easily. She was everything he never knew he wanted until she had showed up on his doorstep.

He kissed her and ran his tongue down her neck to the tops of her breasts, to her nipples and back to her mouth. She tasted sweet, like fruit and spring rain.

"Jarred," she moaned. "I want you so much."

"I want you." His heart pounded. Blood pulsed through his veins. He ached to possess her.

Solange writhed under his touch. A soft moan escaped as the weight of his pelvis ground ribbons of pleasure into hers. Her knee slid up his leg, the material of his pants a rough caress on her skin. Breathless, she began opening his shirt as her fingers gently stroked each button. After a moment she become emboldened enough to transfer the delicate caress to his heated skin. Her fingers grazed the smooth planes of his chest and she felt his stomach clench against her torso. Each hard muscle she touched contracted beneath her feather light attention. Jarred's breath hitched as she trailed her mouth down his chest gently biting one nipple.

Heat engulfed him, along with a level of possessive desire he didn't know he owned. Insanity. He wanted more than her body, wanted her surrender. He wanted every part of her body and her soul. He needed to excise Malcolm Temple from her memory.

Jarred arched. His skin was on fire. "Solange." His voice became garbled, strangled by a moan. Her graceful fingers had freed his pants buttons; her pulsing grasp forced another moan from him as he closed his eyes.

"Tell me what you want, Jarred?" she murmured.

"I want… I want…" His brain shut down. He couldn't think, only react. Each touch of her fingers sent shock waves through him and his knees buckled. He allowed a crushing kiss to become his answer. The bed was so far away. "You." He'd been reduced to one word responses. He'd never been with a woman like this, not one with such roiling passion beneath her calm surface. Her skin, the satiny feel of her exquisite skin, and her deep lavender scent torched his mind.

Unable to stand it any longer, he pushed down her skirt and slid his fingers beneath the pink elastic triangle covering the dark apex between her legs. Her quiet gasp drew his focus to her aching expression. The look on her face made his pleasure-slicked fingers tremble against her. How long had it been since she'd been loved proper? He gently took her mouth. To starve a woman this gorgeous was criminal. Tonight he'd deliver justice… slow, interminable justice, until it incarcerated them both.

"Take them off," she murmured, her voice so smoky it reminded him of aged whiskey.

He knew what she wanted as he looked at her through heavy lids and ripped away the flimsy fabric. A flutter of pink lace pooled at her feet on the floor. His palm smoothed the high swell of her hip. Completely naked, her eyes hunted his, the light from the desk adding exotic shadows to her exquisite frame.

Slowly trailing his hands up her hips, her sides, and slowly over her breasts until she shuddered, he splayed his fingers to cover her jaw, reaching up into her hair to pull her mouth against his. Her lips parted, her mouth eagerly consuming his, her nails digging into his shoulder blades. He could feel the tremor in her abdomen quaking her pelvis as she rubbed her swollen mound against him. Intense

126

pleasure consumed him, and her unmistakable desire blew him away.

Gently pulling her head back, he showered kisses along her throat. She tasted so good, she felt so right in his arms, and the need to be inside her had become an inferno in his groin. His fingers slid into her wetness eliciting a sharp groan from her that dissolved into a low, throaty growl. Her palms flattened against his chest, her eyes seeking. He watched her drop her head back as he slowly slid down her body, his tongue leaving a hot, moist trail, dipping into her belly button, and forcing her fingers to tangle in his hair.

With a gentle tug, he drew her down to the plush Oriental rug with him, easing her back, his eyes locked with hers, communicating all without words. Nuzzling the slick, velvety curls between her damp thighs, he kicked off his shoes then stripped away his pants and boxers. Her heady taste washed his cheeks and chin, the wondrous scent of her arousal drove him to open her soft folds and gently capture her bud with the tip of his lips.

Her nails dug into the carpet, her body arched, heaving against the butterfly flicking sensations Jarred delivered. She was a Lup— gentle, patient, drizzled pleasure was rarely afforded her kind... and *never* on a full moon. The male wolves didn't have The finesse of Jarred's maddeningly slow rhythm... a gentle reminder of insanity. Her beast clawed to be freed as she opened her thighs wider and lifted her hips higher. Strong hands firmly held her bottom while methodically laving suckles built her climax to a trembling inner wave. Her honey flowed, and his groan into her wet valley made her writhe with need. When he reached for her nipple and gently squeezed it, her body spasmed and her legs tightened around him. She chanted his name like a benediction, a sharp inhale, broken in half, like her mind.

She tried to catch her breath as he licked his way back to her mouth. He extracted a condom. Breaking the kiss, she just wanted to see him, needed to watch him sheath himself. Never in all her years had she dreamed being with a human male could be so wonderful. Her inner wolf howled. Jarred winced as he unrolled the condom. She was thrilled he wanted her so badly. The sight of him threatened to make her explode.

Staring at each other for a moment, he took her mouth in a slow dissolve the same way he entered her, then suddenly plunged his tongue deep as he plunged hilt-deep into her. Shocked, she could feel him swallow her muffled groan, causing her inner muscles to clench around his hard thrust. She scrabbled at his back, and then held him tightly. Her legs wrapped around his waist, a howl lodged deep within, drowned by wave after crashing wave of pleasure.

Slowly he stroked inside her. "Baby."

Oh yes, she thought. Her internal muscle began to contract as he moved slowly inside her.

Sweat ran down his face, his eyes shut tightly against the spiking sensations, the need to cum about to split his sac. The first spasm of her completion engulfed him, but now there was only the feel of her and the fire they created. There was no going back. He'd been conquered, turned out… one last stroke, buried deep inside her— her face tucked into his neck, his head thrown back, gasping, he was lost in a molten ocean of pleasure.

For a brief moment he didn't know where she ended and he began as they rocked back and forth while their climax shudders abated. He held her more tightly, possessively, claiming her without words. He prayed she was doing the same.

No matter what it cost him, he had to make sure no harm came to her.

"You didn't go home last night?" Kenny said to Jarred as he wiped down the bar. Jarred nursed a soda. They were both at the end of their shift. Even the casino was slow. The current round of the tournament had ended, and dispirited losers sat at one end of the bar while the winners sat at the other end nursing their drinks and looking drained. Even the vampire who'd won looked the worse for wear, despite the huge glass of blood sitting in front of him. His fellow winners ignored him.

Jarred grabbed Kenny's arm. "Were you following me?"

"Calm down." Kenny twisted away. "Just checking on my investment. Besides, it was hard not to see the way you sniffed around each other last night. Did she change? Did she growl?"

None of your business, Jarred thought with a bubble of anger spreading through him. "If you want this woman on your side, let it go, Kenny. I'm going to get her for you."

Kenny lowered his voice and bent over the bar toward Jarred. "Dude, is she a five million dollar fuck, or what?"

Solange was priceless, and Jarred knew he would have to come clean with the Temples. No matter how good the sex had been, she'd talked about the Temples as though they were blood family. No matter what Malcolm had done to her, she wasn't going to betray her family. He admired her loyalty.

"We need her," Kenny persisted.

"No problem."

Kenny smiled seductively. "I knew you had magic in those pants."

Jarred steeled himself not to move, he refused to back down no matter how he felt about Kenny's behavior. "Jealous?"

Kenny simply grinned, and Jarred finished his soda, pushing the glass away. He half-hoped Solange would just walk by. He wanted to see her, to find out if the sparks between them last night had been real or some sort of dream. He'd never connected with a woman before the way he had with Solange. She frightened him. She had an uncanny ability to read him, and he didn't know if that was a werewolf thing, or just her. All night long he'd resisted the urge to confide in her, to simply tell her the truth. But self-preservation kept him silent.

Maybe telling her the truth wasn't a bad start. He frowned as he pushed away from the bar and stood.

Chapter Three

Jarred stood in the center of Esther Temple's office. She watched him; her dark eyes sized him up like he was her next kill. His palms began to sweat, but his pride demanded he not avert his gaze. He'd never squared off with a woman besides his mother before. If he weren't so scared shitless, he'd be impressed with himself.

Her long elegant fingers tapped on the desk blotter. "So you're telling me the French Quarter has been targeted by the Casino Crasher, who just happens to work for me, over a year ago, and the FBI decided not to inform us about the danger to my children, my employees, or my guests."

Saying a simple "yeah" was just too disrespectful. Besides, he understood her anger. He'd be ten feet of pissed if he were in her shoes. "Because there's always an inside man, and I wasn't sure until a couple weeks ago who the inside person was. For all I knew, it could have been someone high enough up they would know if you found out."

Julius Temple's large hand gripped the back of his wife's chair. "Explain to me how Solange comes into this again?" His prize-fighter body dwarfed his wife's chair

Jarred took a deep breath and started again. "When Greg Mills died, my assignment was to bring her in." He heard the snap of a pencil and turned to Laurel, the security chief sitting next to him. These people could rip him to shreds and eat the evidence. Maybe he should have just kept his mouth shut and do his job. But now he had to be noble. And it was going to get him killed. "I didn't need to come to you."

"Why Solange?" Laurel asked.

Jarred hesitated. They all knew her better than he did. "She's vulnerable." No one disagreed with him.

"Does she know you tried to play her?" Laurel asked.

Now came the guilt. "She's not going to betray you, but her life could be in danger. I don't know how Kenny intends to get away with the money; he keeps a lot of his plans close to the chest. In fact, I think he's pretty crazy to take on a were pack as powerful as you are."

Esther yanked on her jacket sleeve. "That man is not going to touch one of my babies. I'll kill him myself."

"Which is the reason why I came to you, ma'am." Along with a sense of guilt for having seduced Solange. Conflict raged through him, he could have just blown his entire case trying to protect Solange.

Solange opened the door and walked in. "You wanted to see me?" She stopped at the sight of him. Alarm spread across her face. "Is there a problem with the bar?"

Esther motioned for her to come inside. "Solange, we need to talk."

She entered the room; her steps slow, as if she were ready to bolt at the drop of a hat. Her eyes flickered at Jarred, and her bottom lip trembled.

As he spoke, Julius's face softened. "Solange, we'd like you to meet Special Agent Jarred Maitland with the FBI."

The heat of her stare skewered Jarred. "Mr. Maitland." Her voice was controlled, but an underlying growl sent shivers down his spine.

"Solange, I really am with the FBI."

"Why am I here?"

He flashed his badge. He hoped she wouldn't tell these people they'd slept together. If they knew, no one would ever find his body. "You need to know that the casino is going to be robbed."

"Robbed." She shook her head. "No one can rob this casino. No one would dare." She glanced at Esther as though seeking validation.

"Kenny Brooks would dare," Jarred replied.

She held up her hands. "The bartender?"

"He's more than a bartender. He's the 'Casino Crasher.'"

Solange glanced at Esther and Julius, then back to Jarred. "How does this involve me?"

How could he tell her she had started out as nothing more than an assignment that had grown into something much more? "My orders were to bring you into his fold as his inside person."

Solange planted her hands on her hips. "I'm not going to help him rob the casino."

"I know. The Temples know, but Kenny doesn't. He thinks you're a spurned lover looking for revenge."

"Never." She thrust out her chin.

Esther gave her a reassuring smile. "We know your loyalty is above reproach, but Special Agent Maitland wants you to cooperate. And we're going to cooperate with the government," Esther said quietly. "Special Agent Maitland was kind enough to let us in on his plan, and we have agreed to lend you to him. We have a large stake in getting the Casino Crasher off the streets."

"On his last heist," Jarred put in, "Kenny beat a guard almost to death, and the guy is a vegetable. This may be the last chance we'll have to get him behind bars. I need your help. I need you to pretend you're willing to go along with his plans."

She bit her bottom lip. "And if I don't?"

"He will not hesitate to kill you," Jarred said. Just the thought sent a deep, icy chill down his back.

Jarred glanced around the room. "Mrs. Temple, Mr. Temple, do you mind if I have a word with Solange alone."

"Not at all, Special Agent Maitland," Julius responded smoothly.

"We can go into my office." Solange turned on her heel and led the way out of the room to an office next door.

Solange's office was almost as large and comfortable as Esther Temple's office, but contained less flamboyant muted blues, greens and grays. Another row of windows overlooked the casino. Solange stood in front of the windows, staring down at the poker tournament. The players had been whittled down from the original five hundred who had started to twenty tables of six.

She tilted her head at him. "Was seducing me a part of your special plan?"

He deserved that crack. He reached out to touch her, but she smacked his hand away. He had to make things right with her. "Last night I knew—I don't know how, but I knew you were important in a way that surprised me. And the crazy thing is, I barely know you and…" He shook his head, reaching for the right words to tell her how important last night had been. "I don't even have the words to describe last night." That sounded smart and sophisticated. How could he appeal to a woman who was not only older than him by a century, but would outlive him by another century or more? She'd probably heard everything a man could offer her, heard every pick-up line in the book. Yet, something had happened between them neither could deny.

"Because you're a man."

Heat crawled up his spine. "Yeah, and I'm thanking God every moment for the rest of my life that I was a man last night with you." Two seconds alone with her, and he wanted to rip her clothes off.

She chuckled. "Don't make me laugh."

"I want to make you laugh." *God, I want to make her love me. Back up, re-wind, and don't think again. Man on a mission. Man on a mission.*

"I'll help you," she said quietly, "but whatever you think is between us, can't happen."

"But…"

"No, buts, Special Agent Maitland. We're going to talk about this later. But right now, I have to make sure everything is right with Julius and Esther."

She left him in her office. When she was gone he felt lost. He sat down in a chair and glanced around. He had the feeling he'd just screwed up.

Solange closed the door. Her whole body shook. She was of two minds: here was this incredible man who smelled so right, and he'd used her. She wanted to tear his throat out. She wanted to kiss him. She wanted to punch him in the nose, and then toss him on the bed. She didn't know what she wanted.

She stormed into Esther's office. Laurel was gone, and Julius sat on the sofa with a stiff drink in his hand. "Where's Laurel?"

"Gathering the pack members."

Solange walked stiffly to the bar. She needed a drink, too. "I'm so sorry. I brought this to your door." She poured herself a glass of merlot and leaned one hip against the bar as she sipped it. She thought about Jarred waiting for her next door. She thought about the night before and the feelings he'd roused in her.

"You didn't create this trouble, baby," Julius said. "I think it's been waiting to happen for a long time."

"We can't let these people rob the casino and live." Solange sipped the merlot. The wine slid down into her stomach and created a warmth filling her from the inside out.

"We can't eat them," Esther said in a practical tone, "their targeting this casino has put us on the FBI radar. Anything we do will be under their scrutiny."

"Whose law do we follow?" Solange asked. "With you and Julius leaving, the pack is vulnerable. There is no way any pack in the world would let a robbery slide. They'd be on us like…" She couldn't think like what.

"We certainly can't afford a turf war," Julius said. "Dissension between the weres would bring more attention to the packs. We've already had more than we should with the fight. The humans are nervous, and rightly so. We've only been a part of their society for a few years, and already we've created a lot of chaos."

"What do we do?" Solange tried to figure out how they could have gotten caught in such a Catch-22.

Esther closed her eyes and rubbed her forehead. "For the moment, we let Special Agent Maitland guide us."

Julius put his glass down. "I've got to meet with the rest of the pack and let them know what's going on. Maybe someone else has an idea." He opened the door and left, leaving Solange alone with Esther. The last thing she wanted was to be alone with Esther. As children, she and the others had called Esther the relentless because she never let anything go. She would rattle everyone's cage until they told her what she wanted to hear.

Solange tried to ease herself out the door, backing up slowly and sliding carefully across the carpet. She didn't want Esther to play twenty questions. And Esther wouldn't be fobbed off with a lame explanation.

"No you don't, young lady." She pointed to the large Shaker chair in the corner of her office. "You sit yourself down in that chair right this minute."

Solange hesitated, thinking she just might manage to bolt, but old habits brought her back. She sat down in the chair. She always called this particular chair Esther's Inquisition. Whenever any of the children had been naughty, they were put in this chair while Esther thought up a suitable discipline just after the grilling that would have put a seasoned lawyer to shame.

Esther put her hands on her hips, her nose not quite twitching. "You've had sex with Special Agent Maitland, haven't you."

Solange had taken twenty showers between last night and today just to get the smell of him off her skin. "How could you tell?"

"The pheromones shot right off the scale the minute you saw that fine looking young man." Esther poured herself a refill. She glanced out the windows at the casino below, and then turned to face Solange.

Solange covered her face with her hands. "I didn't mean to, but I couldn't control myself. He is so...good." Delicious even. Her body still tingled with the aftermath of their night together. And she thought of him waiting in her office, and she almost bolted.

"What are you going to do about him?"

"You're the one who said we can't do anything."

"Not about the robbery, but about your...exactly what are you having with Special Agent Maitland."

"Nothing anymore."

"Really?"

"He's human, he's an FBI agent and he lied to me." What else was there? She wasn't going to go near him again unless she had to.

"Sounds more like he simply stepped around the issue without really saying anything. After all, he's working undercover. No man is perfect."

Esther was correct. Jarred had never actually answered any of her questions, but seemed to simply change the subject. He'd never out and out lied about anything. She would have smelled the lie. "Other than helping him stop the robbery, I don't want anything else to do with him." *Liar*, she told herself. She wanted...she didn't know what she wanted.

Esther stood at the bank of windows and looked down into the casino, frowning. "He didn't have to reveal what is going on."

"Why are you defending him?"

Esther shrugged. "I like him. I sense he is an honorable man."

"Then you be his play toy."

Esther's eyebrows rose. "My, my, my, you have found a backbone."

Immediately subdued, Solange replied, "I'm sorry." She so seldom showed her teeth; even she was surprised at her heated response.

"Don't apologize. It's about time." Esther patted Solange's cheek and bent over to kiss her forehead.

"We need to explain to him about pack politics and..." her voice trailed away. Humans may know about weres and vamps, but they didn't really know about weres and vamps. Not really. So much of her world was still hidden, a world with so many unrevealed secrets would frighten them, and frightened humans knew only one thing—how to destroy what they didn't understand. "We can't afford a turf war," Solange continued. And especially not now when human society was still trying to figure out if they were civilized or not. "The last time there was a huge, all-out werewolf turf war, we had World War II to hide the carnage from the humans. We don't have anything on a large-enough scale to hide our internal problems right now. You and Julius are modern in your outlook, but what about the South American packs, if Antonio Delgado even had a whiff our pack was having internal issues, he and his people would march through here and leave a bloodbath behind. He doesn't care about collateral damage."

Esther paced back and forth. "My darling, we are stuck between a proverbial rock and a hard place. We are not invulnerable, no matter what we like to pretend."

"This is the twenty-first century, Esther. We're not a secret anymore. We have to think about the future." As much as she dreaded telling Jarred about how were society worked, she had the feeling he would understand. She had sensed something in him the night before. "You're the one who thinks he's a good man, and a good man would understand and do the right thing."

"Darling," Esther said gently, "there is no right thing here. Someone is going to lose, and it can't be us."

An answer had to be found, one allowing the pack to save face and stop Kenny and his people from robbing the casino. Just the thought that Kenny Brooks was willing to take on a were pack made her wonder at his sanity. She stood and put her empty glass on the bar. "If you don't need me for awhile, I'm going back to my office. I need to think, and I need to talk to Jarred. I need to know just how great is the danger to us as a pack." *And to me as an individual.*

Esther slid an arm around her and hugged her tight. "Of course, I understand. Go talk to Jarred."

Chapter Four

Jarred turned onto Tropicana. His car made a jarring sound, and he wondered if he'd make it. His old, nondescript Toyota Camry was generally trusty, but of late had been acting up. "Go through the scenario one more time."

"I've got it." Solange rolled her eyes.

"I don't need Kenny thinking we're just playing him along. You need to be real." Kenny seemed to have a nose for deception. Sometimes, Jarred felt caught in a cat and mouse game with the other man. If not for his years undercover and his ability to change his spots on a dime, he doubted he would ever have been able to get close. If Kenny had harbored any suspicions about Jarred, he would have been long dead in an unmarked grave.

"I survived a whole lot of years by being a good actress. I can make him believe me." She tapped her finger on her cheek. "Oh, I forgot, you don't know me."

Her statement stung. He did know her. He knew about the little mole next to her belly button. He knew about the little Chinese dragon tattoo on her hip, which had surprised him. She didn't seem the type to decorate her body. He wondered if the tattoo stayed when she shifted. She had an antique record collection dating back to the twenties even though she didn't seem like the kind of person to listen to records, but yet she loved South Park and I Love Lucy. She had a hip feel to her that went hand in hand with an iPod. She was sexy, smart and funny. Having met her, a whole new dimension had been added to his life. And for the first time he wasn't thinking about his career, but how he could get her back into bed.

"I didn't start out to sleep with you." He needed her to know. "Seduction is definitely against FBI policy. I'd be in less trouble if I kicked the shit out of you." Though he doubted such a thing would happen. She had a lot of punch in her delicate body.

She gave him a little contemptuous snort. "I'd like to see you try to hurt me."

Okay, maybe he couldn't take her on.

Harry hadn't been happy. He'd been willing to sanction Jarred's action, but he was putting his job in jeopardy, too. He just didn't have as far to fall as Jarred. "My boss isn't exactly riding the happy train in regards to the turn of events in this case. But because he likes me, he's giving me a lot of leash."

She frowned at him. "Then why involve the pack?"

"Kenny's inside people tend to end up dead. He sets them up, uses them, and then kills them. I can't let him kill you." Not now, when he'd just found her.

"Assuming he can," she retorted. "I'm not easy to kill."

"I couldn't take that chance."

"And you didn't think I'd do the right thing."

He smiled. "Five minutes of listening to you wax poetic about how you loved the Temples, I knew you weren't going to turn. So I got on my white horse to come to your rescue."

She slanted a glance at him. "When I stop being mad at you, I'm going to think you're really sweet."

His heart soared and his pulse went wild. He still had a chance with her.

Jarred parked in the visitor lot and got out. As they walked across the hot asphalt, he grabbed her and kissed her. "I have faith in you."

She looked him straight in the eye. "I won't let you down."

They climbed the steps to Brook's apartment. Jarred had to steel himself before entering. He glanced at Solange and could see she was mildly tense. He rubbed the back of her neck while they waited for Kenny to answer the door.

Kenny smiled expansively at Solange as he ushered her into his apartment. "The fair Solange." He kissed her hand, and she giggled as she pulled her hand back.

"I've seen you in the bar, but I had no idea you were so charming," she said.

Kenny almost twinkled at her. "My dear, I have old world manners. Please, sit down."

"The very best kind," she replied as she sat on the sofa. She glanced around and for a second stiffened when she saw the copper box on the side table. Then her manner relaxed, even though her smile was suddenly a little strained.

"Can I get you a glass of wine? Have some snacks." He gestured at a tray set up with crackers and cheese.

Jarred hated the way Kenny mooned over Solange. His hackles rose. He wanted to punch Kenny, even as he realized giving in to his jealousy would take his focus away from what needed to be done. She's on my side, he reminded himself as he sat down. Kenny handed him a beer, but he set it aside, not wanting alcohol clouding his mind.

Solange gracefully accepted the glass of wine, took a quick sip and then set the glass aside on the table with the copper box. Again, her eyes drifted toward it and slid away in the same confused manner Jarred had when he tried to look at the box. And for the first time, Jarred let his fear surface. Something about the box scared the shit out him.

Solange shifted her gaze to Kenny and smiled. "How can I help you?"

Kenny grinned. "You're direct."

She leaned forward, her hands resting on her knees. "I'm a woman scorned."

"Malcolm Temple is a fool," Kenny said.

Oh my God, Jarred thought. He wanted to barf. *Talk about higher and deeper*. Though he had to admit, Solange was playing the game surprisingly well. Maybe all those decades of hiding her identity were paying off.

"Yes, he is." She glanced at Jarred.

"Thank you lovely lady," Kenny crowed, "let's get down to business. What I need from you is the quickest way to the money. I have blueprints of the basements, but they are out-dated. My key man died in an auto accident before he could get me current ones. And I'm certain you have the combination to the vault, the guards' schedules and the best time to strike."

She leaned back. "As much time and effort as you've put into your planning, you have it all wrong. Good thing you came to me."

Kenny stiffened, a frown pulling his face down. "What do you mean?"

She tapped a finger on the arm of the sofa. "You think the money is being stored in a new vault under the glass case, but you're wrong. The money on display is fake, and the real money is in a different vault."

"What do you mean the real money isn't on display?" Kenny asked, confusion written all over his face.

Jarred stared at her. What the hell? The money wasn't the real money. How come that little secret hadn't come out earlier when he'd been with the Temples? Then he realized he might not have acted surprised enough. This lady was clever.

"Do you think the Temples are really dumb enough to display twenty million dollars? What you see on top is decoration. Everything underneath is just paper."

"Then what's the purpose of the display?" Jarred wondered when this bombshell was going to drop. If they had hit the wrong vault, there was no telling what kind of collateral damage there would have been at the French Quarter.

She sighed. "This is Vegas, baby. It's all about the flash."

Kenny rubbed his hands together. "Tell me about this old vault?"

"The new vault has lots of bells and whistles, but the old one is just as solid. The Temples never stopped using it. They keep everything of real value in it, not only the twenty million, but bearer bonds and the family jewels. And let me tell you about Miss Esther's jewelry. Harry Winston has been trying to purchase her Cartier collection for year. It goes back to the beginning of the Maison de Cartier. The collection is priceless."

Kenny licked his lips. "Jewels, I love jewels." Kenny ran his hand down Solange's arm. "You're a godsend."

She gave a schoolgirl giggle, and Jarred tried not to be annoyed. Her flirting with Kenny set his teeth on edge. The only thing saving him from tearing Kenny's spine out was knowing they were both putting on a show. He still didn't want Kenny making her laugh, or feeding her dinner, or involving her in witty conversation like they had shit in common. Jarred was keeping her for himself. So deeply was he caught up in his thoughts he didn't realize Kenny and Solange had stopped talking and were both staring at him. Kenny was amused as though he knew exactly what his flirting was doing to Jarred. Solange seemed irritated.

"Jarred, is something wrong?" she asked.

"I'm good." He just needed to calm himself down and focus on the job. Damn, his career was on the line, and he was reacting like a bull moose fighting to the death over a female. This case and this woman were driving him insane. *You need to get a handle on yourself, or you'll blow everything and get yourself killed, or worse yet, get her killed.*

Kenny and Solange chatted for a little while longer and, finally, Solange stood up to leave. "Look, I have business back at the casino." She handed a card to Kenny. "This is my private number. Tomorrow, I'll bring the current blueprints, a map to the old vault, and the combination. I look forward to doing business with you."

She headed for the door, Jarred trailing after her, trying to keep his emotions under control. Kenny gave Solange a kiss, not quite brotherly, but not quite lover-like and again Jarred had to control his impulse to knock the other man on his ass.

"You were broadcasting in there," Solange walked down the rickety steps to the parking lot. A plane, landing at McCarron Airport, roared overhead. She shielded her eyes from the afternoon sun.

"Broadcasting?" For a while he'd forgotten how sensitive she was to his emotions.

"You don't like Kenny, and you let it show. I doubt he'd do anything because he needs you, but you need to be more careful. You may see him as a bartender, but he's a lot more dangerous than you think."

"I know how dangerous he is," Jarred growled as he stalked across the parking lot to his car.

She gripped the door handle. "No, you don't," she said, and a troubled expression settled on her face as she slid inside the car.

"What's wrong?" he asked after they'd put on their seatbelts, and he'd started the motor.

"Nothing."

"You need to tell me."

"I will, just not until I check something. I need to get back to the casino. How fast can you make this car go?"

"Fast." He turned out of the parking lot and headed back uptown as quickly as traffic would allow.

Solange furiously paced back and forth across Esther's office as she talked on her cell phone. Esther looked mildly surprised at her agitation, but Solange could barely think, much less sit still.

Esther hung up the phone. "What's going on? Your meeting with Kenny didn't go well, did it?"

"I know how he's been getting away with murder and robbery and any number of other crimes we don't have a clue about." She paused a moment, and then blurted out, "He has a demon box."

Esther's face went still and frightened before she schooled it back to her normal composure. "That's not good. Any idea what kind of demon?"

"Not a clue. He just has the standard copper demon box with embossed runes on the sides. When I tried to read the runes, the compulsion to look away was so strong I couldn't fight it."

Esther picked up her office phone and punched in several numbers. "Laurel, I need you."

A few moments later, Laurel arrived. "What's up?"

"Brooks has a demon," Esther said quietly, her agitation showing only in her eyes.

Laurel pinched the bridge of her nose. "Now we know how he's managed to pull off his robberies so easily for so many years." She turned to Solange. "What kind of demon?"

"I don't know." How had Kenny Brooks enslaved a demon? Demons were notoriously difficult to control, and their wild magic didn't conform to the rules of the game set down by the wizards in centuries past.

Laurel nodded briefly. "You probably noticed more than you think. Take a moment to relax, and then try to draw the runes you could make out. I know a demonologist at UNLV. Maybe he can identify what Brooks has."

Solange found herself clasping her hands tight to still the tremors rippling through her. What had she allowed herself to be drawn into? But then again, Jarred didn't know either.

"Did you tell Special Agent Maitland?" Laurel asked.

"No. Humans have a hard enough time assimilating the notion of vampires and the weres, what would he do if he knew demons, and more, walk the earth? He's been pretty broad-minded so far, but there are limits." She thought about the way he made her body sing with passion and knew taking a werewolf to bed had probably been a lot harder than he let on. But getting over his worry about what she might do in the throes of a climax was a testament to the type of person he was. He'd probably handle the idea of demons without too much trouble. Or not.

"You underestimate Mr. Maitland," Esther leaned back in her chair. "You have to tell him."

"I know. I just wanted to have more to tell him," Solange said, and her voice quivered with the cold fear running through her. She'd met a demon once, a pretty girl who looked almost normal until she'd noticed her yellow eyes, pointed teeth and slightly sallow green skin. Fortunately, the demon had been carefully controlled by the wizard who'd conjured her out of her world and into this one. Solange started to shiver, and once started, she couldn't stop. Of all the creatures to import into the human world, a demon was probably one of the most dangerous.

Solange sat down on the sofa and tried to still her trembling. "At least now we know why Brooks has targeted us. He thinks with a demon he is unstoppable."

"Depending on the type of demon he has, he could be," Esther said.

Solange forced herself to relax and get herself under control. Until they knew what they faced, she needed to be prepared. She stood, and despite a faint tremor in her hands, she managed to make it to the door without collapsing.

Solange spent the rest of the day and half the night trying to recreate the runes she'd seen on the copper box. After she had wracked her brains and found she'd actually managed to put together a fair facsimile of the box, she was so tired she could hardly stand.

She picked up the phone and called Esther. "I'm going for a run in the desert after I fax the picture to Laurel's friend."

"Be careful," Esther replied.

"I will, but I need to clear my head. I need to think." She faxed the drawing and then headed out the door.

The desert was cool and dry. The moon pulled at Solange even though it was a couple days past the full moon. Silvery shadows gave the desert an eerie feel. She probably should have gone more toward Henderson where she could run in the canyons and ravines, but she hadn't wanted to travel so far. She needed to run now.

The Hunger Within

After she parked her car at the end of a dirt road, she opened the door to let the night air in. She stood and stretched. The discovery of the demon box had set her nerves on edge. No wonder Kenny had been so successful at not only robbing the casinos he'd targeting, but also getting away with it. She wondered what kind of demon he had. She needed a good refreshing run to clear her mind, then she would head back to her office.

Sand crunched under her feet as she pulled her clothes off and tossed them on the driver's seat. The night air cooled her heated skin. With the sleepy cries of a nearby bird and the deep, melancholy howl of a coyote as her only company, she stood naked beneath the moon.

She inhaled deeply, closed her eyes and let the change come over her. Her limbs twisted and reshaped themselves. A mist clouded her vision as the beast within came out and took over. When she opened her eyes, she saw as clearly as though it was daylight with so much more detail than she saw with human eyes.

The night breeze ruffled her fur, and the desert sand was rough beneath the pads of her paws. The breeze brought the scent of the coyote she'd heard earlier. On four feet, she loped across the desert sand. The scent of small animals in the underbrush came to her. She sorted out the scents of a mouse looking for insects, a night owl floating on the wind, a small deer jumping over a shallow gully. A desert tortoise slept in its summer burrow. A snake rustled its way through the dry desert grass. She didn't feel the need to hunt; she just needed to run, to feel clean again.

She stretched out into a mile-eating lope, searching for the peace running always gave her. She felt exhilarated as she leaped across a tiny depression in the sand. Her problems melted away and she was free of the worries, the confusion over Jarred.

How could she let a human get under her skin the way he did. She felt so vulnerable around him. Her life was in chaos, and Jarred added to it. She'd allowed a human male to get close to her, and he really didn't know what he was getting into being involved with her.

148

A pack of coyotes topped a small hill. Solange skidded to a stop, sand flying out. She was downwind of them, and she wanted to conquer them. The leader, a large, scrawny male with scarring on his narrow head, whirled, growling as Solange approached.

She lifted her head and started to howl. The coyotes looked at her, and then joined her in the howl. She felt their freedom, their uncomplicated lives. If she weren't who she was, her life would be so much less complicated. As a wolf, all she had to worry about was surviving in the wild with no one around to help her, to protect her. As a woman, she had obstacles to hurdle and a life to balance. Maybe she should stay a wolf.

The coyote pack stopped howling and bolted over the crest of the hill and out of sight into a shallow gully. Solange wanted to follow them, to be a part of their lives, but resisted the urge as she always resisted. She never allowed the beast in her to totally take over, no matter how much she yearned for the freedom of the desert.

Reluctantly, she turned back the way she'd come and galloped back toward her car, tired but ready to face what was to come. What had to come? Not only did she have to face Jarred, but the demon. She felt the only thing standing between the demon and her pack— was her.

As she loped across the clearing, she frowned. Another car was parked next to it. She trotted up to the car, but it was empty. As she shifted back to her human form, light suddenly blinded her. She gasped at the brightness, at the heat. Someone was in her car, but the shifting wind and the bright light kept her from identifying that person.

She finished shifting, pulled herself to her feet and started toward her car. When she opened the car door, Jarred's scent rushed toward her.

The Hunger Within

The moon was silver on her skin. Her face was a series of gaunt hollows made secretive by the darkness. The desert behind her looked almost peaceful compared to the turmoil inside him. He'd never seen a werewolf shift, and it had looked painful and had been the most frightening thing he'd ever seen in his life. He couldn't move, couldn't think for a second. But what surprised him most was that he wasn't afraid.

"You followed me." She reached for her clothes.

"Yeah." He didn't want her to get dressed. He wanted to study her body to figure out how she could shift from human to wolf. He'd seen something he doubted any other human in the world had seen. "Are you going to kill me?" He sounded calmer than he felt.

"Did you take a picture?" She hastily dressed, pulling her pants on first, and then her T-shirt.

He gulped, nervously. "Didn't think to bring a camera." He'd read about reporters who'd followed weres for days trying to get photos of them shifting, but weres were a lot more slippery than people thought. Their secrecy made people afraid. He was nervous, too, but he was a special agent and had been trained for every eventuality. Though he couldn't remember a class on what to do when his lady changed from human to wolf inside of a NASCAR second. "I'm still in shock, but trying to maintain my coolness." He was trying to maintain his dinner. "Is it painful to change?"

"Not anymore. But when I first changed, it was pretty awful." She'd left her bra on the driver's seat and pulled her T-shirt on without it. Her nipples poked out from the smooth fabric, and his palms started to sweat even more. Okay, he was sleeping with a werewolf, and she hadn't eaten him, hadn't tried to hurt him. He didn't feel the need to leap out of the car shrieking into the dark Nevada night. He was pretty proud of his composure.

When all else failed and a person was scared shitless—talk sports. "So what do you think of UNLV's chances of making the Final Four this year?"

"I don't care for football."

"Basketball." He paused for a long moment.

"Don't care."

He took a deep breath. "So where do we go from here?"

She tapped the steering wheel. "I don't know."

He wanted to touch her, but the look on her face told him she wasn't touchable at this moment. He wanted to repeat the magic of their previous night. "I know vampires can be made. How are werewolves made?"

She stared out over the desert. "First let me say, I was born in 1853."

He already knew her birth year, but hearing her say her age startled him. "Most women never tell their age, especially when you start hitting the hundred year mark, and you don't look a day over twenty-seven."

She smiled, almost sadly. "How sweet, but I've been around the block a time or two."

"When we were talking about the amber room, you started to say something, and then changed to something else. You saw that room, too, just like my grandmother."

"It was pretty impressive, and like your grandmother, I started collecting amber because of the beauty of the amber room."

"I know what the census figures say, but in actuality, how many wolf packs are there in the world?" The government tried to count them, but the figures never added up. The vamps and weres were secretive beyond belief, and at times he wondered what other secrets they kept to themselves.

"Globally about a hundred and eighty packs with around two thousand weres in them and a couple thousand more not associated with a pack, and there are the rogue wolves which don't allow themselves to be counted even by us. We're probably less than six thousand total. I don't have exact figures. We only take a census every hundred years."

Should he be thankful werewolves weren't about to overthrow the world, or should he be worried. Like most humans, their very existence worried him. Did this mean other creatures of mythology also existed? Did he dare ask?

The question slipped out. "What about mummies, ghouls, and zombies?" Other things that went bump in the night. He tried not to shiver. He had the feeling he was going to learn more than he ever wanted to know.

She shrugged. "I don't know about ghouls, zombies and mummies. The Preternatural Authorities keep all the records."

"The Preternatural Authorities don't play with the rest of us either."

She turned to look at him, her face grave. "We barely let them ride herd on us, but they do a decent job of keeping the peace between us and otherworldlies."

The thought didn't bear thinking, but his blood ran cold. He'd been thinking they all agreed to obey human law, and now he knew they hadn't. "How did you come to be a werewolf?" He hadn't really meant to ask, but she was being so uncommonly candid with him, he had to ask.

"In 1857, the Temples ran away from their slave master, and they took all the orphan children on the plantation."

"Running away was dangerous in those days. I'm surprised you all escaped."

"We had no choice. The master of the plantation was going to sell Esther and all the orphan children. Julius wasn't going to let that happen. We found a tribe of Indians, and they sheltered us and eventually gave us the secret of the wolf."

And how good a thing was that? He wondered. What else didn't he know? What else was she keeping from him? "I know you're long lived. But how long exactly."

"I'm going to live another two hundred years."

He hadn't expected her to tell him. Most weres kept their ages a secret. No human wanted to know how long he or she would live, how he or she would influence the future. "That must be exciting to see the world change before your eyes."

She half-smiled. "Humans talk about World War II, the march on Washington and the Russian Revolution, but my family witnessed it. I witnessed it. Julius helped win the Civil War by fighting for the north. Oliver liberated a concentration camp in Germany. Malcolm enlisted and fought in Korea. We all were there for the march on Washington. Yes, we have a gift, but with our gift comes certain responsibilities."

"I thought the other shoe was about to drop. How is this going to affect my case? Break it down for me."

"In more ways than we anticipated. We can't let Kenny walk out of the casino with one dollar of our money."

"I'm going to be right there to catch him and see him in jail."

She was quiet for a second. "I doubt Kenny will go to jail."

"Why? Because werewolf justice doesn't involve a court of law?"

"Because we protect what belongs to us."

Now he knew he wasn't going to like the answer. Maybe he should have run away screaming when he had the chance. "You're not above the law."

"We walk in the world, but we're not a part of it. A weak pack is an invitation for a coup." She seemed about to add something, but didn't. After a few more moments, she started talking again. "Most of the packs follow the rules because we have taken our place in the human world. Others… They see, they want, they take, damning the consequences or anyone who gets in the way." She stopped, licked her lips and closed her eyes. When she opened her eyes again, she said, "Do you remember twenty years ago in Rio, that bank heist where a hundred people were butchered."

"Yes, the scenario is still being used in hostage negotiation as an example on what not to do. Was that werewolves?"

"In broad daylight in the middle of the most populous city in South America, and two packs went to war. Eighty-five percent of the people who died weren't werewolves, but human. Half the squabbles in Africa in the last thirty years have been packs going to

153

war over stupid things: personal insults, five inches of land. We've managed to keep our battles under the radar, but this is Las Vegas, and everything is on twenty-four hours a day, and if you don't think the French Quarter casino wouldn't be the big, fat jewel in someone's crown, then you are sadly mistaken. The Temples have been fighting off rival packs, mobsters, international business who have more money than God, for more years than you've been alive. And one lone, psychopathic, narcissistic thief isn't going to get away with his drama. We have to squash him like the little ant he is."

"And go to war with the FBI…"

She grabbed him tightly by the neck. "Pull your gun and shoot me point blank. In five minutes, it will look like a scratch. You have no idea how to kill us. In ten, it will be totally healed. How do you fight an enemy you can't kill? Haven't you learned anything about us yet?"

He clamped her hand, refusing to back down. "Go ahead, my bosses will just send somebody else." He leaned into her grip, staring her right in the eye. "Kill me. But I don't think you will. You don't have it in you." He hoped she didn't. He envisioned his death as being something a lot less messy than having his throat pulled out.

Her hand dropped away. "What I don't want is to get my car dirty. Blood is hell on leather."

He resisted the urge to rub his neck. He didn't want to show any weakness, though his stomach was ready to rebel. He took a deep breath and gathered his thoughts. "You agreed to cooperate with the FBI."

"That was before—" her voice trailed away and he thought he actually heard fear in it.

"Before what?" he prompted curiously. What wasn't she telling him? Something about Kenny.

"Before I discovered Kenny has a demon."

The other shoe had finally dropped. His throat went dry. "Demon! As in red eyes, red skin, red tail?"

154

Her voice was low and fierce. "You don't understand. You don't know about demons."

"Enlighten me." If she was afraid, then he should be doubly so. What kind of demon would frighten her? She was strong, fearless and unstoppable. Now he was afraid.

"I don't know what kind of demon he has, so I can't tell you what it does. But it doesn't have red skin, tail or eyes. It probably looks just like you. Demons are masters of disguise and Kenny having the demon's box means he's controlling it. Maybe."

"What do you mean maybe?" His heart was thumping so loud, and his throat had grown so tight he could barely talk.

"Demons usually work as wizards' familiars. They control their demons by keeping them in copper lined boxes. Copper is poison to them. When they are out of the box, they wear copper bracelets, or something copper on them. They can't take it off."

"Wizards? You mean wizards are a part of the game, too." He'd thought she had secrets, and now as he was beginning to discover them he wished they were still secret. Solange was giving him more information than he could possibly imagine. His innocent thought about what other creatures went bump in the night would haunt him for the rest of his life.

"Wizards, mages, necromancers, witches, ghosts, succubi, incubi, dragons, djinn, there's even a phoenix or two burning up every once in a while and being reborn in the morning." She rattled off a few more he didn't recognize, and he started to feel ill. Only seconds ago he'd been thinking werewolves and vampires were all there was to the otherworldly element of his world, but now he knew more than he ever wanted to know about the frightening truths of legend and myth.

Jarred attempted to still the dread creeping through him. He couldn't catch his breath, the enormity of what she was saying felt like a sucker punch to the gut. "I think," He said nervously, "maybe you and I have a bigger reason to work together than we thought.

You have a lot of secrets, and I have a whole world to protect."
Protecting the unsuspecting from their worst nightmares.

"Starting with Kenny."

He wanted to forget about Kenny and his demon. "Okay, we can do this," he said with more bravado than he felt. "I will do what I have to catch Kenny and I won't let any of it taint your family. We don't want a werewolf turf war anymore than you do."

"Do you have a plan?"

"Not yet. But I'll come up with something that will make both of us smell like roses when it's done."

She gave a small chuckle. "To grow good roses you need a lot of shit."

He didn't know what to say. He kept thinking he would wake up in a couple hours and realize this was all a dream. No, a nightmare. Except his nightmare was really pretty, and he'd already explored every inch of her body even if she wasn't totally human and she had just told him about other non-humans walking the face of the earth humanity knew nothing about. "I've worked undercover too many years not to know how to deal with shit."

"We will sell you out if it comes down to it, Jarred. We have to protect the pack at all costs."

Working undercover meant he got his hands dirty in ways that would shock the rest of the world. He understood where she was coming from. And he knew she would choose her pack over anything. If he were in her shoes, he would do the same thing. "Are you still going to drop the plans off at Kenny's?"

"Yes."

"If he has a demon like you say, then I'm going with you." As strong and as smart as she was, he couldn't let her face Kenny alone. Not with the kind of danger she said Kenny had. Maybe a gun wasn't much use against a demon, but he'd be there anyway.

"I can do this by myself."

"I don't trust Kenny, and I'm not sure I trust you." Not anymore. The thought that he'd slept with her and made love to her beautiful body still left him wanting more. Maybe the attraction of being with a woman as dangerous as she was made him insane, but he didn't care. She was the most thrilling woman he'd ever known. Admittedly, she turned into a wolf periodically, but that added to her allure.

"Thank you for such a ringing endorsement, Special Agent Maitland."

"I do the best I can." What would Harry say? Hell, Jarred couldn't tell Harry anything. This was one secret he would have to keep.

He opened the door and stepped out. As he walked back to his car, gravel crunched under his shoes. When he glanced back, Solange sat behind the wheel, making no move to start the car and leave. He had the feeling she was more disturbed, more worried about telling him about the demon than she let on. He walked back to the car, opened the driver's door and at the startled look on her face, bent down and kissed her.

"Maybe I'm a little out of my depth. Hell, I'm a lot out of my depth, but I do know one thing. You and I are going to solve this, and we're going to do it together. We're going to—"

She grabbed him and kissed him back. His hands crept up under her shirt to knead the tight nipples. His pants were too tight; he couldn't breath. And this intoxicating woman, with her bizarre secret life, was not only the source of all his problems, but also the source of all his answers. If only he could just ask the right questions.

She pushed him away and laughed shakily. "I really, really, really, want to take you home with me and make love the rest of the night, but I can't." She pulled back, regret in every move. "I'm sorry, I have something to do. I'll explain it to you later."

He pulled back and stood on the dirt road while she started her car and peeled out so quickly, he barely had time to think. As he walked back to his car, he started to whistle. Things always looked darkest before the dawn. But he had Solange and her family on his side.

"I have made a mistake," Solange said to Esther.

Solange paced back and forth; just knowing she was wearing a hole in Esther's carpet, wringing her hands nervously. Esther sat calmly on the sofa watching, sipping a glass of red wine. "You've fallen in love with Special Agent Maitland."

Solange went very still, and then she whirled to face Esther. "We have a demon to take care of. What makes you think I'm in love with him?"

"Years of experience."

Solange started pacing again. "I don't have time for love. I have the rest of my life to worry about. How stupid would I be if I fell in love with a human? No, I told him about the demon." And a lot of other things she probably shouldn't have mentioned, but somehow it seemed the time was right.

"I suppose we could just kill him," Esther said in a matter of fact tone.

He may know more about the supernatural world than he wanted to know, but killing him would just bring another FBI agent just like him. Besides, she liked him. Maybe more than she should, but she still liked him. "We've had enough violence lately. I'd prefer another solution."

Esther crossed her legs and held her wine up to the light to stare at it. "How about we let him do his job. He's a good man, and he did come to us with Kenny's plans."

Solange had only spent one night with him, but the memory of how he'd brought her body to fulfillment would always be with her. "We can't let Kenny target our casino and get away with it. Our standing with the other packs would be in jeopardy."

Esther took a deep breath and spoke in a careful, thoughtful manner. "If we take one step in the wrong direction, it will be the end of our kind as we know it. We may be stronger and faster, but there is nothing more determined than a mob of frightened human beings who don't understand what's happening. They butcher first and ask questions later. I'm assuming you told him about our unique dilemma."

"I did. But he didn't have a solution."

Esther sighed. "With all this brain power, you'd think someone would have figured out an answer."

"Esther we're all too afraid of making the wrong choice. We have fire on one side, and a tank full of hungry sharks on the other. Choose how you want to die."

"In my bed, next to my beloved."

"That wasn't one of your choices."

"I don't like when things don't go my way."

Neither did Solange. She had never been one for confrontation, and if things didn't go right, the pack would remember that. More than ever, she knew she had to leave, to find her own way. "I don't want anyone to think Jarred is the enemy. Make sure everyone knows."

Esther chuckled. "For someone not in love, you're going to a lot of trouble to keep him safe."

"You've always told me I'm the nice one. It's not in my nature to kill someone. I like Jarred, and I don't want to see him dead because I was careless." She started for the door, but then remembered the demon. "Has Laurel found out anything about the demon?"

Esther rubbed her forehead. "Her friend hasn't called back yet. As soon as she knows something, I'll call you. Let's just get some rest, and we'll tackle it all again in the morning."

Solange nodded, kissed Esther's cheek and left. Though it was after midnight, the tournament was still going strong. A few slots chimed wins and losses. A woman carried a large cup almost overflowing with quarters to the cashier and music flowed from the bar. But Solange could tell the floor was nowhere near as crowded as it usually was, even so late in the night. She hoped Marcus' campaign brought the gamblers back. Though Esther and Julius could survive a downturn in business for a while, they could only last so long. And with Malcolm taking over, the pack would be scrutinizing everything he did, every decision he made and with business off, putting extra pressure on him.

Solange took the elevator to the residence floor where all the weres lived. As she walked down the long hall to her apartment, she could smell the other weres in their apartments with their mates and their children. Some of the single weres had overnight guests, and the scent of sex in the air made her miss Jarred.

Once inside, she stood in the window overlooking the city. She leaned her head against the cool glass. Even at this time of night, the strip was snarled with traffic and lit up as though it were day. This was her home and in a way, she would be sad to leave it. But her choices were few and far between. Better to make a new life somewhere else, than worry about her acceptance in the pack once Julius and Esther were gone. Better to move on.

The French Quarter had originally been situated in a part of town catering to the black population on east Fremont Street. But Esther and Julius had moved the casino to a newer location on North Las Vegas Blvd in the late seventies and built the casino as it was now. Originally, the area had been filled with warehouses and strip clubs. Eventually the big financiers realized they were sitting on a gold mine and started building and eventually built up the strip until it reached the French Quarter. The strip clubs and dives had disappeared to be replaced by casinos. She'd watched the changes in the city the same way she'd watched the changes in the world around her. Las Vegas would go on and so would she.

Chapter Five

Kenny opened the door to his apartment. Solange slipped inside. The apartment was hot, despite the noisy wheeze of the air conditioner. Then she remembered demons liked the heat. A basket of laundry sat on the sofa. Even though Kenny seemed alert and chirper, he smelled of stale sex and the aroma of another man that made Solange anxious to get out again. She shouldn't have come by herself, but she doubted Jarred could protect her any better than she could protect herself, though she found his chivalry endearing.

She handed Kenny the blueprints for the two basements beneath the casino, detailing the location of the old vault and the corridors leading to it. He unrolled them and she stepped back, her eyes drawn to the copper box. Again, the box seemed to blur, and she felt the compulsion to turn her head away. Laurel's friend had suggested she try to look at it from the side of her vision. So she stared at the door beyond it, letting her peripheral vision study the box. Again, the compulsion took her, and she was forced to look away, but she did feel she had a clearer view of it.

He re-rolled the blueprints and tossed them on the sofa. "Let's get to know each other better."

Solange didn't like the way he wrapped his demand in a smiling face and nice manner. "I don't have the time for idle chit chat." She started back toward the front door, but Kenny grabbed her wrist.

When she tried to twist free, his fingers tightened and tiny alarm bells went off in her head. Jarred had said Kenny was dangerous. He was a lot stronger than his lean pale body appeared. Had the demon given him extra strength? For the first time, she felt a ribbon of fear. "I don't think your boyfriend would like you fooling around on him."

"What makes you think I have a boyfriend and not a girlfriend?" He raised his thin blond eyebrow.

For one thing, she could smell him and why anyone wanted to date someone who smelled rank was beyond her. "For one thing," she pointed at the coffee table, "those pants all neatly folded on the table are too big for you. And no man does another man's laundry unless they're sleeping together."

He rubbed his thumb on the inside of her wrist. "I'm flexible."

"I'm not". She jerked free.

"Too bad. I didn't know you and Maitland were exclusive."

She stepped back from him. "None of your business."

He glanced at the plans lying on the sofa. "Why are you so willing to rob the people who have been your family for so many years?"

"Besides a nice payday my little ripple will start a tidal wave, and I can sit back and watch." She took a step toward him

Kenny grinned but took a step back. "I didn't know weres had a sense of humor. That old goat, Julius, certainly doesn't have one. You could give that stand-up comedian playing at the bar a run for his money."

"Way too much pressure."

He stiffened. "And a high-stakes robbery isn't any pressure?"

"This is revenge, not pressure." Did she sound ferocious enough to convince him of her sincerity? He relaxed and she did, too. "I have one request of you."

He glanced at her. "Anything for a beautiful woman."

"No guns. I will take the Temples' money, but I will not be responsible for anyone's death." Especially the humans. She had to neutralize as much damage ahead of time as possible.

"You want me to commit a robbery with no guns. Half the fun is shooting up the place."

"You do this my way, or I take those plans and walk out of here. We are in and out with nobody being the wiser. All you need is enough people to carry the twenty million." Not everybody in the pack was happy with the hands off rule Esther and Julius had imposed. But they had agreed to let the FBI work their own magic, which was a testament to Julius and Ester's strength. This type of situation tore packs apart.

"No."

"Fine, I'm out of here." She grabbed the blueprints and spun toward the front door.

Kenny grabbed her. Growling, she twisted around and wrapped her hand around his wrist. He dropped to his knees, pain on his face. Rage filled her. Her beast awakened, and she had to fight the urge to rip his throat out. Her heart pounded in her chest. How she wanted to let her wolf out and rip Kenny to shreds. "Don't let my delicate looks fool you."

He glanced at the bedroom door, a slow smile spreading over his lips. She took a deep breath, pulling back from the red haze filling her gaze.

Slowly he pushed to his feet, his entire body shook, he didn't back down. "I believe you, little wolf. But do keep in mind, that even the big, bad wolf met his match in the end." Again he glanced at the bedroom door. "I won't bring a gun, but I will tell you this. If things don't go right, you'll be the first one I kill."

Why the bedroom door? She kept thinking. Wouldn't he look at the box where the demon would be? Unless…she didn't complete the thought. "Give it your best shot," she replied in a steady voice, even as the horror of her thoughts filled her. The demon was his lover. How she knew, she couldn't say, but the demon wasn't in its box, but in the bedroom, and was the owner of the folded pants on the table. Which made her wonder who controlled whom?

"I'll win." He gave her a cocky, confident smile.

"Maybe." She yanked him up to his feet, grabbed the tail of his shirt and pulled the wrinkles out. "Now let gets down to business."

She spread the blueprints out on the coffee table and explained to Kenny where everything was. She asked about the other people in his gang, but he refused to tell her anything.

"What about the security codes?" Kenny asked when she was done.

"We generate random codes and change them daily. I won't know the code until I report in to work."

"Too bad." Again he gave her a speculative look as though trying to figure out if she were lying or not.

"Listen," she said, "this is a one-shot deal for me. When we walk out of there, I'm taking my money and I'm out."

Kenny frowned. "I have rules about how the money is divided and used."

"What kind of rules?"

"You have to let the money sit a couple years. Let the heat die down."

Kenny showed more caution than she would have given him credit for. "I can manage for a few years."

"I'm sure you can."

He didn't believe her. He knew she was a were and still figured she was easy, soft and unable to survive by herself. He didn't know much about werewolves.

"How about some lunch?" Kenny asked.

"We're done." She turned and purposely walked slow to the door. Hurrying showed fear, and she'd be damned if she let him see how much she feared him. He trailed behind her, so close, she could feel the bombardment of his body heat. And the more he crowded her, the more her beast wanted out, and she wondered if he were playing with her, trying to see how far she'd go before her beast took over. He reminded her of a man she'd once seen teasing a hungry dog with some food. Before she could do something, the man caught the dog and clubbed it over the head with a brick. She had felt the dog's death in a way she had never felt any other animal's death and had fought hard to keep her beast inside. Her instinct had been to attack, and her anger for the man's actions had almost pushed her over the edge, but Julius had held her back. She hated bullies, and underneath all his smooth talk and easy manner, Kenny was a bully.

She left before he could say anything else. She felt the need to shower, to wash away the feeling Kenny had left on her skin.

Jarred leaned against her car waiting. He worked to keep his anger under control. Though he knew she could take care of herself, he didn't want her with Kenny. Kenny looked mild and easygoing, but underneath he was more dangerous than any man Jarred had ever known. Especially when he had some sort of ace in the hole with this demon. Jarred wasn't certain what demons were, and knew for sure he didn't want to find out.

She exited Kenny's apartment and walked stiffly down the steps. She grew even stiffer when she spotted him. As she approached, Jarred opened his mouth to speak. She held up her hand. "Don't speak. I don't know what I want more: a shower, or something to eat." She pointed her remote at her car, and it beeped back at her as it unlocked.

"He has the same affect on me." He couldn't keep the irritation out of his voice. "I told you to wait for me." She hadn't needed his protection, but Kenny might have backed off if Jarred had been with her.

"We may have slept together, but you don't own me."

Desire flamed in him. Her eyes went wide. She wanted him as much as he wanted her. "As much as I'd like to join you in the shower, right now, I think you should eat something safe."

"Sushi," she replied.

He laughed. "I know a great place over on East Sahara."

"Works for me. I'll follow you."

He pulled out of the parking lot with Solange following him. He kept glancing in the rear view mirror as he drove, half expecting her to change her mind. But she didn't. She followed him all the way to Sushi Palace and parked next to him.

Sushi Palace looked like a run down fast food place on the outside, but inside it was decorated in a muted Asian theme, was exceptionally clean, and Jarred knew the sushi was exquisite. Several sushi chefs stood behind a long counter, putting together orders for the few customers who sat at the bar. A hostess led them to a booth at the back of the room, half empty with the noon crowd having just left.

Solange seated herself with a smooth, flowing grace. She had a predatory glitter in her eyes as she glanced over the menu. Her fingers, long and slim, held feral strength and constrained violence. The waitress deposited glasses of water in front of them, took their drink order and departed. Jarred glanced through the menu. "Why did you go to Kenny's apartment alone after I asked you not to?" Especially with a demon on the loose. Not that he knew how to kill a demon, but he didn't like her putting herself in danger.

"Funny, you almost sounded like you care about me."

Did he? He had to admit, he did and that bothered him. She interlaced her fingers, rested her chin on them and flirted with him. She looked so normal. If he had just met her on the street, not in a million years would he have though she was a werewolf. The world wasn't all cut and dried anymore.

"What are you thinking about?" she asked.

"You," he replied honestly. He was thinking about how the moon had given her skin a silver luster and how her black hair had flowed about her face as she had changed. Excitement filled him, and he though about their wild night in bed and how the sex had been so incredible and how hot she was and how hot he was and... He ran out of breath, thinking about all the things he still wanted to experience with her.

Frowning, she glanced through the menu. "No matter what you're thinking, you need to know there can never be anything between us because of what I am."

Her ability to read him so accurately troubled him. "Do werewolf skills also contain mind-reading? Because, sistah, you are way off." He had to protect his man-ness. He couldn't give up any emotional crap to her. She was seducing him. What had happened to the nice, shy woman he'd met only two days ago? "I thought you were all hung up on the boss's son."

Her mouth dropped open, and then she laughed. "You're thinking I loved Malcolm."

"Werewolves don't marry for love?"

"Some do. I guess the easiest way to explain this is that it's like the nobility in old Europe. People were always trying to marry better than where they started."

He remembered a documentary he rented the other day. "To advance your status in the pack, right."

She gave him a dimpled smile that sent him spiraling back into lust.

She wagged a finger at him "Special agent Maitland, have you been watching the Discovery Channel."

Caught red-handed. "I needed to know what I was up against. One thing I've noticed about wolves—they don't back down. Even a lone wolf will take a stand."

She touched his hand. "The pack is who we are. All my wolf life, I've been raised to be a part of a pack. Every decision I've ever made, was made for the better of the pack."

The waitress came and they ordered their food. Silence fell between them. He thought of all the past years, the times he called BVW—before vamps and weres—that she'd spent hiding what she was, moving when people started to notice she wasn't aging like normal humans. He could understand why the pack was so important. The pack had been the only stability she'd had. The same type of pack mentality was evident even in the FBI where decisions were made for the better of the organization. "What I don't understand is why you want to leave. Isn't the pack your security, your protection from the world? It's not like you have to pick up and move anymore. The world knows you exist."

"Why," she asked softly, "do you think Kenny chose me to be his new inside person? Because even he knew I'm a weak link. Malcolm is going to be the alpha after Julius and Esther leave. I'm the omega, the bottom of the pack—everybody's friend, therapist, and go-to girl. If I had decided to stay, I could end up as everybody's punching bag."

Jarred decided maybe he didn't understand pack politics after all. "Malcolm would allow that."

"He would allow whatever he needed to keep the pack strong and his position secure. Most of the time it's the same thing."

"But the way you talk about everybody, you all seem so close."

"Never forget this. We act human, but underneath we're still wolves. The veneer of civility will be tested when Esther and Julius leave. I don't think anyone will challenge Malcolm, but…"

"You wanted him for protection."

"I wanted him for security."

"You make yourself sound so different from everyone else. You're a lot stronger than you think you are."

She licked her lips. "What do you see that I don't?"

"People perceive kindness as weakness. I see it as strength. And even if you weren't a werewolf, you would have helped me because you always do the right thing. You're not only moral, but also brave. I like that about you, more than I should."

"How did you ever end up as an undercover agent?"

How did he explain his desire to make the world a better, safer place? He was like his grandmother who'd had an adventurous spirit. Working undercover was a different adventure every day. He didn't sit behind a desk pushing papers. He didn't teach numb-nuts newbies how to be decent agents. No, his life changed from minute to minute. He had no patience for the mundane, which was probably why he'd fallen for this sexy woman who was a wolf in her spare time. "You didn't answer my question. Why did you go to Kenny's house by yourself? I told you I would go along."

"There has never been a major crime at the French Quarter. No rapes, no assaults, no murders. Do you know why?"

He couldn't resist teasing. "Because you eat the bad guys!"

She had the grace to blush. "Admittedly, that has happened in the past. But because we take it as a sacred duty to protect everyone who walks through our doors. We can smell chemical changes in the body and know when people are afraid, or angry, or in love. We've been able to avoid trouble."

"If so, then why didn't you neutralize Kenny long before now."

"Just because we smell these changes, doesn't mean we act on it. Kenny is a very good actor. There's not much going on inside him. He's a sociopath, and the most emotional reaction I got from him was when I told him he couldn't use guns."

Jarred blanched. He struggled with the effort not to shout. "You told him what?"

"If he starts blowing the casino up, the pack will revert to instinct and do what needs to be done to protect ourselves and our patrons. Esther and Julius have some control over us, but we have werewolves from all over the world who vacation at the French Quarter, and we wouldn't be able to control them when the bullets start flying. And Kenny has a demon and I don't know if he controls the demon or the demon controls him."

How did he do research on a demon? "Can demons be killed by bullets?"

"Some can. Some are killed by magic."

Magic, he thought. Well, he'd just learned another piece of information about the new world order he hadn't known about. "Then I'm definitely not going in unarmed." The demon was an unknown factor, and he didn't know what he should be doing to neutralize it, if he could. But he would start with a powerful gun.

"Have you ever met Kenny's lover?"

For a second he was silent, wondering why she'd asked. "Yeah, a few times. He's a little strange, but nothing to write home about."

"Does he wear copper bracelets or a copper necklace?"

Funny he couldn't recall the guy's name, but he did remember the jewelry. "He has a copper necklace. Why do you ask?"

"I think Kenny's lover is the demon."

"But you don't know for sure."

"I haven't seen the demon. No matter how human a demon may look, I would be able to spot it if I'm in the same room."

"What's so important about the copper?"

"Copper controls a demon. If he wears copper, he's probably the demon."

He took a deep breath and held it before letting it out slowly, trying to control the worry. *A demon lover. That was one for the books.* Fear settled in the pit of his stomach. "Did Kenny agree to the no guns rule?"

"He agreed." She nodded. "But I don't trust him."

"You're smart not to trust him," Jarred said. "What will you do then?"

She leaned toward him. "Just so you know, if I want to take a gun away from someone, I can." Her voice was low and dangerous.

Jarred had no illusions about what she could and couldn't do, and Kenny was damn lucky he was going to jail. "You don't have to leave the pack to feel safe. From where I'm sitting, you have taken care of everything. The pack is damn lucky to have you."

"Maybe, but I don't belong."

How could she not belong? She took care of things in the pack and kept everything moving smoothly. They'd be fools to let her go. "Why not?"

"My biological father set me aside from everyone else. He was the master of the plantation, and my mother was his mistress. When I was born, I was another piece of property, but with a higher status than everyone else. Even as a toddler, I was taught to speak in a more refined manner. I was taught to serve tea, had my own room, fine clothes to wear and eventually when I was old enough, I would have been sent to Paris to be educated. My future was to end up a rich planter's play toy. Had Esther and Julius left me behind when they ran away, I would have been nothing but an expensive whore sold to the highest bidder at the Quadroon Balls. Even though the Civil War did interrupt a whole way of life, we didn't see it coming. Everyone in the pack, besides Malcolm and Simone, were born before we left. And my father was responsible for selling their parents off to other plantations, or working them to death."

"So you think they look at you and see your father. You've been carrying a pretty big burden around for all of your life." And he felt the heavy weight of her sorrow and wished he could ease her burden. He knew how the past could shape the future and saw the results in what he did.

"Esther and Julius protect me."

"Why would you leave them?"

"Time to grow up."

"And I thought I was a man when I got my driver's license."

Suddenly, Solange laughed. "Thank you, sometimes I tend to feel a little sorry for myself."

He held her hand, feeling the strength in her grip. "What are you planning to do?"

"Travel. I'm young, wealthy and I still have a lot of years ahead of me."

So she didn't think they had anything going for them. He felt a stab of sadness that she considered him nothing but a fling. "How many?"

"About a hundred fifty to two hundred years."

"How does one plan for a life that goes on so long?" He ran his thumb up and down the back of her hand. Her skin was so smooth, like satin. "I live in the now, that's why I'm a good undercover agent."

"What are you proposing?"

"I want to go back to your place and see your sheets again."

She looked startled, and then she grinned at him.

"Look, I'm a guy. I never thought I would appreciate the feel of Egyptian cotton sheets and a beautiful woman at the same time."

"I like that idea, but first, I do need to eat. Something as raw as this place can provide."

The Hunger Within

Their food came, and he watched as she licked her lips and dug into her sushi.

Afterward, he followed her back to the casino. For most of the drive, thoughts of her dominated. He was playing with fire. Only two days ago, his life had been relatively normal except for Kenny. And now…now he was consumed with a woman he couldn't have, and involved with a sociopath who had a demon for his lover.

Maybe he needed to more afraid than he truly was.

Sensual heat rose inside her, surprising her. Jarred Maitland had gotten under her skin, and just looking at him made her want to tear his clothes off and have him right there and then.

Her stomach somersaulted, as he loomed nearer. God, she wanted him. She closed her eyes for a second, reliving the intense pleasure of his hands on her body, and his lips on hers. Jarred Maitland embodied every fantasy created in her love-starved imagination.

He backed her up against the wall, and she realized she could not get away from him. She didn't want to escape.

Jarred braced his large hands on either side of her shoulders. Solange curled her hands into fists forcing them to her side, not trusting herself to touch him. She inhaled the subtle, woodsy notes of his soap mixed with the heat of his body. She remembered the salty taste on his skin, the texture of his smooth flesh, and the hardness of his muscles. Shivering, she pressed harder against the door.

Jarred took another step closer. His mouth was only an inch away. She could feel the heat of his breath on her lips and see the darkness of desire in his eyes.

"The moon," he said, "is still full, and the stars are still straight."

She tilted her head at him. "Are you saying throw caution to the wind?"

He pushed back a strand of hair off her cheek, answering her with a silky smile. The tip of his finger left a trail of fire on her cheek. "I'm saying go with the moment."

Her body trembled, and the intensity of her emotions frightened her. "This might be a mistake."

He kissed her neck, and then ran his hot tongue along the line of her cheek. "The only mistake," he said, "is not letting our attraction play itself out." He nibbled the soft skin at the base of her neck.

A shuddering moan escaped her lips. Heat danced up her spine, and she squeezed her eyes shut, wishing she could mark his seduction up to one of her flights of fantasy. But Jarred was flesh and blood real, not one of her nocturnal musings. He was human and she wasn't. Yet the need for him wouldn't go away.

"I want you." He pressed her hand to his erection.

He felt so powerful and ready. She took a quick breath, hoping some witty comeback would spill from her mouth, shattering the mood. But her trusty brain failed her. Probably because the old girl was in cahoots with her heart. She wanted him. She loved him. Nothing could change her feelings. Solange felt his rhythmic grind against the palm of her hand and was lost.

Jarred slid his hand up inside her T-shirt. Both shirt and skirt gave him easy access to her body. His warm hand teased her flesh, and her belly quivered under his touch.

Taut skin stretched over his cheekbones, and his eyes radiated passion. Her heart demanded she give herself to him without reservation. She would deal with the wreckage in the harsh light of tomorrow. Right now, they belonged to desire.

He knew the truth about what she was, and still his eyes burned with desire for her. He liked her for herself. Not because she agreed to help him in his plan. Not because he thought she was pretty. Or nice. Or kind. He knew what very few people even suspected. Solange was much more than the good little wolf, trying to win everyone's approval. The time had arrived for her to let her wolf out and feed her beast.

"Damn, I want you." Turning her gaze to Jarred, she realized he was still trying to assess her. He wanted her but was respectful and just a tad manipulative. His game was good. "Is that the best you can do?"

"I don't understand."

"Sure you do. You want me. In your bed. Go ahead and make your move." Solange stopped herself from smiling. Good. Let him see her in action.

"Lady, I'm trying to treat you with some respect. I'm still not sure what to make of you being a wolf."

"It is what it is."

Grabbing Jarred's hand, she led him through the maze of hallways in the casinos. She wanted to hurry and get to her apartment before the real sensible Solange reemerged and took back control.

They stopped and waited for the elevator to take them to the lower level where the family apartments were on site rooms.

Jarrod slid his lips across the back of her neck, and Solange's knees almost buckled under his seductive assault. He pressed his entire body against her back. She could feel his erection pressed against her rear end. My God he was a whole lot of man.

The doors opened and Laurel was standing there. She nearly dropped her handful of papers. "Solange."

Solange giggled. "Hi, Laural." She felt Jarrod smile against her neck. His warm breath kicked up her body temperature about six hundred degrees.

Laurel stepped out of the elevator. "Special Agent Maitland."

Jarrod didn't say anything; he just pushed Solange into the elevator and followed behind her. When the doors closed, he pushed her against the wall just as she hit the button to take them to her floor. He started kissing her again, running his hands over her body. His fingers explored her with skill and ease. He curved his hand around and palmed one of the cheeks of her butt and gave a squeeze. Her body arched toward him, and he groaned.

"You are so beautiful."

He made her feel beautiful. She knew her hormones were working on him, but she didn't care. Chemistry can only take a girl so far. If he generally wasn't attracted to her, she would have never gotten this strong of a reaction from him. "Thank you."

Before he could say anything else, the elevator door opened, and she pulled him outside and down the corridor to her apartment. Her hands shook as she dug the card key out of her jacket pocket. And it took her three tries to get it to work and unlock the door. He pushed her through the entry with a gentle shove. The door slammed behind them, and he grabbed her around the waist. Solange stopped thinking as he hauled her against the door. Her feet left the ground, and she locked them around his waist. She heard the sound of ripping fabric and felt a cool sensation of her thighs. Their lips crashed together, and she felt his tongue slip past her lips. Her head was full of heat, desire and the sheer masculine smell of him. He was like running free in the desert on a hot summer night.

The sharp rasp of a zipper caught her attention. She felt herself get wetter just waiting for him to get inside her. He made quick work of stripping and putting on a condom. She wanted him naked, but this first time had to be quick, rough, and mindless. She didn't want hearts and flower. Not now. Not with him.

The tip of his penis breached her. He was so wonderfully big.

He thrust up again. "Jesus, you are tight."

Solange tightened her legs around his waist and tilted her pelvis. "Yes," she whispered against his lips.

His breath was ragged as he thrust up inside her again.

She felt her muscles clutch on to him. Her head lulled back until it touched the smooth wood of the door. Her body took over. She grabbed his long braids in her fist to steady herself.

The Hunger Within

She tried in vain to catch her breath. Her whole body was ready to incinerate, but she wanted more. More of this. More of him. The silk of her blouse clung to damp skin. She could feel him working her hard nipple through the silk and lace of cloths. She didn't want it to stop.

His strokes continued to bombard her. He increased his tempo and depth. Harder and harder he moved inside her. Deep inside her a tremor started to build. Wave upon wave of pleasure grew, and Solange revealed in it. Her internal muscles clinched around his cock. His lips burned on her body. With one final stroke, he pushed her over the edge, and she came with a fury not even another wolf had been able to provide.

Chapter Six

The next night after his shift at the bar, Jarred knocked on Solange's apartment door. He was going to miss the French Quarter. He actually enjoyed working at the club, even though it wasn't what he wanted to do the rest of his life. But since meeting Solange, he'd been questioning a lot of his life decisions.

The door opened, and she stood there looking calm and collected. How could she be what she was? But then, the image of her changing from wolf to human form came back to him, and he tried not to shiver.

"Missed you," he said as he stepped inside and drew her into his arms.

"Me, too," she said, "but the farewell party is consuming all my time at the moment." She rested her head against his shoulder and sighed. "Do you know what Paris Hilton demands just to come to a party?"

"You mean money?"

"No, I mean in just…stuff. If you invite Hollywood people to a party, you have to give them gift baskets. And she wants a wallet costing five thousand dollars. Luckily, a lot of the casinos are donating things, but for heaven's sake. A five thousand dollar wallet she'll only carry for a week, and then probably toss in the trash."

Desire flamed in him. He didn't want to be understanding, he wanted to push her toward the bedroom. "What's wrong with a wallet costing $29.95?" He'd caught glimpses of her during the evening as she'd rushed back and forth always with someone in tow who worked hard to keep up with her. She was a dynamo, and watching her had made him tired.

"Well, I guess because it wasn't massaged by the tender young hands of Japanese virgins."

"I don't get it."

"Neither do I. I've had the same wallet since 1964."

She had a wallet older than he was. *Damn*, he thought, *I'm in love with a senior citizen. This is a light bulb moment.* Screw the light bulb, this was a lighthouse moment.

She stepped back and pointed at the dining room. "I ordered dinner."

"Good, because I'm hungry." He grinned as the aroma of fresh food filled his nostrils. Okay, sex could wait for fifteen minutes. He did appreciate a good meal, too.

He sat at the table and filled his plate with food.

"And then," she continued on her rant as she filled her plate, "you have to be certain about who's dating who so the exes don't cross paths. If you invite Brad, you can't invite Jennifer because he might bring whoever he's dating at the moment, and then there'd be fireworks."

"There's something to be said about birthday parties at Chuck E. Cheese. A slice of pizza with a Star Wars toy and I was good to go." Hell, he would have been happy with a party at McDonalds. Chicken Nuggets were his favorite comfort food.

"You like Star Wars?" Amazement spread across her face.

He remembered they'd only known each other a few days, and didn't really know each other yet. "Yes, one of my guilty pleasures."

"What do you have?"

"This great Darth Vader head that talks to you. An electronic Yoda. Posters, X-wings and a great model of the Death Star."

She leaned forward. "I have the original Pez dispensers still in the wrappers."

His eyebrows shot up. "You! A Star Wars nut!"

"Luke," she said in a gravelly voice, "I am your father."

She sounded just like Darth Vader. "How?" He stared at her, his fork halfway to his mouth, his food forgotten.

"Howling at the moon all night." She ran a hand through her hair and tilted her chin up her mouth forming an O.

"I am not worthy."

She laughed. "Wayne's World."

"No!" This sophisticated woman was too much for him. How could she look like a goddess and have the heart of a stand-up comedian?

She held her fingers to her lips. "Don't tell anybody."

"Party on, Wayne."

"Party on, Garth," she replied.

They both dissolved into laughter. Jarred could hardly stay in his chair. Who would have thought the elegant and almost aloof Solange to be a closet Star Wars and Wayne's World fan. How could he be so lucky? "Have you found out anything about the demon yet?" He hated to bring up business, but the heist was only a day away.

"Nothing," she said. "Laurel's contact at UNLV couldn't come up with anything from the drawing I made of the runes on the box."

He hated the idea of not having all the information he needed. All he could hope for was a demon easily killed with bullets.

His cell phone rang. For a second he contemplated not answering, but a glance at the display told him it was Kenny. He answered.

"Maitland," Kenny said in a curt tone. "Plans have changed. Tonight's the night."

"What?"

"We're hitting the vault tonight. You have one hour to meet me at the employee entrance behind the mall. And tell your pretty little piece of ass, too." Kenny disconnected.

Jarred dropped the cell phone. "Shit. Shit. Shit."

"What's the matter?"

"Kenny has upped the timetable twenty-four hours. We're hitting the vault tonight."

Chapter Seven

The tournament was coming to a close. Only one more day and the event was down to a dozen tables from the hundred that started. Solange stood at the service entrance, waiting for Kenny. She had expected more people, but only Kenny, his demon lover and one other person had shown up. They were changing into wait staff uniforms in the storage room.

She tried not to shiver. The demon had looked at her as though she'd been food and the knowledge that Kenny had some sort of trick up his sleeve worried her to no end.

She slapped at a dining cart, wondering if Jarred's people were going to get into their places in time. Jarred had only had a half-hour to get things rolling. He'd alerted his boss, and Solange had called Esther and alerted her.

A few employees passed her, going out the service door. Everyone nodded. No one was surprised to see her. The genius of being Esther's assistant was the ability to have all her fingers into everything. As she leaned against the wall, she could hear the murmur of Kenny's voice in the storage room as he gave last minute instructions. Solange's only function was to get everyone into the vault and explain their presence should anyone question them. As long as she was with them, she doubted anyone would ask her what she was doing. The Temples' party was an excellent cover for her being everywhere.

The door opened and Kenny stalked out. She could smell his excitement. Behind him stood the demon, its face closed and secretive. The demon had been a surprise. He looked male and very human except for his eyes, a deep bronze glinting with a liquid gold. Most people would consider the color a trick of the light, but

Solange knew better. She could smell the faint sulphur aroma surrounding him. The demon knew she knew what he was and appeared amused by the knowledge. He had a supercilious manner about his thin aristocratic face and a calm expression belying the excitement in him. He was tense and kept clenching and unclenching his hands while Solange wondered what he was.

Besides Jarred and the demon, the only other person was Mitchell Edmonds, a four-year employee who had been much praised for his dedication to his job in the security office. Solange had been so surprised at Mitch she kept staring at him and wondering how he had passed his background check. Laurel was very thorough and would be truly pissed when she discovered a trusted employee had betrayed them. Mitch stared right back at Solange, not the least bit concerned. But then again he didn't know Solange wasn't on his side. What really surprised Solange was that Kenny had been planning this job for several years, getting his people into positions of responsibility. He was a devious one.

"Ready?" Kenny asked her.

She nodded and started down the hallway too aware of the demon behind her. She kept wondering how Kenny controlled the demon and how the power would allow Kenny to challenge a were pack. Fear churned in her stomach as they stood in front of the bank of elevators, waiting. The doors slid open soundlessly and Marcus exited.

"Solange," Marcus said with a hearty, almost too friendly grin, "we're still on for our eight a.m. meeting tomorrow, aren't we?"

This was her signal that everyone was in their place just in case Jarred's people didn't get where they needed to be soon enough. She almost took a deep breath in relief until she felt the unsettling gaze of the demon on her. "Right," Solange answered. "This time remember, fat free cream cheese for the bagels. Some of us have to watch their girlish figures."

Marcus laughed and walked down the hall to the service entry. He let himself out to the parking lot. As the door automatically closed, Solange saw him skirt the big delivery van Kenny had brought for his getaway. Jarred gave Solange a curious look, and she just gave him a slight smile.

Even though everyone was in place, she still felt tense. She sniffed at Kenny and was relieved to know he hadn't brought the gun. At least as far as she could tell. They stopped briefly in one of the other storage rooms, grabbed dining carts and wheeled them into the elevator taking them down to the second basement.

Solange led the way to the vault down deserted hallways. Few people came down to this floor after hours. The laundry occupied a large part of the basement, and most of the staff was gone for the night. The rest of the floor was storage.

She approached the vault. Kenny crowded her as she dialed in the code to open the door. When it swung open, the lights came on automatically. She disengaged the alarm, and then stood with her back to the wall while Kenny entered and gazed around in awe.

The tournament money was stacked on a pallet inside metal cases smack dab in the center of the vault. Kenny grinned as he touched the metal storage cases.

The surrounding walls were lined with shelves containing the pack's treasures. One wall contained Esther's collection of art deco jewelry, which included her Faberge eggs and Cartier jewelry. Julius's collection of antique swords occupied several shelves below Solange's antique amber, including a dollhouse made of amber given to her by the Princess Anastasia as a Christmas gift in 1916 just months before the revolution. Solange treasured the dollhouse. Princess Anastasia had been a huge practical joker, and the house had been as much an apology for one of her jokes as a Christmas gift.

Kenny gave the dollhouse n speculative glance, but passed it by for Esther's jewelry. He opened the storage box containing the Faberge egg and smiled greedily at it. "Nice."

Solange swallowed her rage. The egg had been a gift from the Empress to Esther.

Kenny opened the egg and a wolf snarled back at him. "A wolf! This has never been documented. It's priceless and going on my shelf." He cast a half grin at the demon, who grinned back.

Solange wanted to object, but if she did, he'd wonder at her commitment. "Look in this box." She opened a long walnut box. An emerald-eyed panther symbolizing the house of Cartier was nose to nose with the yellow diamond eyes of a wolf standing for the house of Temple. The dazzling display rested on the velvet and Kenny's face went blank.

"The necklace is over a hundred years old," she said, leaning over his shoulder. She whispered in his ear, "None of the diamonds have ID numbers."

"Ka-ching." He slipped the necklace into his pocket with a wide grin. "Cartier and Faberge. I've hit the jackpot. Who knew wolves would have such good taste in bling."

Solange shuddered as he patted his pocket, uneasy that he'd touched Esther's pride and joy. Kenny opened yet another box to reveal a beautiful wolf carved in white jade with sapphire eyes. He pocketed the jade wolf, as well.

Jarred, Mitch and the demon-loaded carts with the metal suitcases. Kenny was still rifling through the jewelry, his greed was so strong and disturbing, Solange found herself withdrawing from him. She leaned against the amber dollhouse, caressing it, locking out his emotions, trying to ignore the demon who seemed to watch her out of the sides of its eyes.

Just as Jarred started toward the door, Kenny turned to the demon and nodded.

The demon stepped into the center of the vault and started to chant. Solange felt a ripple of something pour over her skin and she tried not to gasp. Sparks flew from the demon's fingers, whirled about his head, and then shot out toward Solange, Jarred and Mitch. Solange flinched when the spark struck her. She felt a tingling in her chest that slowly radiated outward toward her hands and feet. When the chant ended, she somehow felt different, but didn't know how and Kenny looked oddly pleased. "Okay, everybody, you have ten minutes to unload this vault before the time distortion wears off, and then we're out of here." He headed for the door. The demon reached into his pocket and pulled out a gun.

Kenny took the gun with a smile and pointed it at Solange. She'd expected this, but was still surprised. She stood straight up, tension vibrating through her like a drum.

Then she understood. "You're a time demon."

"Correct," the demon rumbled in an otherworldly voice, his eyes now liquid gold.

Time demons did not totally stop time, but caused a distortion in time for short periods. How simple. Stop time, rob the casino and get away. In the time it took for a normal person to take a single breath was ten minutes for Kenny. Even though Solange wasn't up on her demonology, she'd read about time demons. Ten minutes was the maximum, and the range was usually only a thousand feet or so. Most people wouldn't worry or even notice about the loss of ten minutes. And late at night, no one would notice that the casino was running in slow motion while the world outside was still at normal time.

Laurel wasn't going to be able to stop Kenny from doing anything. By the time the spell ended, they'd be gone and Solange would probably be dead. Solange's heart pounded loudly. She had to stop Kenny.

"Just a little extra insurance, little lady." Kenny gestured for Solange to move away from the door. "Come on, Nicholai," he said to the demon.

"Where are you going?" Solange asked.

"I have something to do," he said. "Maitland, keep the lady occupied. I'll be back in a second." He giggled and left the vault with the demon in tow.

Solange looked at Jarred and he simply smiled. He turned to Mitch and when Mitch began to wheel his cart out, Jarred walked over and slugged him. For a second, Mitch looked surprised, and then he crumpled onto the floor.

"Let's go," Jarred said, grabbing Solange's hand as he reached behind his back for his own gun.

"Wait." She grabbed one of Julius' ornamental swords. Every demon had a weakness. Even though she didn't know this demon's weakness, there was copper forged into the sword. She closed the door to the vault, trapping Mitch inside. When he came to he would be in for a big surprise.

Solange and Jarred ran up the stairs, passing people who appeared frozen in the act of moving one step. Solange dodged around Laurel who had one hand inside her jacket gripping the butt of her gun. They were all caught in the spell and Solange could do nothing.

"What is Kenny planning?" she asked as she shoved open the door to a main corridor following Kenny and the demon's scent.

"I don't know," Jarred said, with a frown, "but this appears to be a change of plans."

They raced down the hallway, dodging Laurel's security teams. Up two more sets of stairs, and they were on the office floor.

"They're in Julius and Esther's apartment." Solange flung open the door and raced inside.

Julius and Esther sat in their living room watching TV. The television flickered unaffected by the time distortion.

Kenny stood in the center of the room pointing his gun at Esther's head and smiling while the demon lounged against a wall. They both whirled when Solange and Jarred burst in.

"I told you to keep her occupied," Kenny snarled at Jarred.

"No can do," Jarred said, pointing his gun at Kenny.

The demon snarled and jumped up. Jarred fired at the same time Kenny did. Kenny's bullet hit first and Jarred crumpled, blood rushing from him in a geyser. His shot had gone wide, missing Kenny completely.

"You can't kill me," Kenny said.

"Sure I can." She flung the sword at the demon, impaling him against the wall. The demon glanced down at the sword protruding from his belly, a look of stunned surprise spreading across his narrow face. She hadn't killed him, but she had immobilized him. Her copper sword trumped Kenny's copper necklace, and she now controlled the demon.

She sprang, changing partially to wolf form; her hands outstretched shifting to claws. Kenny pulled the trigger a second time. A bullet skimmed past her as she reached for Kenny. Her claws dug deep into his neck and he screamed. She sank her claws deeper and Kenny went down groaning. She savaged him until she knew he wasn't going to get up again. Then she ran to Jarred.

His blood leaked out. Too much blood. Kenny had hit a major artery in Jarred's stomach. She glanced at the demon. "End the spell. Now."

The demon nodded unable to disobey her. He chanted and time snapped back to normal with a pop that hurt her ears.

Esther and Julius looked stunned as time rearranged itself. Julius took one look at the demon, Kenny groaning on the floor in a growing pool of his own blood, and Jarred cradled in Solange's arms. He reached for a phone.

"You didn't have to protect me," Solange told Jarred.

He coughed. Blood dripped out of the corner of his mouth. "It's the alpha male's job to protect."

"Esther," Solange cried, "he's dying."

Esther knelt down next to Solange. As she did her jaw began to elongate and her canines extended.

Solange grabbed her arm. "Esther, you can't risk this. The Preternatural authorities will hunt him down and—" .

Esther stroked her arm. "Do you love him?"

Solange looked down at Jarred's face. His color fading as the life slowly drained out of his body. "More than anything."

Esther smiled. "Then he's one of mine now. I take care of all my babies. And is there a beastie on the council who doesn't owe me a favor?"

Maybe they would turn a blind eye, but she was putting the entire pack at risk just for the man she loved. "Thank you."

Pain filled Jarred's eyes and he grasped her hand. "I have to tell you something before I die. I love you."

"I know, but you're not going to die."

He shook his head. "Trust me, I'm dying. Dumb ass me, I didn't wear my Kevlar vest."

Solange grinned at him. "Tell me you want to be with me forever."

"If I could arrange it, I would." He coughed and more blood dripped down his chin and spread across his collar. The blood from the gunshot wound spilled out into a growing pool beneath him.

"A hundred years from now," she said, "we're going to laugh about this night."

He gave her a strange look. "No."

"Yes. I'm going to give you, besides my love, the gift of the wolf."

He smiled. The light started to fade in his face.

"Now, Solange," Esther said.

She let the change come over her once more and with a sad look at Jarred's face, she bit his arm, her life-saving saliva pumping into his veins.

Epilogue

Jarred stood at the microphone. Every TV station in Las Vegas was there, including every reporter from the national stations. He pointed at the reporter from CNN.

"Is it true the Temples knew nothing about the sting operation?" the woman asked.

"Absolutely not," Jarred replied. "Without their help we could never have arrested the Casino Crashers gang. As you know, ladies and gentlemen, attempted robbery does not carry the same sentence as an actual robbery. The Temples were more than willing to let their money be stolen so the perpetrators would do more jail time. The city of Las Vegas owes them a debt of gratitude for their forbearance in this investigation."

The reporter from the Las Vegas Review Journal raised her hand. "Is it true you've resigned from the FBI?"

"I have been an undercover agent for many years, and with my mug splashed all over the media, I think I'm out of a job."

"What are you going to do next?"

He laughed. "I'm going to Disneyland." He glanced back at Solange who stood next to him looking very beautiful. He leaned into the mike and whispered, "on my honeymoon." He left the podium to Harry who stepped up to answer the rest of the questions.

"Going to Disneyland is your big plan," Solange said as they walked back into the casino.

"Now the other packs know you're not only a bad-ass pack, but that you're smart."

She took his hand as the front doors whispered open. "Are you going to challenge Malcolm for leadership of the pack."

"Hell, no," he replied. "You and me are going to start our own." He leaned over and kissed her.

"Meet me in my room," she said with a breathless little start, "in ten minutes. And we'll get started on our pack."

"Make it five." He spied Esther and Julius waiting patiently for their moment to speak to him.

Solange headed toward the elevators as he walked over to them. They smiled, all showing their teeth, and all he could think of was that his life was going to be very interesting from now on.

Before the elevator door opened, Malcolm stepped up to her. "Solange," he said, "you're wrong."

"About what?"

"About the pack and the value they put on you."

Solange simply studied him. "My decision remains." Though suddenly she felt better and didn't know why.

"I had to do what was right for the pack," Malcolm said. "And that was no reflection on who you are."

"And I have to do what is right for me," she replied.

"You'll be missed."

"Thank you for telling me."

"You and Jarred always have a home here."

She glanced at Jarred still talking with Julius and Esther. Even though he was relaxed, she could tell he was anxious to be on his way up to her. "We'll be just fine."

Malcolm followed the line of her gaze and nodded gravely. "I think you're right. Jarred loves you in a way I never could. And you deserve better than anything I could give you."

Solange smiled. "Thank you, Malcolm."

As Malcolm walked away, Solange found a new lightness in her as the elevator door opened, and she headed up to her apartment. She would miss the French Quarter, but she had a different path to follow.

The Hunger Within

As the door started to close, a hand reached in and the doors slid open again. Jarred jumped in and even before the doors were fully closed, he reached for her, his hands sliding under her blouse.

"I don't think I can make it up to your apartment." He groaned deep in his throat. His face phased in and out, the shadow of the wolf in his eyes. He was young yet and the change would and he would have almost a month before the next full moon.

"You'd better. I don't want to scandalize the hotel guests now that Marcus has managed to bring the business back up to normal."

He licked her ear while his fingers reached under her bra. "Hmm. I guess we'd best not scandalize the guests."

"We have our whole life ahead of us."

The doors opened, and Solange leaped out and raced for her apartment with Jarred on her heels. They might never make it to the bedroom, but she knew the carpet was a pretty comfortable place to consummate her marriage and the beginning of the rest of her life.

The door slammed behind them and Jarred pounced on her. They rolled across the floor, and Solange found herself laughing with a carefree abandon she hadn't known in years. God, she loved this man. She would love him forever.

J.M. Jeffries

Double Down

by

Seressia Glass

Acknowledgements

To my friends, magical and mundane.
To my muse, awesome and strange.
To old fans, along for the ride.
To new fans, giving me a try:

Thanks to you all.

Chapter One

"I'm sorry, Ms. Temple."

"Sorry?" Simone stared at the agent, doing her level best not to growl at the man. "What do you mean, 'sorry?'"

"Kadim extends his sincerest regrets, but he's not interested in doing the special."

"Not interested." Simone knew she sounded like a parrot, but her only other option was to rip the poor man's throat out. The last thing she wanted was a dead agent in her office and blood covering her Versace skirt. She'd never get the stains out.

Decades of practice to not reveal any signs of weakness made her uncurl her hands and paste a pleasant smile on her face. "Does Kadim understand the importance of this special, not only to the French Quarter Hotel and Casino, but also to his career as a magician? The Mystery Channel hasn't approached anyone else; they want Kadim."

"I know, Ms. Temple." The agent looked positively green, not flattering against the olive-gray of his suit.

"This is a golden opportunity for Kadim to reach international stardom if he wants; to receive prestige and acclaim that most entertainers on the Strip wished they had," Simone continued.

"I told him that, too."

"The amount the Mystery Channel is offering is extremely generous, even after the hotel's share."

The agent's sickly hue deepened. "I know. I've told Kadim all of this. He's adamant about not having any of his performances recorded, even for something like this. I've done everything I can to convince him."

Simone was sure the agent had. He'd receive a very healthy commission, if only he could get his client to agree to the deal.

She swallowed another growl. This deal was important to her, to the hotel. Marketing was banking on announcing the Mystery Channel deal at the end of the Texas Hold 'Em tournament, riding the publicity the twenty million dollar contest garnered. She'd told the network and her family that she'd have the deal done.

Losing the deal would be a major blow. The news would get out, as it always did, costing her and her brother the display of control and status quo they needed, especially with their parents due to retire at the end of the week. People needed to see that Simone and Malcolm could and would keep the hotel going.

Rival packs were sniffing for any opportunity to exploit a weakness and steal the hotel. Just because they'd recently fended off a couple of attempts didn't mean that other packs wouldn't keep trying. It was much easier to take over an established moneymaker than try to build one, and the French Quarter Hotel and Casino was the jewel of downtown.

It wouldn't happen because of her. It sure as hell wouldn't happen because of Kadim and his agent.

"Ms. Temple?"

She flicked her attention back to him. The agent swallowed hard. Simone could hear his heart beating faster; hear the blood rushing though his veins. One of his arteries was partially clogged; she wondered if he knew.

The agent was a professional, protective of his client's best interests. They'd played hardball before. This was the first time he'd smelled of fear, and it was all she could do to not sniff the air, revel in the endorphin rush. She didn't know the cause of his fear, aside from the fact that he probably knew she was pissed. Idly, she wondered if she could make him run. With that partially blocked artery, she'd down him in seconds.

"Thank you for coming by," she said abruptly, rising to her feet. "I appreciate the courtesy of being given the news in person."

"Of course, Ms. Temple. Have a good day." The human

climbed to his feet, revealing his round stomach. One swipe of her claws would rip through jacket and shirt, exposing the soft belly. Warm intestines, hot blood....

Simone realized the man held a hand out to her. For a moment, she forgot what she was supposed to do with it. Then, she blinked, shook his hand. Thank God her nails hadn't lengthened into claws.

The agent quickly released her hand, bobbed his head, and then headed for her office door. Simone gripped the edge of her desk to keep from following him. Correction— *chasing* him.

The heavy oak door closed behind the man, and Simone breathed a short sigh. Her wolf rode her hard. It had been too long since she'd changed, since she'd allowed herself a full-out run. She hadn't been on a hunt, not to mention an all-out fight, in more than five years. Her lupine nature was beginning to ripple through her self-control. The moon hadn't controlled her changes since puberty, but she could feel the need to get wild growing inside her, becoming relentless.

That was a problem with being a born werewolf instead of turned. The wolf was as natural as the human form to her, and at times she had to struggle against her other, wilder half. She didn't need a forced change in the middle of her office because she was pissed off.

Damn Kadim! She stalked around her desk to stand before the bank of windows. The magician was the hottest act on her entertainment roster; his shows booked three months out. Only Mardi Gras got more press, because of the Hollywood and music world A-listers that liked to see and be seen in her nightclub.

She'd made few demands on Kadim since booking him as the French Quarter's headliner a year ago. He had access to all that the French Quarter Hotel and Casino had to offer, including a suite that rivaled those of the family, though he only used it the nights he worked in the hotel's amphitheatre.

Despite his moneymaking status, he'd made little in the way of demands except for requests for privacy. She'd honored those requests because Kadim's publicity phobia only added to his mystique—and their bottom line. Let him be eccentric, let him be mysterious, but don't let him fuck up her ability to handle her business.

Her phone buzzed, snapping her out of her sour ruminations. "Malcolm's here," her assistant, Lisa, informed her.

Simone fingered the lacy strands of gold around her neck, reining in her mood. She barely had time to paste a pleasant smile on her face before the prerequisite knock came a second before her door opened.

"What did you do to Kadim's agent?" Malcolm Temple asked, looking every inch the alpha male and heir in his navy Armani shadow-striped suit. "The man left here looking like a frightened rabbit."

"Nothing." Simone heard the defensiveness in her voice and tried again. "We were just discussing Kadim's schedule, and doing the usual contract dance."

"Is he refusing to do the Mystery Channel performance? Or thinking about jumping ship?" Her brother frowned as he closed the office door. "What's the point of always having dinner with the man and giving him a suite if you can't get him to agree to a simple business deal?"

"You make it sound like more than it is." She pulled herself straight. "Those dinners happen right after his last show of the week, and they're about business. Besides, he's got another year on his contract, so there's no danger of him leaving. And even if there were, I could handle it."

"Under normal circumstances, yes you could." Malcolm ventured further into her office, pausing beside her at the window. Vegas at midday didn't have the same luster as at night, but the power and money ran strong twenty-four-seven. "But nothing's normal right now, is it?"

Simone remained silent for a moment, staring through the glass. The hotel's managing offices boasted an amazing view of the city and foothills beyond. The landscape called to her, called to the wildness inside her, and she desperately needed to let it out.

"No, it isn't," Simone said, letting her brother see a shadow of her anger. He wasn't alpha yet, and she didn't appreciate him questioning her ability to do her job. "I can hold my own, even now."

Malcolm swung around. "Can you? When's the last time you changed?"

"Excuse me?"

"I can smell your wolf all over you." He sniffed the air for emphasis. "I know you haven't hunted since Xavier... in more than five years, but I figured you were at least calling your wolf."

Simone stiffened at the mention of Xavier, the only male of the pack who hadn't tried to mate her at every opportunity, and the only one she'd considered a friend.

Her brother, of course, noticed her reaction. *Damn it.* "Simone, no one blames you for what happened with Xavier. His death hurt all of us, but no one blames you for it."

"Of course not." She folded her arms across her chest, holding back the pain of memory. No one blamed her for Xavier's death—out loud, anyway. But everyone knew that if he hadn't followed her to Paris, he'd still be alive. Any other wolf at his back, and he'd have survived. But it had been her, and he had died. The only reason she wasn't Omega was because her best friend Solange was still in the pack and no one wanted to cross Malcolm or their parents.

"I don't have the luxury of hiding out in the desert for a couple of days right now," she said, managing to keep her voice even. "Especially with the Westwood human and two rival packs breathing down our necks. Remember?"

Malcolm frowned, the dark slash of his brows lowering over his midnight eyes. Great. With everything else going on, she didn't need her brother snapping at her. Literally.

Of course, he knew the threats facing them. While Laurel ran the hotel's security, everyone knew Malcolm was the pack's enforcer. He was GQ fabulous in his designer suits, but he didn't hesitate to get his jaws bloody when need demanded. Lately, with their parents' imminent retirement, Malcolm had to get bloody more and more often. Sometimes Simone thought her brother enjoyed the action a little too much.

"Damn it, Simone. Do you have any inkling of how important this week is for us? I don't need you losing control of your wolf in the middle of a multi-million-dollar poker tournament!"

Simone looked down at her gold and copper Giuseppe Zanotti sandals in an outward display of submission. She would have loved to argue with her brother, but she knew that would only encourage her wolf, not suppress it. The days when she could freely tussle with Malcolm were long gone. Any attempt at a skirmish at this particular time, with so much on the line and her wolf barely suppressed, would have one of them bleeding. She had a feeling it wouldn't be Malcolm.

Still, she lifted her chin and met his gaze. "I'm not Solange. Don't treat me like an Omega or a newborn pup."

Malcolm actually bared his teeth, and then quickly collected himself, straightening the gold and onyx cufflinks on his couture silk shirt. "Westwood's going to be here in a couple of days. The Howlers are here already."

Simone felt her heart drop. "Here? As in, in our hotel?"

"Yeah." Malcolm bared his teeth again. "Having them stay here seemed to be prudent."

"Or suicidal."

He ignored her comment. "We can keep an eye on them, and inviting them here shows that we aren't afraid of them."

Malcolm may not have been concerned about the Howlers, but Simone was. Their leader, Dwayne "D-Money" Hudgens, creeped her out. He'd been a gang leader before he turned, ruthless and vicious because he liked to be, not because he needed to be. Adding a Were's abilities to his warped mind only made him more dangerous.

She'd had a run-in with him during a West Coast wolven conclave. The way he'd looked at her, as if gutting her or mating her were equally appealing, still made her stomach churn.

A violent splinter off the Los Angeles pack, the Howlers gang was filled with young hotheads who'd been dangerous as humans, and they'd set their sights on the bright lights and money of Vegas. If D-Money succeeded in taking over their hotel and their pack, it would be because Malcolm lost a challenge for alpha. Neither Malcolm nor D-Money would let a contender, especially a defeated contender, live.

Then there was the human threat, a technology hotshot named Vernon Westwood. Even though he already owned a couple of properties closer to the Strip, he'd set his sights on the French Quarter for some unknown reason. Their parents had refused his buyout offer a few months ago, but he'd vowed not to give up. Sure, they'd disposed of more than one shady businessman who'd attempted to strong-arm them, but something about Westwood made Simone's hackles rise.

She licked her lips, trying to find moisture in her suddenly dry mouth. "Do you—do you want me to approach D-Money?"

She felt his gaze on her as if he'd reached out and tapped her shoulder. "Do you really think anyone in the family would want to offer you up to D-Money?"

"Both of us are unmated," she said, stating the obvious. "Without pups, we're vulnerable. An alliance would be in the best interests of our pack."

Malcolm actually growled. "This isn't the Dark Ages, Simone. I'm not about to throw you at that thug just to keep this place. I'd rather go down biting and clawing."

Relief had her nodding in agreement. "So would I."

Malcolm studied her. "You haven't been in a fight in five years."

"I haven't needed to fight in five years," she clarified, feeling a sting despite every effort not to. Did Malcolm think her weak like everybody else did? Sure, she preferred pedicures to showing her claws, but that didn't mean she couldn't throw down if she had to. "Just because I'm not an enforcer like you or Laurel doesn't mean I can't handle myself if push comes to shove. I'm still a wolf."

He sighed, turning back to the window. "Mony, I know you can take care of yourself," he said, his voice soft. "And I know I can count on you to have my back. That doesn't mean that I'm not going to worry about you."

Simone took a breath. Her brother hadn't used her nickname in years. It was as close to an apology as she was likely to get, and so unusual that she didn't know what to make of it. "Malcolm."

He didn't turn, but she knew he paid attention. She was worried about him. They'd both had easy lives with their parents as the Vegas Alphas. Her brother had been as reckless and confident as an unchallenged alpha-in-waiting could be. Now, with threats from Weres and non-Weres alike, Malcolm had traded his unruliness for cold calculation and deadly vigilance. That he excelled at it made her proud and worried.

"Today's our slow day," he said, turning toward the door. "I think tonight will be a good time to go for a run. Stretch your legs, clear your head."

Simone wasn't sure if her brother was trying to get her off the premises for a while or really was concerned for the health of her wolf. Getting wild was the only form of therapy Weres believed in. "Is that an order?"

He turned his head, baring his teeth in a wolfish grin. "Would you rather talk to Mom about it?"

"Uh, that's all right." Esther Temple was definitely the diva of the Vegas pack, but Simone had seen her mother take down a bighorn ewe by herself. The last thing she wanted was her mother sniffing around her troubles.

Speaking of troubles... "You know, I do have to leave the hotel for a couple of hours," she said, making a decision. "There shouldn't be any emergencies that Lisa can't handle. I'll get in a run while I'm gone."

Malcolm stepped back, his face softening with relief. "You do that."

Her brother left. Simone looked out the window again, resolute. If Kadim thought she'd take his refusal as final, he was sadly mistaken.

She pressed the intercom on her phone. "Lisa, get me Kadim's home address, then have someone bring my car around. I'll be out the rest of the day."

She crossed to her black laminate credenza, opened one of its deep drawers, and removed a small overnight bag. Even though she hadn't run in years, she still kept a change bag handy, packed with a tracksuit, sneakers, and toiletries. As much as she loved her designer heels, they were the last things she wanted to slip her feet into after a run.

Exiting her office, she retrieved the directions from her curious assistant, and then headed for the elevator. Moments later, she exited into the main floor of the casino.

"Well, well, if it ain't Miss Thang."

Simone stopped in her tracks as Dwayne "D-Money" Hudgens stepped in front of her, flanked by his ever-present Mutt and Jeff flunkies.

"Gentlemen." She forced pleasantness into her tone. In the center of her hotel, there was nothing Hudgens and his flunkies could do to her. "I trust you're taking advantage of what my casino has to offer?"

Hudgens frowned at the veiled insult. "Just imagining some of the changes I'd make if I was running the place," he said, running his oily gaze over her. "Maybe make the waitresses wear a little less."

She wondered how the gold tooth fit his canine when he changed, and then decided she didn't care enough to find out. "Then it's a good thing you're not running our casino, isn't it?"

"It may not be your casino for long." Hudgens smiled. "Your parents are about to leave, your brother doesn't have any kids, or a strong second. If something were to happen to Malcolm, the Temple pack would be in trouble."

"You don't scare me, D-Moron," she retorted, even though ice slid down her back at his words. "I've met Siberian Weres before and after Chernobyl. Compared to them, you're toothless."

"I think you need to show some respect," Mutt said, stepping up on her.

She instantly stiffened as her wolf fought to claw to the surface. Mutt must have seen it in her eyes, because he took an involuntary step back.

She bared her teeth in territorial irritation. "And I think you need to get your wannabe ghetto fabulous ass out of my face."

Two dark jacketed members of security, one human and one Were, both huge, appeared beside her. "Are you in need of assistance, Ms. Temple?" the human asked.

Simone turned an icy glance to Mutt. "Not at all, it's just a *small* issue," she replied.

Hudgens sidled back, his eyes flat with anger. "Just 'cause you own this casino doesn't mean that you're all that, bitch."

"That's Ms. Bitch to you. Carl." She acknowledged the Were beside her. "Arrange for the house to give our guests a starter account. After all, we're equal opportunity when it comes to hospitality."

Reining in her adrenaline rush and sudden need for blood, she turned on her five hundred dollar stilettos and stalked out of the hotel. Luckily, her silver convertible sat at the curb waiting for her, top down and purring.

Simone thanked the valet who handed her into the car, controlling herself long enough not to peel out. Thankfully, Kadim lived an hour northeast of downtown. He'd better hope like hell she had control of her wolf before she got there. God help him if she didn't.

Chapter Two

She obviously paid The Great Kadim too well.

Simone stepped out of her car, pushing her sunglasses up into her hair. Mountain air filled her lungs, musky and sweet. Being halfway up the mountain easily made it twenty degrees cooler here than in the valley, which put the temperature somewhere around eighty-five. Practically freezing, unless you lived in casinos.

Kadim's estate—she wasn't sure it could be called anything else—disappeared into a copse of pine and other trees that hugged the curve of the mountain. The Temple pack owned land closer to Mt. Churchill to the west of Vegas, but looking at this view, Simone suddenly thought it worthwhile to scope out property nearby. She could run on her own land, without fear of encountering other wolves.

The front door opened. Kadim himself appeared in the doorway, at-home casual in beige linen pants and a brown and beige madras-style shirt. He stood six-three, on par with her male pack mates, though leaner in the shoulders. His skin tone reminded her of the most decadent Belgian chocolate, dark and nutty, making his smile a brilliant, sensual pearl against the darkness of his skin.

As she left her car, slamming the door behind her, she noticed that his feet were bare, long, and lean. *Obviously not expecting company*, she thought, though he didn't seem surprised to see her.

He gave her another wide, welcoming smile. "Simone, a pleasure to see you."

"Really?" she answered, lifting her sunglasses into her hair as she took the handful of steps to reach the ornate entry. "You don't seem surprised to see me."

"Bruce called shortly after he left your office," he explained, stepping back to let her inside. "He told me you weren't pleased with my decision."

Simone grimaced, and wondered if Kadim knew how much she'd unnerved his agent. "I wouldn't say that I wasn't pleased, more like confused. I decided it would be better to go right to the source. Seeing as we're friends and all."

"I suppose, given our friendship, that's a reasonable decision." He shut the door behind her. "Bruce, of course, thinks I've lost my mind by not accepting the Mystery Channel offer. What do you think?"

"I think you think that you have a good reason for not filming the special." She followed him deeper into the house. "Something based on your extreme need for privacy."

She stopped, stared. "Which explains why, after a year full of dinners, you've never invited me to see this spectacular view."

It *was* a spectacular view. The paneled entryway flowed into a two-story great room with one wall composed entirely of windows. Cedar beams framed the ceiling and windows, giving the room an alpine lodge feel, even with the wraparound deck visible through the glass. A large stone fireplace dominated the right wall, with a short hallway that she guessed led to bedrooms. The great room narrowed to an intimate family room that spilled into a huge, tile and timber kitchen on the left, with an open switchback staircase leading to a loft-like upper level.

Simone's gaze returned to the large windows, drawn like a lodestone. The mountain and its copse of trees dominated the view, calling to her wolf. Kadim's home would be perfect for Weres, she thought, venturing further into the room decorated in a mix of warm earth tones. Step onto the deck beyond the glass wall and you'd be inches from forest. If she could manage to stay until nightfall, she'd be able to get in a run here, far from her pack. After the incident at the hotel, she desperately needed the release of running wild for a couple of hours.

She turned, catching Kadim watching her. "You have a gorgeous home."

"Thank you." He gestured her into the seating area closest to the windows. "Maybe I didn't invite you before because I didn't think you'd show."

"And miss an opportunity to visit the reclusive Kadim in his private sanctuary? Not on your life."

"I don't think there's anything wrong with keeping a few things private," he answered. "After all, we all have secrets, don't we?"

She gave him what she hoped was a blank look as she wondered what he meant by the question. She'd assumed that Kadim was human—his smell, a curious combination of spice, earth, and smoke, certainly wasn't Were. She'd never told him about the multiple threats facing the hotel. Even though he was a good friend, he wasn't family, wasn't pack.

He smiled at her again. "Relax, Simone. You're a guest in my home. I'm not going to dig for your secrets, but I would like to invite you to stay for dinner. I happen to have a couple of steaks marinating."

Convenient, Simone thought. Her stomach, however, thought it was an excellent idea. With her wolf hard on her she had to eat more than usual, almost doubling her number of meals. The medium-rare burger she'd devoured on the drive up was almost gone.

"I'd love to." She smiled. "Though I can honestly say I understand why you'd like to keep this view to yourself. It's simply stunning." She turned to look at him, raising an eyebrow. "Do you keep it to yourself?"

His slow grin brightened his face and melted her insides. "Would you believe me if I said you were my first visitor?"

"Not for a moment."

He laughed. "I didn't think so. Bruce, of course, has been here once or twice to drop off paperwork, but that's about it."

He looked out the windows. "Truthfully, as decadent as the suite at the hotel is, this place suits my need to relax, to be myself. Would you like something to drink?"

"Merlot, if you have it, thanks." As Kadim headed for the bar,

Double Down

Simone strolled through the open French doors that led onto the deck, and the wild land beyond. Afternoon sunlight warmed her skin, no less intense for being an hour before sunset. The deck extended a dozen feet or so from the house, providing plenty of room for entertaining. The loft area she'd noticed inside had a balcony, and a lower level of the deck opened right into the woods.

Simone closed her eyes, hiding her jealousy. As much as she loved the hotel, she wanted a place like this, a place that could be hers. Her wolf needed a place to be herself, and despite the property the pack and her family owned, Simone didn't feel comfortable running wild there.

She frowned, opening her eyes to stare out into the forest. How depressing that she didn't feel comfortable running with her own family. Then again, no one in the pack had asked her to run with him or her either. Not since she'd gotten Xavier killed. She knew they didn't trust her to have their backs, and she supposed she couldn't blame them for it.

With a sigh, Simone folded her arms atop the railing. So she was unreliable when it came to fighting. That didn't mean she couldn't contribute to the pack in other ways. She was good at her job, the bottom line proved that. But losing Kadim and the special would be seen as a weakness; reminding people of other times she'd failed the pack.

Turning her head, she spotted Kadim at the bar near the kitchen, uncorking a bottle of wine. His gaze met hers, and maybe it was her imagination or simple longing, but she swore she felt something in his gaze. His eyes were a soft black, full of mischief and mystery.

His eyes had gotten to her from the beginning, almost a year ago. His eyes had lured her as few could, causing her to cross the line from employee to friend so smoothly she didn't know when it had happened.

Sometimes during their weekly dinners, she'd found her mind wandering beyond Kadim's latest inexplicable feat and the crowds that packed the amphitheatre to see it. Instead, she'd imagine those full lips moving over her skin, those hands weaving a seductive spell on her. Kadim's body moving like magic inside her.

She shook her head again. It wasn't fair to think of Kadim as a potential lover, simply because it couldn't happen. Apart from the whole pseudo employer-employee relationship, Kadim was human. Maybe a decade ago she could have afforded taking a human as a lover, but not now. Now she had the future of her pack to consider.

That didn't mean she couldn't pretend that something more was possible between them, especially if it netted a signed contract.

Kadim took his time opening the bottle of merlot, watching Simone thinking furiously out on the deck. She was curvy and leggy, filling her designer skirt and skimpy halter-top beautifully. Her skin had a warm brown tone, like toffee-coated pecans, eyes dark and intelligent and way more observant than most. The spiky cut of her dark sable hair, streaked with browns and copper that glinted in the sunlight, gave her a pixie-ish appearance. Except he didn't know any pixies so earthily sexy.

Simone Temple.

She'd come, just as he'd known she would. If he'd learned anything about her during their dinners, it was that she was a woman who didn't take no for an answer, especially in business. As valid as his reason for refusing the broadcast, he knew it would seem lame to Simone, even lamer coming from his agent. So of course she'd come to his home to confront him.

He poured a generous glass of the dark wine, and then filled a cut crystal glass with ice, enjoying the sight of her in his space. He'd been planning his moves carefully for months, ever since he'd entered the French Quarter Hotel and Casino. He'd been drawn there inexplicably, when there were plenty of hotels on the Strip that could have fit his plans. Once he'd seen her, however, he knew.

She was the one.

Not that he could tell her that, of course. Not yet, anyway. She had to think he still had the advantage in their negotiations. Once she realized that he needed her as much as she needed him—or perhaps more—he'd be in trouble.

Double Down

Reaching for a crystal decanter, he poured himself a healthy measure of Di Saronno. He'd have to play his cards just right. Simone wasn't skittish—none of the Weres were—but she was certainly cautious with her emotions. He'd have to take one step at a time, reveal his secrets one by one. Beginning with the fact that he, too, could shift into a wolf.

Cradling the glasses in his hands, he joined her out on the deck. She turned at his approach, giving him a slow smile that made him think dangerous things.

"I suppose I don't blame you for not staying in your suite on your off days." She accepted the glass of merlot, wrapping her fingers around the bowl. "A girl could get used to this."

He certainly hoped so, since he'd built the place with her in mind. Not that he could tell her that either. Instead, he leaned on the railing beside her, holding his glass to catch the last of the sunlight peeking through the trees. "Yes, I enjoy living out here."

He turned to her, the better to see her reaction as he said, "But I enjoy our dinners more."

She looked down into her wineglass. "Laying it on pretty thick, don't you think?"

"It's true," he insisted, hiding a smile at her discomfiture. "I figured that I'd get that out of the way before you rip me a new one over not signing the Mystery Channel contract."

"I'm not going to rip you a new one." She shifted, took a sip of her wine. "I'm perfectly capable of having a rational discussion about this."

"So you think I'm being irrational?"

This time she looked up at him, her dark brows lowering. He had no doubt that she'd probably just swallowed a growl. "I didn't say that."

"But you're thinking it, aren't you?"

"Kadim." Her wineglass settled on the railing in a deliberate motion. "I understand your desire for privacy. Believe me, I do. It adds to the hype and the mystery surrounding you, making you the hottest act in Vegas. Which is why the Mystery Channel wants to tape a special on you. Don't you think you're taking it a little too far?"

"Actually, no I don't." He took a measured sip of his Di Sarronno, almost wishing he'd brought reinforcements out. Getting either of them drunk wouldn't help his negotiations with Simone, however. "Believe it or not, I have my reasons."

She folded her arms beneath her breasts, pushing them up in a movement he'd have to be blind not to notice. "Do you mind sharing those reasons?"

He paused before answering her, pretending to consider her question. He did have reasons for not shooting the special, very valid reasons. The exposure wasn't something he wanted or needed. Only a handful of people worked behind the scenes on his shows. He paid them ridiculously well for a few hours work, and he trusted them as much as he trusted anyone.

And if loyalty and money didn't keep them from recording his act, the electronic disruption field he'd installed guaranteed it.

"I'm content with where I am and what I do," he finally said. "I have no desire for the exposure or the money that they're offering."

Simone took a deep breath. "So what is it that you do want, Kadim?"

He stroked the rim of his glass. "What do you have to offer me, Simone?" he asked, his voice soft, amused, sexy.

Simone watched his finger make lazy circles on the glass. It was all too easy to imagine him making lazy circles around her nipples. Her breasts perked in response.

She sidled closer, looked directly up at him. "I'm sure you realize, even though you're not an employee in the strictest sense, that we offer an excellent benefit plan, very competitive."

She reached out, resting her hand on his. "I'm confident that I can make this arrangement as good for you as it will be for me." She dipped her finger into his drink, brought it to her lips.

His gaze tracked the movement of her finger. "Good for you?" he whispered.

She smiled, licking the last drop of Di Sarronno off her finger. "I mean the hotel, too, of course."

"So we should enter into an agreement that will be mutually beneficial. Explore all the opportunities such an agreement has to offer."

"Exactly."

"Why?"

"Why?" she echoed. "What do you mean, why?"

"Why should we deepen our relationship? Why should I allow myself to fall victim to your ample charms?"

Stung, she backed off him, put a hand to her hip. "Trust me, if we went there, you wouldn't be feeling like a victim."

"Really? How many times have you used your generous gifts to get what you want?"

Before she could think about it, she swung. He caught her wrist easily, eyes sparking. That surprised her. No human should have been able to see her swing, and certainly no human should have been able to stop it.

"That was uncalled for," she ground out, pulling at his grip.

"So was thinking that I'd be seduced into signing the agreement so easily," he said, relaxing his grip enough to let her pull free. It rankled her enough that she balled her hands against the urge to leap at him again.

As if reading her mind, he stepped out of arm's reach. "If you want to play games, Simone, then let's play. If you win, you get your cable special."

"A game, huh?" she asked, stalling. The fact that he didn't fall for her seduction ploy so easily upped her respect for him, though her ego had taken a hit. The wolf in her knew stealth could be just as effective as a direct charge, and she actually liked the idea of a challenge. It had been a while since she'd hunted. This would do until she could get outside.

"So, what are the rules for this little endeavor?"

"I have three confessions to make to you," Kadim said, his voice mellow as he placed the rocks glass on the ledge beside her wine. He held up his hands, spread his fingers. A fan of playing cards appeared. "Of course, the only way you get to hear them is if you win a bet. One bet, one confession. If you win all three, you not only get the confessions, you also get the contract signed."

Simone stared at the confident expression on the magician's face. The offer he was making benefited her in every way. Not only would she get the show for the Mystery channel, she'd also learn more about her mysterious magician.

"What's the down side?" she asked, watching him manipulate the cards.

"There isn't one," he said, his smile putting her on alert. "We can alternate the parameters of each wager. I'll even let you go first."

Simone stopped herself from scenting the air for a lie. There had to be a catch—Kadim wouldn't be this generous if he didn't think he'd have a chance of winning and sending her home empty-handed.

"What do you want?"

He arched a brow, and even that looked good on him. "What do you mean?"

"That's some serious bait you're dangling in front of me," she told him, settling her hands on her hips. "Everything I could want from you, and all I have to do is win three wagers. You act like I'm a tourist fresh off the bus."

He actually looked offended, and stopped shuffling the deck. "I don't think of you like that. I know very well you've got a mind like a trap. You wouldn't be able to manage the French Quarter's entertainment or your brother otherwise."

"Then lay it out straight," she retorted, trying not to blush at the compliment he'd given her. "Everything you've said is in my favor. It looks like you're getting the crap end of the deal, which you seem unusually content with. That tells me that you're getting more than I can see, and until I figure that out, I'm not agreeing to this at all."

"All right." He turned to face her, his dark eyes glittering in the last of the sunlight. "If I win, I get you."

It was what she expected, but the way he said it made her insides clench. "I get the cable show that'll make us both a lot of money, and you get me. That seems a little lopsided, don't you think?"

He gave her that heavy-lidded glance again. "Not from my perspective."

She licked her lips, watching as he watched the movement. She knew then that he did want her. Knowing the stakes were as high for him as they were for her made it more agreeable. More than agreeable. It would almost be worth it, to lose deliberately.

Almost.

With a little thrill of excitement, she reached out, took the deck of cards from him. "All right, you have a deal. Since I know what I'm getting if I win, I think it's only fair to give you a taste of what you could expect in the unlikely event you best me."

"A taste, huh?" His gaze felt like a caress as it moved over her features. "All's fair in love and war, or something like that."

She put the stack of cards beside their glasses, then stepped closer, her hands flat against his chest. "Something like that."

Keeping a whisper of space between them, Simone stood on tiptoe to brush her lips against his. His hands settled on her hips, neither to pull her closer nor push her away. The moment her lips touched his, warmth stole through her, like a sip of expensive liquor. Her eyes slid closed as one hand reached up to cup the back of his neck.

Then he started kissing her back.

His lips bowed against hers, heating her senses. With a little moan she angled her head, wanting more of him. Wanting to taste him. She traced the sweet outline of his mouth with her tongue, smiling as she felt a shudder pass through him. When he mimicked her gesture, it was her turn to shudder, especially when his tongue glided against hers in a heated, sensual dance.

His hands kneaded her waist as if fighting the urge to roam. Then her hands wound their way around his neck, pushing her breasts against his chest. His hands slipped, cupping her buttocks, bringing her closer. The feeling of the hot, hard length of his body pressing against hers caused Simone to widen her stance as his mouth continued to devour hers.

They needed to stop, but God, she didn't want to. Kadim seemed to come to the same conclusion, slowing the kiss, giving her opportunity to pull away. She did, loosening her grip as she breathed, kissed, breathed again, her hands sliding back to his chest. Kadim's hands felt like they were burning through her skirt, his fingers inches away from discovering that she wore a thong beneath her short skirt.

Her feet were planted on the deck, but she definitely felt like she floated on air. She looked up at him, at her lipstick marking his mouth, and decided that before the night was over, they'd both get what they wanted.

"Let's get started."

Chapter Three

As the sun dropped behind the mountain, she beat him at blackjack. He didn't seem too upset about it, though.

He folded his cards onto the glass tabletop of the rattan patio set. "All right, I'll give you my first confession. Run with me."

She looked down at her strappy heels, then back up at him. "I'm not dressed for running."

Kadim smiled as he rose to his feet. "Who said anything about being dressed?"

Simone's mouth dropped open as he pulled his shirt over his head. As she watched, mouth still hanging open, Kadim hooked his fingers into the waist of his loose cotton pants. With a knowing smile on his face he turned away, then pushed the beige material off his hips.

Damn. Simone's mouth went dry as she watched the smooth expanse of Kadim's backside come into view. He had the most perfect ass she'd ever seen, well-muscled, juicy and firm like a dark plum she very much wanted to sink her teeth into. *Turn around*, she silently willed him as he stepped out of the pants and his boxers. *Please, God, make him turn around.*

He turned around.

Heat that had nothing to do with desert summer swept up her body, coalescing solidly deep inside. Kadim was very happy to see her. And getting happier by the heartbeat.

Somehow she found her voice. "Is this a three-legged race? Because you have me at a disadvantage."

He laughed. "I was thinking of all fours, actually."

Simone warmed again as a picture of Kadim taking her from behind filled her mind. Moisture filled her panties, nothing to do with sweat. "All fours?"

"Yes. Here's my confession, Simone. Run with me the way you want to, the way you need to. And if you beat me, you get the second confession."

As she watched, his outline blurred. He bent over double, sleek chocolate fur sprouting through his skin. By the time he hit the floor, his human shape had been replaced by that of a wolf.

Kadim was a werewolf.

Simone stared at the gorgeous creature in shock. Why in the world hadn't she scented his wolf on him? And he wasn't a Turned or young Natural—not with the fluidity with which he'd changed form.

A mature Natural werewolf living in Vegas—working for their hotel—and none of them knew about it? Incredible. If this was the first confession, what were the other ones about?

She held out her hand. The large animal padded over to her, cautious. She sank her fingers into its coat, feeling the very real thickness of it. He felt like a wolf.

Laughing, she straightened. "You are full of surprises, aren't you, magician?"

The wolf yipped, nosed her thigh, and then turned toward the lower deck in obvious entreaty. Night beckoned just over the railing, the mountain air filled with promise. Her wolf squirmed inside her, eager to break free, to run wild.

Without another thought, Simone bent to remove her heels. The wolf watched her with golden eyes, tail wagging, as she removed her jewelry, then rose to her feet. She untied her gold halter, and then in a teasing turn of modesty, turned her back to him to slip it off. Next came the skirt, which she folded neatly onto a chair, then her thong.

She shifted, shedding her human form as easily as she'd shed her clothes. Her body, mind, and DNA had been shaped for this in the womb, making the transition less painful and more fluid than the bone jarring rearranging that Turned Weres had to endure.

Colors faded to shades of gray, but losing colors was insignificant compared to all she gained with her wolf senses. Sounds rained on her: night insects, the house settling, and the gurgle of rushing water. Her muscles tightened with the urge to go bounding into the night, but she shook herself and padded over to the large male instead.

He scented her in greeting and she returned the favor, her nose filling with the scent of burning spice instead of wolf musk. Before she could react to the strange scent, Kadim nipped her in her left flank before bounding over and down to the lower deck.

She immediately gave chase, leaping over the railing to the ground below. Adrenaline flooded her veins as she stretched under-used muscles in the joy of running flat out. She caught up with Kadim, then pounced, sending them both rolling.

They wrestled, played tag, and explored their surroundings. Simone was having the time of her life, reveling in her lupine side, feeling the underbrush beneath her paws, scenting pine and scat and prey and the wolf beside her. She paused to howl with the pure, unadulterated joy of being completely alive.

A jackrabbit broke from the brush in front of them. Simone immediately gave chase, Kadim keeping pace beside her. He broke left as the rabbit zigzagged. Simone instantly mirrored him to fence their prey in. Fresh kill would be so much better than rare steak.

A large dark shape struck Kadim's flank, sending the wolf crashing to the ground. Simone turned, canines bared, only to be knocked over by a smaller shape.

Wolves. Dwayne Hudgens and his partners.

Kadim regained his feet, snarling, but the two betas attacked again. Simone leapt forward to intervene, but the third wolf blocked her, knocking her off her feet with brute force alone. She twisted, but he bit her, hard, between throat and shoulder.

Pain bloomed, causing her to howl in response. Behind her, snarls and growls coerced a loud yelp of pain, a yelp she recognized as Kadim's. He was down, the two wolves circling, preparing for a fatal strike.

Faster than ever before, Simone turned human, flinging herself between the wolves and Kadim. She curled over him, unmindful of the rocks and twigs digging into her bare skin. "Don't you dare hurt him!"

The alpha, a large gray, growled. The other two wolves joined their leader, then one at a time shifted back to human. "Well, well, well, lookie here," Hudgens said, a nasty smile on his face. "Miss High and Mighty ain't all that anymore."

Kadim didn't shift, a fact that scared Simone more than Hudgens and his flunkies. She could hear his heart racing, his breath laboring. They must have hurt him badly.

I'm so sorry, Kadim, she thought, guilt threatening to choke her. Against her will she thought of Xavier, how he'd died defending her. She couldn't let that happen to Kadim.

Clasping her wounded shoulder, Simone climbed to her feet, keeping herself between Kadim and the others. "What do you want?"

"You know what I want," Hudgens said, licking his lips as he slowly ran his gaze up her body. "And when I'm done, you do my boys. Then we go back downtown, stop at a chapel to make it all nice and legal. Then you and your half of the hotel will belong to me."

Her stomach roiled at the thought. "No."

"No? You think you can tell me no, bitch?" He grabbed a fistful of her hair, dragging her closer. "I'm Alpha here. You do what I tell you, when I tell you, or the wolf dies."

Simone closed her eyes, fighting the pain, the fear. She couldn't do it. She couldn't give herself to Hudgens; she knew enough about him to know that death would be preferable to being tortured by him and his packmates. But she couldn't make that decision for Kadim. She couldn't let them hurt him. No one else was going to die because of her.

If she submitted to Hudgens, she'd give Kadim time to recover, to escape. As much as he liked her, he wasn't Alpha. She didn't expect him to challenge Hudgens over her, but maybe he'd make it to the French Quarter and Malcolm before she was too damaged to be of any use. If she were lucky, maybe Hudgens and his crew would get wasted and pass out, and she could kill them all before she—

Simone.

She stiffened, uncertain if she'd heard Kadim's voice inside her head, or only imagined it. *Kadim? Is that really you?*

Yes. I'm a telepath. We can finish this, if you can distract Hudgens long enough for me to regain power.

How long?

Seconds. He'll pay for touching you.

"Well?" D-Money demanded, showing her roughly away. "Are you going to give me an answer?"

Simone bared her teeth. *I can distract him, but I really want to kill him.*

Kadim's warm laughter filled her mind, reassuring her that he would indeed soon be fine. *Not if I kill him first.*

She had two advantages on Hudgens and his crew: she was older and a Natural Were. Even though this marked the first time she'd shifted in nearly five years, she was willing to bet she could shift faster than they could. She could also partially shift her form, something only Alphas and a handful of Naturals could do. Besides, they needed her alive, at least long enough to get her share of the casino. They'd try to hurt her, but they wouldn't kill her.

So she hoped, anyway.

"You want an answer?" She raised her hands. "Here's your fucking answer."

She spun away from Hudgens, her hands instantly lengthening into scythe-like claws. She swung with deadly intent, catching Mutt across the throat. Blood sprayed like a crimson sprinkler as the Were grabbed at his throat, slowly sinking to his knees. Beside her, Kadim sprung into action, leaping past her to crash into Hudgens. The third Were turned tail and ran, heading for the road.

She couldn't let him get away. She wouldn't let him live.

A howl spilled from her throat as she shifted on the run, leaping across the clearing. She ripped into the back of the Were's thigh, bringing him down. He was trying to change back to human form, but she didn't care. They'd encroached on her pack's territory, tried to hurt her, hurt Kadim. Her wolf wanted blood. Now.

Her claws dug into his sides, broke through sprouting fur and knotting flesh. He managed to twist beneath her, closing his half-formed jaws on her right foreleg. Yelping in pain, she rolled, taking him with her, exposing his belly to the sky. Just for a moment, just long enough. With claws and teeth and no finesse, she gutted him, not giving him the honor of taking his throat. He didn't deserve it. None of them did.

Pain radiated through her leg and shoulder, causing her to limp. Shaking herself to jettison some of the blood and gore clinging to her fur, Simone turned back to the clearing, determined to help Kadim. Hudgens was an Alpha, and a dangerous one at that. Kadim wasn't, but she knew there was power in him, power he could tap to defeat Hudgens. The Alpha couldn't be allowed to live.

She limped back into the clearing as fast as she could, driven by the fierce sounds of mortal battle. Light glowed through the trees, light that didn't come from the moon. At the edge of the clearing she stopped, transfixed.

The darker wolf was on fire.

She watched in amazement as the flaming animal leapt onto the remaining male, jaws closing on throat. The gray wolf yelped once before claws, teeth, and flame overpowered him.

The fiery wolf brightened, flames elongated to a human shape. The dead wolf began to burn as the flaming shape picked up the man she'd killed earlier, threw it on top of Hudgens. Somehow the second body caught fire.

Simone crouched in the undergrowth, her animal instinct screaming with the urge to run. This was unnatural. This was wrong.

The figure straightened and turned toward her. She whimpered despite every urge not to, shuffling backwards into the protective cover of the forest. The acrid smell of singed fur and charring flesh assaulted her nose. She needed to run, but her leg wouldn't obey. When the figure took a step toward her, she growled in warning.

Fire seemed to sink into skin as Kadim regained his normal human form. "Simone?" he called, spreading his arms wide. "It's me, Simone. It's all right. You can change back now."

Simone overrode the wolf's instinct, wrenching slowly back to human form. She stumbled to her feet, pain causing her muscles to scream in protest. It hurt like a bitch to change forms so much in such a short time frame; she'd be paying for days, if she lived that long.

"Kadim." She stumbled again, unable to figure out how to make her human legs work. "Kadim. Thanks for not dying."

"Simone." He caught her around the waist. "Simone, your arm."

"He bit me, the bastard. Good thing I'm already a werewolf," she said, trying not to gag on the stench of burning flesh. The two bodies in the flames were almost completely ash, yet she couldn't feel heat, and the surrounding vegetation didn't burn. "How is that happening?"

Kadim's image blurred, but not so much that she couldn't see worry in his expression. "Simone, do you realize you're stuck in a halfway state?"

"Huh?" Blinking away the blood and gore on her face, she looked down, surprised to see that her legs were bent the wrong way. And covered with cinnamon-brown fur. "Oh crap. That explains the trouble walking."

"Can you change back? Either way?"

She looked at her legs, concentrated. Nothing happened, except pounding inside her head. "Apparently not."

Kadim frowned down at her. "Has this ever happened before?"

"No." She tried to take a step, faltered, and would have fallen if not for his arm around her waist. "My fault, for going too long between Changes. My wolf wanted to take over, wanted blood. I couldn't let them hurt you; I couldn't let them take you away from me. I must have burned out."

Her breath hitched as the night spun. "I think—I think I'm going to freak out now."

Kadim swung her up into his arms. "I'll take care of you, if you wish it."

She looked up at him, at his eyes so warm and sincere. Warmth. He was so warm, and she remembered the column of flame moving over Hudgens. No Were she'd ever met could command flame, not even some of the European Weres who practiced magic.

"Who are you?" Her hand reached up to cup his face, but she touched his cheek with a claw-tipped paw instead of fingers. "Oh, shit."

She tried to wriggle out of his arms, but his hold tightened. "Simone, don't."

"You should put me down and walk away," she said, sudden fear clogging her throat. "Once the pack finds out about this, I won't be able to stay in Vegas. They'll try to put me down, and my instinct will be to fight them. I don't want to fight my own pack."

"You won't have to, I promise. If you wish it, I'll help you."

"No, Kadim." She hiccupped, her vision blurring again. "Something like this was bound to happen, since I haven't shifted in five years. I'm going to cancel our bet. You didn't cause this, so you don't have anything to worry about with the pack. They won't blame you; in fact, they'll probably accept you. My brother needs a strong second. You're a good fighter, and you bring in money for the casino. You're worth your weight in platinum."

His dark gaze seemed to burn with an inner fire. "And you are more precious than rubies."

"No, I'm the pack fuck-up, one step away from omega." She looked at her arms, tried and failed again to shift. A bubble of hysteria made her shiver. "Actually, I'd say this wins me the position paws down."

"Simone." The growl in his voice forced her to focus on him and not the pain numbing her senses. "Wish yourself into my care, please? Just wish it."

She sighed, her eyes sliding shut. Why not? Hoping and praying and concentrating hadn't brought on her Change. All she had left were her wishes. If Kadim needed those in order to help her, so be it.

"All right," she whispered against his chest, her energy gone. "I wish… I wish you could help me."

Chapter Four

Kadim stared down at the woman sleeping soundly in his bed. She looked the way he'd imagined, as if she belonged there with her coppery skin and dark hair beautiful against the gold of the silk sheets.

He'd been trying for the better part of a year to get closer to her, to unravel her mysteries, only to have her reveal them all in one bloody, emotional hour.

Simone had defended him as fiercely as if he'd belonged to her pack, as if he meant something to her. And she'd truly believed that he'd be accepted into her pack while they ostracized her.

As if he could be content without her, when she was the reason he'd come to Vegas in the first place.

With a wave of his hand, he refilled the brazier of loose incense beside the bed. The fragrance had helped recharge him, and in turn allowed him to help her; to smooth her transformed arms and legs back into their human shape. She'd slept through it all, for which he was grateful. She'd have questions enough when she awakened.

She was right about one thing, though. Their bet was off. He'd wanted more time before giving her his last confession, but he no longer had the luxury of time. She'd seen his true form; she now knew he wasn't a Were. He had to tell her everything, but how would she handle the truth? Would all his careful strategizing come to nothing, like a house of cards?

No. He hadn't come this far, planned this carefully, to lose her now. Not now, when he needed her even more than he had when she'd first arrived. Not now, when his very existence depended on her making the right decision.

No sense in putting off the inevitable. Expelling a breath, he leaned over to stroke the back of his hand down her cheek. "Simone. Wake up, Simone."

She blinked slowly in response before her dark lashes swept up, her gaze finding him. "Kadim." She took a deep breath. "Is that wolfsbane I smell?"

"It's a special healing incense," he explained, searching her face, wondering when the pointed questions would start, and how he'd answer them. "Besides the wolfsbane, there's dragons blood and nag champa, among other things."

A smile bowed her lips as she inhaled again. "I'm going to have to tell Claire to order some. One of the shops at the hotel really needs to stock some of that. Much better than drinking wolfsbane tea for rough Changes, that's for sure."

She stiffened suddenly, her eyes again finding his. "Healing? Am I okay, then?"

When he nodded, she pulled her hands free of the gold silk sheet, holding them up in the candlelight. Both arms had reverted to their normal toffee-almond color; her fingers their usual length and not elongated claws. He'd even healed the bite wounds on her wrist and shoulder. Like she'd said earlier, it was a good thing she was already a Were, because he wouldn't have been able to stop the lycanthrope virus from infecting her. Even he had his limits.

A gasp escaped her lips as she threw back the sheet, revealing her bare body. Her beautiful shapely legs stretched along the bed, with the knees bent the proper way for a human and completely fur free.

"You fixed me." Her smile spread like cozy heat through his insides. "You actually fixed me."

Before he could answer her, she rose to her knees to throw her arms around his neck. Laughter bubbled from her as she scattered exuberant kisses across his face in enthusiastic thanks. Despite knowing that he shouldn't, Kadim dragged her close, needing to feel her skin against his. The soft warmth of her naked body pressed against his, causing an immediate and unmistakable reaction.

Her kisses began to slow, to change, until she lingered over his mouth. When she pulled back, he instantly released her and opened his eyes, apology ready.

She stared up at him, her eyes dark with something far from upset. "Why aren't you kissing me back?"

He ground his teeth as her left hand pushed open his robe to lightly stroke his chest. "You were thanking me," he managed to say. "I didn't want to take advantage."

Smiling, she pressed closer, brushing her belly against his erection. "You're not taking advantage. You bested a rival, won a challenge. That means you get a chance to mate with me, if I want. And I very much want. Don't you?"

"Months," he said, as she pushed his robe off his shoulders. "I've been wanting you for months."

"Then let's not waste any more time, okay?" she asked, wrapping her fingers around his erection. He took a deep shuddering breath as she stroked him, causing him to thicken in her hand.

"Make love to me, Kadim," she whispered against his lips, her voice urgent, hypnotic. "Let everything else wait for a while."

Growling, he threaded a hand into her hair, keeping her in place as he took over the kiss. He pushed his tongue against her lips, needing to taste her. She responded eagerly, parting her lips so that their tongues slid together. One of them groaned.

He slid a hand down her spine, giving in to the urge to stroke the satin of her skin. She moaned in response, hot and open against his mouth. When she shifted against his erection again, his brain short-circuited.

Simone felt a change in him, as if a switch had been thrown. His fingers sent tendrils of heat sparking through her as his hands slid up her body to cup her breasts. She moaned into his mouth again as the pads of his thumbs brushed across her nipples. "Where are your condoms?"

"What? Oh, of course." He waved a hand toward the intricately carved nightstand beside the bed. The drawer opened, revealing a box of condoms.

"Neat trick," she murmured, sliding away from him to get the box, open it.

"I have more," he offered.

"I don't doubt that for a minute. Let me show you one of mine." Sitting on the edge of the bed so that her knees flanked his, she tore open a foil packet, removed the condom. His entire body tensed as she reached out, wrapped her fingers around him. She stroked him with gentle pressure, enjoying the hot, hard feel of him.

"Simone…" his voice held a definite note of warning.

Taking her time, she unrolled the condom onto his erection, teasing herself as much as she teased him. Anticipation puckered her nipples as she stood; needing to press her body against his again, press her mouth to his again.

His hands immediately slid down her back to cup her butt as his mouth slanted over hers. Every nerve ending in her body flared to sensual life. She had to have him.

"No more games, Simone," he said, his breathing harsh against her neck. She could hear his heart pounding, sending blood into the thick hardness pressed against her belly. "Do you want this? Do you want me?"

"Kadim." She pushed against him, straining upwards. So close, so very close…

He pulled away, and she nearly howled in protest. "I want to hear you say it."

She'd say she was the Queen of England if it would get him inside her. But she knew what he meant. Cupping his face in her hands, she stared unblinkingly into his eyes. "Months," she growled, repeating his words. "I've been wanting you for months."

"Turn around," he demanded, his voice hoarse with barely restrained desire. "On your knees. Now."

The desire boiling in him, a perfect counterpoint to her own, made her hot. She dropped to all fours on the bed, and then turned, waiting. She needed this, needed him wild, demanding, dominant.

His hands wrapped around her hips, dragging her to the edge of the bed. She shivered as she felt his fingers glide over her skin and between her thighs, testing her readiness. After everything that had happened, she was more than ready, and pushed against his hand in blatant hinting.

He removed his fingers, and then she felt it, felt the thick head of his penis pushing between her thighs, sliding. Rubbing along her lips. Widening her stance, she angled her hips, eager for him to fit them together. With one short, sharp thrust, he did.

"By the flames of a thousand fires, woman," he exclaimed. "You feel incredible."

"So do—yes." Air left her lungs as he pulled back slowly and just as slowly reentered her, fully this time, burying himself deep.

"Kadim." Heat pierced her body as she dug her hands into the bedcovers. It had been too long, but this was worth the wait. He was worth the wait. "Again. Just like that—God."

She shuddered as his hands burned a path down her back to capture her waist. He rocked against her, again leaving her breathless. Sweat broke through her skin as he settled into a maddening, driving rhythm that stoked the pleasure into a roaring flame. God, it had never been like this. She'd never been filled like this, taken like this, enflamed like this.

He shifted behind her, a slightly different angle. One moment she burned with pleasure, the next she exploded, tossing her head back with a howl as ecstasy flared like a sun through her system.

Before she could catch her breath, he turned her onto her back, and then entered her again. Her eyes flew open as he wrapped his arms around her waist and lifted her against him, mouth seeking her breast.

Her hands roamed his back before her nails scored his skin, needing some way to hold on, to anchor to reality. He hissed in pure male appreciation, his thrusts quickening. Thrilled, she ran her tongue along the side of his neck, taking his taste into her mouth, smelling the spicy scent of him, the blood pounding just beneath his skin. So delicious, so tempting.

"Yes," he whispered, pressing her into the mattress, thrusting faster. "Mark me, sweetness. Just before you come, do it."

"Kadim." She stumbled over his name. "Harder." She wrapped her legs high around his waist, driving him further inside her. Her breath caught on a sudden eruption of pleasure, her nails digging into his back as her teeth closed over the side of his neck.

Kadim's entire body shuddered in response as he thrust into her wildly, his body burning beneath her hands. He cried out something guttural and foreign as he came. She broke her hold on his neck and fastened her mouth to his in a bruising, almost vicious kiss as he continued driving into her. His final rolling thrust sent her over the edge again, screaming this time, as wave after wave of orgasmic pleasure burned her alive.

They collapsed against the mattress, breathless. After a few heartbeats, Kadim turned so that Simone lay atop him. She could still feel him deep inside, and her muscles clenched in response. She echoed his groan as his hands clutched her buttocks in pure reflex, grinding her pelvis against his as if he had to get every last sensation he could from their pleasure.

Simone closed her eyes in languid surrender, listening to the frantic pounding of Kadim's heart. So much had happened in the last few hours. It was almost too much to comprehend. She never would have thought when she'd left the casino that she would end up lying in Kadim's bed, with him still inside her, thinking she was half in love with him.

She lifted her head slowly, to stare down at him. Sparks glittered in his eyes like tiny embers as he returned her gaze. "Simone?"

For a moment, words failed her. Stalling, she lightly traced his beautiful lips with her fingertips. "I'm here. I think."

He smiled against her hand. "Yeah. Me, too."

Lowering her lashes to hide her expression, she lowered her head, brushing his lips with hers. His hips flexed against her, letting her know that his erection hadn't eased in the slightest.

"We should stop," he whispered, his mouth brushing against hers as he slowly drew out of her and just as slowly pushed back in. "But I need more of you. Do you want me to stop, Simone?"

"No. Oh, yes," she hissed, gripping his shoulders as heat curled around her. God, the man knew just what to do. "I wish you would keep doing that."

He laughed, his voice warming every intimate place inside her. "As you wish."

Withdrawing, he spilled her onto her side. She heard the drawer open, the sound of a new condom being unwrapped. Then, he curved in behind her. She shifted to help guide him inside, aching for that beautiful fullness again. She pressed back against him as he rocked into her with slow, sensual intent.

His left arm curved under her to cup her breast; his right hand entwined with hers to slide between her thighs. "Show me how you like it, Simone," he whispered in her ear. "Show me what makes you feel good."

She shuddered as their fingers worked in unison, making softly pressured circles. "You were doing a damn good job without my help," she gasped as currents of pleasure flooded her senses again. Heat swamped her, driven by his lips moving across her shoulders, the top of her spine, her neck. She'd have a matching love bite soon, and she reveled in it.

He whispered to her in that foreign language again, sounds that were almost familiar to her pleasure-scrambled brain. Maybe he'd chanted while she slept. She found herself responding to those words, warming beneath his hands, his mouth, his fingers. "Kadim."

"I'm here," he answered, his words strained. "I'm right here with you."

Desire coiled inside her, the familiar pressure spiraling tighter. How many times could he give this to her before her senses simply overloaded? "Hurry, God, you have to hurry."

With a thrust of his hips, he pushed her flat against the mattress, their hands caught beneath her. She turned her head enough to breathe, lifted her hips enough to hold him inside her. His knees pressed into the mattress as he increased his pace until their bodies slapped together. She guided his hands, those wonderful hands, faster and faster, gasping for breath as her whole body tightened. "Now, Kadim!" she screamed as her body clamped down on him.

He slammed into her again, and then froze, his entire body stiffening above her, inside her. He cried out, and she felt him come, felt him deep inside her most secret place. She knew then that the love bite on her neck wasn't the only mark Kadim would leave on her.

Deep inside, in that most secret place, she knew she'd never again be the woman who'd driven up the mountain to see him. Whether that would make her stronger or break her forever, she didn't yet know.

Chapter Five

"**I** owe you an apology."

Kadim looked up in surprise. Simone sat opposite him at the dining table, dressed in a pale pink tracksuit and sneakers she'd had in her car. With her face freshly scrubbed and hair slicked back from her shower, she looked all of twenty, though he knew she was at least four times that.

"What do you think you need to apologize for?" he asked, noticing that she'd eaten very little of her blood rare steak. Not that he had much of an appetite himself, despite their energetic love-making.

"Hudgens." She drew her knees up, wrapping her arms around them. "I had a confrontation with him at the hotel, but I didn't think he'd follow me. I didn't think he'd try... that he would...."

"It doesn't matter," he interrupted, pushing his plate away. "He's no longer a threat to you or your pack."

"Thanks to you." She looked at him, her eyes shiny. "Thanks to what you did. What, what are you?"

The question, at last. Taking a deep breath, he pushed to his feet, and then held a hand out to her. "Will you come sit with me by the fire? I have a lot to tell you."

Her expression shuttered with caution. "I suppose, considering we just lived through a life or death experience and mind-blowing sex, we should be truthful with each other."

She slipped her hand into his, allowing him to pull her to her feet. He kept his fingers wrapped loosely about hers, grateful for the contact, the implied trust. Remembering how quickly she could shift, he knew he couldn't relax completely just yet.

"I don't have anything to hide from you, Simone," he said, leading her to the leather couch in front of the fireplace. "Not anymore."

"Obviously, given that you've shown me that you can change into a wolf," she observed, picking a spot on the couch that left her plenty of maneuvering room, he noticed. "And let's not forget the whole human torch thing, and how you were able to… to burn them like that."

Kadim removed the fireplace cover and took his time selecting another log for the small fire he'd started as she'd showered. It was completely unnecessary, even with the cool night air flowing off the mountain and through the open windows, but he'd needed something to do after retrieving her bag from her car.

"I'm sorry you had to see that," he said, knowing she wanted him to say something. "But I won't apologize for what I did."

"I don't expect you to," she said, surprising him. "I know it was necessary. I just… I've never seen anything like that before. Like you."

She took a deep breath. "What are you? I know you're not a Were. And you don't smell like any of the vampires I know. Besides, I don't know any vamp who can turn into a wolf."

Kadim replaced the grate, then stood, dusting his hands off against the legs of his jeans. The night was half over, but he didn't feel tired. Instead, he felt on edge. Too much depended on Simone, and he didn't like relinquishing control. Not after he'd fought so hard to get it in the first place.

"You're right. I'm not a were or a vampire. By the way, some of the older ones can change into a wolf. As for myself, I can change into any animal I choose, but I prefer a panther or a wolf."

"That just tells me what you're not," she pointed out. "You smell of exotic spices, or a good fire on a cold night. Are you going to tell me or not?"

He forced his shoulders to relax. "If you ask me a third time, I'll tell you."

"Fine. Tell me straight up," she said, her voice flat. "What the hell are you?"

"We come to my third confession." He felt something inside him loosen. His ability to lie to her, he supposed. "I'm one of the Djinn."

"Djinn." Simone sat back against the chocolate brown leather. "Magician, I'm starting to think that you're a card short of a full deck, but maybe I'm the one hallucinating. Maybe I'm in my car in a tangled mess at the base of the mountain. There's no such thing as Djinn."

He didn't find her words or the picture they painted amusing. "You're a werewolf," he felt compelled to remind her. "You aren't supposed to exist either."

"Duly noted." She stared at him with rounded eyes. "You're really a genie?"

"A question thrice asked receives truth," he said. "Djinn are as real as vamps or Weres. Didn't you wonder how I could do those more amazing tricks?"

"I just assumed you were a master of misdirection and sleight of hand."

"I am," he said. "For the most part, my show is mundane in the sense that I use all the tools that human magicians have. Occasionally, I enhance my act with Djinn magic."

"Djinn magic," she repeated, as if tasting the words. "Trickster spirits. Fables from a simpler time to caution simpler folk."

"I am no fable," Kadim told her, beginning to wonder if he'd overdone it with the wolfsbane. "My people were born of the smokeless fires of creation, after angels but before humans. We live, love, and die just as humans and meta-humans do, only not in this world. The Djinn live between."

"Between. You mean like another existence?"

He nodded, taking a cautious step closer. "Djinn can see into this world, but this world cannot see the Djinn. Sometimes we can pass through to this world, though not always with the best of intentions. There have been a handful of humans, sorcerers, who have known of our existence and have attempted to capture us in order to harness our magic for their own ends."

"That's where the whole 'genie in a bottle' thing comes from, I take it?"

Kadim nodded again, his eyes fastened to her face, trying to gauge her reaction. "Some Djinn have been careless over the centuries, drawn to this world like moths to the flame. Still others have allowed themselves to be captured because they want diversion. Humanity provides endless entertainment, simply because they are so easily swayed by empty promises and their own greed."

Simone tilted her head, clearly assessing him. "And your deal is?"

He looked away. "I was curious, and my curiosity made me careless."

She snorted. "You don't really expect me to believe that, do you?"

"It's the truth."

"It's not all of the truth though, is it?" she asked, and he could hear the anger slicing through her words. "You're obviously free now. Free to indulge your curiosity and experience a little diversion. So you chose me."

Okay, she'd obviously moved from acceptance to anger. "That's not why I chose you."

Simone allowed her anger to push her to her feet. Anger felt good, better than the confusion, better than the scary half-formed feelings of tenderness toward this man she suddenly didn't know. "Right. You were hoping that my greed would get the better of me, that I'd do anything you wanted to get that Mystery Channel contract signed."

He didn't answer, and the emotional direct hit stung. She took a faltering breath. "But what you didn't realize is that my wanting the deal had nothing to do with greed. It never did."

"I know." He looked away. "You wanted it for your pack."

"I wanted it for security," she informed him, fighting to keep her voice under control. "I wanted it to keep my place in my family."

He turned towards her. "I could give you those things, if you wish it."

"No." She shook her head. "I don't want you to grant me any wishes. I don't think I could afford them."

She looked away, toward the hills. What would she wish for? Hadn't she stared up at the night sky countless times, wishing that wishes could come true? Wishing that there were a way to make the pack safe that didn't involve her brother fighting or her entering a political marriage? Wishing that she could be a full contributing member of her pack, and not just a step away from omega?

She paced a few steps away from him, struggling to wrap her mind around everything he'd told her, everything she'd learned. Everything they'd done. She could accept that he was a genie because she simply didn't know what else he could be. But she was having a hard time with the trickster part. "Tell me honestly, what would you really have demanded, had my greed cost me the bet?"

"Your hand."

She stopped in mid-stride, looking back over her shoulder at him. "What?"

"I would have demanded your hand. In marriage."

Simone spun to face him, shocked. He'd said he wanted her, but she'd just assumed he'd meant sex. "You wanted to trick me into marrying you? Why?"

His expression grew uncomfortable. "I want to live here."

"Isn't that what you've been doing for the past year?" she asked, settling her hands on her hips. "Or is this place part of the trick, too?"

"This place is just what I told you, a retreat," he said, his words earnest. "And it hasn't been a full year yet."

She felt a frown wrinkling her forehead and forced herself to stop. "You have a time limit or something?"

"I've been in hiding from my former master. An accident freed me, and I took full advantage. However, he's not the sort of man who likes to lose—possessions, contests, or face. My escape cost him all three, and I have no doubt that he will do everything in his power to find me and bind me again."

Something in his words, the way he said them, made Simone shiver. "So you came to Vegas to disappear."

"As so many have done."

"Except you decided to hide in plain sight by being a world famous magician," she pointed out. "A Djinn masquerading as a human magician. Doesn't that seem the least bit suicidal to you?"

"I'm Djinn," he reminded her, a smile curving his lips. "It's what I do."

"It's what you do." She felt herself growing angry again. "You've made yourself a target, that's what you've done. You might as well have painted a freakin' bull's-eye on the hotel!"

"You and your people aren't in any danger, Simone, I promise," he said, stepping closer to her. "I've done everything to cover my trail. My name and my appearance are different from when I was bound."

Another trick. "Is nothing that I know about you real?" she asked, hating the plaintive sound in her voice. Hating what he was making her feel.

"You saw my true form out in the forest," he said gently. "And Kadim is a name that I chose for my new self, for my new life here."

He reached out, and she was unsettled enough, undecided enough, that she let him wrap his hands about hers, pull her closer. "Being in hiding is the only reason I refused to tape the special, Simone," he said then. "Trying to trick the cameras as well as the human audience would require too much magic. I have no doubt that my former master has been waiting for just such a magical spike. Unfortunately, fighting and disposing of Hudgens and his men did just that."

"So you think your former master will come looking for you?" Simone's stomach tightened with guilt. He'd revealed himself because of her.

"I know he will," Kadim said, his voice sobering. "And when he finds me, he'll try to bind me again."

Her hands tightened in his. "Can you stop him?"

"I can, with your help."

"My help? I only have Were magic. How am I supposed to keep this guy from binding you again?"

"By marrying me."

She blinked at him. "You're actually serious? Even now, you still want to do this?"

"Marriage bonds are strong, no matter the species." He paused. "Well, maybe humans don't revere it as much as they used to, but the concept is still there. Djinn fall in love and marry and reproduce as well. Because we can be bound against our will, we place a greater value on bonds made freely, bonds made for marriage."

Simone pulled away, her mind whirling. She'd been thinking about marriage, but not to Kadim. She thought she'd have to marry for power, for the pack. For protection. Marrying a non-Were—a Djinn!—had never crossed her mind. If she married Kadim, he'd be safe, but what about her? What about her family?

She faced him, wanting to see his eyes, see his intent clearly. "You want to marry me for a metaphysical green card."

His expression blanked. "If you want to call it that, then yes."

Well. She certainly didn't harbor any fantasies that they'd marry for love, but he didn't have to make it seem so cold. "Why don't I just bind you instead?" she asked, trying to sound reasonable even as she said the words. "That's all it will really take, right? This guy can't bind you if you're bound to someone else. I could just say the words or make a wish, and it'd be done."

His dark eyes remained steady on her face. "You could, if you knew the spell," he admitted. "Would you do that, Simone? Bind me so that I'd be powerless except by your will, instead of equal partners in a marriage? Would you enslave me, do to me what was done to your parents?"

She blinked as sudden, frustrated tears crystallized her vision. She'd had enough horror stories from her parents about slavery to automatically reject the idea. "The human in me wouldn't, but the wolf will do anything to protect the pack. It's survival instinct."

"It's the same for me."

"Why didn't you just ask me?" she wondered. "After nearly a

year of dinners and conversation, why didn't you just ask me straight out to marry you?"

A half-smile crooked his lips. "Because you would have refused me," he answered, simply. "You wouldn't have chosen me on my own merits, even knowing I'm a Djinn."

"That's not true!" she exclaimed, stung by his soft accusation. She wanted to think that she'd have said yes to him in any other situation but this. But hadn't she dismissed the idea of being lovers, simply because he wasn't Were?

"Are you sure about that?" he retorted, his anger flaring. "You were considering giving yourself to a rival pack leader to protect your pack, simply because he was a wolf. Do you not think me capable of making the same contribution, even though I am not a Were?"

After what she'd seen earlier, she knew he was more than capable. He'd helped her fight her enemies, helped her heal. He'd claimed her as a wolf suitor would have, and better. By wolf logic, they were already mated. It was her stupid human side that had to nitpick everything.

Apparently, she'd been silent too long. He strode toward her, his brows lowering. "Fine, you need convincing? Perhaps this will convince you."

At the snap of his fingers, a document appeared on the coffee table. She recognized the contract she'd stuffed into her purse before leaving the hotel. Another snap of his fingers, and a pen appeared in his free hand. Before she could speak, he bent, scrawling his signature across the bottom of the last page. "Here."

She didn't reach for the contract. "I want a ring."

"What?"

"No one's going to believe I got engaged if I don't have a ring," she explained, wrapping her arms around her waist. "I'm already going to be hard-pressed to convince my parents that we had a whirlwind courtship. They probably assumed I'd try to catch a beta's eye in order to back up my brother, if I didn't marry for love."

He focused on her face, his eyes searching hers. "You're agreeing to marry me. Even though you already have what you want?"

"If I marry you, I'm off-market," she said, amazed at how cold and rational her voice sounded. Her wolf logic had made the decision easy. "You get your Djinn free pass, and my pack gains a powerful ally."

His expression drained to nothing. "Are you trying to trick me?"

"Me, trick the master of deception?" She gave a half-laugh. "That's rich, coming from you. No, I'm not trying to trick you. I'm just being pragmatic. We each have something the other wants. We can protect each other. It makes sense for us to approach this as a business deal between friends, a business deal with bonuses."

"Bonuses." He made the word sound distasteful.

"Yeah." She looked away. "We're going to be engaged. Once we spread the story of a whirlwind courtship, people will expect us to continue to sleep together."

He snorted. "Heaven forbid we should disappoint them."

She winced, but didn't back down. "We were friends before we got physical, we can still be friends now. And lovers."

"And husband and wife."

"And husband and wife," she repeated, managing not to stumble over the words. "Just because this isn't about love doesn't mean we should ignore the fact that we're good in bed together. A lot of marriages don't start this well."

"Then I suppose we should make this official." He reached into his pocket, withdrew a navy velvet box. A box Simone knew hadn't been there before, since she'd watched him pull the pants out of a dresser drawer.

He stepped closer to her, opening the box before turning it toward her. Nestled on the dark blue velvet was a princess-cut diamond, perched atop a simple platinum band. Simple and elegant, except for the fact that the flawless stone was easily three carats and gleamed like a searchlight.

"It's beautiful," she said, feeling as if she should say something. It looked real, but then a lot of things in Vegas looked real, if you chose not to examine them too closely.

Double Down

"I'll be as real to you as this ring is," he said, pulling the ring free of the box. "No more tricks between us, no more games. Will you marry me, Simone?"

She looked up into his solemn face, and gave the only answer she could. "Yes."

Something flickered in his eyes. Relief? Joy? She had no clue, and she didn't want to ask. No more tricks probably also meant no more lies, and she didn't want the truth of his answer just then.

"There's just one thing," she said as he slipped the ring over the tip of her finger.

His hand stopped, his eyes boring into hers. "What thing is that?"

"Cheat on me, and I'll rip your throat out."

The smile he gave her almost made her forget he wasn't a wolf. "Glad to hear it. As long as you realize I feel the same way."

He pushed the ring home. The diamond sparkled on her hand like the most brilliant of lies.

Awkward silence fell. Simone tried not to look at her hand, tried not to think about how heavy it suddenly felt. Was she supposed to hug and kiss him, or shake hands and say thank you? Things were a lot more complicated than they'd been when she'd awakened earlier.

"There's no way I can make it back to the hotel tonight," she said then. "It's been a long trip of a night, and I can't face my parents until I've had a good night's sleep."

"Of course." He stepped away from her. "There's a guest room just down the hall, a bathroom across from it." He headed for the dining table.

"Uh, Kadim?"

He turned, his expression polite and non-committal. She missed the sparks in his eyes. A few hours into being intimately involved with her, and he'd already lost his smile.

Inexplicably feeling near tears, she tried to lighten the mood. "You don't really expect me to sleep in the guest bedroom?"

"I don't know what to expect with you, Simone," he said. "You are the most unpredictable woman I've ever met. It's much safer to never assume anything about you."

"Thank you, I think." She stepped closer to him, pulling down the zipper on her jacket. She wanted to feel his arms around her, feel his warmth surround her again.

"Stop." He settled his hands on her shoulders, preventing her from removing the jacket. "There's no one here for you to keep up appearances for."

It would have been too easy for her to be hurt by his words or think that he was refusing her, but she could hear the pounding of his blood, hear his heart rate increase. He still wanted her, and that knowledge gave her courage. "To hell with appearances. I have no intention of giving up those silk sheets of yours. Or anything else of yours, for that matter."

There. Desire rekindled the sparks deep in his gaze. He scooped her into his arms, began climbing the stairs. "As my lady commands."

Chapter Six

"So you're a Djinni, and you want to marry our daughter."

Simone sat next to Kadim on the couch in her father's office, trying not to tense up under her father's scrutiny. She shifted closer to Kadim, forcing herself to relax into the crook of his shoulder. She couldn't feel any tension in him, couldn't scent any unease. How could he be so calm when her brother and parents were sizing him up as a possible hunt?

Her parents sat beside each other on a plush brocade couch the color of dried blood, Malcolm standing behind them. They'd been silent as she'd told them everything that had happened the previous night, including the fact that Kadim was Djinn. Almost everything, that is. There were some things she wouldn't share with her relatives, like how many orgasms she'd had in twenty-four hours.

"I do, sir," Kadim said, holding her father's gaze for a heartbeat longer than necessary or prudent. "I want that very much."

"Why?" Malcolm said from his place behind their parents. "You're already making bank on your stage show alone. You can't inherit Simone's part of the hotel. If she dies, it goes to the pack."

"He doesn't care about the hotel," Simone interjected, not liking the way they were ganging up on him. She wondered where Solange was, or Laurel for that matter. Then again, this was core family business. Laurel didn't think much of her anyway, and Simone didn't want her best friend witnessing her getting chewed out.

Simone, Kadim's voice circled through her mind. *It's all right.*

No it isn't, she retorted, not even questioning him projecting his thoughts into her mind. It wasn't the same as being a mind reader, not really. If he knew what she was really thinking, really feeling—well, not only would he know more than she knew herself, he'd probably be on the first express to Djinn-land.

His fingers reached out, wrapped around hers. *It will be all right, Simone. Trust me.* His thoughts were as warm as his voice, she realized, and forced herself to relax.

"She's right," Kadim said, his voice like warm honey. "I don't want a part of the French Quarter, other than to continue my show. I'm more than happy to sign a pre-nuptial agreement to that effect."

"So you'd leave my daughter wanting?" her father wondered, the mildness of his tone belying the fierceness of his expression. Malcolm had inherited more than looks from their father. Simone knew her father planned to spend a great deal of his retirement hunting in Alaska. On all fours.

"Not at all." Kadim glanced at her, his dark eyes solemn. "Simone knows that she could have anything she wishes for. Within reason, anyway. There are some wishes even I cannot grant."

Simone swallowed, trying to breathe around the lump in her throat. The change in his tone sounded sad to her. Why would Kadim be sad, when she'd agreed to everything he'd wanted?

Her mother shifted on the couch, drawing her attention. "I'd like to ask you a question, Kadim, if I may."

Kadim straightened. "Yes, ma'am?"

"Why would a Djinn want to marry a werewolf? For that matter, out of all the female Weres in the hotel, why choose our daughter?"

Simone watched a smile brighten Kadim's face. "You'd do better to ask me how could I not choose her. She wasn't the first wolf I saw. But I saw no one else once I saw her."

His voice dropped as he lifted their entwined hands, captured her gaze. "I remember how you walked across the casino floor, outshining every game, every light. I remember how soft your eyes were when you looked at me, the way you smiled at me even though I was just one person out of hundreds you'd passed. I saw the fire inside you, and I wanted it. I wanted you."

"Kadim," she began, and then stopped, unable to speak past the sudden tightness in her throat. He sounded sincere, so sincere that she wanted to believe him. God, she needed to believe the slow and steady pounding of his heart, his bluntly eloquent words. But the master trickster was just saying these things to convince her parents, not because he meant them, right? Then why couldn't she smell his lie?

He squeezed her fingers, lightly, and then looked back to her family. "I meant no disrespect by concealing my true nature from you," he said, his voice clear. "And once I fell for Simone, I wanted her to want me as a man, not a Djinn. She showed me just that, when she faced down Hudgens and his men in the woods. I will be a good partner for her. I will protect her as she will protect me. The Temple pack will become my family, and I agree to be ruled by the laws of the pack."

Malcolm, of course, snorted his disbelief, but Simone knew if she couldn't scent Kadim's falsity, neither could they. Her father sat back against the sofa cushions, his expression polite. Then he turned to her mother. "Essie?"

Esther Temple nodded, her hand resting lightly on her husband's knee. "Simone, what do you say to Kadim's words?"

She rose, keeping his hand tangled in hers. "Kadim doesn't have to prove his words to me," she declared, determined to speak nothing but truth. "He defended me against Hudgens. Healed me when I got stuck between. Claimed me in the way of the wolf. He's done everything one mate would do for the other."

She turned slightly, catching his gaze. "He's the most amazing man I've ever known. I couldn't ask for more in a mate."

"Except a wolf," Malcolm pointed out.

"He's better than a wolf," Simone retorted on a snarl. "And if you'd take the stick out of your ass, you'd realize that."

"Simone." Kadim's voice slid over her skin, but it was his laughter in her mind, warm and luxurious as a hot shower, that truly warmed her. Without another word, she sat beside him, curling into his natural heat. She smoothed down the skirt of her bronze silk halter dress, remembering how Kadim had conjured it for her after she'd frantically ransacked his closets looking for something to wear to this all-important meeting. It reminded her of his silk sheets, and the magic they'd made in his bed. The dress had been a deliberate choice on his part, no doubt.

Feeling a sudden increase in heat, she looked up to find him watching her. *You know exactly what I'm thinking about, don't you?*

I see your hand stroking your skirt, and I'm reminded of other things your hand has stroked. His thoughts simmered in her mind. *I was simply hoping you were thinking what I'm thinking.*

Heat suffused her cheeks, and she had to drop her head to hide it. This would work, she thought. With this much sexual energy between them, she could make him forget that he'd decided to marry her out of necessity.

He stiffened beside her, a heartbeat before her father cleared his throat. "I think I've heard—and seen—enough," Julius Temple said, rising to his feet. "Welcome to the family, son."

Kadim rose to his feet, and clasped her father's outstretched hand. "Thank you, sir. It's an honor."

Malcolm edged his way around the couch. "I want to thank you for taking care of Hudgens," he said to Kadim. "If I'd known what he'd planned, he wouldn't have left the building alive. And I like that you have no qualms about protecting and defending my sister. You extend that to the pack, you'll be a welcome addition."

"I can and I will." They locked hands and eyes, longer than necessary. Then Kadim dropped his eyes, and Simone breathed a sigh of relief. Challenging the alpha-in-waiting wasn't the way to get on the family's good side, but Kadim owed Malcolm for those digs.

"So," her mother slid forward on the couch, capturing her attention. "I think it will be perfect to announce your upcoming nuptials at the party at the end of the week. Do you want Vera or someone else to design your gown?"

"Gown?" Simone's hand fluttered upward, tucked a nonexistent stray lock of hair behind her ear. "As in wedding gown?"

"Of course, dear," her mother said. "This will be the event of the year, one of the Temple children finally getting married. We'll have to do it up right."

Simone swallowed, looked to Kadim. She knew he wanted the deed done sooner rather than later, but she hadn't said no to her mother in the last hundred years. It would be a hard habit to break, if her mother didn't break her first. "We were hoping for a simple ceremony."

"Even if it's just the pack at the ceremony, there won't be anything simple about it," Julius said. "I know it's your day, sweetheart, but it's an even bigger day for the standing of our pack. We'll have to invite the who's who of the Were community, whether that's to the wedding or only to the reception afterwards."

Simone bit her lip. Like every other girl child, she'd dreamed of having an elaborate wedding, complete with a ridiculously expensive and ornamental gown. That was years—decades—ago, though, before the political responsibilities of being the Temple Pack heiress began to weigh on her.

Kadim put his hand on her shoulder. "I wouldn't be opposed to a fairytale wedding, should you want it. Wedding celebrations among my people can last more than a week."

Simone almost snorted. Fairytale wedding, indeed. She could see the laughter in her trickster fiancé's eyes. Though she supposed marrying one of the Djinn was as close to a fairytale as she would get.

"There's no harm in doing this up right," Malcolm said. "The lawyers are going to want to take their time on the pre-nups as it is. Besides, it's not like you two are waiting for a preacher's blessing before doing the deed. Your scents are all over each other."

Simone jumped to her feet. "Well, at least I've got someone's scent all over me!"

"Kids." Esther rose as well, smiling at Kadim. "Are you sure you want to marry into this?"

"Absolutely."

"Then welcome to the family, crazy as it is."

Simone watched Kadim's face as her mother hugged him. He looked happy.

Her heart gave a little trip. Kadim was going to be her husband. They were going to spend the rest of their lives together, and she had no clue how long that would be. As a born Were she had another two centuries or so before she hit old age. What was the lifespan for a creature of pure magic and fire?

Not only that, but also what were their children going to be? Could they even have children? What the hell had she gotten herself into?

Kadim looked up as Simone made a sound close to a sob. The panicked expression on her face tore at him. "Simone?"

"Great, here come the waterworks," Malcolm said to no one in particular. "Good thing I have a business meeting to go to." He beat a hasty retreat.

Kadim ignored everyone but Simone. She looked ready to bolt. What had she been thinking of to bring that expression to her face? "What is it, sweetheart?"

"I'm sorry, I'm just—I'm just—" She took a deep breath. "I need to get you alone."

He knew she didn't mean it as suggestively as it sounded, but her parents obviously didn't. "Go on, kids," Julius said, wrapping an arm about his wife. "Just don't let your alone time affect the business. We've still got a hotel to run."

"Julius," Simone's mother admonished her husband lightly, but her eyes were concerned.

Simone mumbled something, and then headed for the door. Kadim turned to her parents. "Thank you so much for your blessing. It means the world to me."

He followed after her as she headed to the private elevator. "I'm sorry, Simone."

She pressed the call button. "What are you apologizing for?"

"I don't know," he answered honestly. "It seemed like a good idea."

She gave a sniffling laugh as the elevator opened. "I'm the one who should be apologizing," she said, stepping into the car. "I didn't mean to flip out at the end like that."

He followed her into the elevator car, pulling her into his arms as the brushed steel doors closed. "Talk to me."

"I'm fine, really. It's just… it was easier to handle all of this when I thought we'd have a quick Vegas wedding. Inviting high Were society and turning it into a major event, I realized how important this is to my family and my pack. Then I started thinking about how I'd be married to you for the rest of my life, and how long that is for me, and then I realized I don't even know how long you live."

She looked up at him, her dark eyes shiny with tears. "I don't know you. You're not the person I've had dinner with for the last year. He doesn't really exist."

"He does exist," he insisted, tightening his grip, suddenly afraid that if he let go, he'd lose her. "I am Kadim, the magician. I'm still the man you revealed pieces of yourself to like precious treasure over the past year. I'm the Djinni that will kill anyone who tries to harm you or your pack, the Djinni who will give you whatever you wish for. I'm the man eager to discover everything that makes you sing with pleasure. You know me, Simone, in all the ways that matter."

"Kadim." She pressed her face into his shoulder, and he sighed as her arms tightened around him, grateful that she didn't push him away.

He whispered his true name into her hair. "I signed the contract with that name, and I'll sign our marriage papers with that name as well," he said. "Everyone else will see Kadim, but I'll always be true with you."

She pulled back, staring into his eyes. He wanted to tell her that he loved her and that he'd meant every word he'd spoken to her parents. The words flared inside him but he held them back, doubting that she'd believe him.

Her hand reached up, cupping his cheek. "Kiss me, please."

He complied instantly, covering her mouth with his. With a little sigh of appreciation, she pressed closer to him, her arms encircling his neck. Passion, pure and elemental, ignited between them as he poured everything into the kiss.

The elevator pinged, stopped. The doors slid open onto the private hallway between the amphitheater and the backstage area. He pulled away from her slowly. "We'll make this work, Simone," he whispered, his voice ragged with need. "I swear we will."

"I believe you," she said, her voice breathy. "You're very convincing. I guess I just needed reassurance."

They stepped into the hall, heading toward the dressing rooms. Just outside the door with his name emblazoned on it in fiery lettering, Simone touched his arm. "You don't need to worry, Kadim. I promise I won't back out. I'm a big girl, I can handle this."

Those weren't the words he wanted to hear from her, he realized. He wanted to hear her say she loved him. It suddenly mattered more to him than being protected from his old master. If she could come into his arms so willingly, there was hope for more. In time, she'd come to love him.

"If you want to take time, we'll take time," he said, pushing open the door to his dressing room for her.

"We don't have time," she replied as she entered the room. "Not if your master's on—" her voice broke off abruptly.

Kadim stepped into the room, and then stopped, ice filling his veins.

His former master stood in the center of the room, a gun held to Simone's forehead.

"Hello, Hassam. If you ask me, I'd say your time's up."

Chapter Seven

Kadim saw Simone tense, ready to spring. "Don't move, Simone!"

She kept her gaze on the older man, seemingly unfazed by the gun at her throat. *Why not? He's only human. He'll be dead before he can pull the trigger.*

Aloud, she said, "Pointing a gun at me is not going to make my family sell the hotel to you, Westwood."

He laughed. "I like your courage, girl, stupid as it is. Trying to buy your hotel was just a means to an end. It's always been about getting my property back."

"Excuse me? I don't think you have any property here. And even if there was some property available, it's not for sale to you."

"Simone, please," Kadim said, acid boiling in his gut. He'd planned for everything. How had he not planned for this? "My former master doesn't draw a gun unless he's already made up his mind to use it."

She stilled, her eyes wide with surprise. "The guy that's been trying to take over our hotel is your old master?"

Westwood grinned, a smug bearing of teeth that Kadim had always hated. "And about to become his master again, isn't that right, Hassam?"

"My name is Kadim," he growled, "and you aren't my master."

"I don't give a damn what you call yourself," Westwood declared. "I already know what it takes to bind you. And I promise, no more glass bottles this time."

"I'm not going to let you have him," Simone vowed. "I'll kill you first."

"You might want to think twice before jumping me, little wolf lady," Westwood claimed, the gun held steady in his hand. "Same goes for you, Hassam. You see, I have specialty shells in here, silver shells, held back by a hair trigger. I'll drop you before you even think of shifting. And I promise, if I hit you with these, you're staying down."

Damn! Kadim felt hope draining away. Westwood was one of the few humans he had met who could sense magic, which was why he'd kept his magic to a minimum since escaping. The older man would pull the trigger as soon as he felt Kadim call his magic. He also couldn't risk attacking Westwood now, not without risking Simone. Even if a bullet only grazed her, silver residue would infect her system like a poison.

Westwood smiled as if he could see Kadim's every thought. "You should have just let her bind you."

Kadim balled his hands into fists, but he didn't dare make a move on Westwood. Simone spoke before he could. "What makes you think I haven't?"

Westwood's thick face reddened with laughter. "He hasn't told you anything, has he? If you'd married or bound him, I'd already be dead. Genies have an obligation to protect their masters, since only their masters or accidents can free them. I'm guessing he hasn't given you his true name or told you how a Djinn marriage ceremony works either. Means he's only marrying you for necessity. It's his insurance against being bound against his will. Course, making a bargain with you is close to the same thing, just better benefits."

Kadim would have given anything to wipe the stricken expression from Simone's face. He'd botched everything. He should have courted her properly instead of tricking her. He'd forced her into the engagement as surely as Westwood had forced him into servitude. If he hadn't, maybe Simone would believe that he truly did love her.

"Your word," he said, not looking at Simone. "Give me your word that you won't harm her, and I'll do what you say."

"Are you out of your mind?" Simone gagged as Westwood tightened his arm about her throat. "You can't do this. You can't go back to him!"

"And I can't let him hurt you." He kept his gaze on Westwood. "Despite everything, he is a man of his word. If he says he won't harm you, he won't."

Westwood beamed. "That's right. I give you my word that I won't harm your little Were-bitch."

Kadim, I can smell his intent. If he doesn't kill me, he'll make you do it after he binds you.

Kadim shuddered as something close to physical pain wracked him. He wanted to believe that he wouldn't hurt Simone, but he simply wasn't sure. He'd done things for Westwood he'd never tell Simone about, things as a bound spirit he'd been powerless to stop.

Simone, you'll have to bind me.

No!

You must. If I must be a slave, I would be yours. Say my true name, and then say these words—

"Wait!" Simone exclaimed.

"Why should I?" Westwood demanded.

"Because Kadim owes me another wish."

Kadim frowned. *Simone, what are you doing?*

You gave me three wishes right? When you told me to wish myself into your care? I couldn't do that unless you'd granted me wishes, and I know you like doing things in threes.

Aloud she said, "When he revealed his true nature to me, he gave me three wishes. I've only used two."

Westwood looked at him. "Is she telling the truth?"

"You're holding a gun to my head. Why in the hell would I try to lie to you?"

Kadim turned to Westwood. "She speaks true. I do owe her another wish. I gave my word as a Djinni."

"You think this is checkmate?" Westwood demanded, digging the barrel of his semi-automatic into Simone's forehead so roughly she winced. "You're in no position to bargain, neither of you."

Kadim forced himself to bank the rage that had exploded inside him. He'd kill Westwood for hurting Simone. He'd kill him slowly and painfully until it seemed his screams would echo for all eternity.

"I don't want to bargain," Simone said. "I want to make my wish, and then get the hell out of here."

"What?" Kadim took a step backwards, staggered by her words.

"He knows I didn't want a part of this," she said, speaking to Westwood. "All I wanted was a damn magic special and the money it would bring in."

Westwood pressed the gun into her temple. "Don't screw with me, wolf. The moment you wish me dead is the moment a silver bullet enters your brain."

Simone swallowed past fear and pain, unable to watch the look of betrayal seeping into Kadim's features. She said a silent prayer of thanks that he could only hear her thoughts when she projected them, not read her mind. "I'm not going to wish you dead, Westwood. Promise that you'll leave my pack and the hotel alone, and I'll give you a Djinni present."

Kadim said something she didn't understand, but she clearly understood the tone and the intent. He wouldn't ever forgive her, but she had no other choice.

Westwood chuckled. "This is the woman you pinned your freedom on?" he asked, obviously relishing the moment. "That's what you deserve for thinking you could betray me and manipulate others into doing what you want."

Simone felt him loosen his hold on her neck. "He manipulated you from the start. It's all his kind knows how to do. That's why they need to be bound, or else they'll just cause chaos. Of course, if I get rich in the process, so much the better."

He shifted the gun to the back of her head. "Go ahead, make your wish. I must admit, I'm curious to see what you plan to do to him."

Kadim's dark eyes bored into her. "Wish well, Simone," he said. "Once I'm bound to him, I won't be able to help you."

"I know what I want to wish for," she said. There was only one wish she could make, one wish that would protect him. And if it didn't work, she'd rather be dead anyway.

Simone pressed her left hand against her thigh, out of

Double Down

Westwood's view. Slowly she shifted it, her nails lengthening into claws. Taking a deep breath, she quickly spoke Kadim's true name, then added, "I wish for you to be set forever free by being impervious to any and all attempts to bind you against your will."

"You bitch!" Westwood screamed. Simone heard the unmistakable sound of a gun's hammer being cocked.

With a silent prayer, she ducked and spun, raking her claws at Westwood's chest before throwing herself to the floor. Shouting a curse, Westwood fired, the sound loud in the dressing room. She tensed against the impending strike of the bullet. If it passed through, she might still be able to completely change and rip Westwood's throat out.

No bullet struck her. She looked up, stared. "Kadim."

Roaring filled Simone's ears as Kadim rose above her in his natural form, a whirling dervish of wind and fire. He moved toward Westwood. The human fired his gun again, but the bullets bounced harmlessly away.

Then Westwood aimed the gun at her. She jerked at the collar of her halter dress, ready to shift, when he screamed.

The acrid smell of burning flesh filled the room as Westwood dropped the gun to the floor, his hand blistered and sizzling. With his good hand, he grabbed for his throat, his face turning a dangerous shade of reddish purple as his skin bubbled with heat. Simone watched, transfixed, as the human fell to his knees, and then collapsed onto his side. She heard it when his heart burst as he roasted to death inside his own skin.

His body erupted in flames. Within heartbeats, he'd disappeared, as if he'd never been. Shaken, Simone tried to climb to her feet, but her body refused to obey.

A hand, still wrapped in flame, stretched toward her. Without hesitation, she reached out her left hand.

The diamond flared, heat stinging her fingers. Before she could cry out, the ring turned to dust. She knew then that her wish had worked completely.

"Simone, what did you do?"

256

She reached out to him, but neither skin nor fire touched her hands. "I gave you what you wished for. You're completely free now."

"Why did you do it?" he cried out. "Why did you include yourself in that wish?"

The ceiling above their heads split open in golden light. Kadim's form flowed toward the rift with a sound as terrifying as a tornado. In the space of a blink he was gone, the silence loud.

"I did it because I love you."

Sinking to the floor, she wrapped her arms about herself, trying to hold the pain in. It swirled inside her, gathering strength and purpose until she had to let it out or be consumed.

She threw back her head and howled.

Chapter Eight

Three days later

Simone waited until the celebration was in full swing before putting in an appearance, hoping the Weres would be too deep in full moon fever to notice her arrival.

She was wrong.

The entire pack fell silent as she made her way through the crowd, heading for her parents. Whispers followed her, and even though she couldn't make out the words, she knew what they were saying. It still surprised her when one of the females, Vivianne, stepped into her path.

"I have no quarrel with you, Vivianne," Simone said, wanting nothing more than to congratulate her parents and return to her suite. She'd emerged only because she'd lose face if she didn't. Life and death were natural occurrences in the pack, and no one mourned someone who wasn't their mate or part of the alpha pair. But then, Simone had never stuck to hard and fast pack rules.

Vivianne didn't budge. The other woman, turned some forty years ago, had never liked any of the women in the Temple pack, though Simone and Solange had both tried to make her feel welcome. Simone wondered now why she'd even bothered.

"First Xavier, and now the magician," Vivianne smirked. "Aren't you tired of being a black widow?"

Simone didn't think; she reacted. One moment she faced the female, and the next she had Vivianne pressed into the carpet, her claws poised above the other woman's throat. Four deep gouges in the woman's cheek filled the air with the scent of fresh blood.

Silence fell as the pack pressed close. "This is my parents' time, a time of celebration," Simone said, her voice just human. "I don't want to disrupt it with a fight, but I will be more than happy to oblige you. My wolf hasn't had nearly enough blood."

Vivianne stared up at her with wide, wild eyes. Simone had to suppress a smile. Vivianne hadn't expected an attack, just like she hadn't expected an offer to fight. Simone knew then that the days when she'd back out of a fight were gone.

Thanks to Kadim.

She dropped her face closer to the other woman's, grinning as she scented the sharp spike of fear. It was all she could do not to taste the blood running down the other woman's cheek. "Fight or yield," she whispered. "Right now, it's all the same to me."

Vivianne looked up at the people surrounding them. The pack wouldn't intercede, and they both knew it. "I paid a lot of money for this dress," the turned Were said, then averted her gaze. "I don't want to ruin it."

Simone backed off, rising. "Go lick your wounds, then come back to the party," she suggested as Vivianne made it upright. "But if you ever mention Xavier or Kadim again, I won't go for your face."

Without another word, Simone turned her back on the other woman, effectively proving that she'd won the dominance fight. Holding up her transformed hand, she turned in a slow circle, waiting to see if someone else had something to say. To her bitter disappointment, no one wanted to challenge her.

With a fluid, dance-like wave, she shifted her hand back to human. "Hey, weren't we having a party?"

The pack dispersed to go back to celebrating. Having shown her respect to her parents by showing up, Simone headed for the elevators. Solange started walking toward her, but Simone shook her head, waving her off. After three days, she still wasn't ready to talk to her best friend about Kadim. She doubted she ever would.

A swipe of her key card turned the elevator express, but on a sudden urge, she pressed the button for the main level. Within moments she stood in Kadim's dressing room, needing to feel close to him.

She hadn't returned to the dressing room since her parents had found her sprawled on the floor, howling her head off. It had taken her another day to tell them everything. They'd canceled Kadim's shows, spreading the word about a family emergency and offering a free night's stay to the week's ticket holders. She hadn't been able to find it in herself to care, relying on her assistant and marketing to manage the crisis. How could she care about business when her heart had broken?

She sank onto the couch, struggling against a fresh onslaught of tears. She'd had Kadim for a year, and hadn't done anything about it. She'd fallen head over paws in love with him, in just a day. And in a day, she'd lost him.

She'd tried calling for him, wishing for him, demanding, and cursing. Nothing had worked. She'd even gone to his house, a trip that had damn near killed her. If there was a way to get to him or make him hear her, she couldn't find it.

"I thought I would find you here."

Simone looked up, catching sight of her mother in the doorway.

"I'm sorry, Mama," she said, carefully wiping at her eyes. "I didn't mean to mess up your party."

"What's a pack party without a fight or four?" Esther Temple said, entering the room. "Besides, I'm surprised that you lasted as long as you did."

Simone picked at the fabric covering the couch. "I know we have so much to be thankful for right now, but I just didn't feel like celebrating."

Esther sat beside her on the couch, reaching out to brush Simone's bangs from her face in a gesture she'd done countless times over the decades. "The way you're sitting here down in the jaws, someone would think you actually loved that Djinn of yours."

"I do love him," she confessed, wrapping her arms around her mother's waist. "I thought I loved Xavier, and it hurt when he died, but this… I've never felt like this before. I loved him, Mama. I loved him so much, but I didn't tell him. And now he's gone."

"It may not be forever," Esther Temple said, her voice soothing. "He came to you once, he can show up again."

Simone shook her head. "I don't think so," she whispered,

throat tight. "I think when I wished for his freedom, it sent him back to his homeland. I don't know if he can come back. Besides, the wish turned my engagement ring to dust. That must mean he's free of me, too."

"You don't know that for sure. Miracles can happen when you least expect it."

Her mother draped an arm around her shoulders, pulling her close. "I do want you to know that I'm proud of you, for what you did. It's the worst thing in the world to be owned by another person. I would rather die trying to be free than live as someone else's property ever again."

"That's what I was thinking of," Simone said, curling her hands into fists. "I thought about what you and Dad went through, how you risked everything to be free and be together. I knew I couldn't let Kadim go back to that horrible man. Nothing was worth that."

"Come back to the party, baby," her mother urged her. "I think it'll do you a world of good. We've got some beautifully aged steaks we can walk through a warm room."

"I'm not hungry, Mom. If it's all the same to you, I think I'll just go for a drive. Clear my head. Heck, maybe I'll even get another run in."

"I think that's a great idea," Esther said, making Simone think her mother knew exactly where she'd go. "Try to make it back for our big send-off tomorrow, okay?"

"I wouldn't miss it for the world."

Simone watched her mother go, then sank back into the couch, closing her eyes. She had to find a way to get Kadim back. Somewhere, there had to be a book or scroll or whatever with instructions for calling up Djinn. Westwood couldn't have plucked the information out of thin air. Surely, you had to call them before you could bind them.

She'd go to Kadim's, rip apart his office. If that didn't pan out, she'd head to North Africa, to the Middle East, track down every magical being she could find. She'd find the right spell and call up Djinni after Djinni until the one she wanted actually showed.

Kadim's true name welled up in her mind, her thoughts, and she released it on a soul-heavy sigh. "I wish you were here with me, so I could tell you how much I love you."

"Finally."

Jerking her eyes open, Simone leapt to her feet, whirling around. Kadim stood in the center of the room, resplendent in a classic black tuxedo.

She actually felt faint, hope and disbelief swirling inside her. "Is it really you?"

He smiled at her. "If you don't believe your human eyes, use your wolf's nose."

She did, scenting the air. The current of air from the air conditioner brought her the scent of exotic spice, the whiff of smoke.

"Kadim." She clapped her hands over her mouth, choking back a sob. Her body jerked forward a step, then stopped. "Kadim."

He swooped down on her, wrapping his arms about her waist, lifting her off her feet. "Simone. Beautiful, brave Simone."

She threw her arms around his neck, drawing his scent into her lungs, nuzzling her cheek along his, reveling in his warmth. "You're here. How are you here?"

"Your last wish sent me back to the Djinn," he explained. "Believe it or not, no one's ever wished a Djinn forever free before. No one knew what to make of it. I wanted to come back, but the passageways I knew were all blocked. The only certain way I could return to you was if you wished for me out of love."

"You mean I could have made this wish three days ago?" Three days." She'd wasted three agonizing days.

He nuzzled her cheek, his arms locked securely about her, comforting. "You didn't know, Simone, and I had no way to tell you. But I'm here now. And I intend to stay, if you want me, that is."

"If I want you? Of course I want you!"

"I was hoping you'd say that." He knelt in front of her, a velvet box in his hands. "Simone Temple, will you marry me?"

She stared down at the box, tears fracturing her vision. "No."

His smile froze. "What?"

"I said no." She shook her head for emphasis, not caring about the tears running down her cheeks. "I wished you forever free of any attempts to bind you. The ring you gave me is gone. That means that we can't be married." The thought of watching him disappear again made her choke with grief.

His gaze was like a caress. "Do you love me, Simone?"

"So much," she whispered, fighting back tears. "So much that I think it will kill me if you disappear again. I don't need the ceremony, Kadim, I just need you."

"Then have me. Marry me."

"But the wish—"

"Had a loophole," he told her, his smile wide. "You wished me free of any attempts to bind me against my will. Marrying you is something I very much want to do. I want to spend the rest of my life with you, whether that's two centuries or two millennia."

He opened the box, showed her the ring: a very large and very flawless ruby in a gold Etruscan-style band. "I didn't lie to your parents when I said that I love you. I bought this ring for you, from the money I made as a magician, because I want you to always remember that you are more precious to me than rubies. I built my house for you, because it's a place we can both call home, where we can both run free."

With shaking fingers, he removed the ring from the box. "I thought being free was the only wish I'd ever want granted, but that's not true. I wished for your love, and you've given me that. Now I have just one more wish, another wish that only you could grant: marry me. Bind our hearts and souls and lives together in love and magic. Will you grant me that wish, Simone?"

She knelt in front of him. "Of course I will," she choked out, tears streaming down her face. "On one condition."

"What condition is that?"

"We get married tonight. Right now."

"But your parents—"

"Will be happy for us. I stupidly lost you once, I'm not going to lose you again." She managed a teary smile. "Besides, the next time

Double Down

I make love to you, I want to be your wife."

He slid the ring home on her finger, and she felt something blossom deep in her spirit. The smile he gave her fired her senses. "Did you know there's a chapel just down the street? We can be there in ten minutes."

"I wish we could make it in five."

His laughter wrapped around her as securely as his arms. "As my lady commands."

Out of the Dark

by

Natalie Dunbar

Acknowledgements

I want to thank Parker Publishing for the opportunity to let my imagination run on this one. I also want to thank my husband and my boys for their love, patience, and support. I also want to thank the other authors in this anthology for sharing the journey with me.

Chapter One

The inherited ability to focus inwardly and cast out her awareness allowed Kellie to sometimes capture a little bit of what was to come. She concentrated. *They're coming for me.* There was no time to escape.

Her feet ached, and she was tired and sad that she had missed the chance to say goodbye. She'd spent all day shuffling back and forth between the hospital and the coroner's office in search of Nana's body and come up empty. In her heart of hearts, she wondered if the missing body had anything to do with what was going on outside.

Waiting on the couch, Kellie Monroe shivered, despite the rising temperature in Nana's suburban home on the outskirts of Las Vegas. She'd tried the phone, and it was out of order. Someone had cut the cables. *Not someone, them.* If only she'd charged the batteries on her cell phone.... She needed help, damn it! She hoped that someone in one of the other homes being ravaged had managed to call the police.

Lit candles scattered the room from coffee tables to counters, pooling light, throwing shadows, and filling her nostrils with the soothing fragrance of lavender. The electricity was off again, and the generator didn't seem to be working. With the eerie howls and screams she'd been hearing in the darkness outside the house, she knew better than to go out to check. No, she trusted her instincts and senses too much for that. If she died tonight, it would be because someone or something broke in and took her life. She was damned if she even thought of opening the door.

Rotating a shoulder, she tried to loosen the muscles. Her body was strong and fit from her early years of studying and competing in gymnastics, and then moving on to tennis into her late teens, but she was no match for what threatened outside. Hopefully, the weapons Nana had left for her would even the odds.

Once more, she made her rounds, checking every door and window, making sure they were locked. She idly wondered how long they would hold.

A bead of sweat slipped down the side of her face. She stood at the edge of the window, fear, determination, and anger warring with common sense and making her crazy. She needed to see what was going on with her own eyes.

The knob on the front door rattled. A shudder rippled through her as she grabbed the shotgun she'd loaded with the silver coated buckshot she'd found in Nana's kitchen drawer. It wouldn't kill, but it would maim or cripple the ravaging band of werewolves outside and make them think twice about attacking her.

Nana never used guns, so Kellie was certain that the weapons had been left for her. Kellie didn't know if it was fate or destiny that her ex-boyfriend had been a gun enthusiast who had taught her a lot. Then there was the fact that she'd been dreaming of Nana and wolves for weeks now. Dear Lord, she wished she'd known that Nana was dying.

She'd stuffed the automatic pistol in the waistband of her pants—it too, filled with silver bullets she'd found in the drawer. Then she added a little silver knife that had been handed down in her family for generations. If she went down, damn it, she was taking some of them with her.

In a sudden explosion, the front door splintered. Wood slivers flew as the door disintegrated beneath the claws and weight of two enormous wolves with bark colored coats. *Werewolves.* They leaped into the entryway, sniffing the air, growling, and snapping viciously. In the candlelight, the medallions on gold chains around their thick necks glinted.

Staring down the sight and pressing the trigger, Kellie wasted no time giving each a spray of the silver buckshot. They dropped and howled, writhing in pain on the ceramic tile floor in the front hall. *Two wolves down.* Another leaped forward. She shot it. *Three.* But for how long? They could recover fast.

She was still trapped. How many were there? Not taking the time to reload, she dropped the shotgun and drew the .38. Several quick steps put her back to the wall.

Gripping the gun with slippery fingers and training it on the opening, she focused, using a tentative combination of her awareness, her eyes, and her ears reminiscent of a scene from an action movie. Had she gone into attack mode? Kick-ass mode? Whatever it was, she was determined to survive.

The growling thunder grew to a deafening level. Two more wolves, a steel gray and a black, burst into the room at near-lightning speed. Kellie squeezed the trigger. The rat-a-tat sound of the automatic filled the air as she fed them silver bullets. Two headshots and both fell dead to the floor.

Sudden silence raised the hairs on the back of her neck. They were going to rush her. Kellie swallowed hard, mentally preparing herself. This was it. She turned to face the window on her left, split seconds before a huge caramel-coated wolf smashed it inward. Glass showered the room. She squinted against the sharp rain and prayed, wishing she'd thought to put on her safety glasses.

Behind her, she heard the window on the right explode simultaneously. Gripping the pistol, she fired at the caramel-coated wolf leaping gracefully into her living room. One bullet caught it mid-air in the center of the forehead.

Split seconds seemed to stretch into minutes. She had the satisfaction of seeing the caramel-colored wolf fall.

A murderous growl erupted inches from her face.

"Bitch! You're going to pay for that!"

The fact that she could understand the snarled words stunned her. Had she killed the alpha's mate? Thick paws knocked her backward, the sharp nails ripping through the fuchsia silk of her blouse and the soft pecan colored flesh beneath it. Dropping the automatic, she fell onto the white carpet.

Gasping for air, Kellie fumbled for the pistol. She found herself staring into the furious gray eyes of a wolf with a coat the color of tree bark. Her hands closed on carpet and air.

His mournful howl cut through the air, sending tremors running through her.

The heavy weight of the wolf landed on her, pressing her into the carpet. Intent on protecting her throat, she threw her arm up in a move she'd seen used against attacking dogs. Hot breath raised goose bumps on her arm, seconds before his sharp teeth sank in.

Kellie screamed in pain and rage. She felt the delicate bones in her right wrist snap beneath the pressure of those powerful jaws. Sharp pain cut through her, making her dizzy with the need to get away. Was she going to be eaten alive? She'd heard stories of what the ravaging bands of werewolves could do, but never saw herself in the victim role. Even now, her left hand punched and hit at the wolf with no visible effect.

A rumbling sound vibrated through the wolf and carried through the room that was now filled with wolves. There were at least forty of them. Were they laughing at her?

Instead of ripping her apart and feasting on the remains, he was taking his time and prolonging the pain. Was this her punishment for taking so many of them out? She felt his tongue against her injured flesh, licking and savoring her life's blood. Elongated canines moved up her arm, sinking into new flesh.

Gathering what was left of her wits and strength, she fumbled with the waistband of her pants, searching for the soft leather sheath that held the silver knife. She almost smiled when her fingers closed on it and drew the knife.

Kellie tensed as the wolf bit into her shoulder. Sharp, excruciating pain, the likes of which she'd never known, pierced her body. Her ears rang. Shaking, she struggled frantically, knowing her life depended on getting away. Razor-sharp claws ripped burning shreds of agony from her shoulder to thigh. Horrible screams filled the room, shutting out all else. Stunned, it took precious seconds for her to realize that the screams were her own. *Dear Lord, how can I live through this?*

The claws lifted once more.

Gripping the silver knife in her palm, Kellie struck. She brought the knife up from her side to plunge it into the wolf's chest.

Blood splattered Kellie and the floor.

Then she stared. *What the hell?* A flash of white lightning appeared around the edges of the place where the knife had gone in, growing and lighting the wolf from within. The wolf's surprised howl of pain threatened to burst Kellie's eardrums.

Twisting and turning her body, she started to maneuver out from under him. His claws extended like fingers in an eerie blend of wolf and human. With a burst of savage energy, he reared up, grabbed her, and threw her across the room.

Disoriented, Kellie sailed through the air, struggling to work her injured body to enable her to land on her feet. She was used to working with pain but this was beyond anything she'd imagined. In the middle of a somersault, her back hit the living room wall. Winded and stunned, she fell to the floor, trying to think of something to do when they came to finish her off.

The white carpet was turning red with blood. The smell of burning flesh threatened to choke her. On the other side of the room, the alpha werewolf who had attacked her burned from the inside out. She stared in wonder, trying to remember what Nana had told her about the knife. The normally closed-mouthed old woman had spells where she talked a lot. Unfortunately, what she said then made little sense because she was out of her head. Kellie hadn't known what to believe.

While trying to connect the fairy stories Nana told her with hard facts, she'd had the little silver knife appraised, they'd told her it was very old and considered a valuable artifact that should be in a museum with the sword of Arielle. Kellie pushed her brain. Had Nana warned her about the knife's potency? Things she shouldn't do? The memory wouldn't come.

Guns fired outside the house. It could only be the SWAT team they sent out when the roving bands of wild werewolves attacked the humans. It was about time they showed up. Kellie took stock of herself. The werewolf's claws had scored deep onto the flesh of her arms and torso. The bones in her arm and wrist were crushed, and she'd injured her back in the fall. She'd lost a lot of blood. Would she live to be rescued?

A menacing slate gray wolf with pale irises came so close that she felt his hot breath on her face. "Later, bitch. You'll be one of us or we'll be back to finish this."

No. It wouldn't happen to her. She wouldn't let it. Kellie lay there struggling to move.

In silent agreement, the wolves leapt out of the windows and doors in mass. A hail of gunfire greeted them, but Kellie knew better than to think they'd all been exterminated.

She felt *weird*. Almost like she was floating on an undulating bed of molasses. A rushing sound made her ears all but useless and her stomach oscillated between bouts of hard tension and bouts of threatening to toss its contents. Blood soaked the carpet beneath her. Dark spots invaded her eyesight and spread. Her vision darkened until she lay unconscious.

Kellie came to on a stretcher. A group of emergency technicians were putting her into a red ambulance. Her vision was blurred, and she shivered with cold despite the thermal blanket covering her. She'd missed the arrival of the ambulance's lights and sirens. A full moon shone down on them as the rest of the stretcher went in and locked in place. How long had she been out?

In the background, a cleanup crew was gathering the bodies of the dead wolves that had returned to human form and loading them into the back of a coroner's wagon. There was an IV in her arm. They were giving her blood and liquid sustenance.

A pudgy-looking emergency technician in red and white leaned in close to her face, a smile lighting his roughly pleasant face. "Glad to have you with us. You okay, little lady?"

"Dizzy, weak," she mumbled. She was definitely too weak to give him hell about calling her "little lady."

"You've got an IV, and we cleaned and bandaged your cuts, but the doctor's gonna want to look at that arm. He'll probably have to operate."

She wondered, who was he kidding? The arm throbbed and was twice its normal size. They must have given her something for the pain. She was probably going to lose the arm. Kellie's eyes grew shiny with tears. "Lucky to be alive."

"I'll say." The tech leaned closer. "It looks like you put up a hell of a fight. The SWAT team found four of 'em dead inside your place, and I hear that two limped out and got finished off by the team."

"How many humans died?" she asked, trying to put things in perspective.

"Eleven." The tech chose that moment to look away and check the monitors. "Of the homes that were attacked, you were the only survivor."

"How many wolves got away?" she bit out hoarsely, knowing that many more were out there, waiting to terrorize the humans still brave enough to live in the area.

Not bothering to comment further, the tech gave a signal, and the ambulance doors swung shut. Soon they were careening down the road at top speed with the siren wailing overhead.

Kellie closed her eyes. A ride like this had been a childhood dream, but being here on the stretcher meant she would never be the same again. Did they think she was going to die? In the darkness behind her lids, she saw her Nana watching her with a concerned expression on her face. It was strange, because the old woman had been very stern. Kellie rarely saw a look of concern when Nana had been alive.

At the emergency room, the doctor's decision to operate was immediate. "We'll put some pins in it, but we can't promise anything as far as what you'll be able to do with it," he explained. "The nerves in that arm will never be the same." He glanced at the screen with her vital signs, and then stared at her. "You've got a fever, which is to be expected with an injury such as yours, but it is extremely high. You have had your shots for the lycanthrope virus?"

Kellie shook her head. "Nana wouldn't allow it. She said it would kill me. I didn't survive the attack just so I could die from a vaccination."

"It's the law!" he snapped, ordering the nurse to fetch the required dosage for vaccination. "Unless you're a vampire, already a werewolf, or have applied to the council for membership in one of the werewolf clans, you must be vaccinated. Do you want to be a werewolf?"

Kellie gripped the sheets with her fists. "No. Hell no."

Becoming one of those thieving, murdering werewolves that roamed the countryside terrorizing the human population was not an option.

As if he could read her thoughts, the doctor's expression softened. "The wolves that attacked you are not representative of the clans who are a part of this city, its government, and businesses. My concern is following the laws of this city and making sure that what happens here, medically speaking, is in your best interests."

Nothing he said soothed her uneasiness. Her best interests involved never coming into contact with the bastards. Nana had been adamant about the vaccination, even before she'd started losing her senses. "No vaccination," she told him.

When the nurse returned with the shot, the doctor swabbed Kellie's arm with alcohol. His green eyes bored into her. "Did your grandmother tell you why she was so adamant about you not getting this shot?"

"My blood chemistry is different. The vaccination would cause a negative reaction that could kill me," she said finally.

The doctor eyed her skeptically. "Are you trying to say you're not human?"

Kellie met his gaze. "Yes, I am."

The doctor laughed. "Well that's an interesting tale. I had blood work done on you, and our techs have tagged you as human. There are some unusual elements that could not be identified, but you're as human as I am!"

Kellie shrunk away, dazed and confused. She'd avoided doctors for most of her life because of what Nana had said about her blood. To hear that she'd been living a lie was more than she could comprehend. The doctor had to be wrong.

Still talking, the doctor grabbed her arm.

Kellie tried to fight him off. Two nursing assistants held her down.

"As you know, we have the legal authority to force you to take this vaccination. This shot has worked successfully for thousands. It won't kill anything but the lycanthrope virus," he insisted. Pulling the plunger back on the needle, he pushed the liquid into Kellie's arm.

The nursing assistants released Kellie.

Acid fire rampaged through her veins and ate its way up to her throat. She curled inward, not certain how much more she could take. Something was happening, something unforeseen by everyone except Nana. Joints locked as massive convulsions shook her body with the force of an earthquake. Her lips moved. She tried to talk, but the only sounds that came out were pain filled grunts and screams.

In the background, the doctor thrust a flat stick deep into Kellie's mouth and ordered twenty ccs of Melizone.

The serum or her body's reaction to it? She didn't know. Whatever it was ravaged through her, raising her blood pressure until her veins jumped with it and her head threatened to split.

The two nursing assistants held her still while the doctor administered the shot of Melizone.

It slowly eased the fire inside her. Kellie actually felt the serum moving through her system. Her stomach clenched. Dry heaves caught her throat. In a violent burst, her stomach tossed its contents. The nurses worked with her, talking softly, wiping her face, and cleaning her up. When her head hit the pillow, she sank into the darkness.

Chapter Two

The relentless sound of nurses paging doctors on the PA system in the hall outside Kellie's hospital room was the first thing to penetrate the quiet darkness. Then it was the tapping sound of footsteps in the hall and murmured snatches of conversation between nurses, patients, and visitors. She felt the spongy hospital mattress beneath her and the crisp cotton hospital gown and sheets against her skin. At scheduled intervals, the nurse came in to see if she was awake or to change the IV. The normality of the sounds and actions lulled Kellie into a peaceful sleep.

Something rustled close to her bed. The sound was barely audible. She tensed, suddenly sensing a waiting presence. Someone was in her room. She breathed in the fresh, clean scent of a man's cologne and another, indefinable scent with a powerful draw.

The sensual sound of a man's voice skated along the edge of her senses, as intimate as a touch. "You're awake now, Kellie. Will you open your eyes and talk to me?"

Accepting the challenge, she opened her eyes, blinking against the sudden influx of light. A man sat in the chair by her bed as if he were holding court. Soft ebony waves topped a dream of a face in milk chocolate butter. Deep-set bedroom eyes the color of heated cognac, a sculpted nose, and full, well-shaped lips on a wide mouth filled with white teeth all combined to make him the best looking man she'd ever seen. From what she could see of his custom suit-covered body, it was all she'd ever wanted too, with wide shoulders, trim waist, and strong, lean muscled thighs. She could spend hours just looking at Mister Oh-so-fine.

"How long have you been in here?" she asked, one hand instinctively rising to the knotted mess of her hair, and the other drawing the sheets she'd kicked off back over her legs. Lord, she knew she had to look like death warmed over, but she felt good. Looking at him made her feel even better. Something about him affected her as powerfully as the proverbial siren's song.

Distinct interest and amusement glittered in his eyes as he answered her question. "Long enough."

Whatever that meant, she hadn't heard him come in or even known he was in the room until he'd wanted her to. Abruptly, she realized that she'd asked the wrong question. "What do you want?"

The glitter in his eyes became more pronounced as his lazy gaze covered and lingered on her. The corners of his mouth threatened to turn upwards. "Many things, but for now I need to talk to you about the attack. My name is Garen Roy, and I'm working with the Preternatural Police."

Kellie's lids slid downward. She wasn't sure she wanted to deal with anyone from that shadowy organization, especially one as powerful as Garen Roy. For several precious moments, he'd taken her mind completely off herself and the werewolf attack. The man had to be giving off some heavy pheromones to make her forget about that. Kellie reached up to touch her right arm. It was no longer covered with bandages. She examined the soft caramel colored skin. There were no bruises or signs of surgery or the attack. "How long have I been out?"

"A couple of weeks. Your case is unusual."

"For sure." First the attack, then the damned doctors had nearly killed her with that vaccine. She examined her arm again, flexing her fingers, silently rejoicing in the fact that she hadn't lost use of either. The specter of being handicapped had been heavy on her mind when she arrived. "It doesn't even look like they operated on it," she remarked.

"They didn't."

His words stopped her cold. With a quick intake of breath, she hugged herself beneath the covers. Her fingers stroked the smooth warm skin on the healed wrist and arm. What did it mean, her healing like that, without any surgery? She'd never been able to do that before. Did it mean she was a werewolf? Or would she become one with the next full moon?

"Although you were violently ill, Dr. Casey isn't sure the vaccination worked," Garen said, apparently sensing her thoughts. "You're the wild card, Kellie, because there are… *elements* in your blood that he's never seen before."

Those words echoed in her ears and slammed around inside her head. She sat up, suddenly, letting the covers pool at her waist as she rejected all thoughts of the scientific arm of the preternatural police working with her doctor to try to make her into a science experiment. She had to get out of here.

The room tilted, and her world shifted abruptly. She fell back against the pillows, closing her eyes against an attack of vertigo. Her breath came out on a hiss.

"No sudden moves," he ordered, suddenly standing by the bed. "You've been out on your back for two weeks. First the attack, and then who knows what effects that serum had on your body."

She didn't have an answer, and there was no one who could tell her. Nana had died a few days ago, and Kellie had never seen or heard of any other relatives. The old woman she'd called Nana had raised her alone, insisting that Kellie's parents had died in an accident. Other than that, she'd been incredibly stingy with information until close to the end of her life.

The unique scent of Garen and his cologne filled her nostrils. Her heart sped up. Behind her closed lids, she heard him pouring water. There'd been a pitcher on the tray by the bed.

Garen's hand touched hers, hot and filled with the energy of life and something that made her want to grab onto it and press it to the aching tips of her breasts. She was no virgin, but neither was she a slut. She didn't jump into bed with every man who made her hot, but Garen Roy made her want to break that rule.

Something in his eyes told her that beneath his calm exterior she was wreaking havoc with his senses and his ability to maintain his professionalism. It said that what had started and was growing between them wasn't fleeting or casual.

He pressed the cool glass of water into her hands. "Drink this," he ordered. "They took the IV out this morning. You must be thirsty."

She lifted her lids, and their gazes met and locked. Warmth heated and sizzled within her, melting her insides and pooling slick moisture between her legs.

Kellie blinked. She'd never reacted to anyone like this.

His eyes glittered. The rings around those heated cognac colored eyes seemed to glow.

"We're attracted to each other," his voice deepened. He inhaled, nostrils flaring. "Your scent is an invitation I can't ignore." The pitch of his voice dipped so low it came close to a growl. "Do you know what I am? Can you accept it?"

Kellie eyed him, examining him with all her senses. He was no ordinary man. His potent personal magnetism was something she'd previously only read about. The breathless answer bubbled up from her gut. "Werewolf."

"Not one of the rogue gang of werewolves doing home invasions, savaging humans, and robbing banks, but a werewolf just the same."

Nodding, Kellie ran her tongue across her dry lips. She wasn't afraid of him, and she knew that there was bound to be a criminal element in the werewolf population, just like the human one.

Something in Garen's eyes deepened. He seemed to be waiting.

She put the glass to her mouth and forced herself to drink the water. It cooled her dry throat, leaving the rest of her hot and wanting Garen Roy. She drained the glass.

"Kellie, you and the mystery of your ancestry are intriguing," he murmured. Steadying her hand on the glass with caressing forefingers, he refilled her glass with water.

From what she knew of werewolves, he was surprisingly gentle with her. Kellie felt a resulting vibration low in her belly. He knew exactly what he was doing to her. *Enough.* She had no intentions of letting Garen Roy jump her bones right here in the hospital, probably not at all. Collecting her wits, she shot him a look of frustration. "Garen, stop. I'm not myself."

He momentarily froze. "True. At this moment, neither am I. I look forward to an interesting encounter once you've recovered." With an apologetic smile, he placed the pitcher on the stand and stepped backward to drop down into the chair beside her bed. "In addition to being with the Preternatural Police, I belong to the Roy clan, Kellie, and I am related by blood to several others. We are known in this community for our businesses and our work in the community. You will need our protection, and we can provide you with a safe place to stay—"

His offer was more than generous, but after all that had happened, she didn't think she wanted to be taken in by a clan of werewolves, no matter how upstanding. Her attraction to Garen was unsettling enough. She knew of no attacks in the tourist areas of Vegas she reasoned inwardly. Maybe if she stayed there and was careful until her business for Nana was done, she'd be all right. "I appreciate the offer, but I think I can manage," she answered.

"Can you? I admire your strength and determination, but you're a lone woman, and the only survivor out of all the attacks that have occurred within the past months. You don't think they'll come back for you?"

"That would depend on the reason they attacked, wouldn't it? I think you're forgetting that I killed a bunch of them," she reminded him.

"True." He paused. "The other victims were torn limb to limb, but the alpha merely savaged your arm. Why did they let you live?"

She shook her head, unconsciously rubbing her arm. "I don't know." Having her arm chewed was not something she wanted to relive, no matter how Garen Roy sought to minimize it. *I was viciously thrown into a wall, too.* But what was that when the others had likely died within seconds of their encounters with the band of werewolves?

He leaned forward, his face animated with emotion. "Do you know how volatile the balance is between the different species here? This is my home, and I will not see it destroyed. We must catch this gang of rogue werewolves before all hell breaks loose in this city."

Deep down something inside her wanted to help him. It warred with her need to finish Nana's business first. Kellie locked gazes with him. "I can only tell you what I know." She admired his single-minded strength of conviction and wondered briefly what it would be like to have all that energy and determination focused on her. He drew a pen and a small black notebook from his pocket and leaned forward. "Tell me how the attack started."

Placing the glass on the nightstand, Kellie began her story. Reliving the attack wasn't as hard as she'd imagined. It was almost as if it had happened to someone else. She marveled at her calm and hoped she wasn't simply in shock.

Garen was silent for most of her story, stopping her only to ask questions about the gold chains or collars she'd seen around some of the wolves' necks and the silver knife she'd used on the alpha werewolf.

He gave her the pen and opened a new page in his notebook so that she could sketch the emblem on the pendant she'd seen on some of the wolves' gold chains.

"I've seen this somewhere," he remarked, studying it carefully. "I'll give it to the research arm of our group to study. What about the knife?"

"What about it?" she asked, deciding right then that she wasn't giving it to the Preternatural Police to study. She needed it for her own protection.

"We examined it, but we're still not sure what makes it work."

"It's silver," she answered, her tone hardening. "That should be all you need to know."

"But from what you've said, and the report filed by the SWAT team, there's more to it than that. The alpha was burned alive, from the inside out."

"Maybe he had severe allergy to silver," she quipped lightly.

"An expert in the research arm of the Preternatural Police claims that the knife has some of the same markings as the sword of Arielle, an artifact in the Louvre. What do you know about that?"

She answered his question with one of her own. "Is it so unusual to see markings copied from famous artifacts?"

Garen wasn't ready to drop the subject of the knife. "It's not unusual to see artwork copied from museum artifacts, but when objects like your knife exhibit unusual properties, we take note. Can you tell me anything about the knife?"

Out of the Dark

"Nothing except that it's been in my family for several generations and belonged to Arielle, a mythical warrior princess. As a child, I sometimes pretended that I was Arielle. Nana said that I really was related to her." She saw that Garen was studying her, obviously not sure what to believe. "Look Garen, as you've already pointed out, I'm in danger. That knife may have saved my life."

"Against an entire pack?" Garen shook his head. "No way. There was something else they wanted from you." Letting that sink in, he was silent for several moments.

Kellie considered it. What could they have wanted from her? They hadn't asked her anything or bothered to search Nana's home. Except for the fact that she hadn't been torn to pieces and she still lived, her attack had mirrored the others. "No, you're wrong."

"Am I?" Garen's lips tightened and his brows furrowed as he scanned the drawing of the medallion once more, his fingers tracing the markings. His lips moved soundlessly.

Garen stood. "Thank you. I'm sure this will help. We appreciate your cooperation. Are you planning to stay in the area for a while?"

"Long enough to clear up Nana's estate, do the funeral, and head back to Detroit," she answered truthfully. After being attacked, she couldn't wait to leave.

"Be careful," he ordered. "I'm almost certain you're still a target. If I were you, my first stop would be the police station, to retrieve the knife and the guns from the evidence room."

"I'll do that," she assured him, wishing he'd leave so she could get dressed and get out as soon as possible.

He placed the notebook and pen in an inside pocket of his suit coat. "Kellie, refusing our protection is not wise at best. At worst, it is just plain suicide. Don't you want to reconsider?"

As reasonable and convincing as he sounded with his soft southern lilt, Kellie shook her head. Nana had never liked or trusted the Preternatural Police, and some of it must have rubbed off on her. Nana had likened them to having the fox watch the hen house to keep out other foxes.

Something within her urged her to trust Garen. That in itself

286

was suspicious.

Finally accepting her refusal of protection, Garen nodded. With one last regretful glance, he said his goodbye and left.

Chapter Three

As soon as the door closed on Garen Roy, Kellie carefully got up from the bed and stood on rubbery legs. A strong sense of self-preservation fueled her determination. The attack of vertigo had taught her to move slowly and deliberately. Making her way to the room's tiny closet, she found a fresh pair of jeans, green tank top, and clean underwear and socks, compliments of the Nevada Department of Social Services. There was even a pair of new tennis shoes in a plastic bag. On the shelf she found an envelope with her name on it. Her money, charge cards, and ID were inside. She headed for the shower, hoping it would enable her to move a little faster.

In the shower, Kellie stood beneath the hot spray and checked her body for signs of cuts or bruises. There were none. Still, her body felt stiff in several places, and her legs were unsteady. Holding on to the rail in the shower, she imagined that spending weeks unconscious in a hospital bed could do that to a body. Then there was the fact that she smelled different. She'd even lost a layer of pudge.

In the bathroom mirror, she blow-dried her thick hair using the hairdryer mounted on the wall and the little plastic brush in her patient kit. Her facial features had changed. *More striking?* She couldn't put her finger on the difference, but there was an innate vitality or glow there that she hadn't seen before. She'd never been beautiful, and still wasn't, but the whites of her mahogany brown eyes were bright, and her hair seemed more lustrous and full. She'd certainly get more masculine attention.

Closing her eyes she prayed that the changes in her were not because she was becoming a werewolf. There was still hope.

Kellie dressed as quickly as possible. Surprisingly, the clothes fit almost perfectly. The jeans were a little tight, but Kellie had noticed that tight jeans were always in style for women. On the way out, she stopped at the nurses' station to get discharge instructions and some official word on her condition. The head nurse, an obvious veteran of many patient battles, did her best to convince Kellie to stay for more tests. When that didn't work, the head nurse called Kellie's doctor.

"You nearly killed me," she said, facing the man who'd administered the vaccine.

The doctor flinched. He addressed her sincerely in a low tone. "I'm sorry. I was doing my job as required by the laws of this state. We tested your blood, and there was no evidence to support your claim that you would have such a violent reaction. Could we please speak in private? There's something you should know."

Kellie followed him into his office and took one of the chairs.

"Ms. Monroe, again, I'm sorry about what happened. I've been monitoring your condition closely and am pleased with your recovery thus far and hope to see it continue."

Kellie shook her head in denial. "I need to get all of my strength back, but other than that, I'm fully recovered now."

"On the contrary," the doctor said, leaning forward to place a hand on hers, "the vaccine apparently caused some sort of chemical reaction. Your blood is changing."

She felt the prick of tears behind her eyes, and she withdrew her hand from beneath his. "You mean I'm becoming a werewolf?"

He struggled for words. "I mean I don't know. Our hematology department has never seen anything like it."

Kellie narrowed her eyes. "And what is *it*?"

The doctor's eyes gleamed.

Kellie realized then that he was struggling to contain his excitement.

His words tumbled out. "The nonhuman elements in your blood are multiplying. Soon, you will no longer be human."

Kellie got to her feet, shaking. "And what will I be then?"

"We don't know yet. That's why we'd like you to come back periodically for tests..."

"No. Hell no." Kellie turned and strode for the door. "This hospital and its staff have all it's going to get of my blood and I will sue you and this hospital for millions if any of this private information gets out."

"We'll keep all your information private, of course," the doctor called after her, "but you're going to need our help."

"You don't even know what is wrong, how can you help?!" Kellie opened the door and stepped back into the corridor. Slamming the door behind her, she headed for the exit.

Cell phone glued to his ear, Garen sat in an unmarked car on the corner where the hospital's street intersected the main road. He kept his eyes trained on the front entrance. A contact inside would phone him the minute Kellie approached the nurses' station.

He admired Kellie's strength and spunk, both traits admired and displayed by true alpha werewolves, but there was no way he could let her go it alone. Kellie was one intriguingly powerful package of pure woman. She was nothing like the women he usually went for, but something about her drew his mind and his body.

In his bid for nonverbal convincing, he'd decided to let her experience a taste of what she would face without police protection. At the same time, it would be interesting to see who approached her. He'd make sure she didn't get hurt.

Momentarily glancing down at the notebook on the seat beside him, Garen described the picture Kellie had drawn of the medallions that the wolves had been wearing to Elio Whitfield, his boss in the preternatural division.

"Mind if I take a look?" Elio asked in a light tone.

Being a powerful psychic, Elio got more out of reading Garen's mind as he stared at the picture than listening to the verbal description. What he asked was something Garen only allowed in an emergency. He gave permission and felt the touch of Elio's mind. Elio never tried to control him or read anything other than the subject at hand, but Garen dreaded the invasion all the same. It simply wasn't natural.

"I've seen that damned medallion somewhere," Elio muttered, cursing under his breath. "And quite often, too. It's just something you don't notice after a while, this being Vegas and all."

Garen assured him that he'd had the same reaction.

Elio made a clicking sound with his teeth. "Did she give you anything new on the knife?"

"Yeah. She called it a family heirloom, handed down for generations. She also said that it once belonged to the real Arielle. "

Elio's voice was gruff on the other end of the phone. "Killing the werewolf the way it did, we already know that the knife is a thing of power. Arielle was also a sorceress. Her mate was a shape shifter."

Garen frowned. A shapeshifter? As far as he was concerned, it was another name for a werewolf, like himself. "Was her mate a werewolf?"

"Not just a werewolf. Legend has it that he could also shift into a bear, a leopard, and a snake. Maybe even more."

"How? How could one being master so many life forms?" Garen asked as he tried to wrap his mind around the concept.

"We don't know a lot about her mate, but remember, Arielle was a sorceress and rumored to be one of the Fey. She was neither werewolf, vampire, or human."

Garen thought about Kellie and the ruckus at the hospital over her reaction to the lycanthrope vaccine. He'd talked to the head of the hematology unit and heard that there were elements of Kellie's blood that were not human, werewolf, or vampire. If

Kellie was "other," then how did she get here? The more he heard on the puzzle, the more the idea grew that she was actually related to this mythical figure, Arielle. He even allowed himself to wonder, what would it be like to be mate to a descendant of a sorceress who was also one of the Fey?

Just then, his cell phone beeped, and he saw his hospital contact's number pop up on the screen. "Elio, I've got to go. I'll get back with you later."

Several minutes later, he saw Kellie walk out of the hospital's front entrance.

Outside the hospital, a punishing wave of Vegas heat hit Kellie hard. *Damn!* She realized that she should have called a taxi from inside the hospital. Wasting her strength by going back inside was not an option. Besides, she reasoned, taxis were plentiful in Vegas. Squinting against the bright sunlight, she scanned the man who'd just walked out of the hospital behind her. In a tan golf shirt, he strolled along the side of the building as if he didn't have a care in the world. More than once she caught him watching her, and it didn't feel good.

Kellie didn't know why the man was staring. She *hoped* he was a cop because she wasn't really in any shape to protect herself. She recalled her conversation with Garen Roy and tried to remember why she'd been so obstinate. She liked her independence, the freedom to do as she liked, but that didn't usually make her stupid. Mentally kicking herself, she decided that Roy had not only appealed to her sexually, he'd also gotten her back up by insisting that she needed protection. Too bad it was true.

Kellie balled her hands into fists. She had nothing, not even a purse, to fight with. And who was she fooling anyway? She was as weak as a limp noodle now. Refusing protection had been a mindless thing to do. A yellow taxicab turned onto the street; she hailed it.

The taxicab stopped at the curb, just shy of her. Approaching it, she kept an eye on the man.

He walked toward her, his speed increasing as she pulled the passenger door open and climbed in the air-conditioned interior. Leaning forward, she reached out to grab the handle and close the door.

Standing outside the cab, Tan-shirt countered her effort by holding it open with a large hand.

"Let go of the door," she demanded in a tone that had gotten her out of trouble more than once.

With a cunning grin, he bent down and maneuvered to get into the cab.

"Can I get some help here?" Kellie shouted at the surprised cabdriver. "This man is trying to attack me!" She used her hands to scoot to the other side of the cab as fast as she could.

Tan-shirt followed, reaching for her. He smelled like—wolf. His hand closed on her wrist.

"Leave me alone!" Kellie eyed that hand, twisting her wrist and shaking it off angrily. She weighed her options. At the very least, she knew she could bite that hand if he kept it up.

Like a knight in shining armor, Garen Roy suddenly stood outside the car.

For a few seconds Kellie even let herself appreciate the fact that he hadn't listened to her BS and he'd let her see the danger for herself. He was still fine, but now she watched him with a different sort of appreciation.

Jerking the intruder out of the car by the arm, Garen dropped him onto the hot pavement. "What are you doing here? Let me see your identification."

Tan-shirt scrambled to his feet, all but bowing and scraping. "Just a misunderstanding, sir. She looks like a woman I know named Samantha," he whined. "I thought it was her."

"He's lying," Kellie snapped incredulously. "He got a good look at me in the back of this cab. I told him to leave me alone."

Garen studied her, and then slung his gaze back to the man who was scrambling to his feet. "Did he touch you?"

"He grabbed my arm." She massaged the area where a light bruise was starting to fade.

Garen motioned to the uniform cops who had just rounded the corner. The hospital was part of their beat. They came, checking the badge Garen displayed and talking briefly. Each took one of Tan-shirt's arms.

As Garen leaned into the car to talk to her, she saw one of the cops reaching for his handcuffs.

With a smooth, agile movement, Tan-shirt twisted out of the officer's grasp and ducked back into the hospital. The two uniformed cops ran after him.

Straightening, Garen watched, apparently torn between helping them and staying with her.

The cops were human. Somehow Kellie didn't think they would welcome Garen's help.

Cursing under his breath, Garen bent down into the doorway to address Kellie. She won that battle. "Perhaps now you'll let me give you a ride to the station so you can retrieve your things?"

She nodded and accepted his help, getting out of the cab.

"You look tired," he murmured. "Maybe you should have stayed in the hospital a little longer."

Lifting her brows, she fixed him with a challenging look. "And become a science experiment and stationary target? I don't think so."

Garen took her arm, urging her to lean on him.

Garen had managed to earn a measure of her trust. Kellie suppressed a small sigh of relief as she sagged against him. She desperately wanted to close her eyes and sleep, but rest would only be allowed to come on her terms.

"You were under our protection while you were in the hospital," he reminded her on the way to his vehicle. "And you were safe."

Was she? Kellie thought of the werewolf who had followed

her out of the hospital as she got in Garen's unmarked car. Lulled by the motion of the vehicle, she soon dozed fitfully against the seats. The automobile's lack of movement eventually caused her to awaken.

Garen sat in the driver's seat, watching her silently. "Ready?"

"No." Bracing herself for the coming ordeal of getting her property back from the police, Kellie combed her hair with her fingers and hugged herself against a sudden chill that raised goosebumps on her arms. She wondered how long he'd been watching her sleep. It had to have been at least half an hour. The little nap had done wonders.

Extending his long arm to the back seat of the car, he retrieved a navy T-shirt with the letters "LVPD" stamped across the front. "Here."

Touched by his thoughtful gesture, she thanked him and drew the soft cotton over her head. When she climbed out of the passenger seat, the shirt fell close to her knees. Problem solved.

Inside the cool station Kellie was at a loss. People of all colors, shapes, and sizes were everywhere, and most of the civilians seemed to be waiting. She straightened, trying to prepare herself to deal with the bureaucracy of a big city police department.

Leading her to one of the clerks manning a desk, Garen flashed a badge and used his knowledge and contacts to push through the process of getting her things back.

"I'll be back," he murmured, disappearing while she stood in a long line for another clerk to retrieve her property.

Garen made his way to Captain Platt's office. Staring at his computer screen, Platt stopped typing on his keyboard to glance up. "I heard about you tackling and handing over a perpetrator trying to get to Kellie Monroe," the captain began. "Good work."

"Thanks, but he managed to run back into the hospital. Did the uniforms catch him? Is he here?" Garen asked, trying to remember if the man had been wearing a gold chain or collar.

Platt sighed. "No. They lost him. Was he a werewolf?"

Garen nodded. "Yep."

The captain tilted back in his chair. "You and Ms. Monroe should talk to our police artist and have a look at the pictures we have on file. If we find him, we could at least get him on assault."

Garen said nothing. He knew that unless the perp had a record, the likelihood of the cops finding him were next to none. The group, whoever they were, apparently wanted Kellie alive.

Platt pushed a document across the desk at him. "Did you know that Ms. Monroe filed a police report on her relative's missing body?"

Garen scratched his head. "Yes, the body disappeared somewhere between the hospital and the city morgue. I can't imagine what anyone would want to do with the body. We're still checking to see if it's got something to do with the attack."

"You never know. Platt's head inclined toward a chair. "Have a seat. Tell me what you've found out."

Garen sat. Working the preternatural division of the force meant that he had another boss in the regular LVPD. He was still getting the hang of having two bosses. So far, he'd been sharing information more or less equally with both men. He related Kellie's story and showed Platt the drawing she'd made of the medallions. Casually mentioning that the Preternatural Division was pursuing references to the knife, he noted that other than the color of the wolves' coats, Kellie hadn't been able to distinguish one from another. Only another werewolf and sometimes a vamp could do that.

Platt looked grim. "None of the werewolves left on the scene survived. There are no human survivors except for Kellie Monroe, and we lost that werewolf at the hospital. What have you got to go on?"

"Just Ms. Monroe and her sketches of the medallions," Garen

answered, deciding not to mention the mythical Arielle. That was the Preternatural Division's forte after all.

"I know that the vaccine injection nearly killed her. How is she doing?"

Garen shrugged. "Her physical injuries have healed, but we'll have to wait until the next full moon to see if the vaccine worked."

Platt frowned. "I can't see why her family would have skirted the law. Why leave your loved ones vulnerable to the lycantrope virus?"

"Some people apply to the council to willingly become werewolves." Garen observed Platt's facial expression. He worked well with Platt, but the man had prejudices he wasn't aware he had.

"Ms. Monroe wasn't given that option," Platt reminded him.

"No, but she is alive and well, thanks to something extraordinary. The vaccine made her violently ill and nearly killed her. Maybe her family knew the effects it would have on her body."

Platt shook his head. "I doubt that. I've never heard of that vaccine hurting anyone. It's actually kept more than a few people from becoming involuntary werewolves."

Garen shrugged, deciding not to argue. This was not an issue that they would come to agree on.

Moving on, Platt thumped his fingers on his desk with a staccato beat. "Until we catch this pack of wolves, your number-one job is to protect Ms. Monroe at all costs. We both know how important catching this pack is to maintaining the peace for all of us. We'll run that sketch of the medallions through all the police and government databases."

Nodding, Garen told Platt that he'd be in touch.

Kellie accepted the envelope with the things taken from Nana's home. Cradling it to her chest, she took it to one of the counters and poured out the contents. The knife and the guns Nana had left her were there.

Garen had come back and was standing with her. He claimed to have previously examined the knife, but it still fascinated him.

Was he wondering if it could burn him from the inside out as it had the alpha? Kellie mused. She hoped he'd never have the chance to find out.

Grateful for his help, she allowed him to examine the knife.

Raising it to his nose with a gloved hand, Garen sniffed.

How strong was a werewolf's sense of smell, Kellie wondered. Since wolves were kin to dogs, she imagined it would be strong. "What does it smell like?" she asked, curiously.

Garen's eyes were dark and dangerous. "Silver, werewolf blood."

"Did… did you go to the house? Did they find anything to… to—"

"The forensics team on the scene gathered all the evidence we needed," he answered. "But a tracking team went in and examined the house. I was there."

"And you didn't track them down?"

"Our trackers lost the scent in the park near the house. This group knew what to do to cover their tracks."

Biting her lip, she watched him examine the knife.

"It's beautiful," he said, carefully turning it over in his hands and examining the engraved designs of flowers and symbols. Then he surprised her by drawing a camera from his jacket and taking a series of pictures.

Kellie placed the little knife back in its sheath and fitted it into the waistband of her jeans.

"Where can I take you?" Garen asked as they exited the station.

Listening to the rich timbre of his voice and that soft southern lilt, the nature of their interaction suddenly seemed all too personal. She studied him, asking herself what did she really know about him other than the fact that he was a cop, a werewolf, a member of the Preternatural Police Force, and her protector? The longer she stayed in his company, the more right and natural it felt, the more it felt like something that should be. Kellie's right hand formed a fist. Now that she had the knife and her guns, couldn't she protect herself? "I can get a taxi."

Shuffling his feet and rotating a shoulder, Garen all but rolled his eyes. "Do we have to go through this shit again? You're tired, weak, and you just got out of the hospital. You seem intelligent. Think this through."

Kellie set her jaw. "I am intelligent, Mr. Roy, but I'm also stubborn and used to taking care of myself. There's no need for you to get nasty."

He eyed her silently, testosterone coming off him in waves. "I'm coming with you. Fact. We can go in my car, or I can follow your taxi. What's it going to be?"

Kellie could have screamed in frustration. She didn't like the way she felt physically, and she didn't like the way Garen made her feel like putty in his strong, capable hands. All she wanted was a safe, quiet place to rest and heal until she was well enough to handle her business.

She studied the man who fascinated her so much it scared her. What was it about Garen Roy that made her want to simultaneously kick his butt and jump his bones? She'd have to learn to deal with it if she was going to survive. Kellie swallowed her pride and backed down. "I'll take the ride, thanks."

Pivoting, he led her back to his unmarked car. "Where to?"

She'd been thinking about that one for a while. Nana's house with its ruined furniture, busted windows and doors would not be safe. "The Ocean Blue," she said, picking the first hotel and casino on the strip that came to mind.

Garen's reaction to her choice was almost imperceptible, but she caught it. Something flickered in his eyes, and his shoulders dropped.

"Bad choice?" she asked as he opened the passenger door. She climbed inside.

"Excellent choice. There's only one better." He shut the door and got in the driver's side.

"What's that?" she asked curiously.

"The French Quarter," he replied, driving off.

Chapter Four

Despite his family ties to the owners of the French Quarter Hotel and Casino, which was next door to the Ocean Blue Hotel and Casino, Garen didn't believe in luck. Still, Kellie's hotel choice made his life a hell of a lot easier. He suppressed a smile. Stashing her in a room there would enable him to check on the family business next door and call on trusted clan members to help him protect her. He'd also have the pack's best fighters and fastest healers available to take down the rogue band of werewolves.

Garen maintained silence all the way to the hotel. He didn't want to push Kellie or scare her off. Besides, he could see that she was exhausted.

Leaving the car parked close to the door, he held her arm and gently led her past the rolling waves and man-made beach that characterized the lavish hotel. Inside the blue marbled lobby, Coco, on the desk, barely hid her surprise when he stood and waited while Kellie checked in.

"Where will you be staying?" Kellie asked as he led her to her room. "I thought you might get an adjoining room."

Garen shot her a knowing glance. "I can't protect you if I can't see you."

She actually glared at him, her mahogany eyes all but sparking with emotion. "Did it ever occur to you that I might need a little privacy?"

"You'll get it." With an effort, he banked the fire building inside him. Because of his looks, his family, and what he was, he was used to women throwing themselves at him. Here was a woman who interested him more than any he'd ever met, and she couldn't wait to get rid of him. What was wrong with Kellie? "Would you prefer me switching places so that someone else could guard you?"

His ego took a beating as he watched her face show signs of the war going on within her. She did not want him around. Finally, she shook her head. "You can stay. I—I know you're just trying to protect me. I'm starting to get used to you, believe it or not."

That surprised him. This seemed to be a case of a lady protesting too much. Maybe Miss Kellie wasn't as immune as she pretended to be. He followed her to the room, his glance straying time and again to her surprisingly lush behind and graceful legs in those tight jeans. He usually went for the big and voluptuous women that were the Vegas standard, but something about Kellie kept his balls humming. The little head had been talking to him from the moment she'd awakened in that hospital room. At about five-foot five, she was a small, but exciting package of pure woman.

He made her stand at the door while he sniffed the room and checked it out. It was clean and free of intruders and electronic bugs.

She stepped into the room, sparing the king-sized bed a longing look and letting her glance fall meaningfully onto the plush sofa bed.

"I'll take the couch," he said, intent on easing her mind.

She relaxed visibly.

Does she think I would attack her? Garen set his teeth. He'd never wanted or pursued a woman who didn't want him, and he wasn't about to start. "There's a hot tub in the bathroom. Maybe that would help."

"Yeah, I am a little stiff," she murmured, zeroing in on the bathroom. She closed the door.

Surprisingly, she didn't lock it. It wouldn't have mattered. Garen knew how to open the hotel's bathroom doors, locked or not. He heard the water running.

He imagined her stripping naked and stepping into the tub. Kellie's unique scent, mixed with the hotel's signature bath salts, Ocean Breeze, wafted on the air, making him curse his keen sense of smell.

Sighing inwardly, he pushed back in the luxurious recliner. It had been a long but rewarding day. He allowed himself to doze lightly, knowing the slightest sound would awaken him. Thirty minutes later he stood, somewhat refreshed. Kellie hadn't moved.

Standing outside the bathroom, he called to her. There was no sound on the other side of the door, except for the jets busily churning the water. He turned the knob.

She was asleep with her head against the pillows that surrounded the bath. Her pretty caramel breasts with chocolate colored tips jutted out, the rest of her shapely form reflecting up from the depths of the water. He drank in the sight. His imagination hadn't done her justice.

He called to her again, aware that he couldn't leave her like this. She could drown.

She didn't even move.

Garen stepped forward and shut off the jets. He covered the bed with a couple of the luxurious cotton towels. She was so warm and soft in his arms that he felt himself hardening. His hands secured her beneath those shapely thighs and the inward curve of her waist. Her head lolled against his shirt.

Garen placed her on the bed. Her succulent lips were slightly parted. She looked fragile and petite, yet she'd stood alone against a pack of werewolves to put up a fight worthy of many alphas he knew, and lived. The puzzle of her ancestry pulled at him. Was she a descendant of Arielle and one of the Fey?

Her body curled against the soft cotton, an unconsciously issued erotic invitation.

His mouth watered. Desire shook him, gripping him like a boy chasing after his first piece of ass. He could barely think of anything besides the need to thrust himself into the soft folds of her sex. Ignoring the tightness in his pants, he quickly rubbed the moisture from her skin with the towel and covered her with the sheets.

Her soft moan was almost his undoing. *Damn.* She'd called his name.

Garen moved away. He needed to stay sharp. Right now, Kellie was the bait and he would not see her hurt because he was too busy burning up the sheets to protect her.

Satisfied that she was asleep, he opened the pullout couch and stretched out. It was a hell of a way to spend the night. Garen slept for hours. Much later he opened the door to the room. Paul was outside. He'd guarded Garen for most of his life. These days, Garen could take care of himself, but Paul refused to retire. He was like a father to Garen "Watch her. Guard her," he ordered, carefully closing the door. "I'm safe here, but she is a target."

Paul nodded, his light eyes keen as he studied Garen. His nostrils flared, catching the scent of Garen's arousal. "She is yours?"

"I need to talk to the others," Garen said, ignoring the question because he wasn't ready to admit his growing feelings for Kelly, even to himself. He strode down the hall with the weight of Paul's gaze riding his back. The sharp sense of smell shared by all his people was not always a blessing.

In the French Quarter's private club, his father, Dwayne, and the other alphas in the clan were waiting for him. His father appeared calm as he sat at the table swilling whiskey and joking with the rest of them, but Garen saw the tension in the set of his shoulders. Concern weighed in the depths of his brown eyes. "Did you get her?"

"Yeah, but she's anxious to get away from here."

"How's she doing?"

Garen shrugged. "The physical injuries have healed, but she's weak and exhausted. A Were tried to attack her at the hospital. I put two of the uniform cops on him, but he got away."

Dwayne's lip curled in disgust. "We got to get more of our werewolves into the department, 'cause unless they're using deadly force, the human cops can't handle werewolves. What's worse is that the way things are going, we're going to have a war on our hands."

Garen tilted his head. "Senator Ross?"

"Yes." Dwayne's glass hit the table hard. "At a press conference this morning, he used the growing wild werewolf problem to propose that all werewolves be registered and fingerprinted with the government. He even wants to add a chip, so that we can be identified anytime, anywhere."

"No!" Garen dropped down into a chair. "There's no way they can make us come in for that."

"They could do it if the vamps helped," Garen's younger brother, Gil, put in.

"They'd have to kill me first," Garen snarled. The room reverberated with similar comments from the other alpha males.

Werewolves and the vamps weren't buxom buddies, but they weren't exactly enemies either. The bottom line was that vamps needed blood and werewolves had plenty to give in addition to the ability to heal fast. What better way to get fresh blood without killing people and pissing off the government?

The bartender, Harry, set a shot of tequila on the table in front of Garen. Garen downed it in one gulp. "If that band of werewolves weren't going around terrorizing everyone, no one would bother listening to Ross's crazy ideas," he fumed as the warmth of the liquor slid down his insides.

"That's why we've got you working with the Preternatural Po-Po, cousin," his cousin Ralph said, leaning forward to get in his face with a lot of attitude. "Are you saying you can't handle it? Do you need help?"

Garen's right fist shot out so fast that Ralph didn't see it coming. It connected with the side of Ralph's face and sent him flying through the air, chair and all. Without a sound, the group parted like the Red Sea. Ralph slammed into the empty table behind them and hit the floor. He got up, cracking his jaw and stretching his neck.

"I can handle *you*, anytime," Garen said in a soft, deadly tone. "And when I need help, I'll ask for it. Got that?"

"Sure cuz." Ralph's smile was as phony as a seven-dollar bill. He seemed to think it was his job to challenge Garen regularly. They'd had some knockout drag down, hellacious fights, but Garen always managed to win. He'd finally decided that Ralph was acting as his personal trainer, and keeping him on his toes.

"What about the girl?"

"Her name is Kellie, and she came to town to bury her grand-mother and settle her affairs. Then the wolves attacked." He spread his notebook in the center of the table. "Some of the wolves that attacked wore gold chains with medallions like this."

All studied the sketch, but no one seemed to recognize the medallion, so he continued. "The pack of wildings still wants her for some reason. She was nearly attacked as she left the hospital. Right now she is our best chance of catching them, so until we find and eliminate the bunch, I will protect her."

"She is yours?" his cousin Ria asked, apparently sensing some-thing in his manner that the others didn't.

Garen hesitated, unwilling to claim what he felt without some word or encouragement from Kellie. "She is under my protection. Until she is safe, no one else approaches her unless I say so."

"She is one of us then?" Ria pressed, drawing more conclusions from his hesitation. "A werewolf?"

Garen shot her a warning glance. Not only were her questions annoying, they drew attention to the fact that there was or might be something between him and Kellie. As far as he was concerned, Kellie was still an unknown. "We won't know for sure until the next full moon."

Kellie awakened on a bed of soft, slightly damp towels and sheets. Rubbing herself against them, she stretched luxuriously. Sunlight poured in from the sheer panel in the middle of the gold drapes to illuminate the room. She was alone.

She sat up in the bed, surprised to find that she was naked. Then she remembered falling asleep in the hot tub. Garen had taken her out of the tub and put her to bed. By agreement, he was acting as her bodyguard, and it was something she'd never experienced. She'd fought hard against it, but his affect on her, the things she needed to do for Nana, and her need for independence had been at the core of her struggle. With the other, growing connection between them, she was beginning to think of him as hers and wonder what it would be like to have him around once this rogue werewolf business was settled. It put a new twist on her perceptions.

She'd dreamt about him. Her body warmed at the memory. That wide mouth of his had covered hers, and then covered her skin with kisses....

Wrapped in a towel, Kellie got up to get her clothes from the bathroom. They weren't there. Grumbling to herself, she all but tore the room apart, searching for them. The more she looked, the angrier she became. Her clothes were gone. Garen Roy had taken her clothes to make sure she'd stay in the room.

Stalking around the room, she finally noticed the big box in the chair by the bed. It was filled with clothes. Garen had obviously left it for her. Inside, there were two of everything, from underwear to jeans, shorts and tops. She went through them, her lips twisting wryly at the lace thongs and matching bras. The prospect of fresh clothing was too good to be ignored.

Freshening up, she dressed hurriedly. Too much time had passed since she'd been at Nana's. She needed to go back and retrieve the packet of things she found and replaced in Nana's hiding place behind the artificial fireplace.

She'd come to Vegas to bury Nana, but she hadn't been able to find the body. Nana had been declared dead at St. Mary's and moved to the morgue, but somehow the body had disappeared before the funeral home had a chance to pick it up. Kellie didn't know what to think. Nana had been powerful in her day, and so much so that in addition to the private service she wanted, Kellie was still bound to hold an official sort of ritual service and invite all Nana's friends of power, whether she found Nana's body or not. The service would have to be scheduled per Nana's will.

Working through her tangled hair with the little comb she kept in her purse, she tried to decide what she should do next. She'd already been to St. Mary's and talked to the staff. She'd even made a police report and did an escorted search of the morgue at the hospital and coroner's office. Dead bodies didn't get up and walk unless they were vamps. Nana had been something else. Exactly what, Kellie had never been able to determine. Nana kept most of her secrets. As far as Kellie could determine, the old woman had been at least a couple of hundred years old.

Going back to St. Mary's was a dead end. Going back to Nana's would be dangerous. The wolves were obviously still after her. She still didn't know why. There had been attacks across the country before she came to Vegas, but none in Nana's neighborhood. If the wolves had had something to do with Nana's disappearing body, she'd know, wouldn't she? There was nothing subtle about them.

Kellie went to the door. She would go back to Nana's under Garen's protection, but that didn't mean she had to cower in her room until he returned. Outside the room, a chunky young man in a navy suit stood. He was built like a wrestler with dreadlocks that reached his shoulders. At the sound of the door opening he turned, his body blocking the entrance.

She stopped short, weighing her options. He smelled like werewolf, but if he was one of her attackers, he'd missed a prime opportunity to kill or kidnap her in her sleep. "Where's Garen?" she asked, startled at how easily the name rolled off her tongue.

"I am Paul," he said in a voice that grated like rough sandpaper. Light brown eyes sized her up curiously. His nostrils flared briefly as he caught her scent. "I work for Garen. He had a meeting. I will guard you until he returns."

"I'm going to look around the hotel," she announced, moving around him and starting down the hall.

After a second, he followed.

Kellie strolled around the hotel and casino, taking in the plush surroundings. The complex contained a full gym that she vowed to return to, a full service spa, and several restaurants. Ignoring the deep rumbling in her stomach, she lingered in her favorite place, the serene white carpeted lobby where the glass walls and alcoves were filled with blue salt water and all sorts of live creatures from the ocean. After all the excitement of the past days and weeks, the visual beauty was calming.

"Would you like to get something to eat?"

Garen's voice broke in on her revelry.

She didn't hear him approach, but she certainly caught his earthy, outdoorsy scent mixed with cologne. It sent excitement strumming through her body. Glancing at him in surprise, she could see that he knew the effect he had on her senses and wasn't immune to her either. There was a light in his heated cognac eyes.

"I want to get my things from Nana's, but I am hungry," she said, getting up from the white leather couch. "What did you have in mind?"

He ran down the list of the restaurants in the complex. Kellie shook her head to every one. She couldn't make things too easy for him, could she?

He eyed her silently, and then led her back to the casino and through a set of double doors to the hotel/casino complex next door. It was the French Quarter and built to emulate the French Quarter in New Orleans.

Chapter Five

The atmosphere changed as soon as they stepped through the open doors. Kellie felt a sort of energy in the air that seemed to be centered on several of the people gambling and lounging about. They were werewolves, she realized, inhaling the earthy scent in the air. When had she gotten such a sharp sense of smell? She moved closer to Garen, noting that Paul had followed them.

"You are safe," Garen said softly so only she could hear. "My cousins own and run this place."

Taking her hand, he drew her into the Bayou Restaurant.

His hand felt hot on hers. The physical sensations she got from the contact started the vibration low in her stomach. As if he physically explored her body, currents of sensual heat ran up her arms and spread all over her. She was wet.

Garen breathed in deeply. One of his fingers massaged her palm. That damned light in his eyes grew more pronounced.

Kellie swallowed. Sooner or later she knew she would be sleeping with him. What was wrong with her? She really didn't know him; he was a wolf, damn it and she'd been hurt by werewolves, but logic did nothing to dispel her desire for Garen. She simply didn't know how long she could hold out. She had needs, but this compelling attraction and need for him surpassed anything she'd ever experienced. Even worse, she was falling in love with him. "Are you seeing someone?" she managed.

"Nothing serious. Were you?"

"No." Kellie shook her head.

Garen's lips brushed hers. They were soft. Laced with mint, his breath mingled with hers.

Kellie shivered, her whole body tingling. They were in public, and she wanted to grab him and disappear beneath the table. "So this is serious?" she asked, feeling a tremor go through the hand that held hers.

"Yes." The warmth of his breath tickled her ear. "This is the beginning of something deep and lasting for both of us. Have you felt this way before?"

She shook her head. "No. You?"

His hand tightened almost painfully on hers. "I enjoy being with women, it is our way, but this thing between us is different. You are different."

"And if I stayed here with you, what would my life be like?" she asked, trying to picture it.

"I have a home in the hills nearby, and my family is large and welcoming. As next in line to lead the Roy Clan, I am always protected, but you've had a taste of that with Paul. Your life would be whatever you wanted it to be. What do you want Kellie? What do you dream of?"

"I want to take care of Nana, the way she wanted me to, and I want to verify the legend of Arielle, once and for all," she answered honestly. "But the last time I slept, I dreamed about you."

His mouth caught hers in one, two, three teasing little kisses.

She wanted more. The pure masculine power of him washed over her.

"We should have gone to the room," he said an impatient low voice dangerously close to a growl. "Now it is too late."

Kellie blinked as the waiter approached the table with a set of menus. He addressed Garen by name.

Waiving away the menus, Garen ordered Cajun Steak extra rare for both of them.

She didn't often eat steak, but her stomach wasn't turning over at the thought, so she only gave him a sharp glance. "I know how to order for myself."

He apologized. "It's a big menu and I knew how hungry you were. I can call our waiter back and cancel your order."

Kellie shook her head. "I'm too hungry for that."

Garen stared at her, a new element in his gaze. "Yes, you're changing, becoming one of us. Do you know that?"

She nodded. It fit with her heightened senses and the quick way she'd healed. When the new moon came, she'd be a werewolf. Tears pricked her lids. She would have liked to have a choice. Deep inside, she stubbornly nurtured the hope that Garen was wrong.

As if he sensed her thoughts, Garen stared at her intently. "You will be a welcome part of a loving group who cares for their own and you will have a longer life and freedom from disease. Kellie, it is not a bad thing."

The waiter returned with their food. Using her knife and fork, Kellie dug in, chewing and swallowing the barely cooked meat with gusto. Afterward, she pushed the plate away, surprised at how much she'd enjoyed it. There was no salad or potato, and she didn't want them.

A tall, attractive couple approached the table. Garen stood and the men greeted each other by grinning, teasing, shaking hands, and clapping each other on the back. The smiling woman had toffee-colored skin and big gray eyes. She hugged Garen briefly and kissed his cheek. Garen introduced her as his cousin Laurel. The man, had hazel eyes and softly curling hair that came all the way down to shoulders. Garen introduced him as his cousin Marcus.

Both were friendly, but Kellie caught their scent with her heightened senses as they settled in added chairs on the other side of the table. They were both werewolves. She wondered if werewolves had surrounded her all along and she'd been simply oblivious to the fact.

"Garen spends a lot of time out in the field with the Preternatural Police, so we don't get to see him much," Laurel confided. "He's always working."

"You're always working too, Laurel," Garen returned.

Laurel nodded. "Yes, but running security here has a bonus. At least people can find me here when they need to. The extra work you do with the Preternatural Police makes you hard to find."

Marcus put a beefy hand on the table and leaned forward.

"Speaking of the Preternatural Po-Po, Dawg, the heat's on all of us because of this rogue band of werewolves."

"Have you got any leads?" Laurel interjected. "Anything we should be looking for?"

Garen reached into an inside pocket and drew out the sketch Kellie had made. "Our lone survivor saw these gold medallions around the wolves necks," he said smoothing it out and passing it to them. "I've already given the details to the Roy Clan. You guys were next on my list."

Marcus and Laurel studied the sketch of the circular disc with a wolf's head in front of a full moon.

"I've seen this damned thing somewhere," Laurel remarked. "I just can't remember where."

"Me too," Marcus echoed.

Garen sighed. "That's been the consensus so far. Hopefully someone will remember soon."

"Can I get a copy of this right now?" Laurel asked, "I can show it to the clan and my staff and get back to you."

"I'd appreciate it," Garen said. "We're getting copies to trusted people in each of the known Vegas clans."

While Laurel excused herself to go copy the sketch, Garen ordered drinks for everyone. Kellie sipped wine.

"You must be new here, 'cause I haven't seen you around the casino. Garen is taken with you. How did you meet him?" Marcus asked between sips of ginger ale. He'd said that he didn't drink when he was working.

She hesitated, aware that Garen had avoided telling the couple that she was the survivor of the attack. "I'm the one who made the sketch," she confessed.

"Oh." His expression changed to one of compassion and regret. "We're glad that you've survived your ordeal. I hope you know that what happened is not the norm...."

Kellie nodded. "Garen told me, and soon, what I think is the norm won't matter much. My body is going through changes, and Garen is certain I'm already starting to change into a werewolf."

Marcus eyed her sharply. "But your scent is different and the vaccine...."

"Didn't work and nearly killed me," she explained.

She was interrupted when Laurel reentered the restaurant at a fast clip. Her face was flushed with excitement as she reached the table and leaned in to talk in a low tone. "I was talking to Janet, and I remembered. I saw a gold medallion like this on a human who got into a fight in the casino with one of the Tanetti brothers. They came in together and were friendly until the fight broke out. The police happened to be nearby, and they made a report..."

A human? The thought that humans could be mixed up in the business with the rogue werewolves put a nasty slant on things for Kellie. She noticed that everyone looked upset.

Garen whipped out his cell and dialed a number. He identified himself, then he ordered a check of the police reports for altercations at the French Quarter Hotel and Casino within the last two years. When he'd switched off the phone, he gazed at everyone at the table. "We all know that the Tanetti brothers worked for Cutter, Fang, and Mad Dawg, the local drug lords. Cutter died the same week those werewolves attacked that suburb, but new alphas are already stepping up to take over. This could get ugly."

"It already is," Laurel told him. "We had a little problem a couple of weeks ago with some wolves, some vamps, and some tainted drugs. Someone tried to set us up to get wiped out by the vamps. We didn't involve the authorities because it was a family matter, but I'll share the details with you later."

Garen nodded. "I hope to have this mess with the rogue wolves cleaned up before the next pack meeting." He glanced at his watch and turned to face Kellie. "We need to get going."

Taking leave of Laurel and Marcus, Garen and Kellie exited back through the casino to the Ocean Hotel and Casino Complex. Garen's car was still parked close to the building. As they climbed into it, Kellie noticed that Paul was still shadowing them and had climbed into a dark gray sedan. "Is Paul extra protection for me? Or is he your bodyguard?" she asked.

His eyes crinkled at the corners, his lips spreading into a smile that warmed her insides. "Paul is family, but he has been my body-guard since I was an infant. We've offered him other jobs, but he insists on keeping this one. My father is Dwayne Roy and he heads the Roy Clan. We own several properties in Las Vegas, and you've already met some of my cousins who own and run the French Quarter Hotel and Casino."

She returned the smile. "I played right into your plans by picking the Ocean, huh?"

"You made it easier for us to protect you," he agreed, taking off. "You will find that werewolves are very territorial. The strength and leadership of the alphas in the Vegas area's clans has preserved the peace, but there are always others, looking for an opportunity to upset the balance or grab a piece of our turf."

In the closed space of the car, his earthy scent filled her nostrils, making her a little dizzy. She was careful not to touch him. *Good Lord.* She caught herself. *Could the man be that good?* She hoped to find out soon. Maybe then she could clear her head and make a decision about going on about her business.

Kellie turned up the fan on the air conditioning. That seemed to help. She thought ahead to what she would do when they reached Nana's house. There was no way she could keep Garen from seeing her retrieve the envelope and Nana's instructions. She didn't want to keep secrets from him because they shared a connection, and she knew he was trying to help her, but Nana's secrets were not Kellie's to share.

They parked outside the house and cut through the yellow tape to crunch up the driveway on broken glass. There was no one around, but Kellie figured that Paul was somewhere close, granting the illusion of privacy. The doors and windows had been boarded up to discourage vandals. Garen used the tire iron from the car to pry the boards from the door.

Inside Nana's home, the lights were on. The power had been restored to the area. Kellie stepped into what remained of her battle with the werewolves. Broken candles and melted wax littered the floors. It was a wonder that the place hadn't burned down.

Shattered glass and splintered wood lay as it had fallen.

"You can hire someone to clean this place up," Garen muttered as he surveyed the damage.

An odd sense of déjà vu gripped her as she stepped past the couch and the area where the werewolf had savaged her arm. She was a different person now, forever changed by her ordeal.

Sensing something, Garen came over and put an arm around her shoulders. His touch steadied her, enabling her to focus more on the job at hand. Their gazes locked. Her eyes narrowed. He'd known that his touch would have that effect.

"We're connected," he said, answering the question in her eyes. "There's a bond growing between us."

"How? Why?" she asked, sensing that she'd already missed the closing of a trap around her.

He shrugged. "You and I were meant to be. The growing mental, physical, and emotional bond is what happens when you meet your mate, the one who is meant for you. Wolves mate for life. Finding your mate is a blessing. It cannot be ignored."

She huffed in disbelief.

Garen tailed hot fingers down her arm.

She cried out against the sudden wave of desire shooting through her veins.

"Stop pushing me, Kellie," he ordered. "We cannot make love here. It's not safe."

Swallowing a biting reply, she said instead, "I feel... something, but the truth is that you just met me."

"Does that make my feelings any less valid?" Garen turned away from her. "I'll pack your things."

She watched him walk back to the guest room she'd been using without another word. She guessed that he'd followed her scent.

With him out of the room, she hurried to the fireplace and removed the camouflage cover from a brick where the mortar had been chipped away. She saw that Nana had warded the area with magic against intruders. Thrusting her hand into the opening, she drew out the envelope. She didn't dare check the contents with

Garen so close. Kellie replaced the cover and turned around. She stifled a quick intake of breath.

Garen was standing behind her with her suitcase. She wondered how'd he manage to pack so fast. Then she wondered how long he'd been standing there.

"What's that you've got in your hand?" he asked.

She swallowed and tried to get by with a limited version of the truth. "Nana's papers, things she left me, and instructions for what to do after her death."

"Did you check it? Make sure nothing is missing?"

Kellie shook her head. "It's been well hidden. I found it a little while before the wolves attacked and put it back."

His gaze sharpened. "You don't think the werewolves...."

"No." She cut him off. "Let's get out of here."

Glancing around, he said, "Make certain there's nothing here you want."

He scanned the floor of each room, hoping one of the wolves had dropped their medallions or a clue. He found nothing.

Taking Garen's suggestion to heart, she looked around, finally pocketing a little ivory figurine that she'd loved as a child and the thick journal that had been on Nana's nightstand. "Let's get out of here."

Garen drove them back to the Ocean Complex, certain that Kellie was keeping something from him. It had to do with the envelope she'd protectively clutched to her chest. He fought the urge to coax her into talking about it. They were still too new to each other.

At the hotel, she stifled a low moan when he took her hand to help her out of the car. His pants tightened at the sound.

The look she gave him was a carnal invitation of the utmost urgency.

The intoxicating scent of her sent blood pounding through his veins. He could only think of the softness of her skin, her pretty breasts and fine ass; and what it would feel like to explore her body and the welcoming warmth between her thighs.

Careful not to touch her, he strode to the room. She followed, almost running to keep up. Just inside the room he closed the door and drew her close. The entire length of them touched; soft feminine curves to his hard muscled body and thick, burgeoning sex. His pants tightened painfully.

Her hands smoothed up and down his arms and slid under his shirt. "Do it," she whispered. "It's all I can think about." Her head tilted up, her mouth opening on a gasp as he gripped the soft globes of her ass and squeezed.

Garen drew in a harsh breath and covered her mouth, his tongue tangling and tasting the exotic sweetness within. She tasted like ripe mangoes. Licking her lips, sliding his tongue against hers, he feasted. He thrust an open palm between her legs and cupped the warmth of her sex beneath the jeans.

Panting and opening her legs, Kellie trembled as he rubbed his open palm along the center seam of her jeans. It was damp. Her knees buckled, and she fell against him, making soft sexy noises in the back of her throat.

With a low growl, Garen picked her up and took her to the bed. Ripping back the covers, he placed her on the sheets.

"Garen." She reached for him, her body curling and undulating in erotic invitation.

He pulled her tank top up. She hadn't bothered with the bra. His eyes took in the caramel-colored mounds of her cone-shaped breasts. The dark, hardened tips reminded him of raisins. His mouth watered. He laved the mounds as he would an ice cream cone, suckling the tips as his fingers worked the button and zipper on her jeans.

He felt her hands at his waist, pulling the zipper on his pants, releasing the tightness against his erection. She reached in to stroke him.

His sex was so hard it was painful. Garen inched backward. He was too close to the edge. Bending at the waist, he tugged off her sandals and drew the jeans down the length of her legs. Then he stepped out of his pants.

Kellie bent her legs at the knees. The peach lace thong was soaked with her essence. The sweet, musky scent made him crazy. Holding her soft thighs, he traced the edges of the garment with his tongue and sucked the essence from the center.

Kellie undulated against him, her fingers clutching his head and tangling in his hair.

In a swift movement, he ripped off the thong and covered her with his mouth. He dipped his tongue into her hot center, laving the delicious folds of her sex. His groans and her high-pitched cries echoed in the room. Like honey-spiced mango, her juices filled his mouth; sweet, musky, and exotic.

When she lay breathless, limp, and boneless on the bed, he lifted her legs onto his shoulder, and pulled on a condom. Then he hesitated. The sum of him was more than man or wolf. "We should try something else. This has been building ever since we met, and I don't trust myself to take the care you need."

Kellie gripped him with her small hands. Her gaze locked with his, filled with a scorching demand. "You've been teasing me, and it's gotten so that I can't think of anything else. I want to experience everything in your nature or desire to give. I want you to be yourself. I don't want you to be gentle."

Still, he held himself on the edge. She was still fragile from her ordeal. He didn't want to hurt her. His body shook with the effort of holding back. He'd never been this deep into having any woman.

Kellie drew his head down for a sensual kiss that made his head spin. He pushed into her slippery heat. Three hard, dizzying thrusts embedded him deep in her core. She gasped. He rocked fast, then slow, alternating between the two until a wild, rambunctious rhythm sent them on a journey as old as time. Thrusting, panting, pushing until their bodies clenched and spasmed in a wet, sweat covered tangle of flesh.

Kellie's arms locked around him, holding tight with her legs and her sex.

Primal energy filled the room. Garen drew in a deep breath and drew the covers over them. That had been some bone deep, nut busting sex. A man could get addicted to something like that. A man could get addicted to Kellie.

She slid under the covers, her hot, wet tongue licking the salt off his skin and sucking his nipples. Dipping low, she squeezed him and took him into her mouth. He tangled his fingers in her hair, the blood already pounding through his veins once more.

Garen slept hard. He'd awakened twice during the night to make love to Kellie. She lay pressed against him, her legs tangled with his.

In the hours before dawn, they lay together on the bed, holding one another in the dark. "What are you Kellie?" he whispered into the silence.

She snuggled against him and whispered. "Descendant of Arielle and one of the Frey, werewolf, maybe both."

"And more? It is said that the Frey has magic. Do you have magic?"

"I never did before." She turned to face him. "Nana had more magic than anyone I'd ever known, but she kept it secret. She wasn't surprised or concerned that I didn't have it because she was more than enough for both of us. She thought it would come with time. I'm changing Garen, but I don't know what it means. The doctor said that the nonhuman elements in my blood were increasing."

"That's what happens when people become werewolves," Garen assured her.

"But I'm not sure that's what's happening to me."

He pulled her into his arms. "If I could take back what's happened to you, I would, but things will work out, you'll see. I'll do everything I can to make it right for you. I promise."

"Even if I become something other than a werewolf?" she whispered, obviously seeking assurance.

"Even if you become something other than werewolf," he answered, repeating her words and giving the assurance she needed.

Kellie was silent. Soon Garen heard her breathing softly in sleep.

Garen dozed only to awaken as the sun came up. He should be weak from exerting himself he thought as he sat up in bed, but he felt strong and energized.

He got up to run a bath for Kellie and order room service. She awakened as he lifted her from the bed, sighing as he placed her into the tub of fragrant, steaming water.

Chapter Six

Garen sat at the table with a stainless steel tray. Kellie was coming out of the bath dressed in the one of the hotel's cotton terry robes. He started having second thoughts about breakfast. His cell phone rang.

With a sigh of regret, he lifted the cover on the tray, pulled out Kellie's chair, and answered the phone.

Bonner's voice sounded in his ear. "Hey, Garen, I went through all the reports filed on Vegas casinos within the last year and there were only two filed on the French Quarter. I'll give you the names and dates from both. Got a pen?"

"Yeah." Garen drew a pen and the little notebook he kept from the pocket the suit jacket he'd thrown across a chair. With his ear glued to the phone, he wrote down the names Paul Bickford and LaToya Collins, May 2 of last year. Franco Tanetti and Sammy Pierson, August 19. "Have you got addresses for Tanetti and Pierson?"

Garen was excited as he wrote down the addresses. Other than Kellie, this was another big lead. He planned to visit Tanetti and Pierson as soon as he finished breakfast.

Settled in the chair beside him, Kellie was helping herself to bacon, eggs, and toast. Just looking at her filled Garen with a different kind of excitement.

Her gaze locked with his. She smiled, a fresh, intriguing window into her soul. When she spoke, the musical quality of her voice fascinated him. He could very well believe that his Kellie was one of the Frey and as magical as they come. He smiled back and forcibly broke the spell to eat the food on his plate. "I've got a lead to follow this morning," he announced over coffee. "I've got to leave right after breakfast, but Paul will be here to protect you."

"I need to go through Nana's things and arrange a memorial service anyway," she said. "I'll probably stick around the hotel."

Before he knew what he was doing, he'd pulled her from her chair and into his lap. His hands slipped beneath her robe to massage her legs.

Curling into him, she sighed with pleasure. "I'm game if you are, but I can't believe you're down for another round."

"I'm not. I just can't keep my hands off you." He kissed her, his tongue going deep into the recess of her mouth. Garen undid the belt on the robe.

The robe fell open as she climbed off his lap to stand. She cupped his cheek. "I'll be in the bathroom for a minute to brush my teeth. If you're going to follow those leads, this is your chance to escape. If not, we can spend the morning in bed."

Garen watched the sensuous sway of Kellie's hips as she strolled to the bathroom. He honestly didn't want to leave, and it wasn't just about the promise of more sex.

Minutes later, Kellie left the bathroom minus the robe to face an empty room. Garen was gone. That bothered her. She needed time alone to explore the contents of the envelope, yet she felt abandoned, bereft, and slightly anxious. She blamed it on the growing bond between them. She missed him already. Going to the window to look out, she acknowledged that it wasn't a matter of the ache between her legs. Garen's presence had become very necessary.

She found her suitcase in the closet. Combing through it, she found a printed cotton tank top and a pair of slacks and put them on. Then she retrieved the brown envelope and poured the contents out on the bed.

Opening the white linen envelope first, she drew out Nana's will and began to read. Nana's number one request was that her body be buried in the earth near the little village where she'd been born. Guilt seized Kellie at the thought the she couldn't locate the body. Nana had set great store in her body, turning to dust in the same place that she'd come from. At least Kellie could have the memorial service and invite all the people listed. According to the will, Nana had left the house and its contents to her. There was also enough money in a local bank account to make it unnecessary for Kellie to work for a long time.

Examining the rest of the items on the bed, she found a parchment with a hand written history of the warrior queen, Arielle. There was even a list of her female descendants. Kellie saw her name written neatly at the bottom, just below Nana's name and a woman named Meloni. Carefully placing the parchment back in the envelope, she examined a beautiful gold ring with inset ruby flowers and emerald leaves.

Although Nana had had a lot of power in her compact form, she'd also been a very natural woman. It was unusual for her to wear a lot of jewelry. Kellie could only remember the twisted gold loops Nana wore in her ears all the time. There'd never been anything else.

Kellie put the ring back in the packet.

Nearly hidden by the rumpled sheets was a gold medallion that made Kellie catch her breath. It was too much like the one she'd seen on the werewolves. The moon and the wolf's head were stamped on the front, but then there were several other animal heads too. She made out the head of a lion, a bear, a horse, a hawk, and a snake.

If werewolves wore the amulet with the moon and the wolf's head, would this amulet's wearer be able to change into the various animals pictured? Kellie pulled out the will and read one of the addendums. Nana referred to the medallion as the shapeshifter's medallion. It would indeed enable its wearer to change into any of the forms displayed on its front. The medallion felt hot in her hands.

The phone on the nightstand rang. Startled, she nearly dropped the medallion. The phone kept ringing an angry, clamoring sound that grated her senses. Garen wasn't calling, she reasoned. He'd just left. She had no known relatives or friends who knew she was here.

Lifting the receiver, she spoke into the phone.

A deep baritone raised the hairs on the back of her neck. "Good to see you're still with us, Ms. Monroe and feeling better from all reports."

She clamped down on her jaw. "Who is this?"

"Who do you think? It's been at least a couple of weeks since we saw one another." He erupted into a devilish fit of chuckling.

Kellie shivered involuntarily. One hand balled into an angry fist.

"Understand," the voice continued, "if we'd wanted you'd dead, we wouldn't be talking to you now."

"So what do you want?" she asked, making her voice as hard as steel.

"Oh I believe we have something you want. Your dear Nana has been our guest for a while now."

Kellie gasped. Hope filled her at the thought of the impossible. She'd never gotten the chance to say goodbye. "She's alive?"

"No." He chuckled again. "But why should we let a little thing like death stops us from enjoying her company?"

"You're sick," she declared, gathering the things on the bed and trying to stuff them back into the envelope.

"If you want to insure her eternal rest by burying the body, you'll meet me alone and you'll bring the amulet."

"What amulet?" she asked innocently, wondering how someone else could know about something private that she'd just discovered.

"Don't play with me," he snapped. "She would have left it for you since it is yours by birthright."

Kellie gripped the phone trying to make sense of his statement. Nana had claimed to be very distantly related to Kellie. "What do you mean?"

The voice took on an edge. "Floyd Lamb State Park in an hour. It's about ten miles outside of Las Vegas. Take US Hwy 95 to Durango to Tule Springs Road. Bring the amulet and come alone or we'll ditch the body, and she'll never rest in peace."

"I don't have a car," she protested.

The dial tone buzzed her ear. He'd hung up.

Kellie stood and pulled on her sneakers. This was an opportunity she couldn't pass up. If things worked right, she could help Garen catch the werewolves, free herself from their threat, and get Nana's body back. Her purse was on the floor in the bedroom.

Checking for ID, charge cards, her guns, and extra ammo, she opened the door to the room.

Paul was in the hallway, watching her curiously.

Briefly she thought of lying, anything to get rid of him so she could get to the meeting place. Common sense won out. Paul was good at watching and protecting from a distance without being seen. All she had to do was make him understand. "I've got to be at Floyd Lamb State Park in an hour, and I've got to go alone or something bad will happen," she began. "Get Garen. I'm meeting those werewolves."

Kicking one opponent in the solar plexus and punching the other so hard his head snapped back and his nose bled, Garen whirled, knocking two of the Tanetti brothers' hired muscle to the ground. The goons hadn't bothered to change, but they were werewolves. He could smell it in them and see it in their unusual strength. Scrambling up, they came back at him.

He was tired of this routine, but he couldn't afford to change into his wolf and be ruled by instinct instead of knowledge and logic. Garen growled low in his throat, filling it with the anger and rage of an alpha male.

The dark haired one answered by growling low in his throat and approaching cautiously. The other whined and backed off.

Charging forward, Garen smashed his fist into his challenger's face, breaking his nose and shattering his teeth. Lifting his opponent, Garen hurled him into the side of the adobe house.

His challenger lay unmoving on the gravel in a pool of blood.

Garen struggled briefly with the wolf inside him and the instinct to finish off the werewolf. Werewolves healed fast. To make sure his opponent stayed down, Garen drew cuffs from a back pocket and cuffed one leg to an arm behind him. It would make it difficult for the werewolf to change and heal his injuries.

Finishing his task, he looked around. The other werewolf had run. Garen had no illusions about the werewolf returning with reinforcements, so he hurried up the steps. Jerking open the screen door, he peered in cautiously and entered the house.

Announcing his presence as an officer of the law, Garen sniffed the air. The place smelled of werewolf. The scent was different from the two he'd fought outside. The interior of the house was filled with trash. He heard the sounds of running outside.

Garen quickly eased back toward the front door for a look. He pushed at the screen.

Shots rang out. A bullet zinged past him.

That surprised him. The two goons hadn't bothered with guns, so who was shooting at him now? He didn't plan on catching a bullet to see if it was silver. It would take too long to heal. Garen drew the gun he kept loaded with silver bullets. This was deadly force for werewolves and would have to be explained.

Someone was running again. Peeping out the corner of the screen, he saw a figure melt into the shadow of a tree. "This is the police. Hold it right there!" Garen called out.

A barrage of bullets answered him. Garen looked up and down the street. He'd called the Preternatural Division for backup on the way over. They were taking their damned time. Aiming carefully for a place where a scrap of dark material stood out from the tree, Garen fired.

A barrage of wild shots went off. A figure separated from the side of the tree, falling to the ground.

Training his eyes on the prone figure, Garen hurried out. He saw the gun in the street. In the distance, he heard a siren. It was about damned time.

A man who looked like an exotic mix of African American and Asian lay on the small grassy area, writhing in pain. It was Pierson. Blood poured from a hole in his side. He moaned, his fingers clutching something beneath his shirt.

Lifting the shirt, Garen examined the object. It was a gold medallion like the one Kellie had sketched. He saw the wounded werewolf trying to effect the change to wolf. Going on instinct, Garen grabbed the chain and snatched the medallion off him.

Pierson groaned and tried to get it back.

Placing the medallion on the ground out of reach, Garen used his spare pair of cuffs to secure the werewolf. "Tell me about this medallion," Garen demanded in a harsh growl. "Where did you get it?"

"It's mine. Give it back," Pierson insisted.

Garen tightened his hold on Pierson's shirt. "The pack of werewolves who attacked several people on the outskirts of the city was wearing medallions like this. You're under arrest for suspicion of murder." He began to read him his rights.

Pierson's eyes got big, and he actually whined. "No, no man. It wasn't me. I wasn't involved in that."

"Tell me who was." Garen's eyes were hard. He didn't like Pierson's smell. It was rank and foul. He liked the werewolf's behavior even less. The dominant males like Garen were alphas and the less dominant wolves were betas. Garen placed Pierson below any beta he'd ever met.

Garen's cell phone began to ring. Between holding and interrogating Pierson and keeping an eye out for the requested backup, he tried to ignore it. When the phone stubbornly continued to ring, he put a knee in Pierson's chest and whipped it out.

Paul was on the other end talking fast, something Garen rarely experienced. When he heard that Paul was following Kellie to the Lamb state park to meet a werewolf, he thought he would explode. After the incident outside the hospital, she'd been more careful. She'd told him that she would stay at the hotel. Garen cussed a blue streak. "Of all the dangerous things to do… And why?"

"From what I could hear, something to do with her Nana," Paul answered.

Garen snatched Pierson to his feet using the front of his shirt. "Her Nana is dead."

"Yeah, but ain't the body missing?"

"Son of a bitch!" Garen's clamped down on his jaw so hard that it hurt for several seconds. Then the natural healing process of his body took over.

"We're almost there," Paul warned. "I alerted the pack, but they're hanging back till I give the signal. Seeing as how she was attacked only a couple of weeks ago, and then she hasn't fully changed yet, it could get scary for her."

"I'll meet you there in a few minutes." Garen got off the phone with his heart thundering in his chest. Again, he was seeing his Kellie as a warrior to her heart, and she didn't let size or odds deter her from her goals. She was precious and more fragile than she knew. He didn't even want to consider what would happen to him if Kelly got hurt or killed. He would be alone for the rest of his life because there was no way he could ever replace her. He drew Pierson close to his face and filled a growl with all of his power. "I'm only going to ask once. What do they want with Kellie Monroe?"

Kellie drove in under the park's sign, checking the clock in the white rental car. A woman on a mission, she was actually ten minutes early. That suited her just fine. Scouting the place, she drove around, noting the four little lakes, the shaded picnic area, walking/bicycle path, and horse pits. It was a pretty place, just perfect for getting away from the glitz and glamour of Vegas for something closer to reality. The place seemed deserted. She knew better.

To feel more secure, she checked her guns and ammo again. They wouldn't even the odds, but they could help her stay safe until Garen arrived. Stuffing the 9mm in the big pocket of her slacks and the automatic in her purse, she switched off the ignition. She was ready.

Grabbing her bottle of water, she stepped out of the car into the oven like heat. It was almost noon. Nevada sun threatened to roast her skin. She hitched up her sunglasses and started on the grass-lined path down to the picnic tables and the shade. Out of the corners of her eyes, she saw shadows moving. When she turned to look, there was nothing there.

Clutching the purse tightly, she kept walking toward the tables at a calm, measured pace. Her tennis shoes echoed on the hardened dirt. Furtive sounds reached her from time to time. She was not alone. Idly, she wondered how long they'd wait before they made a move on her.

At the tables, she took a seat with her back against the trunk of a tree. The short walk had made her thirsty. She sipped from the water bottle and made the most of the shade.

With a slight rustling sound, a tall man walked out of a copse of trees to her right. The slight breeze carried the werewolf scent. He was pretty for a man, with fine features and bronzed skin that made him look exotic without giving any real hints of his ancestry. Chiseled cheekbones and his lean-muscled build saved him from looking too feminine.

"You came alone," he said, deep voice resonating in the air. "Smart woman."

Kellie wasn't so sure. Especially when she knew that more of his pack waited in the copse of trees. How was she going to keep him from taking the amulet and her along with it? Her guns loaded with silver bullets would help, but given the numbers she'd seen at Nana's, she'd be outnumbered. She could only hope that Paul was as competent as she suspected and had been able to contact Garen.

Unusual, peridot-colored eyes surveyed her, summing her up. "I am Armando."

The closer he got, the more the feeling that he walked in the center of a sphere of power grew. It raised the hair on her arms and made him seem impossibly attractive. When Garen came close, it was a similar feeling, but this was somehow different. She wondered if it had something to do with the gold amulet he wore around his neck.

"What do you want with the amulet?" she asked. "It's mine. Nana left it to me."

"We've been looking for it," he replied calmly as he took a seat on the other end of the table. "While your Nana was alive, none could touch it or her, but now that she's dead, you have neither the skills or the power to hold on to it. I can't see it on you, but I can feel its power from here. Who wouldn't want such power?"

Kellie hardened her tone. "You have your own power. I can feel *that* from here."

Armando's lips quirked up in amusement. "Oh but your amulet has more useful properties," he said. "Have you stopped to wonder about the different animals engraved on the surface? Give it to me, and I'll show you how to use it."

She didn't want to give him anything. She could only stall so long. Garen had to come soon. Unzipping her purse, Kellie delved deep to fit her hands around the gun. "Where is Nana's body?"

Armando gave her a measured glance. "Stay calm, Ms. Monroe, and we will get through this without further violence."

He made a whistling sound between his teeth. Two men stepped out of the trees, carrying a body bag, and headed for the picnic table.

Swallowing, Kellie felt sad that Nana had suffered this indignity in death.

The two men carefully set the bag on the table and pulled the zipper open.

She didn't want to look, but how else could she make sure it was Nana? Training her eyes on the bag, she fought a sickening wave of revulsion.

The scent of lavender hit the air and mixed with the decaying scent of death. Lavender had been Nana's favorite scent. The first things visible were the thick waves of Nana's silvery gray hair. The waves of her hair filled the bag, the mass covering her face. Armando gently pushed the hair away from the face.

Kellie stifled her quick intake of breath. Familiar twisted gold loops adorned the ears. It was Nana, but the body looked severely dehydrated, almost as if the old woman had been freeze dried. She shot Armando a scorching look. "What did you do to her?"

He glowered. "We didn't kill her, if that's what you mean. She died in the hospital."

"And after that?"

"She may have lost some blood," he said, looking impatient.

Her stomach threatened to heave. Not even vamps would touch the blood of the dead. So who had taken the blood? And why?

Armando's eyes narrowed. He extended a hand. "Give me the amulet."

With her hand still deep in the purse, Kellie brought it up so that the gun was pointing at Armando. "Put Nana in the trunk of my car first."

Growling low in his throat, he showed her his teeth. "We haven't attacked you, so we won't excuse your action this time. Our alpha was a good leader and much loved. Some of the pack still wants revenge on you for his death."

"Are you one of them?" she asked, not backing down. "I have a gun loaded with silver bullets, and you'll be the first to go if anyone comes near me."

Armando made a snorting sound. "You're hopelessly outnumbered. There's no way you could kill us all."

"But I'd go down fighting and take a lot of you assholes with me," she countered.

Considering it, Armando tilted his head toward the car. The two men zipped the bag and took it to the car. They even opened the driver's door and used the lever to open the truck.

With the gun in her purse trained on Armando, Kellie watched them place the body in the trunk and close it. They hovered near the car for a moment till Armando nodded, then they joined the rest of the werewolves in the shelter of the trees. Now all she had to do was find a way out of the park without getting hurt or giving up her amulet.

Armando extended his hand, palm up once more. "The amulet."

She reached a hand down the front of her top to where she'd stowed the amulet in the shelf bra made into it. It tingled against her fingers. The thought of giving it up made her mad. A savage growl escaped Kellie's throat. *Where had that come from?*

Armando and the two with him broke out laughing. "One wolf against all of us?" He made a clicking sound with his teeth. "Go ahead and make the change."

Standing, she backed toward the car.

"You'll never make it," Armando taunted.

A group of people stepped out of the trees to her right. There were at least thirty of them. They were all wearing those damned medallions with the wolf and the moon on them.

She was fast. She'd spent years honing her body for competition in gymnastics, tennis, and track. With her hand still on the gun in her purse, Kellie turned and sprinted for the car.

Chapter Seven

Howls of rage erupted behind her. Then she heard running footsteps. Sucking in a breath of the open air, Kellie ran, pushing herself to the limit and past. She dodged tree roots and jumped over rocks, staying on the path and praying that the driver's door on the car was still unlocked. She'd lock the doors and fish the key out of the pocket in her slacks.

Where were Garen and the cavalry? Tantalizing yards from the car, Kellie realized that Armando had been right. She wasn't going to make it. In a calculated move that felt too much like suicide, she turned, whipping her hand out of the purse with the gun to fire on her pursuers. Aiming for vital organs with fast, deadly precision, she got four of them before the pack overran her. On the ground in a tangle of bodies, some in the throes of the change, Kellie fought furiously. Kicking, punching, biting, she felt the amulet grow so hot against her skin it burned.

In the background she heard screams, growling, jaws snapping, and other signs of fighting. Paul had arrived with help.

A surge of electricity went through her body. Her body trembled and shook, the bones suddenly aching so much she wanted to scream. She felt weird, as if she were exploding from the inside out. Still fighting, she felt her knees buckle. The cloth in her top ripped as her body expanded. The slacks became painfully tight. A savage howl forced its way out of her throat.

Kellie shook herself, clawing and biting her way out of the slash of bodies. She had fur. She'd lost control of her body. She'd changed into a wolf. Coming apart inside the wolf she screamed over and over again in horror. Ignoring her, the wolf acted on instinct and continued to fight her attackers with deadly skill.

Armando's scent filled her nostrils. He shoved a hand down the remnants of her top to grab the amulet.

The wolf's powerful jaws closed on the offending arm. The bones gave easily, fresh blood slipping down her throat as it snapped the arm off at the wrist. Chewing, she swallowed chunks of his flesh.

Dropping the amulet, Armando screamed in rage and pain, then he began to change.

With a furious growl, a coal black wolf pushed himself between them to attack Armando and the others with his claws and jaws. His ruthless skill and precision made quick bloody work of her attackers.

The wolf had Garen's scent. It was the first time she'd seen him in wolf form, but the pull was still there. Pressing forward, she tried to rejoin the fight. With a snarled warning, Garen nudged her back.

Scanning the area, she saw that several other wolves and humans had joined the battle. The sight of so many wolves in broad daylight should have been scary, but Kellie could see that the majority of them were fighting on her side. The sheer numbers meant that more than one pack fought with Garen against Armando's pack. Wolves and humans wearing the gold wolf's head medallions were being slaughtered.

Gradually, she discovered that if she was calm, she gained a measure of control with the wolf. Kellie dipped her head, edging the bodies of the dead and wounded aside as best she could in her search for her amulet. Some were in human form, others wolf, and still others caught in an eerie in-between. In wolf form for the first time, she found it hard to concentrate on the search. She missed the use of her hands. Frustrated, she settled down to wait for the end of the battle.

It seemed like hours, but a check of Kellie's watch proved that a mere half hour had passed. None of Armando's pack remained alive. Wolves were shifting back into human form, and those already changed had started a clean-up effort. Kellie recognized Paul, Marcus, and Laurel in the crowd.

Everyone seemed to change so effortlessly that she decided that it must be something done on instinct. Garen transformed and stepped into a pair of tattered pants. Watching him, Kellie tried to do the same. Abruptly, she realized that she did not know how. She howled.

Garen came. Gathering her close, he petted her, soothing her, running his fingers through her fur and making sure she wasn't injured. "I'll help you, Kellie," he whispered, scratching behind her ears. "I'll talk you through the change."

Moving her to a quiet spot under a tree, Garen continued talking to her and murmuring encouragements. Listening to the mesmerizing rhythm and tone of his voice, Kellie let herself relax in his arms. He made her focus inwardly on her body and her desire to go back to the way she'd been, and the physical changes that would have to happen.

Kellie's skin was so tight and sensitive that she moved away from Garen's gentle hands. Blood rushed through her veins, making her ears ring. She collapsed on the grass. Bones aching deep inside her, Kellie shook beneath the scary sensation of being turned inside out.

Abruptly she was lying on the hot grass panting and out of breath. Garen covered her with a soft cottony material and pulled the garment on over her head. "Are you all right?" he asked.

She nodded.

Anger lit the heated cognac of his eyes as he gazed down at her. "You could have been killed. What possessed you to run off to meet a pack of werewolves alone? Especially the same pack that attacked you weeks ago?"

"Wasn't it worth the risk?" she shot back. "Armando and his crew can't hurt me anymore, and I have Nana's body for the funeral."

Some of the anger seeped out of his eyes. "You've also learned how to make the change. Do you know how rare it is for a newling to accomplish that before the full moon?" "Did I tell you that wolves mate for life?" he asked, pulling her close and holding her so tight that it almost hurt. "If anything had happened to you…" His voice rang with emotion, and then tapered off.

"I'll be more careful," she promised. "I was so afraid you wouldn't get here in time, and then when you did…"

They shared a kiss.

Kellie curved a hand around the side of his face. "I want to be with you, Garen, but I don't know if I can stay here and be what you need me to be," she confided.

Garen simply stared at her with a volatile mixture of shock and a little hurt. "All I'm asking is that you try."

"I will. I promise." She locked her fingers behind his neck.

Garen helped her to stand. "Let's see if we can find your amulet."

Kellie followed along behind him, aware that he must have realized that he'd have a better chance at getting her to stay if he didn't push or demand. She hated taking orders from anybody.

While he'd been helping her, a cleaning crew had shown up and was helping the others clear away all remaining signs of the battle. The amulets were in a golden pile on the picnic table. Dirt, bloody fingerprints, and fur soiled their surfaces, but her hands still tingled when she touched them. She found her amulet deep in the pile and gave it to Garen to study.

"It has some sort of magic," he observed. "They went to a lot of trouble to get it. What does it do?"

Sunlight reflected off the medallion and into her eyes. Kellie blinked. "I think all the medallions help the change, but mine does more than the wolf. I was holding it when I changed into the wolf."

"And had lost it when you couldn't change back," he added, finishing her sentence.

Kellie nodded.

Garen returned her medallion. "I'd already guessed that they were using the medallions for more than a symbol of their membership in Armando's group. It's almost a shame that Armando's not alive to explain."

"Hey Dawg, I wouldn't go that far." Marcus spoke from just behind them. "For robbing and killing all those humans and bringing the wrath of the government down on us, he and his pack deserved to be exterminated. Because of what they've done, the humans are afraid of us. It'll take a long time to get that trust back."

Kellie absently stroked her amulet. It felt warm in her fingers, but nothing like what she'd experienced before. "What are you going to do with the medallions?"

Garen and Marcus exchanged glances. "I vote for melting them down and destroying them, but we can save that question for the council meeting coming up in a few weeks," Marcus declared.

"We should leave what's left of Armando here to be found along with his amulet," Garen suggested. "Then the Preternatural Division could study him and the amulet. We'll have more information for the council then."

Several in the crowd murmured in agreement. In short order, they all left with the park pretty much as they'd found it except for Armando and his remains.

Garen called his boss in the Preternatural Division with information about his discovery of Armando's body. Then Kellie and Garen drove Marcus and Laurel to their car, and made a quick stop back at the hotel and casino to freshen up before dropping off Nana's body at the funeral home.

When they were alone, Kellie asked the question that had been occupying her thoughts. "Do you think we got all of Armando's pack?"

Garen's expression was grim. "No, but we'll get them with the leads we got today."

Kellie digested that in silence. As long as some of Armando's pack remained alive and free to roam around, she wouldn't be safe. Except for meeting Garen, Vegas had been a very unlucky place for her.

Forcing herself to think past all that had happened today, she drew Nana's envelope from the underneath the seat and reread the parts about her burial. Nana had made arrangements for her body to be prepared for burial at a specific funeral home. Kellie gave Garen the address for the Flowerhill Funeral Home.

The funeral home was a homey little place on the outskirts of Vegas. It looked like a place you'd find in a small town, USA, not Vegas. They mounted the stone steps and rang the bell. A very short bald man with a wizened face that reminded Kellie of storybook pictures she'd seen of gnomes, answered. His fitted green suit high-lighted bright green eyes.

Taking one look at Kellie, he said, "Kelandra, I suppose you've come about Fern?"

Taken aback by the fact that he'd recognized her and known her given name, Kellie nodded. It was a long time since she'd heard anyone use Nana's given name, too.

"Where is she?" he asked, looking past Kellie and Garen as if he expected to see Nana standing there. His gaze reached the car.

"She's in the trunk," Kellie managed. "It... it's a long story."

"It doesn't matter how she got here. I'm just glad she made it," he said cryptically. "Could you open the trunk, please?"

Garen clicked the remote. The trunk popped up.

Surprisingly fast on his feet, the little man moved past them and down the steps. By the time they made it to the car, he was already removing the body bag.

Garen stepped forward. "Let me help you with that."

"I've got her." The little man lifted the bag easily and carried it to the porch. "You might open the door for me," he told Kellie.

Hurrying to the steps, she did. The interior was cool and spacious and filled with greenery and flowers. They followed the little man to a back room where he placed the bag on an examining table.

"My name is Lucas McGilery," the little man said as he unzipped the bag.

Garen introduced himself.

The sight of Nana's body brought tears to Kellie's eyes. She'd known that the old lady hadn't been feeling well, and she'd been planning to come and see about her. Why hadn't she dropped everything right away? Her only excuse was that Nana had always been more than capable of taking care of herself and everyone else she cared about, too.

The first time Kellie left had been in her early teens, and Nana had been staying in Fieldcrest, Ohio. She'd left then to compete with the U.S. Olympic Gymnastics Team. It had become a career. Years later Kellie had come back when she was too old to compete successfully. Nana had seemed the same, and she'd been just as tight-lipped about Kellie's parents and the past.

After a year, Kellie left to compete on the tennis circuit. She'd done well for a while and made it into the top four in women's tennis. When it became an endless grind of work and competition, Kellie quit that career too and came to stay near Nana in Briarwood, California. When California had become a little too perfect for Kellie, she'd moved to Detroit to live alone. Now she took work as a well-paid professional gymnastics and tennis coach when she chose. She hadn't seen Nana in a year, but she'd been dreaming about her.

Kellie didn't know she was crying until a drop fell onto her hand.

Garen used the tissue dispenser on a side table and pressed several tissues into her hand.

"Don't worry about her," Lucas said gently. "She'll be fine with me. I'll have her looking as beautiful as ever. You'll see."

Kellie blew her nose. "You knew her?"

"Of course I did, but it's been a long time since I've seen her. She was a very private person."

That was an understatement. "How did you recognize me?" she asked.

Lucas smiled. "You were just a little one when she came and made the arrangements. You were at my coffee table coloring when you told me your name."

"Did she say anything about my parents?" Kellie asked hopefully, keeping her tone light.

"Just that they'd gone and gotten themselves killed and that she was the only one left to raise you."

Kellie stared at him. What he said fit in with the story Nana had told her of a car accident, but it sounded different coming from Lucas. She'd searched the newspapers and police reports using what little she could get from Nana and found nothing. She wasn't even sure that Monroe was really her last name. Nana had been an enigma and a mystery. She'd also been a woman of wisdom and power. People had recognized it in her and given her a lot of respect.

Lucas gazed back down at Nana. "I'll have her ready for the family hour tomorrow. She prepaid for shipment of her body back to… to? I'll have to look that up."

"Fieldcrest, Ohio," Kellie finished for him.

"So it is." Lucas smiled. "Is there anything else I can do for you?"

Assuring him that there was nothing, they left.

Stopping for steaks at a little restaurant on the way home, they made it back to their room around six. Garen couldn't remember when he'd packed so much into one day. He was certain that he'd sleep as soon as his head touched the pillow.

As soon as the door to the room closed and he touched Kellie's hand, everything changed. One touch and he was hard and aching to get inside her. Filling her mouth with his tongue, he squeezed the firm round globes of her ass and pulled her close to his heat.

"Garen!" With a soft cry, she curled into him, grinding on him. Her fingers fumbled with the button on his pants. She drew down the zipper and fell to her knees, holding the already moist tip of his flesh in her hands.

He was already on the edge. "No, I want it all," he said, bending down and lifting her into his arms.

Her hands delved into his shirt, massaging his chest as she mouthed his nipples through the material.

Garen thought he'd go crazy as he carried her into the bathroom on shaky legs. He turned on the shower. Unable to wait another second, he set her on the wide counter and spread her legs. Her panties were soaked. He drew them down and off gently, massaging her soft thighs, and then her long legs.

Holding her thighs, he placed a kiss on her abdomen and pressed his fingers into her. Moaning, she arced against him, rotating her hips. Her juices ran down his fingers. He withdrew them and placed himself deep inside her with three hard, mind-numbing thrusts.

Kellie screamed with pleasure and wrapped her legs around him. They rocked together, moving so energetically that she nearly fell off the counter. When they reached the plateau, she gripped him with every part of her body. He spent forever thrusting and pouring himself into her. Together, they floated back to earth.

As Kellie lay in his arms with her ears still ringing, she realized that their lovemaking had been more than the physical act. She'd joined her heart, spirit, and emotions with Garen's.

"Shower's ready," Garen whispered after a moment. "Want to try it out?"

Chapter Eight

Despite a full night of mind-numbing sex, Garen had a difficult time leaving Kellie the next morning. He spent the day at the Preternatural Police Division, tiptoeing around the paperwork surrounding Armando's body and the amulet.

His boss, Elio, eyed him suspiciously. He was sensitive enough to know that Garen had lied about a few things, but he didn't know why. This didn't worry Garen since Elio owed him a favor or two. He called one of those favors in.

Schraf, a sensitive in the magical division, told Garen that he was certain the medallions would help their wearers turn into wolves. He even showed Garen a sketch of the wolf medallions in one of his references, the *Book of All Things Magical*. Schraf further insisted that the medallions had been dipped in the blood of a creature that was neither werewolf nor human.

"What does that leave?" Garen asked, giving Schraf a quizzical look. "Vampire?"

"No." Schraf glowered at him and scratched his gray head. "There are several other possibilities. I will try to narrow it down."

At the Vegas Police Department, the forensics division ran tests on Armando's remains. Garen called in another favor to get an advanced look at the preliminary results. Despite the presence of teeth marks and fur on the remains, blood tests showed that Armando had not been a werewolf.

Garen was at a loss in interpreting that information. He had seen Armando in wolf form with his own eyes and fought with him too. He could only draw the conclusion that the medallions had the capacity to turn humans into werewolves on a temporary basis.

Reasoning that it was likely that Armando's entire pack had been humans that used the medallions to become werewolves,

Garen decided to focus on Armando's friends and family. Once they found out what had happened to Armando and the others, remaining pack members would not openly wear the medallions.

Armando and his pack had paid the price for attacking and killing humans and causing a rift between the authorities and the werewolf packs, but Garen wasn't foolish enough to think the battle was over. He would follow up on the new leads and share his information at the clan meetings.

Garen hadn't told Kellie yet, but his keen sense of smell told him that the creature whose blood had been used on the medallions was her Nana. The old woman's body had been drained of blood and as one of the Frey, her blood would have met the ritual requirements. Pierson had admitted that his band of werewolves were after Kellie for her medallion from the start. They hadn't been able to locate it in Nana's place and knew Kellie stood to inherit it. They'd attacked the neighborhood to cover their tracks, but Kellie fought hard and the SWAT team had showed up much too early for them to even broach the subject of the amulet.

Kellie got up early and began packing her clothes. She spent a good part of the day calling the people in Nana's address book, telling them that she'd passed away. Then she invited them to the funeral service in Fieldcrest and gave them the details. Every one accepted the invitation.

Feeling anxious and a bit irritated, she showed up early for Nana's family hour at the funeral home. The event had been posted in the local papers, but Kellie wasn't really expecting anyone. None of the people in the black address book had lived in the area.

Lucas McGilery had laid Nana out in a painted green room filled with plants and flowers. The green dress she wore had been one of her favorites. When Kellie got a good look at Nana's face, she could only stare. Nana looked like a beautiful queen. Lucas had managed to rehydrate her face and skin. Now Nana looked as if she were sleeping.

"You've done a wonderful job." Palming a tissue, she dabbed at her wet face.

Lucas smiled proudly. "She was a wonderful woman. Then of course, I have a gift for this line of work. Some people say I work magic."

Kellie didn't doubt it. She believed in more than she could see and touch and explain. Settling into a nearby chair, she thought about Nana and remembered the good times. Nana had been stern, but she'd taught Kellie to appreciate nature and life and the things that came to you.

The sound of the door opening reached Kellie. Glancing up, she saw Garen looking quite stunning in a black suit, entering the room. It was then that she realized that she'd been crying.

"Sorry. I meant to come earlier, but I got tied up at work," he explained.

She opened her arms and he stepped into them, holding her tight. "I will always be there for you," he whispered. He nuzzled her cheek. She'd needed the contact. She felt loved and the anxious and irritated feeling eased and disappeared. Was that one of the benefits of the bond Garen talked about? She would have to test her theories on that one. "The funeral is in Fieldcrest tomorrow," she murmured. "Are you coming?"

"Of course." Garen released her. "I've got some time off from work. Paul and two of my cousins will be coming, too."

She lifted an eyebrow. "Is that really necessary?"

His gaze was steady. "Yes, it is. Some of Armando's pack is still out there. We're expecting trouble."

"Okay," she said after a moment or two. "When are you going to introduce me to your family?"

"Tonight."

Kellie swallowed hard. The prospect made her nervous. "I don't know if I'm ready for that."

Garen laughed. "I don't think I can keep them away much

Out of the Dark

longer. They've been asking about you."

Taking his hand, she led him back to Nana. "Let me introduce you to mine."

About the Authors

L.A. Banks, author of The Vampire Huntress Legend series, pens a variety of paranormals, crime thrillers, as well as romances under multiple pseudonyms. A full-time author, graduate of University of Pennsylvania's Wharton undergraduate program and holding a Masters in Fine Arts in filmmaking from Temple University, Banks is currently penning more projects across all genres. She lives with her husband and family in Philadelphia. For a full list of her varied work and upcoming projects, visit her websites at **www.LeslieEsdaileBanks.com** and **www.vampire-huntress.com**.

By day, **Miriam Pace** and **Jacqueline Hamilton** are mild-mannered bookstore owners, but by night they turn into the dynamic writing duo, J.M. Jeffries. Miriam has been married for thirty-six years and has two children and a grandchild. Jackie is single and considers Miriam's dogs her children. They live in southern California and have been writing together for eight years.

Seressia Glass currently lives in Atlanta. When not writing, she enjoys good food, good music, and good friends. She's currently at work on her next romance. For more information, please visit www.seressia.com or write to Seressia in care of the publisher.

Natalie Dunbar was first published with Genesis Press and has gone on to write for Silhouette Bombshell and BET Books. With a love and fascination for paranormal fiction, she welcomes the opportunity to develop a plot and characters for the paranormal universe created in this anthology.